T0038907

ADVANCE PRAISE FOR
Morgan Is My Name

"A very real, passionate retelling of Morgan le Fay's story, with detail about political and magical lives, and the women who are such a vital part of the tale."

—Tamora Pierce, #1 *New York Times* bestselling author

"This is the powerfully feminist, intricately woven, and realistically enchanting Arthurian tale you've been waiting for. Morgan is her name, and I love her."

—Kiersten White, #1 *New York Times* bestselling author of the *Camelot Rising* Trilogy

"Compelling and poignant, Sophie Keetch's prose is as mesmerizing as the ocean's tides, illuminating Morgan's life with a deft and attentive hand. Built on the bones of exquisite longing and unsung power, *Morgan Is My Name* portrays a woman forging her own path and reclaiming her story. A stunning delight."

—Rebecca Ross, internationally bestselling author of *A River Enchanted*

"*Morgan Is My Name* is a powerful reimagining of the origins of Morgan le Fay, infusing the familiar tales of Arthurian legend with a fresh voice, profoundly human characters, and an atmosphere both wistful and deliciously ominous. This book felt like a warm hearth in a lonely castle by the sea, and I loved every sentence."

—H.M. Long, author of *Hall of Smoke*

"As fierce and wild as the Cornish sea she is named for, Morgan defies her cruel stepfather King Uther and follows her passions for healing, scholarship, and a handsome young knight. Keetch's deft handling of this ancient tale highlights Morgan's intelligence and strong will, treating readers to a truly delicious tale of self-actualization and vengeance."

—Luna McNamara, author of *Psyche and Eros*

"Sophie Keetch takes us to a familiar destination—Camelot—on a brand-new road. *Morgan Is My Name* has magic, mythology, Merlin, and a Morgan le Fay we've never met before. Here, we meet a heroine who staunchly refuses to diminish herself while negotiating the world of powerful and cruel men. With twists and turns around every bend, you will love the journey of this book as much as its destination."

—Sharon Emmerichs, *Sunday Times* bestselling author of *Shield Maiden*

"Top marks all round for an enthralling new take on the Arthurian legend, beautifully written."   —*The Times* (UK)

"This is the Arthurian legend as you rarely see it: told not by Uther, Arthur or Merlin, or indeed their male champions, but by the complicated woman they condemned. Keetch's Morgan is vulnerable, courageous and defiant. She makes the legend hers, and I can't wait to accompany her on the next part of the journey. For lovers of the untold story, *Morgan Is My Name* is a convincing and compelling read."

—Lucy Holland, author of *Sistersong*

"Evocative, haunting and utterly addictive, this is a book to lose yourself in."   —Tracy Borman, author of *The King's Witch*

"Keetch's Morgan does not disappoint . . . literally fire and a perfect harbinger of the woman Morgan is destined to become!"

—Stacey Thomas, author of *The Revels*

MORGAN IS MY NAME

SOPHIE KEETCH

RANDOM HOUSE CANADA

PUBLISHED BY RANDOM HOUSE CANADA

Copyright © 2023 Sophie Keetch Limited

All rights reserved under International and Pan-American Copyright
Conventions. No part of this book may be reproduced in any form or by any
electronic or mechanical means, including information storage and retrieval
systems, without permission in writing from the publisher, except by a
reviewer, who may quote brief passages in a review. Published in 2023 by
Random House Canada, a division of Penguin Random House Canada
Limited, Toronto, and simultaneously in the United Kingdom by Oneworld
Publications, London. First published as an original audio book by Audible.
Distributed in Canada and the United States of America by Penguin
Random House Canada Limited, Toronto.

www.penguinrandomhouse.ca

Random House Canada and colophon are registered trademarks.

Library and Archives Canada Cataloguing in Publication

Title: Morgan is my name / Sophie Keetch.
Names: Keetch, Sophie, author.
Identifiers: Canadiana (print) 20220252505 | Canadiana (ebook) 20220252548
    | ISBN 9781039006492 (softcover) | ISBN 9781039006508 (EPUB)
Classification: LCC PR6111.E33 M67 2023 | DDC 823/.92—dc23

Text design: Emma Dolan
Cover design: Emma Dolan
Image credits: (swords) larryrains; (hands) Luccy_lapka / both Getty Images

Printed in Canada

10 9 8 7 6 5 4 3 2 1

Penguin
Random House
RANDOM HOUSE CANADA

For Jason

Enter chorus.
I am my own chorus.

—Anne Carson, *Norma Jeane Baker of Troy*

I WAS BORN in the midst of a storm, when the waves rose so high up the cliffs of Tintagel it was feared the entire castle would be dragged into the sea. Though my mother never spoke of it, my nurse, Gwennol, often told the tale—how Lady Igraine's cries fought with the thunder, her pain carried off on the screaming wind, lightning illuminating her struggle and the dangerous labour she never had with my two sisters.

"For a while we were sure she would die," Gwennol would say, holding me rapt, over the music of Cornwall's swirling clifftop breeze. "Hours she lay there, howling like a banshee, bone-tired. We were about to lose the light when your lady mother sat up, staring at the window as if seeing the Angel Gabriel himself. 'The sea has come!' she cried. 'Risen up to bear us away!' And God strike me if it weren't true. There it was, waves crashing at the window, coming to claim us all. I ran to see, but by the time I got there, the water was exactly where it should be, and when I looked back, so were you: born, alive and open-eyed. Your mother insisted it was the sea that delivered you, and so you were named."

Morgan is my name, and its origin true at least—"sea-born" by way of the Welsh tongue. My mother bestowed it personally after the stormy circumstances of my birth, steadfast in her belief the ferocious Cornish waters had saved us both.

"You cried for an hour after she bore you," Gwennol told me. "Raging at the world until that storm blew itself out and the sea settled beneath us. Truly the name is yours by right."

I

"WHY IS MORGAN 'Morgan'?"

My ten-year-old sister spread my hair across my back with orderly hands, proceeding to braid it neatly. "I mean," Elaine added, "it's quite obviously a boy's name."

"It isn't," I retorted, "since I'm *not* a boy." I had not long turned seven and was increasingly disinclined to endure insults.

"Father wishes you had been," Morgause said from across the room. Remote and beautiful, nine years my superior, our elder sister sat gazing out of the window, cloaked in disdain for childish things.

"You're a liar," I snapped.

"Keep *still*," Elaine said. "How will you ever be a lady if you can't sit quietly?"

The three of us were alone in our mother's solar, awaiting her presence. It was a bright, pleasant room, full of well-cushioned chairs and good light, walls painted yellow beneath lively tapestries. The scent of roses, blooming early around the windows, warmed sweetly in the sun until the air was thick with it. Spring had blazed in long before Easter Day, heat seeping through Tintagel Castle's cool stone walls, pervading our chambers and defying the sea breeze.

Morgause rose and drifted across, regarding us down her delicate nose. "Morgana is neither a lady nor even a person. She's half fox cub,

found by Sir Bretel under a blackberry bush and taken in as a kindness by Mother and Father."

"*That is not my name!*"

I flew at her, limbs alight with white heat. Morgause—older,
stronger, experienced in confrontation—easily held me at bay, laughing. The suggestion I was not of my parents' begetting was not what
brought forth my rage—she and I shared the blue eyes and night-black
hair of my father, and were both lauded for echoing our mother's
finely wrought features—rather it rose up at a single sound, the lilt-
ing errant *a* she always placed at the end of my name. My sister chose
her weapons well and kept them sharp.

"What in the name of St. Petroc?" Strong as a moor pony,
Gwennol grabbed me, containing my furious struggles. "Now, Lady
Morgan, not again. Your temper will be the end of you if you let it
rule you like this."

"She started it!" I cried. "Morgause called me a fox cub."

"Really, Madame Morgause. A young lady hoping to be presented
at court ought to know better." Morgause's sneer quickly faded, her
face tinged pink. Our nurse switched her gaze. "You're quiet, Lady
Elaine, as usual. What was your part in this?"

Elaine, never a liar, spoke in cool tones. "I asked why she had a
boy's name."

"What silliness," Gwennol tutted. "Fetch your work baskets, you
two. Your lady mother will be along shortly." Guiding me into a
secluded corner, she knelt and replaited my loosened tresses. "You
shouldn't leap at your sister like that, my duck, no matter what she
says. You're clever enough to know better."

"I can't help it." I sniffed. "When Morgause says those things, it
gets hot in my belly, then up to my head, and . . . I just forget."

"Aye, your mother's the same way, but she keeps her temper hidden
for the most part, like a great lady should. You must learn it likewise."

I nodded, though it didn't seem very fair. It wasn't as if I knew when my fury was coming; I couldn't catch it in my hands, or even bury it deep, because it already lived there, slumbering in my core like a dragon waiting to be woken.

"Gwennol," I said in a small voice, "would Father have preferred a son to me?"

"What? Goodness, no!" My nurse spun me around to face her. "I was there when His Grace first saw you in your mother's arms. You only ceased squalling when he took you up, and he looked exactly as he should—happy as a piskie in mischief."

She waited for my smile, then ushered me into a sewing chair just as my mother glided in with her women. She beamed at her trio of now peaceful daughters, and settled gracefully into her seat.

"I hear the hot weather is set to continue," she said, accepting her sewing basket from Gwennol.

"Aye, my lady, so the fishermen say," Gwennol replied. "They claim it's a bad omen."

Constance, my mother's formidable chamber-mistress, gave a derisory snort. "If I had a gold piece for every one of your omens come to naught, the Duke would be fetching my wine."

I looked down at the kerchief I was hemming, listening to the soft, soothing murmurs of female company. The enveloping heat slowed my fingers until I could barely make another stitch.

Suddenly, my mother's hands slipped, ripping the stitch in the sleeve she was embroidering with my father's standard, drawing blood from her finger and a rare oath from her lips. My chin jerked up, and Elaine's hand went to her mouth. Morgause merely stared, aghast.

Our mother laughed and sucked the ruby bead from her fingertip. "Don't tell the Duke. I'll never hear the last of it."

As if summoned, my father strode in, regarding our amused faces with puzzlement. "Council has concluded for the day, my lady," he said to my mother. "If you are in need of me, I'll be out on the headland with Jezebel."

She was his favourite falcon, a large, glorious peregrine, perfect in line and colour: slate-blue back, breast cleanly barred in black and white, clear onyx eyes encircled with gold. My father had manned her himself after she was caught as an eyas on Tintagel's cliffs, and boasted to all who would listen of her beauty, intelligence and faultless recall. He had named her thus purely for the enjoyment of saying it in the presence of my mother, who never failed to tut and call him blasphemous.

And she did so then, crossing herself and shaking her head. "The things you say, and in front of your daughters," she said mildly. "You'll have much to answer for in Heaven, my lord."

He laughed. "Say a Mass for me, my lady."

"If I thought for a moment it'd save you," my mother rejoined.

He gave her an affectionate look. "I commend your efforts to address my sins, as ever."

She inclined her head, the slightest hint of satisfaction playing across her lips.

I watched them with fascination, sparring in the sunlight. It was their game, and they played it often—she the saint and he the sinner. My mother was devoted to the chapel, but neither salvation nor damnation concerned my father much; his habits were informal, chancy even, harking back to his people in Ireland, who knelt to the gospels but whose hearts, oftentimes, still rode with the Tuath Dé.

"My ladies," he said, bowing. "If there's nothing else, I bid you good day."

"There is!" I threw down my needlework and dashed after him.

He paused just inside the door, raising dark eyebrows above eyes of deep lapis. "Morgan of Cornwall. How may I be of service?"

"I want to go and see your falcon," I blurted out. Then, politely, "By your leave, my lord father."

"I see." He glanced at my mother, who gave a gentle shrug, then back at me with a slow-dawning smile. "Very well, loyal daughter. No harm in you learning to hawk a little early. As long as you pay attention and respect the authority of the bird. Yes?"

At my eager nod he started back down the corridor with his hands swinging loose. Beside him I was barely waist height, and took three strides to his every one, but within, I grew, foot upon foot, out through the courtyard and into the bird mews, until we reached the headland with the falcon on his fist, and I thought my head would scrape the very sky.

*

MY FATHER WAS Gorlois, Duke of Cornwall. He had been born in the land of his dukedom, but his ancestors were Gaelic chieftains of old, who had frightened the Romans from attempting their shores and claimed to be descended from giants.

He met my mother not long after inheriting his title, while lending his banner to her father. They had a striking asymmetry: he a seasoned, raven-haired warrior and she a minor Welsh Princess ten years his junior, fair and delicate as May Day. But he asked for her hand, her father gave it, and it was a good match for them both.

They were married at Cardigan and returned immediately to Cornwall, where my father took his favourite place—the impressive, picturesque island of Tintagel—and rebuilt its fortress into his largest, most comfortable castle, a palace stronghold fit for his new Duchess. My mother always said she could have wanted for no better wedding gift.

Though we had other places, it was Tintagel where we spent most of our time. There, at the windblown, salt-drenched sanctuary my father had made for us, we were home.

*

I HARDLY DARED presume such a treat would be repeated, but my
father called for me most days thereafter, teaching me his way with
birds, out there on the headland with the kittiwake cries and the sweet
smell of seagrass burning under a late Cornish spring. I began to seek
him out as a matter of course, until I arrived at his Great Chamber one
morning to discover he and my mother had left in a hurry.

"They've gone north, to Carduel," Gwennol explained. "For the
High King's court."

"Again?" I said, for they had been there at Advent, barely returning in time for the Christmas feast.

"How unfair!" Morgause complained. "Mother swore she'd have
me presented at the next royal court."

"I wish they *had* taken her," Elaine muttered, making me giggle.

"Peace, my dears." Gwennol gave each of us a kiss on the forehead, which even Morgause leaned into with a reluctant fondness.
"It'll not be long till they're back, eight weeks at most. We're to meet
them at Castle Dore for St. Swithin's."

But they were back long before that, thundering into Tintagel on
horses foaming at the bit, knightly retinue grim-faced with fatigue;
they could not have been at Carduel but a few days before riding the
considerable distance home. Afterwards, my parents kept mostly to
themselves, appearing only at table, without laughter, as if a long,
dark cloud had travelled with them.

One sweltering day, I was haunting a high corridor in the castle's
South Tower, cooling my skin at an open embrasure, when I heard
my father's voice, low and urgent, around the corner just beyond.

"Stay in Tintagel. You, the children and the women. You'll be
safe here with ten knights. It's the best fortress we have. She'll not
be breached."

"Where will you go?" My mother's voice wavered, undercut by a
note of fear that pricked my ears. "Surely we should all stay together?"

"I cannot risk it. I'll go to Dimilioc—it's the only other place we can hope to hold. If I can draw Uther Pendragon there and rout him . . ." He gave a heavy sigh. "It's the only way."

They were silent for a moment and I waited, hardly breathing.

"Gorlois," she said. Never in my life had I heard her call him by his first name, and the oddity of it, the absolute intimacy she conveyed in its use, almost drove me away for fear of what I might hear next. "You know as well as I, it's not the only way. I caused this war—it's me he wants. I . . . I can save Cornwall."

"Good God, Igraine! It's not *you* who caused this, nor is it your cross to bear. Our so-called King, that godless, marauding *wolf*—" His voice dropped, earnest, desperate, thick in his throat. "I'd let him burn ten Cornwalls rather than make you lay eyes on him again, much less . . ." Another guttural sigh came forth. "He will not defeat us. Tintagel will not succumb, and neither will you— I swear it."

My mother's response came as a sob, muffled but bone-deep, reverberating through my body.

"My love," he said, tone low and soothing once again. In my mind's eye, he put a hand to her face—a strong hand, expert at bearing a falcon or wielding a sword. "Stay at Tintagel, keep our daughters safe, and I will come back to you. Or the Devil take me."

"Don't say that, even in jest." But her voice was lighter, and he laughed in return, echoes of his confidence catching on the breeze and vanishing into the sea beyond me, before I balked and escaped on shuddering legs.

*

MY FATHER SUMMONED me a few days later, and we took Jezebel to the headland under a sky full of light—hot and diamond-hard.

The grass beneath our feet grew in tufts, cropped short and bleached yellow, the breeze warm and meandering, tangy with sea.

The falcon was fractious, neck feathers in an irritable ruff, head twitching at every buzzing insect, and eyeing me with more suspicion than usual. My father clucked to her under his breath, stroking the barred feathers of her chest with the rhythmic delicacy of a harpist.

"She should be on her eggs, waiting for the moult," he said as we reached her favourite hunting ground at the cliff's edge. "But I wanted to bring her out one more time before—"

"Before you go," I said matter-of-factly. "Because you're leaving and we're not."

We hadn't yet been told, and he cast eyes down at me that were sharp as the bird's.

"That I am." He raised his fist up to look again at Jezebel. "Hopefully this one will have hatched those eyasses and grown a new set of feathers by the time I return."

In one taut movement he tossed the peregrine into the wind, and she lifted, wings catching the air like a pair of flashing blades. He watched her soar, shielding his eyes against the sun, pacing underneath as she found her path. Reaching her peak, the falcon began to circle, waiting on for her prey to come. She spied something and began to stoop, then thought better of it, tilting onto her side and curving like a sickle up to her observational height.

"The name, *peregrine*," my father said. "It means 'wanderer.' 'She that roams.'" He looked down at me, lines on his face drawn grave. "Do you know what her greatest strength is, Morgan?"

"Yes. Her talons, for the crushing of skulls." He had told me so on our very first flight—the beak is sharp and worth your caution, but never forget her talons: there death resides.

But today, I was wrong.

"Survival," he said. "At any given moment she can fly away,

knowing she can live. She doesn't need me, the falconer, or the shelter of the mews. That is the greatest power of all."

A pair of rock doves flew up from the cliff, twirling inland. Steadying her body as if walking a rope, Jezebel glanced down, folded her wings back and plummeted before we could draw breath, a sleek, dark teardrop against the sky's glassy cheek. A heartbeat before reaching her prey, she pulled back, releasing talons of black and gold in an elegant flash.

The dove was dead before it hit the grass. When we reached her, Jezebel had shrouded her quarry in shadow beneath outstretched wings. At my father's whistle she hopped disinterestedly to his glove to claim her reward—some other bird's chick, sacrificed to her prowess—which she held between her deadly claws, tearing and crunching.

"True power comes from freedom, and the ability to survive what befalls us." He had sent the peregrine up again to wait on, though I saw now it was us who waited on her. "There's nothing keeping her here other than the respect she's been shown."

"Every return to the glove is a courtesy, not a right," I agreed.

Suddenly, my father crouched, his face at my level. Only then did I see how drawn he was: cheeks hollow, forehead etched deep with lines that weren't there before. Hints of silver gleamed at his hairline, threaded through the shining black mane and scattered in his beard along the ridge of his jaw. He gripped my arms and held me steady.

"You are wise, Morgan, you always were. You must use that wisdom, harness it, learn to wield it. Promise me you will not forget."

I loved my father, as much as my child's heart could, so I did not hesitate. "I promise, Father. I won't forget."

"I will come back for you," he said firmly, though his voice shook as it had up in the tower with my mother. "But until I do"—he pointed at the sky—"Jezebel is yours, only yours. I trust you to know what's best for her."

Clapping my arms like I was one of his knights, he rose, and we turned our faces back up to the heavens, my father's hand snug on my shoulder like armour. Still the falcon flew, up to her dizzying height; climbing, climbing, never stopping until she was far above us, farther than we could ever hope to go, scaling endlessly, forever out of our reach.

He left later that day.

2

THE SHOUTING WOKE me instantly, and how my sisters slept
through it I don't know. My chamber was in darkness, only the
embers in the hearth giving off a faint, pulsing glow. The moon—
so bright when I went to sleep—was a mere suggestion now,
hidden behind a slab of cloud. I slipped out of bed, cracked the
door open and eased into the empty passageway. There were no
more voices, only a distant commotion, but I had heard clearly
enough what was said.

The Duke is here: open the doors.

He had been gone for a shade more than three weeks and, of
course, would go straight to his Duchess. They kept their chambers
on the south side of the castle, overlooking the sea, the fastest route
a narrow, twisting stair nearby. One glimpse was all I wanted as
I ran up it, a moment's confirmation that my father was back safe
at Tintagel.

At the last step I paused, arrested by a sudden wrongness in the
air, a queer silence insulating the upper corridor like a drawn bed
drape. Opposite, an unglazed window stood mute, breezeless, the
eternal roar of the waves all but vanished. The only movement was a
light mist whispering along the windowsill, snaking down the wall
like a living thing. Puzzled, I took a step towards it, shrinking back
at the sound of oncoming footsteps.

He was several strides beyond me when I leapt forwards and called out.

"Father! Jezebel hatched three chicks."

I knew it would stop him, and he turned, broad shoulders jolting around, twitching as if his clothes were chafing his skin. Perhaps they were: it was a fair ride from Dimilioc, dusty in the heat, and he had been fighting for weeks. He took me in with unusual severity, a sneer of epiphany unfolding across his shadowy face.

"One of *his*, I suppose."

The voice was my father's in depth but alien in tone, scathing in a way I'd never heard him speak to man nor beast. A thin plume of mist crept across the floor, curling idly around his armoured leg.

"Get to bed, whelp," he snapped, and I fled, his snarl still ringing in my ears.

*

I AWOKE AT dawn, jumping from my bed and running up the same stairway towards my mother's chamber.

"Morgan!" my mother said as I slipped through the door left ajar. She was already risen, wearing a robe of sky-blue silk and a contented air. "My dear child, you must learn to knock."

I glanced around the room; the only other inhabitant was Constance, fussing by the fire. "Where is he?" I asked.

Suddenly, the door swung fully open, to the tune of armoured feet. "Good sir, you cannot come in my lady's chamber!" Constance exclaimed.

I turned to behold Sir Bretel, my father's trusted marshal, halfway up from a deep bow. "I beg your pardon, but this news cannot wait."

"Hush, Constance," my mother chided gently. "It's Sir Bretel. Of course I'll hear him."

"My lady." He paused to draw breath, and when he spoke again his voice was full of tears. "The Duke, your husband, my good and honourable lord, is slain, gone to God at Dimilioc."

All at once, his legs buckled, greaves hitting the floor with a crash. I shrank back, reaching for the closest wall. More than his words, the sudden prostration of such a man drove into my gut harder than a pony kick.

My mother slipped a hand under his elbow, and he clambered weakly to his feet. She was fresh as the sunrise next to his dirt-encrusted mail, golden hair undressed and cascading to her waist, smiling at him with pitying kindness.

"You are a good man, but happily you are mistaken. My husband is here, come to me last night."

"But my lady—"

"He's in his chamber." She gestured at the connecting door between their two rooms. "He rode alone and told no one he was coming."

Sir Bretel's head dropped, gauntleted hand cradling his face. He was my father's best knight and closest friend—they had squired together, sat vigil together and were knighted side by side under the previous Duke. At the dinner table they told long and complicated tales of shared adventures, fit to rival any bard. Sir Bretel loved my father too much to even speak of such a thing unproven, much less lie to his Duchess.

I stumbled towards my father's chamber and pushed my way in. The windows were shuttered, air claggy from the brackish humidity of summer and lack of a fire. The bed hangings stood open, the coverlet obviously undisturbed.

"No!" It was my mother's cry, high-pitched and vibrating with rage. I rushed back in to see her pointing shakily at Sir Bretel. "He was *here*. In this chamber, with me in my—this cannot be!"

Sir Bretel held out his hands in entreaty. "Lady Igraine, my Lord Cornwall is dead. He fought valiantly, but it was night, the enemy troops were too many, and we were savagely overcome. Before the fortress could be burned, the Duke rode out to put them to the sword, but his horse was killed, and a foot soldier ran him through the chest. We carried him to the gatehouse and removed the spear, but it was too late."

He ducked his head; a small tear rolled off his nose, white as a pearl in the dawn light. "Your husband died in my arms, my lady. I watched the life leave his eyes and closed them myself. I will swear on any relic that he could not have been at Tintagel."

Hand at her throat, my mother staggered backwards, landing heavily on the edge of her bed. "No," she whispered. "He was here, he . . ."

Constance ran to her at once. "Now, my lady, you need to lie down."

My mother held her at bay. "Am I mad, Sir Bretel? I cannot doubt you and yet . . ."

I could take no more, wanting only the warmth of my mother's embrace. I flew across the room and flung myself into her lap.

"You're not mad, Mother, you're not!" Twisting in her arms, I pointed viciously at Sir Bretel. "It's *he* who is mad, *he* who tells lies. Father is not dead, because I saw him too. Last night, in the corridor just outside. He spoke to me—it was him."

Little did it seem to matter the *way* he spoke to me, the harsh bark of dismissal that had frightened me away. I glared at Sir Bretel, daring him to contradict me.

He only regarded me with eyes full of sorrow. Extending his hand, he held something out: my father's gold ring, set with three sapphires—one for each of his daughters—his wife's name engraved inside the band. Whether at table, ahorse or with sword in hand, he never took it off. My mother wasn't the fainting kind, but she held fast to me then, gripping my bones like she was dangling off a cliff.

"His shade, my lady," Sir Bretel said softly. "You and Lady Morgan must have seen his soul, returning to his loved ones and Tintagel."

"It wasn't his spirit!" I insisted. "He was whole."

"Enough of this." Constance pulled me from my mother's lap and planted my unsteady feet on the floor. "The Duchess has had a terrible shock. You must leave and let me attend to her." She was already drawing the bed hangings, ushering my mother's weary body underneath the coverlet. "Sir Bretel, if you'd be so good as to take the child to the nursery and tell Gwennol the news. She'll know what to do with the young ladies."

Though I flailed and resisted, Sir Bretel scooped me up like so many feathers, never minding my tears, howls of rage or clawing hands, striking at him like a wildcat.

"Come now, Lady Morgan," was all he said, gently.

Lulled by his steady gait, I relented, pushing my hot, exhausted face against his armoured neck and letting darkness envelop me. The mail was cool and hard as sea pebbles against my skin, and smelled of earth in a rainstorm: rich, vital and distinctly metallic, like the blood of a thousand men.

3

BEFORE MY FATHER'S death, I had barely heard the name Uther Pendragon. I knew he was High King of Britain and that, of late, my parents had been summoned to his northern court with a frequency both inconvenient and highly unusual. Then he declared war on Cornwall, and that name was all we knew.

It was a fortnight before he sent word of whether we were to live or die. We sat in our unbreachable castle with the gates closed until the message came that Uther Pendragon was outside with my father's body on a bier, which he would not return unless my mother agreed to meet with him.

"It was our Duke's wish to be buried at Tintagel," she declared to a full but silent Great Hall, sat on her ducal throne beside my father's empty seat. The sapphires in his ring glinted darkly atop her twisting hands. "If one must enter, then so will the other."

Two long weeks of suffering had sunken her cheeks, grey eyes hooded with sleeplessness, skin sallow and clinging to her bones like death wrappings.

She sighed, sitting straighter. "Let him in."

Soon enough, a man strode forth, stocky and compact, with a bull neck and a ruddy, thick-boned face. He charged up to the dais, powerful chest bulging incongruous as a barrel under his tunic, a vicious golden dragon snarling rampant across the ivory silk.

He bowed briefly to my mother. "Lady Igraine, my thanks for opening your gates to me."

"I had little choice, King Uther." My mother surveyed her husband's murderer with distaste, eyeing the plain gold coronet around his close-cropped head, then glanced up as a second man appeared.

The stranger was slightly built and draped in robes of midnight purple, a twisted black staff in one hand, wielded lightly, like a weapon. Hair the colour of lead fell to his shoulders, beard long and streaked pale grey. His face was lined but ageless, features filed almost to points. Restless eyes, black as a tar pit, moved around the room in quick, calculating flicks. For a moment they alighted on me, and fear, sudden and involuntary, soaked through my limbs.

It was a relief when my mother signalled her knights to escort the High King to their private meeting, drawing the stranger's oily gaze away. As they moved off towards the Duke's Great Chamber, he followed without qualm, as if such things were a formality.

I slipped behind a distracted Gwennol and my gossiping sisters, up the wooden staircase onto the minstrels' gallery. From there, a door in the panelling led to a scribe's closet at the back of my father's council room. I wedged myself onto the high, slanting desk, pressing my ear to the gap in the interior door.

I heard my mother's voice first, dismissing her knights and refusing to sit.

"I don't expect this to take long," she said coldly. "Know that I consented to this meeting only for the sake of the Duke's surviving men. You also agreed this was a private matter, yet we are not alone. Who is this?"

"Merlin is a wise and learned man, my lady, a sorcerer of great repute and my closest adviser." Pendragon's voice was deep, rough as tree bark and halting, as if unused to deference but trying, nonetheless.

"This does not concern him. He must leave at once."

"Every aspect of my rule concerns him," came the reply, still polite but taut, inflexible. "He will be of help to us in resolving our difficulties."

"I doubt King Solomon himself could do such a thing," she snapped, and I swelled with pride at her forthrightness. Then Uther Pendragon laughed, loud and without a shred of care; dread replaced triumph in my chest.

"Regardless, he stays." He switched back to seriousness. "Lady Igraine, let's not tarry. I've done what you asked. The Duke's body lies in your chapel, ready for burial. His death was not my intention. I was away from command, and my men acted too quickly. He was only to be taken prisoner."

"How very generous, King Uther," she said. "What would you have done, sent him back to me? You lie, sir. His death was always your purpose."

"My lady, that is quite an accusation. When I have come here only to make honourable reparation for the Duke's . . . misadventure."

"And how might you offer that, as if I don't know?" she snarled. "Nay, you did not come to Cornwall to adhere to any notion of honour. You came here for *me*."

The long robes of the sorcerer whispered past the closet doorway, staff thumping with every step. A cold prickle took up under my skin. Who was he, this Merlin, the so-called sorcerer? What was his role within the private battle between a Duchess and a King?

"I am indeed offering marriage," Uther continued. "To marry a King, in your position, widowed with however many whelps in your nursery—daughters, at that—is quite beyond reparation. No woman alive could ask for more."

"That, sir, will not compel me. I was a good and faithful wife, and shall be a good and faithful widow."

Uther Pendragon laughed again, a humourless, dishonest sound. "It's your spirit I admire most of all." He chuckled. "You are good,

Lady Igraine, and pious by all accounts. Mistress of the chapel, generous with your benevolences. All the more reason to heed me, given we are already married in the eyes of God."

"*What?*"

"Don't fret, good woman. It wasn't adultery. Your husband was already dead at his fortress. Merlin will confirm everything. It was his clever sorcery that cleared my passage to your bed."

My breath caught in my throat, but the awfulness in her whisper told all. "That was *you*? With his face, his body? How did . . . *How could you?*"

"You rejected my admiration and spurned my advances," said the King. "What choice did you give me, truly?"

I jumped at the sudden crash, followed by another, the sound of metal clattering to the floor, the musical report of broken glass.

"*Get out!*" she screamed. "Get out of my castle, or I'll have my men cut you limb from limb and the Devil take the consequences. I will never marry you!"

No response came from Uther Pendragon, and I had the fleeting hope he was knocked into a stupor by one of the missiles she'd thrown. But soon, a chair scraped across the floor as the High King of Britain sought to make himself comfortable.

"Merlin, tell her."

The sorcerer's voice came forth as a toneless drawl, like a wasp in a bottle. "My lord King has put a child in you, Lady Igraine, one you will bear alive. It is woven into the skies."

"It is a lie." Her words caught, as if she had taken a blow to the stomach. "It's ungodly, it . . . will not be."

"It has already begun," Merlin said.

"So you see, my Lady Igraine," Uther Pendragon said, "marriage is the only pathway to saving your soul. As to the rest, I needn't explain that Tintagel is mine and you cannot order me out of it. In fact, I'll be happy to stay. You've been kept well here, by your Duke. His stables and bird mews alone are fit for an emperor, and I shall enjoy their spoils."

He paused, but she gave no reply. "Therefore," he continued, "either you marry me and love me as your lord, becoming Queen of All Britain, kept safe and in an even higher manner than you are already, or I go from here, as you request. I might even let you keep your rooms at Tintagel. But the gates will be opened, and my men will come in to secure her. My barons need to be paid—they'll fill their coffers and take whatever they feel is due to them. That is, anything I haven't claimed as my own. How many daughters is it you have—three? The things that might befall them at the hands of other men . . ." He gave a short bray of laughter. "Distasteful, reprehensible behaviour, of course. But actions quite out of my control the moment I turn my back."

"You selfish, black-hearted demon," she hissed.

"Loving you as ardently as I do, my lady," he cut in, "I would hate to see you so reduced. But if you refuse my hand and protection, what can I do?" He let out a long, animal yawn, and I knew he was stretching his limbs. "Well, Lady Igraine, what say you?"

I waited, arms rigid against the desk. Suddenly, my sweating palm slid, sending three pots of ink clattering to the floor.

Uther Pendragon's chair crashed to the ground. "Merlin!" he barked. "Are we overheard?"

Footsteps marched towards my hiding place. Pushing frantically at the closet door, I burst free, racing down from the minstrels' gallery and away from the terror of the Great Chamber, deep into the obscuring belly of the castle.

*

"I THINK SHE ought to marry him," said Morgause. "It would make us all Princesses."

"Morgause!" Elaine exclaimed, in a rare loss of composure. "That's no good reason to marry someone. She loved Father."

"It's the *only* reason," Morgause replied. "One cannot eat love, after all. He's a King, and he wants her. She must do it if we are to live. There is no better way to assure our future."

Elaine pulled a considering face, then trotted off to catch up with Gwennol. We had been summoned to the Great Hall, and Morgause had hold of my wrist to ensure I didn't slip away.

"Despite what *you* want, Mother isn't going to marry him," I said. "I've never heard her so furious."

"That doesn't mean anything," Morgause replied with an air of insufferable wisdom.

I yanked my wrist out of my sister's careless grasp. We walked side by side in silence, before curiosity overtook my irritation.

"Morgause, what does it mean to be 'married in the eyes of God'?"

She glanced down at me, eyes like daggers. "If I told you that, fox cub, I'd be saying Hail Marys until my hair turned grey."

"Please. I won't tell."

She sighed, slowing our step so we would not be overheard. "It's a . . . situation a lady doesn't want to be in with a man, unless he intends on lawfully marrying her. And don't ever tell anyone I told you that much."

A crowd had already formed in the Great Hall, Pendragon men mingling with ours, intruders at my father's hearth. A door flew open on the dais, and through it strode the High King, with my mother behind him, her face utterly blank. I did not need to hear the herald's announcement to know that Morgause would be proved right: Igraine, Duchess of Cornwall, had surrendered, and they were to be married in all haste.

The room rang with broken, confounded applause, and Uther Pendragon—liar, King and murderer—smiled, a joyless thing made only of victory; the same sneer I had seen once before, on the face of a dark, hulking figure, in the corridor of my mother's chamber, trailing mist and wearing the skin of my father.

*

THE CASTLE'S BACK corridors were empty, shock keeping Tintagel's household away from their posts. The few people I did see were clustered in corners, murmuring worriedly in Cornish, too preoccupied to notice a slip of a girl.

I crossed the kitchen courtyard and ran into the deserted bird mews. Jezebel, grumpy with moult and suspicious of me as ever, nevertheless allowed herself to be coaxed to my fist with the bribe of rabbit. She tore at the pink flesh as I carried her carefully out of the back door and onto the headland.

She was a weighty bird for anyone, let alone one of my age and stature, and my arm throbbed as I lurched over the soft tussocks, trying my best not to stumble and drop her.

"He will not have you," I muttered. "Never will he take you like he has taken us."

Unsettled, she ruffled ragged neck feathers at me, so I did as my father used to—clucking, tutting, saying her name—when all the while I was not him, could never be him, was barely capable of giving her a steady perch.

But she came with me, with better grace than I deserved, never bating or screeching, and when I slipped off her jesses and delivered her into the wind, she didn't hesitate, curving skywards at my command. Jezebel, the wanderer, went just as my father predicted she would: without a backwards glance, first reaching for the clouds, then gliding over the edge of the cliff, taking flight towards her freedom.

4

MY FATHER'S INTERMENT in Tintagel's chapel was done quietly, with only family and his closest knights in attendance. We had barely said "Amen" over his tomb before we were put on the long road north to Carduel, where the wedding of Uther Pendragon and my mother would take place.

By the time my mother spoke her vows, unsmiling but clear-voiced, she looked almost herself, encased in a smooth marble beauty and clothed in a gown of ivory samite brocaded in gold, reflecting her angelic colouring and the new standard under which she was wed. Two days later, they crowned her in the abbey and she became Uther Pendragon's anointed Queen. It hardly seemed possible that on Easter Day she had taken my father's hand and danced with him in Tintagel's bustling hall, his arms about her and their faces close.

Halfway through a week of wedding celebrations, my sisters and I were called to play our parts in the palace's enormous Throne Room, golden dragons snarling from every rafter. Behind the throne, the sorcerer Merlin hovered silently, prowling, disinterested, occasionally surveying the assembled crowd.

Uther sat on his gilded chair, ermine-swathed, one hand clasping his new Queen's arm. The other, heavy with jewels, beckoned us forth. Morgause went first, kneeling before them, elegant and well practised as she spoke the words we had been given.

"King Uther and Queen Igraine of All Britain, I pledge to you my loyalty as your faithful subject and daughter. It is an honour to kneel before your royal and holy office, and to pay my respects to you as my lady mother and my esteemed lord father."

It was a clever oath, designed to leave no doubt of our fealty, and my eldest sister spoke it exceedingly well. Uther stood and beckoned her to rise, nodding in satisfaction.

"Lady Morgause, I am pleased to call you daughter and hereby confer on you the title of Princess of Britain, in recognition of your status under my Crown." He took up her hand and kissed it. "But as your father and King, I can do far better for a maiden of such beauty."

At his signal, a man emerged from a group of knights at the foot of the dais. He looked tall as a tree next to my sister, better equipped to be wielding an oaken club than the gold-hilted sword at his side. He had about a decade on Morgause's sixteen, and stood fiercely upright, fit and healthy-looking, with a head of dark-red curls and beard to match. His ceremonial mail shone like purest silver, weapon belt flaming with rubies.

Morgause, at first, seemed wary in the stranger's great shadow, then he bowed deep and, at the sight of his modest crown, she transformed, smiling at him in glowing realization.

Uther picked up her hands and placed them firmly in the man's awaiting grip. "King Lot of Lothian and Orkney, I give to you my eldest daughter—Morgause, Princess of Britain, in betrothal. May your union be long and joyous, and bring you many sons." He turned to my sister. "Obey this man as your lord. Honour him with your body and spirit, and prove yourself a worthy Queen."

"I will, my lord father," Morgause replied.

I clamped my teeth together to stop a sob from escaping. Was I the only one to remember our true father, the man who had loved us, given us our home and made us proud?

A small hand, cool and dry, pushed itself into my closed fist, and I looked up at Elaine's steady countenance, so assured, disdainful of indulgent emotion. She squeezed my fingers, enough to make me swallow my tears, then she left me to go speak her oath, accepting her new lands and titles from our father's usurper with her natural indifference on full display. No husband was allotted to my second sister, for which I shivered in relief.

I was next. Uther, seated again, summoned me with a flick of his wrist, and I flinched, cooling balm of sorrow evaporating at once, leaving the only response I knew in its place: fury.

My mother's imploring eyes were all that brought me forwards. I wanted none of his lands, none of his titles, wishing only for my name to stay aligned with Cornwall. I couldn't say a word of it now, of course; I was to make my obeisance, accept the honours bestowed on me and, most of all, keep quiet.

So I did. There, under Uther Pendragon's expectant, smouldering gaze, I stood, straight as a pikestaff, and said not a single word.

At first he sought to fill the silence, awarding me lands for the benefit of my future husband and throwing his title, Princess of Britain, across my shoulders like a poisoned mantle. Still I stood silent, with my knees unbending. I wasn't stupid; I knew it would not sustain. But I didn't care. I was made of stone, as if Medusa's rage had uncoiled within me and caught sight of its own ferocious reflection.

Uther's face darkened with blood. "You should kneel now, Morgana."

I moved not an inch.

"Do as you've been told," he cautioned. "Kneel and speak your oath, like your sisters."

Once again, I did nothing.

"She's nervous," said my mother. "My child, do as the King says. Kneel, touch his mantle and say the words you've learned." But she was not my mother now, rather an imposter made in her image. I stayed standing.

Silence lay heavy across the room. At the back of the dais, Merlin paused and cocked his head in curiosity.

Uther Pendragon held up his hand, perhaps contemplating wringing my neck, and for a moment I willed it—the exposure of his violence, his cruelty, his selfishness—but he only clicked finger and thumb together, sound snapping around the walls. A short-legged knight with a face like a hatchet stepped out from behind the throne.

"Ulfin," Uther growled, "make her kneel."

"My lord—" my mother began.

"Nay, my lady. She's had her chance."

A hard hand fell on my shoulder, driving my small frame down-wards until my knees hit cold stone. Sir Ulfin hooked up Uther Pendragon's pooling golden mantle and shoved it into my hand, before stalking back to his place in the shadow of his master.

"Now speak," Uther commanded. "You are daughter of a King and must act as such. Acknowledge your title, accept my generous boon and address me as your lord father." He eyed me down his much-broken nose. "Say it, Morgana. Say 'Thank you, my lord father.'"

My capacity for hatred has always been great, but unlike my temper it was never innate; not borne in my blood but formed there, on that day, at the feet of Uther Pendragon, being forced to call him "father."

The mantle slipped from my fingers, alive like a snake.

"*You are not my father*," I said, and spat at his feet.

Hundreds of hands seemed to reach out for me as I ran, pushing blindly past row after row of brightly dressed bodies, daughterly loy-alty singing in my veins. I was doomed but victorious.

Or so I thought, until I heard him laugh.

In the midst of my triumph, Uther Pendragon sat back in his

throne and gave a deep, bloodcurdling whoop of joy. My feet turned to lead, the exhilarating aftermath of rebellion already fading.

"Let her go," he chuckled. "She's afeared, overwhelmed, practically an infant. It seems," he added to his audience, "I have a thing or two to learn about managing daughters!"

And the room laughed, though the relief was as thick as smoke from a funeral pyre. In the distraction, Uther made a quick summoning gesture, and a strong hand shot out from nowhere, catching my wrist and yanking me from the room before I could do so much as scream.

*

I HAD NEVER seen the sour-faced woman before, and she didn't look back as she pulled me, twisting and dissenting, down the echoing corridor.

"Let me go!" I protested. "You're not my nurse."

"I have my orders," she said sharply. "Now come along and stop performing. You are not a monkey."

A wisp of fear unfurled in my chest. "What orders?"

"From the High King, of course. You'll come with me, and quietly."

"I won't. I want to speak to my mother!"

With one painful tug of my arm, I broke free. Her eyes flew open in alarm as I staggered backwards and hit something that could not have been the wall but was almost as hard. I bounced off it and onto the floor.

"Thank you, good woman, I will take it from here," said a stony voice. The woman scuttled off, and I looked up to meet the seething, muddy glare of Uther Pendragon.

Scrambling to my feet, I made to run, but his hand flew out and grabbed my hair. My neck and scalp screamed in pain as he dragged me around the corner and threw me into the wide stone window seat. My bones shuddered against the slabs, but I leapt up almost immediately, blood roaring.

Uther loomed like a devil. "Defy me, would you?" he bellowed. "Every man and woman in that room obeys me, yet it falls to *you*, a runt bitch from that feeble peninsula to challenge my authority. But heed me you will, Morgana."

"Never!" I screamed. "You lied to my mother, you murdered my father—"

"If your beloved father was half the man he should have been, he'd have obeyed me and would still be alive. He too thought he could defy me, so I took all he had."

"Not *everything*. I've heard you at Tintagel, asking after his peregrine. *I let her go.*"

I half thought he wouldn't care, but he stared at me like I had confessed to poisoning his meat. "You did *what*? That bird belonged to *me*, you godforsaken hell-cat!"

Grabbing my arm, Uther half lifted me from the ground and struck me clean across the face, rattling my jaw so hard I was sure I felt it break. Dazed, I veered sideways, tasting blood, vision full of underwater stars. A pair of teeth skittered over my tongue, clattering onto the stones like bloody pearls. He jolted me upright, pulling his hand back for the next blow.

"*Stop this now!*"

From nowhere, my mother seized his arm, making him drop me. Curled up on the floor with my vision clearing, I saw the old flare in her cheeks, her eyes gleaming like steel. "She is a *child*. Never did I think you would stoop so low."

Uther paused, chest heaving with unspent brutality. "Your daughter must obey me. If she won't of her own accord, then she must be forced."

"As you said, my lord, she is *my* daughter. You will spare her such harsh treatment for the love you bear me. And on the week of our wedding. *For shame.*"

"My lady, I won't be told how to behave in my own kingdom, much less my house. Such defiance has led your family into trouble before."

I winced, but she stood straight-backed as an archer, placing a calm, stately hand over her belly, above the child that the sorcerer and the skies had promised.

Uther sighed with impatience. "Make no mistake," he continued, less sharply, "you are my wife, my Queen, and I am within my lawful, God-given rights to check you, or any of your nest of daughters, by hand. See that she learns how to conduct herself, or so help me . . ."

With a vicious sweep of his gold mantle, he charged off down the hallway, threat left incomplete.

Rushing across, my mother lifted me onto the window seat, tilting my face gently. "Good Lord, what has he done to you?"

My jaw and cheekbone throbbed under her delicate fingers, soft flesh already swelling into the shape of Uther's kingly handprint.

"Morgan, dear child. It's my fault, this choler of yours. Our blood betrays us when it rises, lights a fire not easily put out." She brushed a thumb under each of my eyes, finding no tears. I braced myself for her comforting arms, but instead she regarded me with a frank grey gaze. "You should heed the King, avoid his ire. I won't always be able to restrain him in such a way."

"He is not my father."

Abruptly, she stood up, brushing creases from her bridal skirts. The evening light seeped through the window, dissolving gold to mauve, rippling across the finely wrought surface of her diadem.

"No, he is not," she said tiredly. "But he is my husband now, and our King. Uther Pendragon is what keeps us out of harm's way, well fed and with clothes on our backs. Whether it pleases you or not."

She turned and walked a few steps, then looked at me over her shoulder. The advancing shadows rendered her suddenly hollow, stripping away the glow of finery and beauty and leaving her empty, like a death's head. Her voice was cold as the grave.

"Submit to him, Morgan, for your own good. It is the only way to survive."

5

MY MOTHER WENT to her lying-in at Tintagel around Candlemas, about a month before she was due to give birth. After a cold autumn spent traipsing around Uther's North, and a drizzly midwinter in Caerleon, it was a relief to all of us to be back home in my father's fortress. Even Uther Pendragon could not destroy the sense of belonging I felt within those sea-swept walls.

"Soon we will be three again," Elaine mused, as we idled in our chambers on the first morning of March. "I must learn to be Morgause, and you will be me, as you're no longer the youngest."

"I'd rather be myself," I replied. "If you're going to be Morgause, then perhaps you should look after her birds."

I picked up a gilded cage from the tabletop. Within, Morgause's pair of red-throated linnets flitted between perches, chirping greedily. After a quick wedding in Carduel, our elder sister had galloped off to her queenly fate in Lothian with nary a glance, leaving the poor creatures behind. "I'm surprised they've survived so long, stuck in this tiny cage."

"You're not to let them go," Elaine warned.

Why not? I thought, as I carried the cage to the windowsill and sprinkled in some seed. Suddenly, one of the birds flew at the closing cage door in a burst of desperate independence. An outstretched wing caught the bars at an angle, trapping it there. The bird thrashed madly until something gave, then fell onto its tawny back, wing oddly outstretched.

"No, no, no!" I cried. Reaching into the cage, I took the linnet's fragile body into my hands and smoothed the jutting wing down. It sprung back out again, helplessly broken.

"What's happened?" Elaine peered over my shoulder. "Oh dear. It can't live like that. I'll call someone to deal with it."

"No!" I exclaimed. "You can't, I—"

"Morgan, be sensible. It's kinder if it doesn't suffer."

I knew she was right—even a caged bird needed its wings. I stared down at my hands; the linnet gave two mournful chirps. It was all my fault, but I hadn't meant it, couldn't bear the thought of causing such pain. I folded the wing back and cupped my hands snugly around the small feathered body; its heartbeat whirred within my hands, mirroring the panicked despair fast rising in my chest.

Do something, I thought. *You have to fix this.*

Elaine beckoned for the bird. I turned away, holding it out of her reach. "If you just let it rest—"

Between my palms, the bird's warmth increased, radiating outwards, gaining in strength. All at once, the linnet gave a great, struggling push, bursting forth from my hands and into the air on perfect wings. Upon seeing its companion, the second bird hopped to the cage door and took flight, the pair of them darting out of the open window to freedom.

"Morgan, what . . . ?" Elaine gasped. "But that wing was broken. How . . . ?"

I stared at the escaping linnets, tiny dots now against pale-grey clouds, my hands still warm, tingling with a faint, pleasant sensation.

I did it, I wanted to tell her. *I willed it and then it was done.*

Before I could decide whether to express such an impossibility, Gwennol burst in and flew past us, striking at tears with the heel of her hand. Elaine and I swung around in unison, birds forgotten.

"All these years," she muttered. "All the children I helped bring safely into the world." She thrashed at my unmade bed, slapping the sheets taut. "Every birth I've been there, and now it's 'She needs help fit for a queen.' From a girl of that age! What can she know?"

The two of us edged closer as Gwennol sank onto the mattress, weeping freely. I nudged Elaine. "What's she talking about?"

Elaine gave me a doubtful look, then, drawing her kerchief from her sleeve, strode across to Gwennol and offered it to her. "Gwennol, what's wrong? Is it Mother?"

"Your lady mother has started her labour, but she's healthful and will bear it bravely, as always." She sniffled loudly into the kerchief. "I'm just being churlish, but I thought I'd be there, as I was with the rest of you."

"Won't you be?" I piped up.

"No. The King has brought his own people." She rose, tucking the kerchief into her kirtle. "Don't take my weeping to heart, my dears. Now, why is that birdcage empty?"

Leaving Elaine to take a scolding, I slipped out of the door and up the spiral stairs. My mother and Uther inhabited a suite of chambers on the castle's north side, overlooking the tiltyard, but for her lying-in my mother had returned immediately to the airy south-facing tower she'd kept as Duchess.

The usual breeze whistled down the stairway, full of salt, and wintry, but less biting now, softened by the expectation of spring. A pair of voices floated down with it, so I slowed my steps, leaping back in horror when I saw who was at the top.

The sorcerer Merlin stood mere feet away, thankfully with his back to me. He wore the same violet-black robes as before, but instead of a staff, he held the arm of a girl. She was older than Elaine—fourteen or fifteen at a guess—and exquisitely beautiful, with long hair of shining copper and the most remarkable skin. She seemed to glow, shimmering from within, and I knew, with sudden, unexplainable certainty, that she was not of my kind.

"The child must live, Ninianne," Merlin said in his colourless tone. "The stars have it written, but we must ensure it. You are to bring all your skills to bear on the Queen."

"She doesn't want me," the girl protested. "She wants her women, those she knows."

"She cannot have them. Remember what I've taught you and become all she needs. It shouldn't be difficult—she has borne many children."

"And I have delivered none." Huffing, she pulled away from his grasp. The sorcerer reached up to touch her face, and she twisted her head in avoidance, emerald-green eyes alighting on me.

I was caught, inescapably. One word and the sorcerer would drag me straight to Uther Pendragon, or worse, punish me himself, and I wondered why the devil I wasn't running away. But I was terrified, stuck, as if trapped under glass, held by the girl Ninianne's gleaming stare.

It was as if time had slowed around us. Gradually, her shining presence seemed to come alive, flowing forth off her skin like tendrils of sun, warm and almost tangible, reaching out for me in comfort and recognition. *I know you*, her eyes seemed to say. *I feel you and you are safe*.

All at once, my fear vanished, tension in my insides dissipating in the wake of her light, setting me free and connecting us in a strange, wordless solidarity.

Ninianne turned her face back towards the sorcerer's hand, still hovering in the air. As if no time had passed, he moved, probing a loose red curl at her cheek, tucking it carefully behind her ear. She concealed it well, but I saw the faint flutter of her eyelids, the controlled shudder of disgust.

If Merlin noticed, he paid it no mind. "Ninianne," he said indulgently. "My fairest Lady of the Lake. I have faith in you. When it is done, cut the cord, get the child fed by his mother and bring him to me."

A thin moan echoed down the corridor: my mother labouring alone, without the comfort of Gwennol, Constance or Tintagel's long-serving midwife. I started forwards at the sound, and Merlin sensed it, dark head swivelling.

The girl grabbed his arm and made him look at her. "I'm afraid," she said plaintively. "I want only to please you."

He smiled, entirely absorbed by her luminous, beseeching face. "You'll please me, my dear, as you always do." Another groan came, louder this time. "Hark, she cries. Go to her, bring Britain's son into this world alive."

The girl nodded, green eyes hooking into mine once more. *Go,* they urged me. *He will look for you next.*

I turned on my heel and ran as fast as I could back to the nursery, accepted my telling-off for freeing the birds and never told a soul about any of it.

Much later, as I lay wide awake in bed, I heard the first cry, brand new and hearty with life, and knew it was over. Outside, the horizon glowed against night's final resistance, before light pushed through the last vestiges of the dark and brought forth the dawn.

*

"STILLBORN?"

"Aye, a son. The red-headed girl said he never drew breath. The King immediately sent him to Carduel for burial."

"By God, my poor Lady Igraine!"

I sat up in bed, head fogged from uneasy sleep. The door to Gwennol's bedchamber stood open, so I swung my feet onto the floor and crept towards it. Gwennol and Constance sat huddled together, still in their nightclothes. A reedy white light filtered in behind their bent heads, like the grief of saints painted on a church wall.

My nurse crossed herself and dissolved into a torrent of sobs. "We should have been there. We've never lost one, have we? Not at full term."

"I know, my dear," Constance said. "One inexperienced girl to deal with a labouring noblewoman. It beggars belief."

"I heard a baby cry," I declared. "Maybe it's a mistake."

They stared up at my intrusion, exchanging a shocked glance. Gwennol shook her head sadly. "You couldn't have, my duck. There never was a baby, not in this world at least."

"I heard it! The red-haired girl might have lied."

"You were dreaming, child," Constance said briskly.

Gwennol rose. "Come along. You're still tired."

She guided me patiently back to bed. I waited until she shut the door, then jumped up and ran as fast as I could to my mother's lying-in chamber, where I would find her and confirm I had indeed heard *something*.

What I found was desertion: bedding and drapes stripped, surfaces scrubbed, not a discarded robe or stray rosary in sight. My mother had obviously been taken hastily back to the Royal Chambers, under Uther's watchful eye.

I crumpled to the floor, defeated. I hadn't dreamed it, I was sure. I knew a child that never drew breath could not cry, yet why would anyone lie about such a terrible happening?

Something cool brushed across my knuckles, soft and sudden like the glancing whiskers of a cat. A pale line of mist trailed across the boards, glowing benignly in the early-morning light. I followed it to the open window, tracking its wispy passage down the tower wall and across the headland grass, where it slithered along the cliffside and disappeared into the cove below. I had seen it before, on the night of my father's death, curling around the leg of the man who wore his face.

I flew from the empty chamber, careening down the nearest stair and through a side door onto the headland, chasing the shrinking vapour down the rocky path and over the shingled sand until I reached the water's edge. A cold wave rushed over my bare feet.

A small rowing boat was rounding the corner of the bay, almost out of sight. Tintagel's lively blue sea—famed for its ferocity in our coves—sat flat and glassy beneath the clouded vessel.

A figure pulled at the oars, made conspicuous by a blaze of copper hair: Ninianne. Opposite her sat Merlin, a dark blot against the brightening seascape, carrying a bundle of white and gold, unmistakable in shape. A child in swaddling, either stillborn and sent for burial, or one I had heard cry, carried off regardless.

I shot forwards, desperate to follow, stopping knee-deep in freezing salt water. I hardly noticed the cold, my entire focus upon the boat and my chance for the truth, fast slipping away.

I wanted to scream, halt them somehow, but I was mute, weighted by failure and useless fury, spreading through my limbs like hot vines. Around me, the sea awoke, smooth surface trembling so hard it broke upwards in jagged peaks, as if disrupted by my own frustration. It rippled out and up, waves rising ever faster, until the tide was churning and leaping as usual, alive once more.

But it was too late. The small boat vanished beyond the cove, undisturbed, trailing mist. It was then I heard it: a defiant keening sound, strong and vital, endlessly fierce, already fading into memory; a wail I had heard before, or perhaps just the renewed protest of the Cornish wind, lost beneath the echo of the roaring waves.

6

THE AFTERNOON OF my eighth birthday, I was summoned to see my mother in her dim, north-facing reception chamber, a few days after she had emerged from her lying-in. She rushed to embrace me, holding us cheek to cheek, and I inhaled her presence, the familiar sweet scent of the rose oil she used to perfume her bath. Her face was drawn and weary, but yielded little of the grief she must have felt.

"My dear Morgan," she said. "What gift would you like for your birthday? The marshal in Caerleon has bred some beautiful ponies."

"Lessons," I blurted out. "Not just letters and numbers. I know all that."

I'd been sitting in on my reluctant sisters' lessons with Tintagel's chaplain for years, absorbing every word, repeating writing exercises on my wax tablet until perfected. I had always wanted more, but my recent experiences had made me acutely aware of my limitations, and hungrier than ever to defeat them. Learning about the world seemed the first step towards greater understanding.

"I wish to learn everything," I continued, gaining in animation. "Other tongues, every story ever told, all about the land, the sky and times past. Father used to say the chapel had many books."

She flinched, briefly. "Very well, dear daughter. I'll speak to the chaplain, see what he can offer you beyond the instruction you already have."

"*Absolutely not.*"

Uther Pendragon stalked out of the shadows. My tongue ran unconsciously over the fresh hard spurs in my gums, where new teeth were emerging to replace those he had knocked free.

"In a few years Morgana will be wed, with a household to run and a lord husband to get children for," he told my mother. "She has enough learning for that. What purpose, education, for a female child?"

"But my lord, she is eight," my mother protested. "She already spends hours with the women, learning for court and house."

"Chapel duties, then," he snapped. "God knows she could do with some instruction in piety."

There was no further argument. I was to hear early-morning Mass with Father Felix, and observe every hour thereafter with prayer, in between learning Scripture and keeping the chapel neat. All this until the midday meal, after which I would rejoin Elaine and the women for the usual music, sewing and ladylike concerns.

The next day, at dawn, I made my way across the headland to Tintagel's chapel. I stepped into the empty nave, morning light streaming through a trio of large arched windows at the altar end. The plastered walls were decorated with frescoes: curling vines, stormy seas, tales from the gospels rendered in vivid detail. The air smelled of burning beeswax and frankincense.

I approached the marble altar on tentative feet. It was handsomely carved with images of the Cornish saints, bordered with gilded lettering. To the left, an arc of shadow stretched down three steps into a cloistered alcove, where my father's tomb stood sleek against the wall. A single window, glazed in checkered sapphire, cast a bluish light over the sealing stone, a smooth white slab thick as a horse hand.

When we went to Mass I tried not to look at it, but there alone in the muted early morning, I found myself inexorably drawn down the steps. I laid my palm on the cool, blank lid and abruptly burst into tears. It came forth in a noisy deluge, pouring out the black grief that had filled my heart daily since my father had fallen to Uther Pendragon's murderous will.

The sound of my cries drew Father Felix from his living quarters within the sacristy. "Lady Morgan, my dear child!" Pattering down the steps, he put a guiding hand on my shoulder. "Come, light a candle for your father and commend his spirit to God."

There was already a candle burning atop the tomb—always had been, I realized. I took the new taper from Father Felix and lit it from the existing flame. "Who ordered this rite?" I asked.

"Your lady mother," he said. "So the Duke might better find his way to Paradise. I also say nightly prayers for him aloud, since she cannot."

He made his way back to the altar, hands clasped behind him. He was a small man, bald and white-bearded, soft in both speech and movement, with keen, owlish eyes.

I followed him, tears dried by curiosity. "Does Uther know?"

"Fortunately for us, King Uther cannot and does not know everything. I will always keep the Duke's secrets." He considered me with a sideways glance. "I hear you wish to be educated."

"I do, but I'm not allowed lessons. I'm here only to assist you and better learn to be pious."

"A worthy endeavour," agreed the priest. "But it was your lord father's intention that all his daughters be educated. A good man's untimely death doesn't mean I should leave his wishes unfulfilled."

I stared at him. His face was tranquil, matter-of-fact, as if his words were common sense rather than bordering on a dangerous treason.

"The Duke always said you were very quick," he continued. "He believed you would be an excellent pupil, keener than your sisters. But is knowledge what you wish for?"

"More than anything," I said.

"Then it's settled. We will begin at once."

"But Uther forbade—"

The chaplain waved the notion away. "We must keep it to ourselves, of course. But even Uther Pendragon doesn't have mastery over the will of a true father, neither yours nor the One above us. And I serve both."

He went to the sacristy doorway and gestured within. Beyond him was a bright, orderly chamber, walls lined with shuttered cabinets, stacked floor to ceiling with bound manuscripts and scrolls of parchment. A long table stood under the windows, a chessboard at one end displaying a game half-begun; at the other, a glazed blue pot, bristling with swan quills. The air smelled warmly of ink, rich with possibilities.

*

FATHER FELIX WAS a learned man; years of study in Britain and overseas had left him in good stead with foreign tongues, but also literature, philosophy, history and logic. For seven years I sat at the sacristy table, immersed in the knowledge a love of Latin allowed: poetry, myth, past lives retold; the wisdom of great thinkers; the trials of Aeneas and the searing letters of Ovid's heroines—endless worlds unfolding before me, just as I had wished it.

When the midday bell rang, I submitted once again to ladylike pursuits, rooms full of chatter, gossip, needles and thread, where I practised plucking a lute and stitched seam after seam. I could share my newfound happiness with no one.

We were much at Tintagel and Uther was not, as he took King Lot of Lothian's men and waged war in the North. But when we could not be in Cornwall, I disappeared to the little-used libraries of

Uther's finer palaces, treasure troves both deserted and surprisingly rich. There, hidden away, I studied: huge books of maps; illustrated volumes detailing the natural world; explorations of land, sea and sky; plants and animals native and exotic; the hierarchy of elemental forces that controlled our entire existence. At night, I leaned out of my chamber window, sketching the stars.

Then one day at Carduel, I found the *Ars Physica*—a large book of medicine, going back to Galen's time, full of diagrams, anatomies, ailments and cures—and fell headlong into its mysteries. Amid the lists of bones, organs, muscles and flesh—and all that could befall them—I discovered the key to the puzzle of human frailty. If one could learn it, master it, then surely no power would ever be of more use? The thought was intoxicating.

The volume was heavy, conspicuous and a great risk to take, but I needed it. In the end, it took my best lanner falcon and a great deal of ladylike charm to convince a Cornish stablehand to be my accomplice, so that when the household rode south a few weeks after my fifteenth birthday, the book was hidden in a sack and strapped safely to a packhorse, on its way home to Tintagel.

7

"I'M GETTING MARRIED," Elaine said, early one midsummer morning.

I turned over in bed and stared at her, mouth open, ready to protest.

"Please, no fuss," she said, with the unflustered equanimity I little understood. "I am resigned to it. But know that I will miss you."

"I'll miss you too," I said, and meant it. Along the way Elaine had given up her determination to be Morgause, and had become an elder sister in her own right, sensible and collected, a panacea to my fury and confusion.

"We found our way somehow, didn't we? And now you're becoming a woman, and . . . well, I am one."

I snorted. "I'm not becoming anything."

She did not smile. "You're fifteen, Morgan, and I'll be of age in a few weeks. Womanhood is already here."

Neutres of Garlot, it was to be: a newly crowned King of a small but prosperous country nestled between the North Wales border and the River Derwent. Two months and Elaine would be wed—by St. Swithin's I would be completely alone, the sole remaining daughter of Cornwall.

"You'll have company," my mother told me that afternoon. She had drawn me aside in the cavernous red room she used as her solar, away from the ever-pricked ears of her women. "There are plenty of well-bred young ladies who would be honoured to attend you."

"I don't want to be attended," I hissed. "I don't know how you stand it, surrounded by these nodding hens. All I want is for my sister to be safe and happy. She isn't like Morgause, hard as diamond and desperate for a crown. Elaine is quiet, and good, and likes things just so."

"Elaine will have all she wants."

"You mean Uther will," I retorted. "Selling your daughters for more gold, more men to wage more wars."

"Morgan . . ." She passed a tired hand across her face. "Morgause is coming, and Elaine is here for a few more weeks. Spend time with your sisters, that's all I can advise."

"I can't bear to listen to this." Turning on my heel, I charged out of the solar and down the stairs.

I emerged onto the bustling main courtyard. Tintagel Castle had been buzzing with wedding activity for a while, I realized; more knights and an increased guard, supplies trundling in at all hours of the day, lords from surrounding manors meeting with Uther's stewards.

I cut left, heading diagonally across the courtyard green, seeking the roar of the sea. An immense crash brought me to a halt, followed by a chorus of shouts and claps from a crowd gathered near the tilt-yard. The long, fenced stretch of grass ran along the curtain wall, a jousting boundary down the middle, painted spectator stands bracketing either end. Inside the stockade, a row of horses idled while two dozen new squires—recently arrived from the usual noble houses—stood listening intently to Sir Bretel as he sat astride his horse, explaining a complex jousting technique.

Since becoming Queen's Knight to my mother, Sir Bretel had given up competing at tournaments, but tales of his sporting prowess were woven through my childhood like a tapestry. Curious, I drew closer, slipping into the shadows at the edge of the stands.

Sir Bretel beckoned to his chosen opponent from the group of jostling squires. A tall figure unfolded itself from the fence and shoved on a helmet. Striding over to a horse, the chosen youth vaulted into the saddle straight from the ground, took up the proffered shield and lance, and set off at a canter to the opposite end of the barrier. Gathering his reins in one hand and steadying the lance with the other, he saluted Sir Bretel and charged.

The squire's form was excellent, the charge fast and immensely controlled. Hugging his horse to the joust boundary, he deflected a hit while lining up the centre of his instructor's shield with quick precision. Sir Bretel just about parried the counterstrike, experience alone allowing him to keep his seat. When they rounded the barrier to take up the second charge, the squire tilted his shoulder slightly inwards before impact, and Sir Bretel found himself sitting on the grass with his shield almost cleaved in two. Grinning, he sprung to his feet and awarded his opponent a round of applause.

"That," he shouted to the others, "is how it's done."

My eyes stayed with the tall squire as he dismounted, pulling off his helm without a hint of triumph and pushing long ash-dark hair off his forehead. He had a strange kind of beauty, with an intriguing, high-boned face, sculptural features arranged underneath a sardonic brow, his top lip slightly upturned, as if in gentle but permanent amusement. He moved the way he rode, rangy and careless, completely at ease with his long limbs and broad shoulders. Upon reaching the fence, he leaned back on his elbows and crossed one boot over the other.

I edged around the stockade, watching him watch the others, his eyes low-lidded, concealed. The squires were all around sixteen, but he seemed older; his dark-blue tunic was well tailored, worn with care, and he possessed an air of quiet knowingness that his boyish, overexcited peers did not. As the lesson went on, he drew a gold coin

from his pocket and toyed with it, flicking it into the air and catching
it again and again.

I stayed until it was over, but saw little of the continuing joust
lesson. Nor did I see much more when I returned the next afternoon, and the one after that. Whether he was in the saddle or not,
my gaze rested upon the tall squire, drawn to his every graceful
movement like a magpie to a shining thing. I didn't know his
name, and finding out was unthinkable, but by the end of the week
all I wanted in the world was to learn the colour of those well-
guarded eyes.

                                     *

"WHAT YOU MUST do, Elaine, is play the part they want you to
play. Be just afraid enough, the coy but loving maiden, and he'll want
to ease your way, rather than simply take what's his. That is all you
need to remember for a wedding night."

"Morgause!" My mother's head jerked up from her stitching.
"Must you speak of these things?"

"Better Elaine be aware of what's coming," Morgause replied.
"She'll be grateful for my advice when stood in the bridal chamber
faced with her husband. I know I would have been."

She and my mother exchanged a challenging look. "Even so,
daughter, we must preserve the innocence of others."

I fell under the scrutiny of Morgause's sharp blue stare. "Morgana
ought to hear it too. Won't be long until she joins the rest of us as
wife and mother."

"Don't assume that I will," I said. "It sounds perfectly horrible to
me, all this pretending and obedience."

"You'll have no choice, Lady Particular. What do you imagine
you'll be doing instead?"

"There are other things, you know, than bearing sons." I knew it would irk her: Morgause had arrived at Tintagel on the arm of her Orkney King, with three healthy boys left behind, bearing the pride of maternal success like a battle standard.

"It's my wedding—can't we have peace?" Elaine said in a bored voice.

"I quite agree," said my mother. "Morgause, keep to your own business. Morgan, your temper, please."

"She started it." I gathered my work and stalked out of the fire's circular glow, taking refuge in the window seat farthest away.

Outside, tilt practice had begun, and my squire was once again ahorse, running demonstration drills alongside Sir Bretel. It was a windless day, the hottest of the year so far, so he rode without helm or tunic in a flowing, open-necked shirt. After a particularly impressive charge at the quintain, he dropped the reins to scrape his hair back, tying it at the nape of his neck with a leather thong. I leaned closer to the glass.

"So *that's* why you came to sit here." I spun around to see Morgause's exquisite profile peering into the embrasure, her lips curved into a knowing smile.

"I came over for better light, nothing more."

She glanced at the dropped work in my lap. "You certainly look busy. So, which boy is it? Or perhaps there's more than one?"

"Of course there's not more than one . . ." I trailed off, cursing internally. Picking up my work, I faced a mess of uneven stitches amid a bundle of loose thread, irrevocably tangled.

"Morgana the fox cub becomes Morgana the vixen." Morgause grinned, tracing a finger across my shoddy stitching. "See how your weakness interferes with what a lady should be? It twists, it spoils, it unravels you at the seams."

"You'll stop saying such things if you know what's good for you," I said feebly.

"I know I'm right. Go on, tell me who it is."

I shuddered with the urge to strike, and change her perfect white pallor to hand-printed red. But that was what she wanted: my anger, confirmation of my transgression. To indulge my temper now would be disastrous.

I took my eating knife from my belt; it was my father's, and big as a dagger in my hand, but sharp and fine enough for delicate work. The handle was polished bone, carved into the shape of a falcon, and every time I held it, I thought of him. I slipped the pointed tip under my failed stitches and began to slice the knotty thread free, wondering how my father would respond to being judged against values that were not his own.

The Devil take them, he would have said, holding true to what was in his heart.

And so would I. Whatever it was—this affinity for a stranger, this bright, peculiar pleasure I little understood—it was mine. I would not let Morgause take this small freedom from me, or allow her to put shame in its place.

I twirled the knife in my palm and resheathed it, smiling with insufferable calm. "I was bored, that's all. Horses running at tilt are far more interesting than women swatting at gossip. But you look at the squires as much as you wish, sister. We've all seen how your eyes rove away from your husband in the banquet hall."

Her jaw tightened. "You have a deal too much freedom, little sister. If I were you, I'd keep my tongue in my head and my earthly purpose in mind."

"I'm sure *you* would." I stood, gathering my work and pushing past her.

"One last thing, Morgana." She caught my wrist in a cold, hard grip. "If you're as clever as they say, you'll heed me. Remember, if nothing else, that you are a Princess."

8

A WEEK BEFORE the wedding, bored and in defiance of Morgause, I decided to venture somewhere forbidden, down the steep coastal path to Tintagel's deeply cut cove. Out of the castle's sight, I explored the caverns and walked the sands, drinking the warm salt air into my lungs as the afternoon sunshine dazzled across windblown waves.

If not for the impulse to bathe my feet, I'd never have seen it: a dark speck in the water, bobbing near the left-hand rocks—a cormorant, perhaps, or an errant seal. Then a hand shot up, fingers splayed, and I realized it was a person. The hand flailed, grabbing onto a rock then slipping off again, straining against the force of Tintagel's savage rip current. Whoever it was, they were drowning.

I stared in dismay; there was no time to get help, and the narrow rock ledge along the left-hand cliff was treacherous at best. If exhaustion didn't kill them first, any large surge could dash them onto the rocks.

Suddenly, the hand appeared again, leaping into the air, along with a flash of bare back, rising and sinking with the rolling sea. They were still alive; I had to try.

I knew of a rope, tangled up with an old fisherman's net just inside the mouth of the largest cave. It stunk so powerfully of rot I feared it would fall apart in my hands, but it was thick and well woven. Pulling my father's knife from my belt, I cut the net away and heaved the damp green coils to the tideline, lashing one end around a rock and tying it fast. I hoisted the rest over my arm and took to the precarious cliff shelf, edging between rows of sharp, barnacled rocks, unspooling the rope loop by slippery loop.

Eventually, I drew level with the drifting figure, sun blazing directly in my eyes. "Hold on!" I shouted. "I'm throwing a rope!"

I knotted the end into a wide noose, then tossed the rope into the water, almost toppling in headfirst. My footing held, but the throw missed the mark by several feet. Reeling the rope in, I tried again, but this time it flew forwards on the wind, landing nearer to me than them. The beleaguered soul disappeared underneath the surface once more, bobbing back up even farther away. One more sizeable wave and they'd be out of reach, doomed.

"Please," I muttered, exhorting the rolling waters. "*Let me do this.*"

I could barely see to toss the noose out again, and it came down behind us both, landing on the crest of a small blue wave. Miraculously, the wave lifted the rope and carried it forwards, hooking it perfectly over the drowning person's head. My spray-filled eyes cleared just long enough to see an arm pushed through the loop.

Thank you, I thought.

I hiked the rope taut over my shoulder and started for shore, skirts soaked and dragging. At first the tension in the rope eased, as if the person was swimming. But soon, resistance took its place, weight dragging against the sucking backtide. When I finally put my feet on the sand and gave one last, muscle-burning heave, the bump and drag behind me felt like the beaching of a corpse.

Exhausted, I gulped just enough air to stagger over to the prone figure. It was male, tall, wearing only breeches, and lay face down in the sand, unmoving.

I fell to my knees, gripping the slack shoulder with both hands. A cold, solid weight flopped abruptly into my lap, and I looked down onto a face covered by a blanket of dark hair. Fingers shaking, I brushed the wet tendrils away to reveal the distinctive features of my oft-watched squire. His skin was white as marble, apart from his lips and nostrils, which were tinged ice blue, eyes shut in their final repose. He was quite dead.

The breath left my body. It couldn't be, of all people, not after all I had done to save him. I contemplated him in quiet despair, this nameless boy I had looked at so much, when suddenly, his lashes twitched under my gaze, the slightest disturbance beneath their long, dark softness. It must have been the wind, or my breath—surely it was—and yet . . .

Instinctively, I shoved him up onto his side, thumping the space between his shoulder blades with the heel of my hand. The body stiffened, lurched forwards and gave a loud, choking cough. Surprised, I scrambled to my feet. The youth spluttered and gagged, spewing out several pints of sea water, followed by a stream of curses in Picardy French.

Thus emptied, he fell onto his back, chest heaving, staring up at the clear blue sky. Still coughing, he sat up, turned to see me standing there and almost jumped out of his mottled skin.

Immediately, he began to shiver and wheeze. I hastened back, placing my hands on his juddering shoulders.

"Hush, it's all right. You're alive, you're safe." I loosened the rope, took off my short summer cape and threw it around him, though it barely reached his waist. "Where are the rest of your clothes?"

He took me in with a squinting frown, as if I were a siren sent to trick him, then pointed over his shoulder to his clothes and boots, tucked behind a rock. I helped him tug on his shirt and tunic, then wrapped his own, better-fitting mantle firmly about his shoulders.

"There," I said, sitting beside him in the sand. "Keep that around you for a while."

He gave a stiff nod, unable to move much, but his lips were less blue, and the shuddering had subsided to a minor tremor. Suddenly, the wind ceased like a candle blown out, dropping warmth and silence between us.

I offered an uncertain smile. "I'm relieved to see you're not dead."

Still he said nothing, only tilted his face sideways, eyebrows raised. Perhaps he had been rendered senseless by his ordeal, or he didn't understand me, so I reached for the language in which he had cursed so eloquently.

"*Parlez-vous?*" I said, blushing right up to my scalp.

He coughed again, then attempted a smile. "*Oui.* I do. I . . . I should thank you. I am . . . fortunate you came along."

"Yes, you are. And lucky I was foolish enough to try and save you. What were you doing out there?"

"I wanted to swim."

"Swim!" I exclaimed. "You can't swim in this cove—it's far too dangerous. Sir Bretel tells all the squires."

He gave a hard-won shrug. "I thought I'd be strong enough."

"Well, that was very stupid. No sensible Cornish boy would see that rising tide and expect to live long by swimming in it."

He scoffed and looked down at his hands, which hung elegantly between his upraised knees. "In case you weren't aware, my lady, I am not a sensible Cornish boy."

In its natural state, his voice was a deep murmur, its accent rich and lazy like a summer brook over pebbles. When I didn't respond, he glanced at me out of the corner of his eye, sighed heavily and got to his feet. "I must go."

I followed, retort to his discourtesy forming on my tongue, but he had moved too swiftly for his weakened body and almost lost his footing. My hands shot out, holding him steady by the arms. He was warm again through the layers of cloth and, fleetingly, his eyes were fully open in surprise. As I'd imagined, they were blue, but also not—darker than mine, changeable in the light, like a peregrine's back, or the sea he'd almost drowned in during a nighttime storm.

I averted my gaze as another ridiculous flush crept up my throat. "You should see the barrack surgeon. Running drills might be dangerous."

"*L'enfer,*" he muttered. "I can't. I'll be whipped for this if they find out."

"Sir Bretel doesn't give whippings. And punishment is better than falling down dead."

"I disobeyed command," he said tersely. "They'll simply send me away."

"But you—"

"I cannot risk it." He looked at his feet, which were busy rucking an agitated trench in the sand. "God's wounds, it is hopeless. I'm soaked, filthy and already late for drills."

I sighed. "There's a path in that cave, leading to steps beneath a trapdoor. It comes out in an old guardroom on the mainland side. From there you can slip into the barracks." I pointed at the biggest cave. "At the back, bear left."

He blinked, studying my face, as if seeing me for the first time. Three small lines of doubt formed between his brows.

"I won't tell anyone," I added. "You're in no danger from me."

"I know," he said. "Just . . . you too are soaking wet. How will you—"

"I'll be fine." I tried not to think about the picture I must have made with my sandy, wet skirts, tangled hair and salt-encrusted face. "But you should take care for a while. If you're dizzy, or sleepy at odd times, don't indulge it. Walk, talk, find cool air."

He smiled faintly. "How do you know that?"

"I read it in a book."

"*Ah, bien,*" he replied. "And thank you, again. For saving me."

He hesitated, as if contemplating the formalities of our situation. The thought of him kissing my hand was unbearable.

"You should go now," I said quickly. "Before they come looking."

He nodded and smiled, fully this time, upper lip arching pleasantly, drawn in the shape of a recurve bow. Then in a heartbeat he was gone, snatching up his boots and loping away, dissolving into the dark mouth of the cave as if he had never been there at all. It was only then I realized that I still didn't know his name.

9

ON THE TILTYARD they called him The Gaul, speaking not only to his birthplace but a certain reputation that went with those of his heritage: well dressed, worldly and louche, along with a careless skill at his knightly calling that charmed and vexed in equal measure.

I didn't see him again until Elaine's wedding, sat at the squires' table, leaning on one elbow and laughing into a goblet at the antics of his cohorts. I was free to watch him from high up on the dais, lithe and languid, wearing his easy demeanour like a vair cape among the rough-hewn, cold-weather boys of home. After our shoreline encounter I expected something, willing him to glance my way just once. But he never did; seemingly, my bringing him back to life had slipped from his mind as readily as it had lingered in mine.

Later, when the tables were pushed aside, I escaped my seat among the ladies, navigating the edges of the throng as the music took up in earnest.

A smattering of applause heralded the arrival of Elaine, Queen of Garlot, blushing happily as her new husband drew her close and carried her off in a lively jig. Short, slight and colourless, King Neutres of Garlot was not as impressive as Morgause's towering Orkney warlord, but as they danced, he displayed a consideration to his bride that made the pair of them quite becoming. Something about their union made sense, captured in their shared smile, and I believed Elaine's future might truly be a happy one.

The dance soon changed to a sprightly carole, and I was considering joining in when a tall, dark presence manifested beside me and I looked up into the stormy blue eyes of The Gaul. Like a fool, I jumped, but he was already bowing and did not notice.

"Lady Morgan, may I speak with you?"

My name in his mouth was as I had never heard it: a low, purring start with sudden emphasis thrown on the last snapping syllable. *Morr-ganne*—true to its essence but lyrical, as if he were placing its rhythms in a song.

My first instinct was to refuse, my next thought the scrutinizing eyes of those up on High Table, catching sight of me unaccompanied and speaking to an older, unknighted youth.

"Of course," I said.

I moved around the pillar at my back, under the pathway of lowered arches between the bustle of the room and a row of large recessed windows. There, the bright lights and noise of the celebrations seemed to fade, enshrouding us in a cloistered, almost private air. I offered the back of my hand, and he took it, briefly brushing my knuckles with his lips.

"I am obliged to you, my lady," he said. "I beg your pardon if I'm too bold. But after what you did for me, I wanted to thank you properly, as a good knight should."

"You're not a knight." I regretted my flippancy at once, but he didn't seem to mind, his face relaxing into a rueful smile.

"No, I'm not, though one day I hope to be." He dipped his head courteously. "*Alors*, I am Accolon, of Gaul, and my lady's faithful servant."

"Pleased to make your acquaintance."

"And I yours, Lady Morgan. You have my eternal gratitude for saving my life, as well as my future spurs."

"You give me too much credit," I replied. "I'm sure Sir Bretel wouldn't punish anyone so harshly for mere misadventure."

"Perhaps not. Sir Bretel is a man of great honour, and I am in good stead with him. But I broke several rules, and without your help I still might have been sent home. I cannot lose my path to knighthood. It is all I have wanted."

My pulse quickened at his sudden candour. "In that case, you're very welcome," I said, swallowing hard. "Accolon of Gaul."

He considered me for a moment down his slope of a nose. The back of my neck began to prickle with heat, so I looked away, pressing my spine into the cool pillar behind me. I watched the blur of guests, whirling, laughing, obscuring us from the world.

The Gaul was still looking at me when I slid my eyes back to him, his face toying with the ghost of a smile. "Would you join me in dancing the next song?" he asked. "It would be a great honour and a pleasure."

"I cannot. Squires aren't permitted to dance with ladies. I shouldn't even be talking to you now."

He inclined his head. "I wouldn't like to get you into trouble. My apologies. There are many unwed ladies dancing tonight—it never crossed my mind one must be knighted to ask. Where I'm from, in Gaul, there are manners to observe, yes, but more freedom to interpret them."

"That sounds . . . easier." Relaxing, I peeled away from the pillar, pacing across to one of the Great Hall's deep-set arched windows, wondering if he would follow. He did, drawing up to my side with his usual fluid grace. Remnants of the sunset shone lilac pink through the windows, casting the fine angles of his face partly in shadow.

"I expect you miss it," I continued. "Your home, your family?"

"If I am honest? No," he replied. "My father is a *baron ancien* of no great importance, and I am his third son. I doubt he can even remember my face." His tone was languid, almost tired. "I miss the countryside, maybe. Our . . . his lands lie in a beautiful valley just north of Paris." Torchlight pricked at the dark fronds of his hair, dishevelled where he had pushed them off his forehead. "It's beautiful here too, but in a different way. Magnificent but dangerous."

"As you discovered when testing our waters," I said lightly. "A lesson, perhaps, in why some things are forbidden here that are permitted in Gaul."

He smiled, his thoughts so deep in some instant, private pleasure that I was envious at whatever memory had caused it. "Possibly you're right, Lady Morgan. Swimming in the lake at our manor, I do miss. It's the main reason I sought your treacherous waves." He turned back to me, secret joy still alive on his face. "The no-swimming rule makes sense. The rest of your strict customs, *non*, I'm not convinced."

I stifled a laugh, and he regarded me with that same brow-furrowed contemplation. Slowly, he leaned forwards and reached around to the window seat left of ours, drawing out a long, rectangular object wrapped in dark linen.

"Lady Morgan, I want you to have this. I was sent here with it, in case an official occasion required a gift. But I'd rather give it to you."

He placed it in my hands, and I unwrapped a sleek wooden box, delicately hinged and clasped, inlaid on each side with alternating squares of shining black and opalescent white. It opened to reveal thirty-two small, expertly carved chess pieces. I stared up at him, blood rushing to my face.

"I've heard that you play," he explained. "So before you refuse—"

"I must," I cut in. "You can't give me this."

"Don't you like it?"

"Of course! It's beautiful," I said. "I've never seen its like. The pieces are remarkable."

He seemed pleased. "Then accept it. A token of gratitude, in exchange for my life."

I snapped the box shut and wound the cloth back around it. "I can't. To begin with, it's my sister's wedding gift."

"Can she play?"

"No, but—"

"Then it's a waste of craftsmanship, its beauty and purpose left unappreciated. Surely that's far worse?"

I rolled my eyes. "You'll be expected to give something. I thought you were eager to avoid trouble?"

"Let me worry about that. I have a roll of my father's finest silk that will do just as well for the bride." Tilting his handsome head once again, he regarded me with beseeching charm. "*Alors*, what do you say? I know I am not yet a knight, but can a person not thank another for saving one from drowning?"

This time, the laugh escaped me, and I brought a hand up to my mouth to stop it travelling too far. "All right!" I declared. "You have me defeated. I gladly accept and thank you. I shall treasure it."

"My lady Princess." A strange voice broke our shared gaze, and I turned to see a white-and-gold-liveried page. "Your lady mother requests your presence, with all haste."

Tintagel's hall flew back to me in all its cacophonous reality. I dismissed the page with a shaky hand, and looked again at Accolon. A slow, draining ache spread across my chest; a swiftly absorbed grief for something never quite begun.

"I must go," I said. With the last of my fortitude, I prised the chess set away and shoved it at Accolon's chest. "I cannot accept this. I . . . I'm sorry."

Snatching up my skirts, I fled, back up to the dais, with regret snapping at my heels. Even if I hadn't been seen and was not in deadly trouble—which, as it happened, I wasn't—after my strange departure, Accolon of Gaul would surely never speak a word to me again.

But hours later, when I returned to my chamber alone and exhausted, slipping into bed by the dying light of the moon, I laid my head on the pillow at last only to feel hardness underneath, and my hand found it there: the chess set, hidden and yet dangerous, now wrapped in a square of Parisian blue silk.

10

THE WEDDING TOOK more than my sister. Father Felix had left too, sent by his bishop to inspect some relics in a newly founded abbey in the Welsh Marches. My summer of lessons went with him—he left me the keys to the sacristy, but by Uther's command, I was not permitted to wander outside of the main castle building alone, so it was of little use.

Nevertheless, the *Ars Physica* was too fascinating for me to go without reading it. I was deep in the subject of poisons: where to find them; how to render them weak or potent; how a dangerous herb, flower or berry could be a cure or an agent of death. Only knowledge and intention stood between the ability to heal or maim, and I was determined to have it all by heart.

The idea came to me a week or so later, as I watched a great stream of knights, squires and attendants march out of Tintagel's main gate. They were headed north, off to another round of Uther's endless battles against the Saxons, snatching up land the former invaders had stolen from those before them.

The long column retreated inland at a steady, military pace, morning sun washing over gleaming mail, dragon standards leaping in the wind. At its core sat Uther Pendragon, gold-armoured and molten in the burning light. I sent my usual prayer up to God, wishing him dead, then waited patiently for the midday bell.

*

"AN ESCORT?" SAID my mother. "Whatever for?"

Stripped of Uther's retinue, Tintagel's Great Hall was uncrowded and peaceful, a few sparsely populated tables spread out along the foot of the dais. My mother's throne had been brought forth for her to hear a few local concerns, the last of which came from me.

She exchanged a look of puzzlement with Sir Bretel, then regarded me with mild amusement. "Well, daughter?"

I drew a deep breath and launched into the speech I'd been rehearsing. "Mother, I am in dire need of occupation. With Father Felix gone, I am unable to perform my usual church duties, and now there are no ladies to instruct me in the afternoons. I heard we're not even travelling to Caerleon for Michaelmas."

"The King has ordered us to keep safe here at Tintagel," she said. "He sent the ladies back to their manors. There is nothing to be done."

"I could still be keeping the chapel neat, flying my bird, walking the grounds for exercise. But without Elaine, I'm not permitted to wander outside the house on my own."

"Some would say that has not stopped you," she said wryly. "But I concede it's not healthy to be indoors so much. Nevertheless, without the women, what escort is there? You can't expect Gwennol to—"

"A squire," I cut in. "Just to follow in my wake and ensure my safety." She was already shaking her head, but I went on regardless. "At the very least, someone needs to keep Father Felix's prayer candles lit, and I'm the only one who knows the rites."

That gave her pause. "But a squire—is it wise?"

"Why not? I won't have to converse with him. Whoever it is can stand outside the chapel door, carry my hawking supplies and walk three feet behind me. They're all training to be knights, aren't they? Some will become protectors of ladies, just as Sir Bretel is to you."

My mother glanced up. "What say you, Sir Bretel? Is it a reasonable undertaking for an unknighted youth?"

"Lady Morgan's not wrong about courtly training," he replied. "They are well taught, and most of them will go directly to someone's court once knighted. A few will certainly be expected to guard great ladies, as is my privilege."

"You see?" I said triumphantly. "You must trust Sir Bretel's judgment, surely, Mother? Let him choose someone." It was risky, but I could not suggest the name myself, instead placing all my faith in what I had seen of Sir Bretel's regard.

My mother afforded me a long, considering gaze, then looked again at her champion knight, who gave a reassuring nod.

"Very well," she said. "If Sir Bretel chooses his most suitable squire, you shall have your escort. You may summon him once a day for the errands we have discussed, and he may accompany you only around the castle grounds, never within the house. This arrangement will last until the King returns. Agreed?"

"Of course, Mother."

She sighed. "Have we a suitable candidate, Sir Bretel?"

"Yes, my lady. Our most highly skilled youth in sword and horse, who will likely make knighthood the day he reaches majority. He also has by far the most experience in courtly manners, due to his continental upbringing. If I had a daughter, I'd entrust him with her safety without a moment's pause."

"Bring him forth, then. The sooner I have my daughter's boredom off my conscience the better."

Sir Bretel took three long strides along the dais. The remaining squires clustered around the farthest table, some still eating, others taking turns playing a rapid game with a knife and splayed fingers.

All except one, who was sitting with his chin propped on his hand, eyes alert to the approach of his master-at-arms. Sir Bretel beckoned to him without hesitation.

"Accolon," he said. "Come before the Queen."

*

IF ACCOLON OF Gaul minded being dragged from his peers to traipse the headland behind me, or wait for hours outside the chapel while I read in secret, I never heard a word of it. After the chess set, I was nervous of our standing, but he was quiet, courteous to a fault, and held himself at a respectful distance, the great sword of Sir Bretel's regard dangling over him like a portent of doom.

However, the more we walked, the more I paused so he would unwittingly catch up to me, the more polite questions I asked that his manners would not allow him to ignore, and soon enough I had us striding side by side. Questions and answers quickly turned to friendly talk, and talk turned to laughter with even greater speed as he assuaged my endless curiosity with stories of knights and his fellow squires, the barracks and the tiltyard—tales that often weren't for ladylike ears, but amused me to no end. He liked to see me laugh, I could tell, perhaps as much as I enjoyed his smile in return.

"You mean to say that you can't even play chess?" I said to him one afternoon, after rehousing my falcon. We had cut our time short, jogging in from the headland to escape an iron pall of cloud that was trundling over the waves on a fractious wind. "When you insisted I accept your set for the sake of the game?"

Accolon regarded me aslant. "You never asked, my lady."

I rolled my eyes at his courteous insolence, which I enjoyed far more than I would ever admit. "Can you play or not?"

"All I will say is, it doesn't suit me to sit still."

"Ah, so you *can't* play, but are too proud to say so." He said nothing, only continued to look at me with an inscrutable neutrality. I smirked. "It's surprising you were never taught, given your much-lauded upbringing. Sir Bretel said they have you learning dance steps and plucking a lute before you can walk."

"It's not . . . unlike that."

A fat raindrop shed itself from the ominous cloud, landing lukewarm on my nose. I glanced around the small inner courtyard between the mews and the kitchen entrance; it was deserted, slumbering, daily life chased off by the threat of thunder and the metallic scent of rain. The only sound to remind us of the corporeal world was the ever-present chorus of the waves, and our own close, whispering breaths.

"This just won't do," I told him. "Come on."

The chapel was still scrupulously clean and smelled of vinegar and beeswax. I had hidden my chess set in the locked sacristy, placed innocently alongside Father Felix's larger board. The square of blue silk I kept as a kerchief, pinned surreptitiously under the neckline of my gown.

The Gaul and I walked towards the altar in silence, footsteps echoing softly across the floor. A rumbling crack of thunder made him jump.

"Cornish weather," he tutted. "It's barely past summer."

I grinned. "How delicate you are! I'd have thought you'd be used to it by now."

The windows brightened with a great sheet of lightning, followed by another terrific crash. The storm was directly above our heads, rattling the roof tiles and lashing hard rain at the windows.

"Sit there," I told him, pointing to the steps that led down to my father's tomb.

"I don't think I should," Accolon called into the sacristy after me. "I'm meant to wait outside for you. Surely we can't be found alone like this?"

"For goodness' sake, it's a chapel. And this storm is so violent, no one would question you taking shelter." I strode across and held out the checkered box. "You're just afraid of looking foolish because you can't play."

He paused, one eyebrow raised, before swiping the box from me and dropping onto the step. "On the contrary, my lady. Make all the fool of me you wish."

I sat down and scooped the chess pieces into my lap, then turned the box over and placed it between us. I proceeded to set out the carved ebony and ivory figures on their correct squares, naming them as I went.

"That much I do know," he said. "I also know the *chevalier* here can jump any obstacle, and the queen can do whatever she wishes."

"All except what the knight—your *chevalier*—can do." I plucked the carved crowned woman out of his fingers and placed her back on her square. "Listen carefully to the rest, then we'll play."

"And I will lose, of course."

"Again and again," I said cheerfully. "But that's how you learn, like falling off a horse at tilt and getting back on. Then, when you vanquish me, think how wonderful it'll feel."

His eyes met mine in wide contemplation; in the sparse candle-light they were almost midnight in hue. Another crash of thunder sounded over our heads, this time making us both jump.

Accolon considered the pieces on the board with renewed interest. "You are too wise for me, Lady Morgan. I'm sure I will never defeat you."

"Of course you will," I said, overly bright. "Now, I'll play white, but you can go first, since I have the advantage." I raised my open hand and flourished it over the board. "So, Accolon of Gaul, let's begin. Your move."

II

OUR SECOND LESSON came a few days later, when the weather turned torrentially wet once again. Accolon had been holding fast to his duty, waiting patiently in the chapel porch and ignoring my teasing that he was afraid to lose any more games. But the wind had blown a wide puddle under the porch roof, and the idea of suffering wet boots all day was enough to persuade him inside.

At length, we sat, and I handed him his pieces to place. "If not chess," I said, as we began, "what did you do during your childhood in Gaul?"

"I've told you," he murmured. "Hunting, swimming, riding with my brothers."

"How many brothers do you have?"

"My lady, I suspect all this talk is to throw me off my game."

I laughed. "What an accusation! Besides, the silence of a monastery couldn't save you from defeat."

He shrugged. "We shall see."

He still couldn't beat me, but had so greatly improved I jested that he could obviously already play. "Confess," I said. "It will save you days of defeat."

At this, he regarded me with mock offence, then picked up his knight and placed it immediately in danger.

"Three brothers, three sisters, not all living," he said. "Burdensome mouths to feed, my father called us, on his kinder days . . ."

*

THE GOLD COIN, he told me, was a relic of Ancient Gaul, found
at the bottom of his beloved lake when he was ten years old. Up close
it was something of a marvel—a shimmering disc of unknown
denomination, bright and unscathed as if it had been struck that very
day. It bore the handsome profile of Apollo on one side; on the other,
the sun god resplendent in his chariot.

Over the years, he had taught himself coin tricks to pass the time:
the idle thumbnail flick and catch, or running it over and under his
fingers in hypnotic, unfaltering rhythm. Lastly, he would swipe it out
of thin air, vanishing it from sight.

I came to know the coin's appearance meant he was thinking
deeply, sometimes on matters of importance, other times merely our
chess game. But I spent hours watching those fine hands oscillating
in the stillness, and at night when I closed my eyes, they were all
I could see.

*

AFTER MUCH TALK and a hundred checkmates, we had reached
his fourteenth year and his final brother, who died at birth with their
mother, just before Accolon was put on a boat and sent to squire for
one of Uther's bannermen in London. Two and a half years later, he
impressed at a royal hunt, and Sir Bretel brought him to Tintagel.

"I'm sorry about your mother," I said. "Do you miss her?"

"Lady Morgan, always the same questions," he said idly. "Forever
'Do I miss this or that?' My mother was a good woman and very fond
of me. I miss her, my sisters, a close cousin who also squires somewhere
on this chilly island. I miss the lake, the trees, the valley where our manor
stands. My old hunting hound. The list, is it long enough for you?"

It was and it wasn't—I was ever hungry for more. So far, he hadn't once mentioned his future, and by then I wanted to know badly enough to be direct.

"Will you go back home?" I didn't dare look up from the board, despite knowing that in three moves I had him beat regardless. "To your father's lands, I mean. When you're no longer a squire."

He picked up his rook, rolling it between finger and thumb before driving it through my pawn, snatching the piece into his palm in one deft movement.

"It's time we were away," he said briskly. "Checkmate me and be done with it."

*

THE NEXT DAY, we played three games in relative silence before Accolon sighed and drew out his coin.

"The truth is," he said unexpectedly, "I cannot go home. There's no place for me there. My father told me before I left."

"Oh," was all I risked saying.

He sent his coin ringing into the air, catching it once, twice, three times. "To the Devil with him. As long as he sends me the armour and two horses he promised upon my knighthood, I care not if I never see him again."

"Then what will you do? Take up arms under someone's banner?" He would swear to Uther, I supposed, much as the idea might gall me. Then again, it would mean that he stayed.

"No. Court life, military life, it's not for me."

So quick had he dismissed it, and it stung. "Then what is?"

He shrugged. "Most likely I'll return to Gaul, perhaps Paris, at least to begin with. I'm familiar with the roads; I have connections there. They'll know where I can find mercenary work."

"And sell your sword to the highest bidder?" My tone, unexpectedly harsh, made us both wince.

"You forget, my lady, I have scant choices," he said tersely. "No land, no title, no gold—what else should I do? Rattle around a drafty British castle as someone's house knight, barely above the huntsman's dog? Far better to sell my blade, my lance, my skill. Earn enough to at least buy a life one day."

"Paid for with blood," I retorted. "A dishonourable life if ever—"

He was on his feet and half the chapel away before I could finish. "I should escort you back to the house now, my lady," he said, rubbing a weary hand across the back of his neck. "We have lingered too long."

I got shakily to my feet and went towards him. "I'm sorry. I shouldn't have said that. I don't know why I did."

He turned, head and shoulders first, like a reluctant horse being reined about-face. "It's of no matter. And my lady's prerogative, of course."

"It *does* matter. I had no right. Never mind my rank, or your supposed duty. I thought . . ." I drew a long breath and looked up at him. "I thought perhaps we were beyond that."

His face remained still, brow pinched in a pained expression. "How could we ever be?" he said.

I found I could not answer. So, instead of explanation, I gathered my fortitude and reached for the truth.

"What I meant was," I said slowly, "that if you go, I will miss you."

My words dawned gradually on his face, dark eyes widening in elation, followed by a hopeless, melancholy smile that felt like a blow to the ribs. Then, suddenly:

"I will miss you too, Lady Morgan."

The musical rendering of my name in his mouth struck me anew, tripping across my nerves like a flourish on a harp. I moved closer, and before I could think too much, I stretched up and sought his lips with my own.

He made his decision just in time. Lifting his head out of my reach, Accolon feinted sideways as if dodging a counterstriking sword, catching me firmly by the elbows as I stumbled into his avoidance.

"You cannot do that," he said, affecting calm. "In a chapel, of all places."

I wrenched my arms away from his grip. "I never took you as being so God-fearing."

"I may not attend every Mass, but I know right from wrong."

"And I am *wrong*?" I had little idea where my anger was coming from; he was well within his rights not to admire me, but his rejection stung in a way I had never felt before.

"I didn't say that. *You* aren't wrong—*we* are. *This* is. How could we ever . . . It's impossible." He threw up his hands. "Before your own father's tomb!"

That was the last of it. With a cry of pure rage, I ran, charging across the headland without a backwards glance and swearing to every saint I knew that I would burn before I ever went near Accolon of Gaul again.

12

I DIDN'T TELL anyone I no longer wished for an escort, but I was neither so good nor so calm as to face Accolon outright, and embarrassment still ran through me like a river in spate. Instead, I ceased to call for him, spending long days languishing in my chambers with only Gwennol and the needle for company.

But indoor life did not suit me, so one dove-grey morning, I ignored the clouds, hanging low and full-bellied with rain, and made my way down the cliff path alone, to Tintagel's deserted cove.

The wind cut across me, blustery and indecisive, blowing sand off the stiff headland grasses, swirling around the mouth of the bay. Waves grey blue and angry rose and fell in points, white-capped like gnashing teeth. I pushed my hood down and stepped towards the water, stretching my arms wide, salt breeze lifting my cape and hair away from my body. I closed my eyes, and it felt like flying.

An urgent voice sounded behind me. Shocked, I spun around to find myself face to face with The Gaul. He was windswept as the sea itself, dark hair whipping around his face, and veering somewhere between irritation and panic.

"*Par le diable*," he said dramatically. "I've been all morning trying to find you."

"It's no business of yours where I go," I replied. "How did you know I'd even left the house?"

"I was in the tiltyard stands and saw you come out. I waited to be summoned, but no one came. Yet here you are, without an escort."

"Yes, here I am," I said carelessly. "Not calling for you was intentional. I have no need for your company, now or ever again."

"And I have no need for *yours*," he retorted. "But it was you who asked for me to walk by your side, and that's where they expect to see me."

"They?"

"Sir Bretel and the Queen. I swore my honour to them and won't desert it on a caprice of yours. If you want me discharged as your escort, you must tell them so yourself."

I raised an eyebrow. "They'd only ask why. The truth would get us both into trouble, and to invent something is risky."

"It's even more risky to run off to the beach, which is expressly forbidden. If we are caught—"

"Then you shouldn't have followed me," I interrupted. "Therefore, we're both forbidden to be here, and I'm not going anywhere with you, but supposedly you cannot leave my side. What *would* you have me do for the best?"

He shrugged, stoking my annoyance yet further. "I am entirely in your hands, my lady, as you well know."

"Not entirely," I said pointedly.

Saying nothing, he looked away, out to sea. Light flecks of rain pricked at his profile, speckling his high, sculpted cheeks and long nose. He bit his bottom lip, and I imagined him tasting salt.

"All right," I relented. "I'll come back."

But it was too late. All at once the clouds ruptured, giving way to their burden with indecent haste, mild drizzle replaced by great sheets of cold, relentless rain.

"*Sang de Dieu*, you'll be soaked," Accolon muttered, grabbing my elbow.

We ran with the torrent slashing at our uncovered heads until we reached the mouth of the largest cave. The downpour ripped in at an angle, roaring towards us and hitting the scattered rocks at the entrance. Accolon ushered me farther inside, just as a white waterfall began to pour across the cave mouth.

He regarded it with exasperation. "This place. I've never seen weather like it."

I unhooked my soaked mantle from my shoulders. Accolon took it from me, snapped it in the air several times, then draped it carefully across a pair of rocks.

"It'll never dry, not in this damp," I said matter-of-factly, drawing an incredulous look from him.

"That is the least of our worries. It was bad enough idling at the seashore by ourselves. Now we are stuck here, like this."

I rolled my eyes and wandered off, seeking the smooth, jutting ledge tucked just inside the first curve of the rock wall. I perched on it, settling back against the sea-scented stone, listening to the rapid *drip-drip-drip* of the rain at the cave mouth, pattering onto the compacted sand. Accolon stayed exactly where he was.

"Go, then," I told him. "Sneak up the cave steps into the old guardroom. I am quite capable of waiting here until it stops."

"And what if they ask me—your supposed knightly escort—where you are?"

"Oh, you do worry so," I scoffed. "I hardly thought it possible when I first met you."

"I think only of your reputation, my lady. Though it seems I care for it more than you do."

"It's not your place to worry about my reputation," I said haughtily, and he fell silent, mouth downturned in sulky agreement. "We're here now; no one knows. We'll just have to wait out the worst of it. Come and sit."

Reluctantly, he trudged over to the ledge and leaned beside me, folding his arms across his soaked chest. His long hair was scraped back from his face, curling around his ears, neat droplets forming at the tips.

"I'm sorry for my words in the chapel," he said. "About your father's tomb. It was hurtful, uncalled for. I apologize, with all my heart."

I nodded, a warm ache galloping through my chest. For once I could think of not a single clever or amusing quip to ease the air of seriousness hanging between us.

"I'll speak to my mother," I said at last. "You won't have to escort me anymore." It came out like a sigh: quiet, with a rush of relief. "I'll see that she and Sir Bretel think no less of you."

Still Accolon said nothing, his form rigid like the rock all around us. I might have believed him magically transformed were it not for his low, steady breaths and the heat of his body mingling with mine, warming our pocket of rain-filled air.

"I know it wasn't ideal," I continued, "for a knight-in-training to be stuck trotting around after me. But it will commend you, even if enduring my company—"

He gave a short, unexpected laugh, and it echoed raggedly around the cave. Standing up from the ledge, he paced a few steps off, hand cradling his forehead.

"What's wrong?" I asked. And when he didn't respond: "Come back here *at once*."

At my command, he wheeled around and strode back, stopping at arm's length. I slipped off the ledge and closed the distance.

"Tell me," I said.

"Do you truly not see?" Suddenly his face softened, blossoming into an expression both anguished and earnest. "I can play chess, Morgan. I always could."

I opened my mouth, seeking words, but none came.

"And I never *endured* you. I only wish it were so. But every day, every hour I've spent in your company . . ." He threw up his hands. "I can no longer imagine wanting to be anywhere else. *That* is the problem."

"But last week, in the chapel," I managed. "You called me unholy."

"If you are unholy then I am damned along with you." He began to rove back and forth, speaking in soft, rapid tones. "I had to reject you—you must see that. We could never . . . I couldn't . . . For both of our sakes—"

"Accolon, stop."

He stopped pacing and looked at his boots. "You know all about me," he went on. "My life, my future, my prospects. And you—everything you are—your wit, your beauty, that remarkable mind . . ." He sighed, raising his eyes to mine. "Your rank. How could I presume to even think of, much less touch, one such as you?"

I said nothing, leaning towards him until our bodies were as close as they could be without touching. Reaching into the shadows, I pushed my hands into his, and felt his strong, slender fingers tighten around mine like ivy. His eyes shone darkly in the vapourish half-light, and in a flicker of his lids I saw it, perhaps felt it too—his giving in, the abandonment of his senses to all but the idea of me.

In one small shift, his body moved against mine, and there was no more need for space, or doubt, or a world outside the small patch of rocky sand upon which we stood. He tilted his head down, warm breath fluttering across my lips.

"If they find out," he murmured, "they'll hang us both."

I smiled, my mouth brushing against his jaw. "Then we'll hang," I said. "We'll hang, or we'll run." It was so easy to say it, so easy to fear neither discovery nor punishment; to believe that our shared, immediate truth was all there was.

So he kissed me, and though we were halting at first, I felt the smile on his lips and it made me bolder, kissing him long and needful, until we were uncertain no more, giving rise to an urgency that betrayed us both.

And we stayed that way, cleaved to one another, until the rain ceased to roar across the cliffs of Tintagel and the skies, once more, came to peace.

13

FROM THAT DAY forth we were lost, within ourselves and to the world around us. Accolon and I exploited our freedom in ways only a barely populated castle allowed; the empty chapel was our shelter, our chess games an excuse to lean close. Some days we sat in the sacristy, I at my books and he beside me, his chin propped on his hand.

"I could watch you read all day," he would say.

But for me, to look at him was to need him, my desire illuminating the restrictions of time, knowing that any day, any moment wasted, we could never have back.

"Come with me," I'd say. "Now. Quickly."

With my hand in his, I would guide us through the sacristy's side door and around the corner to the stretch of clifftop between the chapel and the sea, so I could feel his arms around me, kiss him endlessly or simply gaze upon his face bathed in rich autumn sun. Obscured from the world by the chapel wall, we sat in the sweet-scented grass, fingers entwined, talking for hours on all subjects, but never of the coming end.

Nevertheless, the wild days of our liberty were numbered; news reached Tintagel telling of Pendragon forces advancing down the road to Cornwall. I returned to my mother's red solar with a serrated ache deep in my chest, curling into the chill window seat as, below, Accolon took to the joust with his usual mastery, driving the other squires into the dirt before vanquishing them with a relentless, swooping sword. I knew he must feel my eyes on him, but he kept his word and never once looked up at the window.

"It won't be long," my mother said to her women one waning October day. "There's another band of Saxons threatening our northern borders. The King will be back on the march."

I turned, wondering if I had heard correctly. My mother was bent to her work, firelight casting a halo around her.

"Very soon," she said, as if I had asked. "A week at most."

Her women bobbed their heads, warbling sympathetically. My spine felt strangely coiled. "Where will we go?" I asked.

"We stay in Tintagel. All will be exactly as before."

*

LATER, RECKLESS WITH anticipation, I caught hold of Accolon on the way to the Great Hall, hooking him into a deep side passage when the rest of his party were distracted.

"We'll be seen!" he exclaimed as I pulled him to me, but his resistance was of the token kind. We had not been closer than twenty feet in three weeks, and the hunger of forced absence radiated from us as we kissed.

"It'll be like this again soon," I said breathlessly. "Uther marches north in a few days."

His hands tightened at my waist, familiar grooves of tension appearing between his brows. "I know. I wanted to tell you. I . . . have been chosen to go with them."

I pulled away, back hitting the opposite wall. "How? You're Sir Bretel's squire. He'll be staying here with my mother."

"The King's own guard captain asked for me. I'm seventeen now, by far the most skilled, a decent reserve in a fight. Sir Bretel has bid me go."

"You can't," I said. "It's *war*, not a hunting party. It's not safe."

"Very little is," he quipped, and I had to stop myself from slapping him. He must have sensed it, because he came to me, warming my hands between his own. "It is command, a knight's life. I cannot say no." He bent his head, seeking my eyes, but I refused to look up.

"Morgan," he said in his particular way, though it was deeper now, steeped in tenderness, rich with our secrets. I raised my chin, taking him in, the face that never failed to strike me as remarkable, trying to imagine it was the last time I'd lay eyes on his curved-bow lip. Squires weren't borne back on biers like heroes of war; if he was crushed under a horse, or died bleeding from a sword strike, his existence would simply fade into the shadows.

I could hardly bear it. I threaded my fingers through his, and showed him how to slip from a room unnoticed.

The night air was brisk, edged with the threat of winter. The pale-red sliver of a hunter's moon made way for a dazzling swath of stars, streaking across the darkness like an angel's train. Accolon and I stole away, shifting shadow to shadow, finding safety just inside the low-lit kitchen garden, where we ducked into a long, vine-covered arbour.

"Promise me that you won't die," I said. "Swear it on your life."

It made him smile in the way I liked best, slow and charming. "I swear. Anything for you."

The smell of winter herbs drifted past us, woody and fresh, conjuring days of frost and pine trees; of fur mantles and afternoons watching falcons against an ice-blue sky; of roaring hearths and spiced wine, and thick bed drapes drawn against lengthy nights. For all this he would be elsewhere.

"Do you have good furs?" I said worriedly. "The North isn't like here. It snows a quarter of the year, and the ground is unforgiving. How will you keep warm?"

He smiled softly and put a hand to my cheek. "I shall think of you, of course."

"Fool." I smiled and waited for him to draw me in, his clever hands caressing my back, lost in my hair. He kissed me and I tasted honey wine on his lips, sweet and undiluted. If only I could keep us this way, absorb my being into his somehow so we wouldn't have to part.

I pressed my face into his chest. "You have to come back."

"I will, for you." He lifted my chin and kissed me again. "I love you, Morgan. You must know that."

I stared at him; in our rush of feeling he had flown ahead of me, stealing the confession I had determined to make. But I didn't care: he had said it, I felt it, and nothing else mattered.

"I love you too," I said. "Too much, far too much." I kissed him again, holding him tighter, feeling him pull me even farther in, bone against bone, crushed and breathless, warm enough to thaw a thousand winters.

I heard the footsteps before he did: clanking, officious paces, more than one set. I pulled my head away, trying to hear if they were patrolling or approaching.

"What's wrong?" Accolon asked. I held a finger to his lips as the voices came.

"In the courtyard, stealing away with some lad. Hand in hand, by God." A male voice, gruff, northern-lilted; then another, slightly younger. "What lad?"

"He didn't know, being so far into his cups. But he swore it was Lady Morgan. Sir Ulfin's got others searching indoors."

"It's no harm, surely," said the other. "Remember being that age?"

"Has a mule kicked you in the skull? She's a *Princess*—if she's been touched by more than her nurse's kisses, she's worthless. The lad's good as dead regardless."

Accolon and I had sprung apart, barely drawing breath. He jerked his head in the direction of the kitchens. "We have to go. *Vite*, this way."

"We can't," I hissed. "They're searching the building. If anyone sees us even close to the same place . . ."

Grabbing his arm, I shoved Accolon out of the arbour. "Go," I said. "They're not looking for you."

He stared at me as if I were mad. "I'm not leaving. I love you and we're in this together."

His declaration caught me again, like a soft blow to the chest. I reached up and traced my fingertips across his cheek, as if we weren't in any predicament at all, let alone a dire one. "Would that I could hear you say that every day, forever."

He leaned into my touch. "If you want me to, *mon coeur*, then I will."

Outside the garden wall, the footsteps took up again. "They can't be far," the first guard said. "It's too bloody dark to go any distance from the building."

I dropped my hand. "Accolon, I'll fix this, deny everything, but you *have* to *go*."

"I don't want you to have to deny anything."

"It's the only way," I insisted. "If you love me like you say, you'll trust me."

"All right," he said at last. "But if they try and punish you, you must tell them—"

"They won't, I promise." I gave him a final, swift, incredibly risky kiss, then pushed him towards the kitchen courtyard. "Hurry!"

With a last blazing glance, he dashed out of the walled garden just as the guards wandered through the opposite archway.

The older one bowed. "There you are, my lady."

"What is it?" I snapped. "Can a lady not take the air?"

The second guard began walking around the herb garden, peering into the arbour and half-heartedly checking the shadows.

The older guard looked back at me. "Your lord father wishes to see you, Princess."

"My lord father is dead, sir."

He shifted uneasily. "King Uther, then, my lady. He wants you brought to him, if you please."

There was little more I could do; I'd bought Accolon as much time as I could. "Very well," I said, pulling every last shred of my fortitude into my posture. "Take me to the King."

14

MY FATHER'S GREAT Chamber was little changed from the time he kept it; the furniture stood in the same place, the display of greatswords still mounted above the fireplace. Our ducal arms had been taken down, the rampant beast of Pendragon now hanging in their place.

Uther sat in a gilded, long-backed chair with my mother standing to his right, so solemn I expected to see a rosary dangling from her fingers. They made a strange pair—their grim, monkish expressions at odds with the outlandish luxury of Uther's heavy furs and my mother's ermine-lined samite, sewn thickly at the throat and wrists with jewels.

I glared at Uther, wondering whether this would end the same way as our last confrontation, with me spitting blood and teeth. He returned a mud-coloured, sneering gaze. Hatred ran fiery up my spine, and I straightened, did not even think of bowing.

"Morgana," he drawled. "I hear you've been merry-making abroad."

"I don't know what you mean."

His eyes narrowed. "You were seen in the courtyard with a male member of this household, like some tavern wench."

My mother flinched, but his words bounced off me. "Whoever said so is mistaken. They're all drunk as brewhouse dogs down there. I was taking the air, alone, as your guards found me."

He braced against the arms of the chair, then reclined again with a deep chuckle, which had always unnerved me far more than the expectation of violence.

"It matters not if you deny it," Uther said lazily. "I know the truth. The Devil's spit has always been in you. It's only natural you should turn to the habits of whores."

"My lord!" exclaimed my mother.

He held up a silencing hand. "I know it's hard to hear, my lady. But it is time you did. Most born ladies know how not to offer themselves as temptation, that they are meant for holier things. Not this one, your runt whelp. Her blood is tainted by sin and must be cleansed. Isn't that right, Morgana?"

My lips curled back off my teeth. "*My name is Morgan.*"

"Your name is whatever I say it is!" Uther roared, mask finally slipping. "Manners. Goodness, godliness, chastity. Obedience." He thrust out a finger for every explosive word, veins rippling in his red temples. "All qualities a lady must have to be worth her upkeep, and you have *none* of them. I thought sending you to the chapel would cure you, but I should have known that addled Cornish priest was too soft. A witch's nature like yours requires extreme measures."

I bristled, poised to strike; perhaps I was even hungry for more. But Uther's anger was short-lived, cooling into granite in front of my eyes, and I knew then the battle was already lost.

"Which is why I am sending you to a nunnery," he concluded. "Perhaps the holy sisters will teach you how to repent. Lord knows it will take much godly work to redeem you."

"You're sending me away?" I gasped. "You can't. Mother, tell him!"

She started towards me. Uther grabbed her arm. "Your mother cannot change my decision; it is final. Guards!" The same two guards appeared from just outside the door. "Escort the Princess to her chamber and arrange a constant watch on her door. You will remain there, Morgana, until your departure in three days' time."

*

WHEN MY MOTHER came to my chamber and sat on the bed beside me, I refused to speak to her.

"It's for the best, Morgan," she said. "You'll be safe there, away from—"

I glanced at her sharply, willing her to say it aloud after all these years. But the words died on her lips. She ducked her head, wiping a stray tear from her still-rosy cheek, and for a moment I wondered how she had stayed so beautiful, so preserved, while caught beneath her husband's constant, crushing shadow.

Her hand dropped back into her lap with a glint of blue—my father's sapphire ring, back on her finger. I almost relented and asked how she was able to wear it, hidden as it had been since the day Uther and his sorcerer stalked into Tintagel. Yet I still couldn't speak, the added pain of my father's memory too great to allow me a single furious word.

"I know this is your home, and your father is here. But his spirit, his tenacity, his capacity for love—it is in you, Morgan. Your temper came from me, but in all other ways, you are him. Wherever you go, he goes with you."

It was not what I wanted to hear, and I turned my face away.

Eventually, I heard her sigh. "If nothing else, remember that I have tried."

Gracefully, queen-like, she rose and quit the room. Only then did I see the gold gleam of my father's ring against the coverlet, where she had left it.

Slipping it onto my thumb, I studied it for a while, then rose to find a piece of charcoal. Grimacing, I tore a corner of blank parchment from my *Ars Physica* and wrote a note in stark black: three words to save a life.

I called through to the antechamber. Gwennol's round face, still puffy from crying over my departure, peered around the archway.

"Would you do something for me?" I asked. "It's a secret and will not be easy."

"Anything for you, my duck," she said, and took Father Felix's sacristy key from my outstretched hand with a quizzical look.

"It's a chess set," I said, after explaining my task. "The note goes inside it. Third bed on the right in the squires' barracks. Put it under his pillow."

*

THE ENTIRE HOUSEHOLD turned out for my departure. I stood in the courtyard, cold wind flicking drizzle into my hood, and said goodbye to every person, wondering if it was for kindness they stood there or another cruel trick on Uther's part to show me exactly the extent of his power. By then, it was all the same to me.

The squires came somewhere in the middle and he, The Gaul, was the very last. Pale as a ghost, he looked as though he might sink to his knees in guilt, if not for his love for me, and my note— innocent chess advice to any other eyes—which I knew he would honour.

Protect the chevalier, it had said.

Suddenly he stooped, seemingly in prostration. My heart leapt into my throat, but just as quickly he rose and took my hand, his eyes steady on mine.

"Your glove, my lady. You dropped it."

Swift and artful, he curved his fingers beneath the gloves I already held, as if returning the dropped item to me. His fingers pressed something hard into my palm, then he drew away with an elegant bow, and the smile that would have to last me forever.

"Your *chevalier*," he murmured, and I knew at once what he had given me. Later, far down the road, I would slip the ebony chess knight from inside my glove, and the flourishing *A* he had carved underneath would thrill and devastate me in equal measure. But there, in the courtyard, I still feared for him.

The hard hand of Uther's marshal landed on his shoulder. My insides froze, but Accolon held my gaze, unafraid.

"*Chevalier* indeed," scoffed the marshal, marching him off. "Not yet, boy. An afternoon cleaning mail will do you the world of good."

Then Accolon was gone, and in less than an hour so was I, riding out of the castle gates, a cabal of Uther's knights encircling my solitude, Tintagel and the sea vanishing behind me.

15

IT WAS HOURS past nightfall when Uther's guard captain finally halted in front of a high-gabled gatehouse. It had been raining for the last mile in cold, slanting drops, and the torchbearers' flames hissed and guttered. I dismounted as the gates yawned wide and a dour, elderly man appeared.

"You're late," said the gatekeeper. "The Prioress awaits you."

I followed him into the darkness until a constellation of lights floated up and we entered a large, grassy courtyard lit by outdoor sconces. Across the cropped green, I saw that the starry lights were candles, hung high and glittering through the mullioned windows of the abbey chapel.

"In there." The gatekeeper gestured to a small doorway opening onto shadowy steps, then shuffled off.

Hesitantly, I turned and climbed the stairs.

"You were expected *hours* ago."

I had barely poked my head around the open door when a nun—the Prioress, I assumed—snapped at me. She stood poised in the middle of a neat reception chamber, face clean and austere against the crisp grey and white of her habit. Her pale-blue eyes gleamed with a disapproval that I felt right through to my marrow. "I have sat awake long enough. Come with me."

She led me down a dim corridor past a row of identical closed doors, a ring of keys jangling on her belt like a dungeon-keeper's.

At length, the Prioress swept towards one of the squat doorways, immediately found the right key from a choice of hundreds, and unceremoniously pushed open the door. "You will sleep here. Don't keep the candle lit too long. Wax and tallow are not to be wasted."

I took the light from her and slunk into the room. It was a bare cell and small, containing a roughly carpentered table, a narrow cot with scratchy woollen blankets, and a chamber pot. A plain wooden cross hung at the bed's head, beside a dark slit of window. The room smelled clean, riverish, as if scrubbed with cold water and determination.

"Get some sleep," commanded the Prioress. "The Abbess will summon you in due course."

"What about my things, my bed robe, dry hose . . . ?" I thought of the vair-lined cloak in the trunk sent ahead of me, much needed in this room, where I could see my breath.

"You must make do. Time is the Lord's to keep, and you were unpunctual. Don't forget to say your prayers."

"But—"

Her reply was the slam of the door, the steady retort of her slippers fading away. I sat on the thin mattress, shivering hard. That morning I had woken at Tintagel, in my own bed with its quilted coverlet, the sea roaring beneath my window. Now I could not even be certain *where* I was: my refusal to speak to my mother meant I hadn't even been told the name of this lonely place.

I glanced at the door, shut fast but quite unlocked. I wasn't a prisoner, at least; if I wanted, I could run to the gatehouse, draw the bolt and be gone. But where would I go? I had no coin, no horse, and only my father's eating knife for protection, sharp but useless to a woman alone on the road.

I lay down on my side, clutching my damp cloak around me. A hard, unusual shape pushed against the inside of my wrist. I drew the ebony knight out of my glove; it reared darkly in my hand, alive against the dancing flame.

I held it tightly to my chest and, in the forbidden light of the unsnuffed candle, tumbled into a deep and melancholy sleep.

*

THE ABBESS SENT for me early, a novice waking me from a chill, aching slumber. I was given fresh water, which I gulped directly from the pitcher's lip, then used the rest to scrub my face.

The novice guided me to the Abbess's door, knocked and left. A warm voice bid me come in, and I entered a comfortably furnished reception chamber with a stately desk dominating the back of the room. A short, round woman stood before it, her cheerful, heart-shaped face entirely at odds with the scrubbed severity of the Prioress. Over her grey habit she wore a luxurious robe of blue brocade, trimmed with winter mink.

"Lady Morgan!" She kissed my cheeks as if we had known each other all our lives. "We meet at last. I've heard much about you over the years."

"You have?" I said. "How is that, Abbess—"

"Lady Honoria," she supplied. "Reverend Mother and Abbess of St. Brigid's Abbey. I've known your lady mother a long time— she is our greatest patroness. This abbey wouldn't be what it is without her benevolence, and that of the late Duke. I was sorry to hear of your loss."

"Thank you." My voice wavered at her reference to my true father. "He was very dear to me."

"And you to him, from your mother's word. Which is why you have come here." She gestured to a chair before the desk, then took her own seat. There was a ripple of black and white, and I was surprised to behold a live magpie hopping along a perch behind her. It tilted its head and gave a low, enquiring caw. "Hush, Benedict," she scolded it mildly.

"I beg your pardon, Abbess," I said. "But I am here because my mother's now-husband, Uther Pendragon, sent me."

"King Uther's command is indeed why you were sent into monastic life," she replied. "But being under my particular care is based on your mother's wishes, and those of your lord father."

"What wishes?"

"Lady Igraine wants you to be educated, my dear. Her generosity has allowed us to maintain a fine school for the teaching of young ladies. Her and your father's belief in your quick mind meant your mother ensured that you came here."

I ran a fingertip over my father's ring, snug on my thumb, and saw my mother in my bedchamber, telling me to remember she had tried. A sudden ache washed through me, twin waves of love and remorse.

"Uther said I may not write to her," I said in a small voice.

The Abbess offered me a sympathetic smile. "Rest assured I *can* write to Lady Igraine, and I will. She will hear of your progress, and you of her replies."

I drew a deep breath and nodded. "What will I learn?"

"You will begin with the Seven Arts, along with foreign tongues, the histories, some study of nature, flora and fauna—things like that. Thereafter, we will see where your strengths lie."

My heart fluttered with her every word. "It doesn't sound much like becoming a nun."

"There'll be prayer, of course. And all must take part in the daily running of the abbey. We have gardens, a farm, sewing to be done, our own brewhouse, as well as administrative duties. But most of your time will be spent at your books. Then, if you stay, you take holy vows at one-and-twenty. How does that sound?"

"It sounds wonderful." I ducked my head, overwhelmed. "I never imagined . . . when he sent me away . . ."

"Child." I looked up at the kindly face. "Thank your lady mother every day in your prayers, and do your work diligently. She will be made proud. Now, where were we?" She rose, hurrying across to the door and pulling it open, beckoning without.

A tall, serene-looking girl entered the room. She wore a neat blue surcoat embroidered with ferns—clearly not nun's or servant's attire—her rich brown hair braided like a fishtail down her back. She moved peacefully, like I imagined a nun should, but her golden-brown eyes took me in with a mischievous curiosity that was distinctly un-ecclesiastical. She seemed only slightly older than me, but hooked her thumbs into her belt and regarded Abbess Honoria with a knowingness far beyond her years. I liked her immediately.

"Lady Alys, this is our newest pupil, and hopefully your companion," said the Abbess. "Lady Morgan, formerly of Cornwall, now Princess of Britain."

"I don't claim it," I said quickly. "I mean, I prefer Lady Morgan."

The girl's pleasant, snub-nosed face relaxed into an agreeable smile. "Pleased to meet you, Lady Morgan. I am Alys merch Gruffydd, of Llancarfan. A lady too, just about. How came you to be in St. Brigid's?"

She had a low singsong voice, proudly announcing her Welsh heritage. Upon hearing its warm, lively rhythm, I found myself soothed and instilled with a vicarious confidence—the sense that I could become whoever I wished if I learned to speak my own truth.

I regarded Alys of Llancarfan directly. "I was sent here against my will, for bad behaviour. But I'm happy I've come."

Alys let out a fluting laugh. "I'll keep this one, Reverend Mother."

"That's Lady Morgan's decision." Abbess Honoria turned to me. "As sister scholars, you would be much together, sharing a chamber, lessons and study time. Alys is bright and good, but as you can see, has a jesting, occasionally outspoken streak. Do you deem her a suit-able companion?"

I glanced at Alys's roguish, friendly face, then at her hands, down at her sides. The fingertips were speckled with ink.

"I'm sure Lady Alys and I will get along well," I replied. "Very well indeed."

16

ALYS BEGAN OUR tour of St. Brigid's right away, hooking her arm through mine and pointing out the abbey's main sights: the impressive chapel, the refectory where the nuns gathered for meals, the infirmary and the long, narrow wing where the sworn sisters kept their cells. Lastly, she led me out onto a peaceful courtyard just off the central building.

It was fully enclosed and contained a sizeable garden, diligently kept, plants and shrubs flourishing despite the winter cold. We walked alongside it down a cloistered pathway to where Alys opened one of the doors to reveal our chamber.

It was a vast improvement on the one I'd slept in the previous night: larger, well furnished, with its own fireplace and a scribe's desk under the window. A pair of decent beds stood at the back, behind painted wooden screens.

Alys surveyed me and the room both. "It's not the palaces you're used to, but—"

"It's perfect." I ran my hand over a sturdy lectern. "We can have books in here?"

"Of course! For extra study." She unlatched the window shutters and pulled them open. Chill air rushed in, smelling of rosemary and pennyroyal. I inhaled it deeply.

"Lovely, isn't it?" she said. "In the warmer months it's lovelier still—roses, honeysuckle, lavender, summer herbs in abundance."

She wandered back out, and I followed, closing our door. "It's a very impressive garden."

"I think so," she said proudly. "Tending it is my main household duty, and I enjoy it immensely. You are welcome to join me, if it pleases you."

"If it saves me from stitching shifts, I certainly will." I glanced across to the adjacent row. A few of the windows were cracked open, flickers of candlelight emanating from within. "How many pupils are there?"

"Just us," Alys said. "My former chamber-sister recently took her vows to the order. She assists in the infirmary now." She gestured to the shutters standing ajar. "The widows reside there. Ladies who have chosen to live out their days in seclusion. Or were sent, for various reasons."

"Interesting. What are they like?"

"Friendly. Rather wise. Between them they know all there is to know about menfolk, marriage, motherhood and manorial life." Alys took my arm and guided us back into the main building, towards the central thoroughfare. "How long are you expecting to stay?"

"I didn't even know I was coming until a few days ago."

"Ah yes, the 'bad behaviour.' Can I ask what it was?"

"Lack of piety, disobedience, dislike of the High King of Britain," I said. "What of you? The call of vocation?"

"Something like that. When I was fourteen, a cousin of my father's offered marriage. As many manners as he had teeth, and three wives in the ground already. It was astonishing how fast I realized my path lay with Christ."

I giggled so hard it became a snort. Alys smothered her own laugh, nodding politely to a row of nuns rustling towards the chapel like a column of doves. After they passed, she led me across the main courtyard and up a limestone staircase to a door painted with olive branches.

"And finally . . ." She pushed it open to reveal a long, high-vaulted room, lit by chandeliers the size of cartwheels and a row of huge arched windows. There were shelves everywhere, bearing all manner of books, parchments, jars and pots, curious implements made from metal and glass. "Our classroom."

I gasped. "It's incredible."

Alys grinned, pointing to a doorway at the farthest end. "There's a library too, with more books. Half the day we're taught in the classroom, then time is given to household duties, but once those are finished, we are free for private study. That's why the garden is good work—tending herbs and medicinal plants benefits my learning."

"Medicinal plants?" I said excitedly. "When will I study that?"

"Not yet." Alys strode across and tossed a few split logs into the enormous fireplace, churning the embers with a poker. "You'll begin with the Seven Arts. Grammar, rhetoric, logic—"

"Arithmetic, music, geometry and astronomy," I supplied. "I've heard of them, perhaps even know a little."

She regarded me in mild surprise. "The Abbess told me you had no learning. Some reading, writing and numbers only."

I stiffened, a remnant of caution on Father Felix's behalf. "Not . . . formally. I had other instruction, in secret."

"For how long?"

"Seven years."

"Goodness! And no one knew?"

"I never told a soul." My own lie caught me off guard, the remembrance of the soul I *had* told affording my gut a bolt of pain. I closed my eyes for a moment, distracted by the thought of him.

I turned to the window; the courtyard was deserted, nuns safely ensconced in the chapel. "What about prayer? I assumed there'd be a great deal."

"Scholars are too busy to attend every office. We say Mass at Prime and Vespers, and are trusted to otherwise pray privately."

"It all sounds rather permissive."

Alys shrugged. "It is and it isn't. Our life is less strict than true sisterhood, but there are rules, and we are expected to obey them."

I drifted towards the long table near the hearth. The surface was covered with parchment in banded rolls and flattened squares, ink bottles and multicoloured quills. Someone had left an unrolled sketch, held at the corners with matching lion-head paperweights, and I was surprised to behold a detailed anatomical drawing of the human eye, rendered neatly in crosshatched black.

Alys sidled up. "Good, isn't it? That's by the Prioress herself."

I thought back to the cold blade of a woman who had so abruptly thrown me into my first-night cell. "The Prioress comes here?"

"She teaches occasionally. She's an immensely skilled healer, knowledgeable in physic, some surgery. She instructs me because of my interest in curative plants."

Gently, I unweighted the parchment to reveal a sheaf of similar sketches beneath: a jawbone swathed in muscle; the numerous spiked bones of the hand; a human heart placed in a cutaway torso. "I'd love to learn the healing arts."

"The Prioress is incredibly strict on whom she agrees to teach." Alys reweighted the top parchment exactly as it had been. "It took eighteen months of study before she deemed me ready. But there's plenty of time to prove yourself."

I nodded vaguely, gaze still fixed on the sharply inked eye, recalling my first encounter with the Prioress and her obvious disdain for my failings.

Alys moved off, beckoning. "Come. Brother Kerwyn is on his way up at last. He's always a canter stride behind the bell."

I pushed one of the lion heads until it was clearly off-centre and

strode away from the table as a monk arrived in a flurry of brown, so
flustered he noticed neither one of us.

"Brother Kerwyn," Alys called, and he stopped. "Your new pupil
is here."

"Of course, Lady Morgan." He dipped his tonsured head. "Abbess
Honoria said to expect you. I trust Lady Alys has shown you our
classroom?"

"I have," she said. "Lady Morgan is keen to begin."

"Yes, naturally, yes." Brother Kerwyn rushed off again to a disorderly shelf, pushing and pulling at various manuscripts. "Please, be
seated. Where to start?"

We took our seats at the long central table, backs to the roaring
fire. Alys leaned a shoulder against mine, whispering conspiratorially.
"Brother Kerwyn is rather scatterbrained, but there's none more
knowledgeable when he gets onto a subject."

I smiled, a warm ease enveloping me as I looked around the room
at all the future held: hours upon hours of reading, discovery and
understanding. Brother Kerwyn shuffled over, dropping three enormous leather-bound books onto the table. Library-scented dust
puffed into the classroom's peaceful air, swirling in the candle glow
and steel-white winter daylight.

"Astronomy," he declared. "Lady Morgan, what do you know of
the skies?"

17

AFTER TWO WEEKS of Brother Kerwyn's benign rule, I had settled to his method of encouragement and praise without yet finding myself tested. I memorized simple star charts as Alys sat at her own studies, occasionally pausing to stare comedically at me with her mischievous amber eyes until I noticed and collapsed into silent giggles. Sometimes Brother Kerwyn would glance up, or utter a peevish "My ladies," though this tended to make us worse.

But our days of ease could not last, and a fortnight after I traced my fingertips across her starkly efficient sketches, I faced the Prioress for the second time. Alys and I bustled into the classroom, all elbows and mirth, stopping dead when we saw her, standing gravely where our rumpled monkish tutor should have been. She was upright as a spire, her habit so scrupulously starched it might have been carved from quartz.

Alys dipped her head with unusual deference. "My lady Prioress."

The Prioress nodded crisply at her before sliding her gaze towards me. "Lady Morgan, I trust you are well versed in the ways of St. Brigid's now, punctuality and all?"

"Yes, Prioress," I said, thinking of Brother Kerwyn's casual attitude towards the bells.

"Good. Take your seats. Obviously I am not here to instruct *you*, Lady Morgan." She pointed to a seat several chairs away from

Alys. "Brother Kerwyn informs me you have scribe work, listing the stars?"

"I do, my lady."

She raised a slash of eyebrow. "He must think quite highly of your lettering. Continue with it, in any case."

"Lady Morgan has a great interest in healing," Alys piped up. "It might be fitting to let her join us."

I was aghast at Alys's forthrightness, but the Prioress merely gave a neat shake of the head. "Absolutely not. She is in all aspects unready." Moving around the table, she paused in front of her sketches, spotting the lion-head paperweight I'd moved two weeks ago. She shifted it back into place, then touched the edges of the papers to make sure they were aligned.

"Healing is a difficult art," she went on. "One cannot simply learn it from a page and have done. Most who come here aren't capable of it at all. Now, Lady Alys, the skeleton. Eyes on your work, Lady Morgan," she added, without looking in my direction.

I bent my head to the volume I'd been copying from—names of stars, their relative positions as the year turned and their celestial influence. I filled the well with black ink, picked up my favourite rook-tail quill and took a lined rectangle of parchment.

"Incorrect, Lady Alys," snapped the Prioress. "You've had ample time to learn this."

I pricked my ears as I scribed. *Pegasus*, I wrote, *Orion, the hunter, comprised of . . .*

"From the shoulder," urged the Prioress. "The bones in the upper arm are . . ."

Out of the corner of my eye, I saw Alys turn crimson. Her failure was entirely my fault; she had spent the last fortnight guiding my way at St. Brigid's, like my own North Star. I sat hopelessly, willing the words I knew so well out of my mind and into hers.

Scapula, my hand wrote, *humerus, radius, ulna.* Carpus next, the wrist. Eight bones. Named by the Romans for the shapes they resembled, like so many of the parts that make a body. Language is deep but true, Father Felix had said; it can always tell you more if you listen closely.

I was halfway through my list of carpal bones when I saw what I'd done: wasted my parchment—about the only crime Brother Kerwyn cared for—and rendered the entire page into nonsense.

"God's teeth!" I threw my quill down, splattering ink, then clapped my hand over my mouth.

"*I beg your pardon?*" The Prioress reared up, sweeping around the table. "Those are *not* the words of a lady, or a scholar of St. Brigid's."

I scrabbled at the parchment, fruitlessly trying to cover my mistake. "I apologize for the blasphemy. I pricked my finger with the quill, I—"

She swiped the ink-streaked paper from under my foolish hands, gaze flitting from top to bottom, then fixed me with her acute, wintry stare. "What is this?"

I ducked my head in shame; the thought of losing this place, this happy cavern of knowledge and possibility, was unbearable.

"Lady Morgan," insisted the Prioress, "how do you know these words?"

"Prioress, I . . . I . . ."

"Don't mumble, troublesome girl!"

Her tone of disdain pierced me, and I thrust my chin into the air, flaring with irritation. "I read them in a book," I retorted. "I know every single bone in the skeleton, if it please you."

The Prioress drew back in a tightly controlled recoil, basilisk stare fixed on me.

"You read Latin?" she asked unexpectedly.

"Y-yes," I stammered. "My father's chaplain taught me, along with other tongues. Father Felix of Nantes."

"I know of him. A highly respected and learned holy man. Which other tongues?"

The list I rattled off surprised me as much as it did her, particularly when I detailed further subjects I had studied using Latin. Only then did I fully appreciate the advanced and comprehensive knowledge seven years with Father Felix had given me.

"I don't have much old Greek," I conceded. "And less Welsh than I'd like." Alys unfroze enough to raise an acknowledging smile; I'd been pestering her for her native vocabulary every evening since we'd met.

"I see." The Prioress had lost something of her severity, merely cool now rather than tundra cold. She ran her fingernail down the list headed *Scapula*. "And this?"

I gave the smallest of shrugs. "I wasn't sure if you required clavicles."

Her mouth twitched, whether to snarl or smile I couldn't tell. "Your chaplain taught you physic?"

"No, my lady. I found a book in the Royal Library—collected Roman writings on anatomy, sickness and remedy." I wasn't about to admit I still had the *Ars Physica* in my possession, buried deep in my travelling trunk. "I studied it, memorized it, practised—"

"Practised! How?"

"Just healing notes in the household ledger. And . . ." I cast my eyes down to my hands, woven together in my lap, fingers entwined—just as he and I used to do, when his hands weren't soft at my face, or tangled in my hair. "I saved someone from drowning once, because of what I'd read. Knocked the water from them until they breathed again."

The Prioress nodded. Alys drew her braid over one shoulder, chewing agitatedly on the end.

"This interests you?" asked the Prioress. "Healing, physic, afflictions of the body?"

"Very much." Then, with the last of my bravery, "As I said, I could name you every bone in the skeleton and the organs that sit within, down to the chambers of the heart. And if you teach me, I will quickly learn the rest."

She considered me, eyes pin bright. "My pupils don't volunteer, Lady Morgan. I choose them. Without exception they have been here for much longer than you, with many, many more classroom hours. A few facts do not an affinity make."

I nodded defeatedly. All I could do now was pray my learnedness would be enough to save me from dismissal.

The Prioress glanced at the parchment again. "I will speak with the Abbess."

"Please, my lady," I begged. "I'll do any work you wish, but let me stay."

She tutted. "You can begin with being less dramatic, Lady Morgan. You're not going anywhere. Nor should you assume that I will condescend to teach you. But you will be discussed."

The Prioress turned back to Alys. "Find your list of bones and study it. You have until tomorrow." She pointed briskly to the table in front of me. "Return to Brother Kerwyn's task; ensure it is right this time. And *do not* count on miracles."

I didn't, and never had, but two days later she swept into the classroom, directed me to the seat next to Alys, then introduced both of us to the inner workings of the human heart.

18

MOST OFTEN, I missed him when it rained. From the cold torrents of winter through blustery spring showers, to late summer, when the thunder came, I thought of Accolon—smiling across a chessboard on the chapel floor, or drawing me into his arms in our saltwater cave—and the two furious storms that brought us together, setting my fate in motion.

And what was his fate, I wondered, as I marked his eighteenth birthday at Michaelmas and the first year of my banishment approached. Was he knighted now? Had my Gaul returned to his homeland to trade his sword and lance for gold?

He could have been dead, of course, marched off to Uther's war, never to return. But I could not escape the belief that if he had ceased to exist, I would have known it deep in my bones. So I thought of him alive: flashes of his face as I brushed my hair, ate silent meals in the refectory or knelt at an altar in sacred prayer; of his arching lip; the sardonic affection of his sideways glance; the loose, confident grace with which he carried his body; the way he said my name— *Morr-ganne*—low and tender, like music.

By night, I relived our togetherness, sleeplessly recounting every glance, word and kiss. Lying in bed while all around me slept, I would take the ebony *chevalier* from the hole cut into my mattress and grip it hard in my palm, remembering, until it left marks deep in my skin.

I wondered if he suffered the same. Did he lie awake at night thinking of the time we spent together and what might have been, or look at the incomplete chess set and remember carving his initial—that permanent, violent mark—to make sure I thought of him? Or was the memory defunct, forgotten, shoved into a trunk with the checkered box and left behind?

Perhaps he had found others to share his life with: fellow knights in faraway courts; fair maidens willing and free, who flirted and danced and smiled as Accolon's fine hands fluttered beneath his golden coin. Surely by now he thought nothing of me, the disgraced, hopeless girl, hundreds of days gone, who in her loneliness and longing could not forget, falling asleep every night with his chess piece clutched tight.

And yet, sometimes, I told myself he did think of me, that he must, that he always had. That he too had not forgotten.

*

BY THE TIME my own eighteenth birthday came, I had barely felt the two and a half years of happy confinement, at least in the daytime. My nights were still long and full of marching shades, but between study, prayer and tending the garden with Alys or assisting with Abbess Honoria's accounts ledgers, there was hardly a moment's pause to muse on the passage of my life. Any spare hours I spent in the library, availing myself of its delights.

The majority of our lesson time was spent with the Prioress. She schooled us relentlessly, making us learn list after list of anatomical structures, plants and their properties, how to make and administer hundreds of powders, poultices and tinctures. I could sketch an accurate human heart blindfolded, name almost any sickness and its humoral effect, and argue a case for diagnosis with barely a misstep.

Under her watchful eye we stood, needle in hand, stitching incisions made in the side of a pig, before cutting it open and examining its organs. "The closest one can get to the parts of a man," she told us, "without committing a mortal sin."

Recently, Alys and I had been entrusted with the mixing of some cure-all ointments for minor ailments. Gaining the Prioress's chilly trust pleased me at first, but Alys was deeply dedicated to herbal lore, whereas I had grown restless. To my mind, we had done little true healing.

"What good, knowing that the moon waxes in Aries if I never get within arm's length of examining someone's head?" I complained to my ever-tolerant companion. It was a bright day on the cusp of autumn, and the Prioress had not yet appeared. "I want to examine, I want to diagnose, I want to *heal*."

Alys chuckled, filling two inkpots. "If you feel so strongly, then tell her. Look, here she comes."

I glanced up to see our formidable teacher stalking through the doorway, carrying a large gold book under one arm.

"I wouldn't dare," I whispered.

Alys grinned. "Why not? She won't bite."

"I highly suspect that she might."

"Whispering again, ladies?" said the Prioress. "Pray, what is so diverting?"

"Actually, Lady Prioress, we were speaking of our learning so far." Alys's voice was clear and assured as spring birdsong. "Lady Morgan is eager to know when our lessons might progress to more practical methods of healing." She swung her shins away from my kicking feet, face devilishly earnest.

"I'm sorry, Lady Prioress," I said quickly. "I'm not questioning—"

The Prioress looked up, narrow-eyed like a panther. "Do not *apologize*, Lady Morgan. Your decorum leaves a little to be desired, but never have I been able to fault your work. Never apologize for seeking further wisdom, or for being remarkable. As it happens, the Lord smiles upon you today."

She laid the gold book on the table. Wincing, she raised her left arm to her chest and cradled it, displaying a ring of dark, swollen bruises beneath her narrow cuff.

Alys gasped. "My lady, what happened?"

The Prioress rolled her eyes. "There's no need for alarm. I merely skidded on some tallow and landed awkwardly. Now, may I start my lesson? Concentration is essential, and I have seldom had pupils capable of mastering these arts."

Our teacher laid her palms on the gilt-embossed cover, gave us another crystalline stare, then flung it open. "Adjurations, the saints and the laying on of hands."

I nudged Alys and we both sat straighter.

"Here is where heart meets mind," the Prioress explained. "Where you surrender your learning to your love of God and the holy sacrifices of the saints. Above all, we are a messenger, a conduit, the mortal, physical connection between Almighty Grace and the person you intend to heal."

A sliver of doubt crept into my head. After years of learning to sharpen the forces of my intelligence, abandoning them to become a mere vessel seemed suddenly unappealing. Surely there was more to it—more power, more control?

"There is much theory to be learned," she continued. "But given you are so impatient for practicalities, I will show you the correct form for laying on hands. Lady Alys, you first."

Alys scrambled from her chair and joined the Prioress on the other side of the table. The Prioress pointed to a section of script in the book. "This is the adjuration to St. Cosmas, a plea to a most holy healing saint for his grace in curing an affliction. In time, you will learn each specific adjuration, along with the concentration technique to make your touch effective. But for now, basic placement." She rolled back her right-hand sleeve and extended her bare arm before Alys. "Put your palms side by side, touching the skin, but without pressure."

Tentatively, Alys placed her hands on the Prioress's forearm. "Choose your place and keep to it," said the Prioress. "It is important to hold oneself steady. Now, read the adjuration."

Alys took a deep breath, glanced down at the page and began murmuring.

"Speak clearly!" commanded the Prioress. "Only the most talented and experienced can intone in their minds—the beginner must *enunciate*."

"Holy St. Cosmas," Alys read, "patron of physicians, master of healing and most unmercenary brother, relieve this good woman of her affliction. Bind her injury and make her whole again, with your mercy and grace, in the name of the Father, the Son and the Holy Spirit."

"Good," said the Prioress. "When truly healing, you should feel heat slowly gathering beneath your hands as the saintly power flows through you. But that comes much later, after a great deal of study." She beckoned to me. "Lady Morgan, come."

The Prioress turned the same precise folds on her left sleeve, exposing her bruised wrist and holding her forearm out to me. I laid my palms side by side exactly as Alys had, touching the cool skin lightly but firmly, then inhaled a steady breath in preparation.

Before I could pay St. Cosmas my humble compliments, a rush of warmth ran down both of my arms and into my hands—not overly hot, but sudden, unexpected—a glorious internal burst of light fusing my touch to the Prioress's arm. Alarmed, I broke away, staggering into the table behind me.

"Lady Morgan," scolded the Prioress. "If you cannot take this seriously—" Her mouth snapped shut, eyes flicking to the hand she had raised in admonishment. "How . . . ?" she said to herself.

My heart was still racing from the quick bolt of warmth, sensation subsiding into something softly pleasurable, like sinking into a much-needed bath, or the first sip of a particularly good wine.

"Lady Prioress, your wrist!" Alys exclaimed. The purple-black bruises had faded to a pale yellowish green.

I had never known the Prioress struck dumb, but she stared at her wrist with tranquil eyes, a dazed almost-smile on her face. As Alys gaped, she held out her left arm to me and said, "Again."

I obeyed, wrapping my fingers around it, uncertain. But as my skin began to warm, I recalled the feeling, the rush of strength and light that was, however briefly, transcendent. I fixed my mind on the injury and felt the resistance beneath my fingers—a tangible ring of pain, flexible but tough, like leather armour, and stubborn. But somehow, I knew it would yield to me.

It was not long until it came, not a flash this time but a hot, steady march of light, growing and pushing until something gave way under my hands, splitting the bruise and dissolving it with ease.

I let go, blinking at the Prioress's now spotless skin. My blood tingled with quiet euphoria, and I was intrigued to find myself completely unsurprised at what I had done. A memory fluttered up, faint but echoing: Morgause's broken linnet in my hands; the sudden surge of warmth; its jubilant, unhindered escape. The same certainty, impossible and unspoken, that I had been the cause.

"It's . . . gone." Alys stared at me in wonder. "It's a miracle."

Mustering some semblance of authority, the Prioress set her

shoulders and took two steps backwards. "Not a miracle," she said sharply. "That assertion is blasphemous." She clutched her wrist and regarded me, eyes gleaming with caution. "The saints *are* listening keenly today, Lady Morgan. You barely had time to bring them to mind, so quickly did they rush to your aid."

"But, my lady," I said, "I don't feel like I thought of the saints at all."

"Of course you did," she snapped.

"No, I—" I wanted to say that what happened was natural, powerful, and I alone had done it, but her severe expression held my tongue.

"Be careful, Lady Morgan," she warned. "Other forces are at best subversive. At worst . . . well. Without God's will, there is only the work of the Beast. Necromancy, by any other name."

"My lady, *no!*" I had barely heard the word *necromancy*, aside from Gwennol's cautionary childhood tales and an unwelcome notion of the sorcerer Merlin. "I only did what you asked."

"That's quite enough," she said coldly. "As I'm sure you know, any sympathies or curiosity for anything less than holy would mean instant expulsion from St. Brigid's."

She spun around, gathering the gold book into her arms. "You have overreached yourselves, perhaps. Be sure to acknowledge and thank St. Cosmas profusely in your prayers for the blessing he has bestowed on us today."

Stalking away, she paused at the door. "If I choose to continue this line of teaching, I must be assured of your dedication to my methods. You will learn every scrap of knowledge about the saints, their lives, their holy suffering, but strictly under my supervision. No independent study, practising or discussion among yourselves is permitted, or our endeavours will cease immediately. Is that clear?"

"Yes, Lady Prioress," we mumbled, and she fled the classroom.

"What in Heaven was that about?" Alys exclaimed. "I've never

seen her so rattled. And you, curing that bruise! How did you do it?
Could you do it again?"

I recalled the first, inexplicable golden rush, and the second,
stronger time, where I seemed to gather and hold the force in my
fingertips, sending the bright heat forth of my own volition. So
quickly had I learned to control it.

"I honestly don't know," I said, certain I had to find out.

19

THERE WAS NO further mention of what had occurred; the Prioress merely gave us copious texts to read on the lives of the saints and reiterated that Alys and I were forbidden to discuss things outside the classroom.

Despite this, our curiosity could not be contained, and we soon contrived to recreate the effect, which I did to some success: alleviating the low pains of our monthly courses, or soothing minor candle burns. Once I went so far as to unblacken Alys's thumbnail where she had jammed it in a drawer.

However, I soon discovered my ability had its limitations: Alys lost the thumbnail, and her herbal salves often proved more effective against burns. Practice improved my strange talent, but the wish to understand it stubbornly eluded me: upon searching, we found not a single book outside the Prioress's private gold manuscript that mentioned the laying on of hands.

As Advent began, the Prioress was busy with ecclesiastical duties, but Alys and I were still expected to be in the library, and by the start of the third holy week, I felt that I had scaled the full height and breadth of the well-stocked bookshelves.

"You can't possibly have read *everything*," Alys said, as I dragged the rickety shelf ladder along the landing above her. "You're quick but not *that* quick."

"I certainly am." I paced along the unyielding rows, past histories, speeches and political treatises—dry texts I had used for studying rhetoric. I had half decided to revisit Virgil's *Aeneid* when an anomaly caught my eye, two volumes jutting an inch proud of the shelf edge.

Setting my candle aside, I tried and failed to push them back into place. Exasperated, I pulled out both books, shining my candle into the gap to see what was stopping them. A thick tome sat behind, fallen on its side. It was too far back to reach, so I dragged the ladder to the shelf, climbed a few rungs, then leaned in to grasp it.

"Morgan, what are you doing?" Alys called up.

"Just moving a book that's in the way." Heaving the manuscript out, I clambered unsteadily down and laid it on the floor. The binding was like nothing I'd ever seen: jet-black covers, ornately tooled into a pattern of spiky vines, twisting densely around glossy inlaid onyx. The edges and spine were studded with rubies of all sizes, shining bloody in the candlelight.

I had seen jewelled manuscripts before—our ducal family Bible at Tintagel was similarly ornate—but had never encountered a volume like this, big as a side table and almost alive under my gaze. I brushed my fingers across the surface, nerves tingling.

Alys appeared, kneeling beside me. When she saw the book, she recoiled like it was an unidentified snake. "What's that?"

"I'm not sure." I lifted the front cover and ran a finger along the page edges. They too were black, painted with ink as if to keep the book hidden at all angles. "It's unmarked, completely anonymous."

Gingerly, I lifted the pages: thick, good-quality parchment, covered in a sweeping black script. There were no ruled lines, no embossed letters or colourful illustrations. The script danced across the page at will, running sideways, top to bottom and diagonally, sometimes in arcs and circles around black line drawings. The images were highly proficient, and the Latin far more complex than most things we read.

"Are those . . . incantations?" Alys peered closer.

I kept leafing, turning page after page of charts and diagrams, until I reached a full-length anatomical sketch of a man, with some sort of method beside it. "*To drive out . . . blood-borne ills and drag . . . life from the brink of death*," I translated aloud. "This seems to be some sort of healing chant, but nothing like our adjurations. *Take leaves of the belladonna bush and two tail feathers of the purest black raven. Burn all as twilight falls . . . speak thus three times . . .*"

"By God, stop that." Alys pulled the book from me, turning the pages with increasing agitation. "Spoken fire, entice your beloved into a lust frenzy, bring enemies to madness. Command the wind! Induce barrenness in a woman!" She slammed the cover shut and stared at me in horror. "Morgan, this is sorcery, used only by the damned. How this even came to be here . . ."

"Nevertheless, it's very interesting." I took the book back and opened it again. "Look at this—healing formulae for illnesses we haven't dreamed of treating. If we can learn to speak the words correctly, just think of what we can do."

"Are you mad?" Alys exclaimed. "We must stay well away from this."

"I don't see why. It's no different in theory to what we've been learning—just more powerful, more difficult to master."

"Of course it's different! What we do is within the allowances of nature, under God's eye. This"—she prodded the book—"is unnatural, sinful. It calls upon forces we can have no dealings with. It's *demonic*."

"Now *that* is madness," I scoffed. "It's simply superstition talking, and fear."

"Because it's worth fearing. We can't begin to understand this."

"Lack of understanding is the very reason we *should* explore it. No knowledge can be inherently terrible, surely?"

"Morgan, listen," Alys said firmly. "We don't have the knowledge to take chances with this. What if the Prioress found out?"

She picked the huge volume up and struggled to her feet, pushing it far back into the gap where I had found it.

I stood, torn between my respect for her wisdom and my own sharply twitching will.

Looping her arm through mine, Alys turned us away from the shelf. "I know how dedicated you are. But this is still a nunnery, and the rules are set in stone. You're happy here, aren't you? Why risk everything for a whisper in the dark?"

*

I WAS HAPPY at St. Brigid's, yes, but Alys's so-called whispers fast became their own choral movement. I lay awake at night, trying to recall diagrams and fragments of Latin, lips moving silently as I attempted to rebuild the incantation with the power to drive out sickness. But even I could not summon what wasn't there, so it remained in pieces, a useless torment, and eventually, what was inadvisable soon became inevitable.

One evening, I returned to the library on a false errand and took the red-jewelled volume from its hiding place, painstakingly copying down the mysterious healing method on a scrap of parchment, repeating its chant in a whisper until the language was a tune in my mind.

A few days later, kneeling alone in the cold garden beds, I slipped my father's knife from my belt and sliced into the mound of flesh just under my thumb. The pain felt far away, the welling blood like that of another, more sensible creature, one who would never maim herself to ask a question that might never be answered.

I scooped a handful of soil from beneath the mint bush and pressed dirt into the wound, then used my kerchief to bind the injury. Later on, I told Alys my knife had slipped while trimming dead leaves, but the cut was minor and I'd treated myself.

Within a few days it began to fester, waking me in the middle of the night, throbbing like a furnace. The next morning I unwound the makeshift bandage, gritting my teeth as it pulled at the puckered wound, edges now ragged and yellow-raw. The smell of earthy decay caught in my throat, affording me a moment of revulsion followed by grim satisfaction.

I bound it back up and watched for another week as darkness spread down my wrist, blood vessels wine red, angry and aching. I hid it well; I wore overlong sleeves, chewed valerian root for the pain and assured Alys it was healing as intended. Once or twice I wavered, considering what would happen if my clever plan failed. Amputations, we'd learned long ago, were near impossible to survive.

When at last the day came, I sent Alys off to the refectory in the evening with the excuse I was feeling unwell, unhungry and in need of extra sleep. By then my left arm hurt bone-deep, hanging against my side, inert and rotten. Alys went with reluctance, vigilant to my barely concealed fever, and I knew she was trusting my word for the last time. No matter, I thought, as my blurring eyes watched her long braid swinging out of the door; if this didn't work, I would need her to carry me to the infirmary anyway.

I kept my eyes on the window, waiting for twilight, then pushed the rush mats aside, laying a pile of belladonna leaves and two raven quills before me on the hearthstone. The feathers caught fire quickly, the leaves not so easily, flaming briefly before curling with dreadful slowness, filling the air with an acrid green scent. When all was finally reduced to ash, I blew the heat away, peeled the bandage off, and pushed my good hand into the smoking pile.

The afflicted limb was almost as blackened as the char-covered one, wound bluish, peeling like onion skin. The stench struck me anew, recalling the stink of dead sheep in the rain. Swallowing a bubble of disgust, I closed my eyes and laid my ash-covered fingers across the pulsating wound. Then, as the book's method had instructed, I began reciting the incantation.

Not a nerve twitched at the first saying, and by the second I was sure I'd made a horrifying mistake, the chant summoning not even a spark of feeling or shift in my blood. A sob caught in my throat at the third repetition, bringing the words forth in a tearful, breathy garble.

I opened my eyes to see my wretched, mangled arm, still lurid with rot, faintly reverberating under clumps of ash. I had failed, and was likely dead. Another cry fought its way up, but I shoved it back down. "No," I whispered. "It *can* be done."

Releasing all thoughts of how it *should* be, I closed my eyes, braced my fingers against the wound and drew deep, restoring breaths. The fear fell away, along with the world, until all that remained was a single channel from my core to my fingertips, like a golden rope made from light.

Voice deep and rhythmic, I repeated the incantation three times, drawing new breath for each. At the final word, my arm shuddered, filling with a white-hot pressure, sickness drawing in on itself like a pupil contracting to light, the ache in my bones pulling towards my ash-dusted fingers.

I opened my eyes to see the blood vessels fading, the veins in my wrist restored to pale blue, the tide of necrosis drawing back and up into the wound. The skin dried, the edges of the cut shrinking and binding, the livid flesh lightening. A thin plume of jet-black speckles poured upwards through the closing incision, dissipating into the air like smoke. By the time I took my right hand away, all that remained was a thin red curve, slightly upraised, a barely discernible future scar.

I stood, pacing around. Other than a mild thirst and a gratifying sleepiness, I felt entirely restored, euphoric, blood tingling throughout my body like a high river; the same triumphant pleasure as I had felt after healing the Prioress, multiplied tenfold.

I fell back onto my bed, holding out my arm in all its healthful glory, rotating my wrist, squeezing the flesh, marvelling that I felt not an ounce of pain.

I had done it. I was healed.

20

I AWOKE FEELING refreshed and joyous, and turned over to see Alys sitting up in her bed, staring blankly into the middle distance. Something dark green against the blanket caught my eye. Panic shot up my spine like a loosed arrow; in her hand was a sheaf of belladonna leaves.

She turned, eyes stained red. "I found these. What did you *do*, Morgan?"

For the first time I felt inclined to lie outright, but I saw from her face she believed I had done so already, many times. "Alys, I—"

"Belladonna leaves were part of that spell. From that awful, dangerous book."

"It's not awful, or dangerous." I threw back the blankets and leapt from the bed, thrusting my arm at her. "See what it did—what *I* did—using that *awful* spell. My arm was festering, black, rotting away."

Alys glanced at my arm, which gleamed with health and strength in the thin sunlight. Her eyes widened, then she turned her face away. "But at what cost? Don't you worry what you've wrought upon yourself?"

"No," I said firmly. "Nothing has struck me down. I won't burst into flames at morning prayer. I don't feel the least bit demonic—I feel *better*."

She sighed bitterly at the wall. Exasperated, I swiped the belladonna leaves from her and shoved them into my trunk, next to the *Ars Physica*.

"The incantations in that book are just words and recipes, only more powerful," I went on. "It may frighten you, but I'm not afraid. Knowledge cannot be bad, only misused. And if we learn it, lives will be saved, dreadful injuries repaired. This abbey's healing reputation could become a thing of legend."

She slid out of bed, curiosity piqued. "What do you mean?"

"I'm going to the Prioress to tell her about the book. It has techniques that will greatly aid our understanding of healing. If she doesn't know of them, she should."

Alys put her arm out, blocking my way. "You can't. I dread to think what she'd say. Remember what happened when I expressed an interest in midwifery and suggested we could help women in the nearby villages?"

"Yes," I said reluctantly. "She told us that our learning was only to reflect God's glory and associating with bodily sin would compromise the morals of the entire abbey."

"And that's delivering innocent children," Alys said. "When you healed her bruises, her mind immediately went to necromancy! If she thinks you've even *looked* at that book, she'll expel you without hesitation. Is that what you want?"

"Of course not. The path I follow is the same as yours." We had talked of it often—our intention to take the veil together at twenty-one. Thereafter, Alys and I would keep studying, tend the garden, assist in the infirmary and see if there was more we could do with our scholarship, perhaps educate the novices. "I still want everything we've planned."

"Then you cannot speak of this. Please, Morgan. For the sake of our future, we can never look at the black book again. It's not worth the risk to either one of us, *cariad*, is it?"

I considered her fawn-like expression, the face I trusted most. I wouldn't have endangered her for anything.

"All right," I said. "For us."

"Thank you." She reached out and squeezed my hand, drawing a deep breath. "Then, *for us*, I will solve this once and for all. After I'm dressed, I'm going to the library, getting that book and taking it directly to the Abbess."

The book was burned and, despite knowing better, I dwelled on its lost secrets at length.

*

THE MORNING OF our classroom return after Christmastide was an oppressively grey one, icy fog hanging low and thick over the chapel spires. The air inside sat stagnant with disuse, cold creeping damply up our sleeves.

Alys shivered, seeking the hearth. "We're late. The Prioress should already be here."

As if summoned, the Prioress swept in. We braced for her admonition, but she merely beckoned with unusual discomposure. "Ladies, come with all haste. You are needed urgently in the infirmary."

"There's been an outbreak of sickness," she explained as we followed her through cloister and corridor. "Two novices and a sworn sister have taken to their beds with it in the past three days, and four more have succumbed this morning."

"What's the ailment?" I asked.

"Some form of lung malady, spreading rapidly, more sudden and severe than anything I've encountered. High fever, rawness of breath, terrible aches in the bones and endless fatigue. Some are coughing blood. You must mix and administer remedies, pray to the Lord for relief, all you have been taught."

We stopped at the infirmary's oaken door, silence falling like a portent. The Prioress gave an uncharacteristic sigh. "Do what you can."

Thus she left us, to face whatever we might find inside. "Well," I said doubtfully, "we have our great healing challenge, though I didn't imagine it would be like this."

Alys slid her arm through mine. "We will rise to it. Now, let's put our skills to good use. We'll have the infirmary empty in no time."

Her optimism was heartening, getting us through the first day, and the second, and the third, even as the infirmary quickly filled to bursting. Eventually, some ailing sisters had to be confined to their cells, and we visited them individually, Alys bringing poultices and tinctures she mixed from dawn until sunset, while I cooled fevers, administered pain relief and prayed for mercy until I was hoarse.

We soothed some and could not save others.

"Where do you think it came from?" I said a week later, as we dragged ourselves towards the infirmary. Progress had been made; the earliest sufferers' fevers had broken, but the stock of tinctures was running dangerously low, the herb garden near obliterated.

Alys drew her mantle tighter about her. "I heard it came from a horse messenger, who returned to the inn at Brigid's Ford and died in his bed. But those are just rumours." Her eyes were cavernous, and she wore a tired flush down her long throat. "What does it matter? It's here, and if we cannot stretch the medicine, the effects will be catastrophic."

I put my arm around her, pulling her warmth towards me in the chilly corridor. "You've done all you can, far more than that. If anyone, it's me who should be cursing my lack of action."

"How can you say that?" she said. "Without you tracking symptoms so expertly for accurate treatment, those extraordinary instincts of yours . . . I dread to think how many more would be dead."

Perhaps it was true: two of the widows, four elder nuns and one sixteen-year-old novice had sadly been lost, but seven deaths were far fewer than we had expected. And maybe it was nearing its end. But as I looked at Alys, the wretchedness on our respective faces said all.

"I could have cured this," I muttered. "Banished it right from the start."

Alys drew away. "Not the book again. The Prioress laid on hands."

"That incantation was so much stronger. All this could have been prevented."

"You swore you'd forgotten . . . you promised me . . . not to risk . . ." Her voice caught between the words. At first I thought I'd made her breathtakingly cross, but suddenly she stumbled, sliding to the ground.

"Alys!" I cried. "What's wrong?"

She pressed a hand to her breastbone, gulping for air. "Nothing. Just tired . . . long days . . . I'll be fine."

I put my palm to her forehead, the dread surge of heat burning my palm. "You're riven with fever. How long have you felt this way?" I put my fingers to the side of her throat, and her pulse raced away from my count. "Tell me, *how long?*"

She let her head loll back against the wall. "Two, maybe three days."

"God's blood, Alys! Why didn't you say?"

"You needed my help, the sisters . . . There were too many sick . . . too few of us." She shifted against me. "Help me up, I can carry on."

"You'll do no such thing," I said stoutly, though my insides were quivering. Arm around her waist, I took her sagging weight across my shoulders, inching us back to our chamber and to her bed. She fell sideways onto the pillow, so I heaved her legs under the blankets and tucked her in tightly. "I'll be back with the remedies as soon as I can, bringing the Prioress herself if I have to."

"Really, Morgan," she croaked, "there's no need. I'm not as bad as all that."

But her speech was slurred, and by the time I returned with cold muslins, her own poultice mix for her chest and the strongest elixirs we had, Alys had fallen into unconsciousness and would not wake.

21

FOR THREE DAYS I sat vigil while Alys twitched and muttered with fever, skin growing hotter until I could barely touch it. I did my best to give her water, lifting her head and spooning it down her gullet, praying she would not choke. She seemed to take it, but never woke enough for a true mouthful. Her lips grew cracked and sore, her skin chalky, slackening around the bones.

"If she doesn't wake soon, she will die," said the Prioress, standing over us at the end of the third day. She had laid hands on Alys five times now, to no saintly effect, and the plaintive note in her voice terrified me.

"She'll wake," I said. "She has to."

Unbeknown to the Prioress, I'd already sat for hours with my hands against Alys's breastbone, babbling to every saint I could think of, forces of healing jamming my nerves. I had felt the tingle of the fever, the clogged lungs, the savage blood-borne pain under my fingertips, trying to dislodge it just an inch. But the sickness would not budge, as immovable now as the very first day, when I was so much stronger.

The Prioress's cool hand fell on my shoulder. "Change your prayers, Lady Morgan. Fetch your rosary, cry your tears and commend her soul to God. It is all you can do."

I made no answer. Eventually, her hand left me, but I didn't hear her retreating steps or the closing door. I kept my gaze fixed on Alys's hollow, ashen face, pulse jerking at her throat. Somewhere across the herb garden a bell rang, heralding Vespers. Outside the window, the last arc of sun vanished, slipping towards night. I glanced down at my hands; the left palm flashed upwards, my scar a gleaming crescent moon, curving insistently, like a smile.

It was *not* all I could do.

I still had belladonna leaves and two more raven feathers on the scribe's desk. The scrap of parchment with the black book's method was safe in the slit in my mattress, rolled around the ebony knight, but I didn't need it; the formula was burned into my mind like a brand.

I hardly waited for the ash to cool before plunging both of my hands into the smouldering pile. I stood over Alys, limp in her bed. Her breathing had shallowed yet further, and beyond it, I made out a faint rattle deep within her chest: the disease's killing blow.

Placing both hands on her breastbone, I closed my eyes, pushing and pulling at my breaths until they were steady as a longship's oar stroke. The beacon of my consciousness tightened and shrank until all that remained was a gem of pure light, glittering hard in the centre of my being. I began to chant.

I felt it at the third: the same warm rush of power, as if light were pouring through my blood and into my hands. Darkness rushed towards me, the forces of Alys's sickness scraping through her as I held fast and demanded it obey. Three chants were too few, but I kept intoning, commanding the scourge in her blood to yield to me. My voice became harder, stricter, the cords of my neck standing out with the effort of battle, sinews stiff as I wrestled with the illness's ferocious resistance.

Alys's body arched under my hands, and she gave a great terminal wheeze. Invisible vines of sickness twisted about my knuckles, wrenching me forwards, seeking to draw itself back into her. I became aware of my own extreme fatigue—the desperately dry throat, the searing ache of my limbs, the wave of sheer futility surging fast. If I didn't release the disease now, not only would it take Alys, it would kill me too.

Fury shot through me at the idea of defeat. With the last of my strength, I pushed my blackened hands harder against her skin and screamed in rage, one final incantation in defiance of death's imminent victory, before collapsing to my knees, arms slung across Alys in exhaustion. When my eyes fluttered shut, I let them, not caring if I ever woke again.

I didn't know how long I had been that way when a cool hand patted the back of my head, rousing me from my stupor.

"Morgan." The voice was croaky but calm, its lilt impossible. "*Cariad*, what are you doing?"

I shot up to see Alys's golden-brown eyes open, tired but clear with life. "Alys!" I cried. "By God, you're alive, you're here, you're—"

"Covered in ash?" She rubbed her throat in confusion, fingers coming away grey.

I grabbed a cup of water and held it to her lips. "Drink. You need it."

She sipped obediently. "I was dreaming, burning, made of flame. I could hardly breathe."

"You had the lung fever," I said. "It's been days. There wasn't much hope."

"Then how am I alive?" She hoisted herself into a sitting position. "Even in survival, I should feel far weaker than this. Did you heal me?"

I had turned away, and felt her stare on the back of my neck. "I did all I could, and now you are better."

"That is not an answer."

"Lie back down," I said. "You've just woken up; it—"

"Morgan, look at me."

She had me, clear as day; I was mad to think she wouldn't know me in an instant.

Reaching out for my hands, Alys turned the palms up to reveal thick ash caked from fingertips to wrists. Her returning colour drained. "Mother of God, what did you do? What did you risk?"

"Everything!" I snatched my hands away. "I risked my place here, my reputation, my life. And I'd do it again, a thousand times over."

"You used the dark spell? You risked your *soul* to—"

"I wasn't going to let you die!" I said fiercely. "I had the method, the ability—why wouldn't I use it to save you?"

"But it's sinful, against nature. You'll be punished."

"I don't care, Alys. I couldn't just watch you fade away. It can't be sinful if it saved you, can it?" I sighed, sitting beside her on the bed. "I love you, and you are the good in my heart. It was worth anything to keep you safe."

Tears rolled down her sunken cheeks, cutting a pink trail through the streaks of ash, and I braced myself for her rejection. Then her arms were around me, clutching me so tightly it was as if I'd been the one in death's hungry jaws.

"You headstrong, precious fool," she sobbed. "Will you not learn to think before you act, you rash, brilliant woman?"

"Peace, silly thing." I stroked the matted tangles of hair at the back of her head, happiness washing through me like a sudden high tide. "Rest first, then you can praise and denounce me later. All is well now."

22

THE PRIORESS DESCENDED on us early the next morning, expecting to see me in the presence of a corpse. Alys did her best to appear wheezy and deathlike as our stunned teacher took her pulse and examined her, while I made excuses—she broke and sweated the fever in a matter of hours; the poultice was particularly potent; she awoke enough to take some ground willow bark.

"This is wonderful news," the Prioress said. "But nothing like the others. Even those almost recovered don't have the colour or breath that Lady Alys has."

"She is young, Lady Prioress, strong and blessed by Heaven itself. I prayed all night for her soul, and the Lord God answered." I raised a painfully innocent smile. "Truly it is His miracle."

She regarded me narrowly for an agonizing moment. "Perhaps you're right, Lady Morgan. We should not question His ways. If you're *certain* that's what occurred."

The Prioress returned every day for a week, Alys often having to leap back into bed from being sat by the fire, and though her visits got shorter, it never left me that she had read guilt on my face and was seeking proof to brand me a heathen.

"She knows," I was still saying ten days later, after waking up with a horror I couldn't shake.

Alys went to the table, devouring a hunk of the previous night's cheese. "Don't be silly," she said with her mouth full. "There's nothing to know anymore."

A soft knock came from behind us. I waved Alys back into bed and opened the door. A slip of a novice hovered at the threshold. "Lady Morgan, Abbess Honoria requires your presence in her reception chamber."

My stomach lurched. "N-now?"

"Yes, my lady. In all haste."

I glanced at Alys; her eyes widened. The novice shifted uncomfortably, and I realized she had been told to accompany me, guiding me to my fate like a tiny, wimpled Ferryman.

"Very well," I said. "Lead on."

I followed her down the vaulted corridors, past the chapel doors, open again since the sickness had left the abbey. The rich scent of frankincense came from within, alongside the swells of a chanted litany.

The Abbess was alone at her desk, aside from Benedict, sitting shiny and inquisitive on his perch. She rose, unsmiling, but her tone was kind. "Lady Morgan, you look perplexed."

"I thought the Prioress would be here."

"Why's that?"

The idea of more subterfuge was exhausting. "I have displeased her recently. She has spoken of expulsion."

She put a hand around a sapphire-studded cross at her bosom and rustled over to the fireplace. "You are not being expelled, Lady Morgan. You are a brilliant scholar, perhaps the best we've seen. Your wish to take vows to St. Brigid's is as much my desire as it is yours."

The relief was instant, crashing through me so hard I had to take a step backwards.

Until the Abbess turned, looked directly into my eyes and said, "If only I could keep you here," and the world went cold.

"But you said—"

"It is not my decision."

"Whose decision if not yours?" I asked. "Not even Bishop Summerland tells you how to administrate. I can't imagine anyone who—"

"Uther Pendragon, of course."

The name hit me like a sword to the chest.

Abbess Honoria sighed. "The High King himself has recalled you to Tintagel, by Royal Decree. You turn nineteen on the spring equinox, do you not? And on that day, you will leave us."

Two weeks, in fact, but I had not remembered it until then, my sights firmly set on taking the veil at twenty-one. The outside world and its arbitrary touchstones had pleasantly ceased to exist; that Uther Pendragon still had control over anything I did was more shocking than the news itself.

"Why?" I said dazedly.

Abbess Honoria guided me to one of her fireside chairs. "Some legality to be addressed, so the decree says. As God is my witness, I wrote to your lady mother, explaining your learning, your plans to take holy vows. But she wrote back saying a decree from the King is absolute. Defying it is treason."

I rested my chin on my fist, thinking. A spark of survival, small but potent, lit up my hope. "I have land bestowed on me, manors, useless if I take the veil. The King must need my presence to officially sign them back over to the Crown. Which I will, then return right away."

Abbess Honoria visibly paused. "Certainly, you can return if you wish . . . but if your intentions do not please them, losing the Queen's . . . blessing may make things difficult."

The benevolences, of course. If Uther forced my mother to withdraw her generous charity, the abbey's circumstances would be seriously reduced.

"I assure you, Lady Abbess, my mother will be overjoyed with my taking holy vows." I looked down at the scar on my palm, grinning, certain. "I will sign over my land, declare my loyalty to this sisterhood and be back in St. Brigid's by Pentecost. Nothing will prevent me."

*

ALYS MET ME just inside our chamber door, looming like a ghost. "Did she expel you?" she demanded. "If so, I'll go to her, explain—"

"Be easy, it's not that."

"So you're safe?"

"From her, yes." It hit me then, the implications of my departure, the savage possibilities I could be returning to. Nausea washed over me, fear I had not felt for over three years. "But I am leaving for a while. Uther has summoned me to Tintagel."

Alys stared. "But why?"

I swallowed hard, tasting bitterness. "It's a legal matter—signing away my land and Princess status, I assume. I'll still be taking the veil, don't worry."

"Except it's Uther Pendragon who summons you." She placed her hands on my shoulders, thin face lined with concern. "I don't like this, Morgan. Stay here; refuse the call."

"I can't. The summons came by Royal Decree. Abbess Honoria will be accused of treason if I don't go."

"Not if you stay under the laws of sanctuary." Alys pointed at the door. "Go back to the Abbess. Tell her everything you've told me, exactly what the High King has wrought on you over the years. She won't refuse, and there's nothing Uther Pendragon can do about it. Even he won't defy the laws of God and Church."

Alys's argument was compelling, but knowing the man himself, I wasn't so certain. "That would put the whole of St. Brigid's at risk,"

I said. "He'll stop my mother's benevolences and make his barons' wives do the same. The abbey will be bankrupt by autumn, the sisters turned out into the road. I cannot be responsible for such a thing."

Alys brought a horrified hand up to her mouth. "He can't do that."

"He absolutely can."

"Very well. Then I'm coming with you."

"Alys, you can't. You're not fully well. The journey alone might be too much."

"I'm perfectly fine," she retorted. "You saw to that. Now it's my turn to watch over you. Take me along as your lady-in-waiting. I won't let you be alone in this, Morgan, not for all the stars in the sky."

*

THE DAY OF our departure dawned brightly, skies entirely opposite to those under which I had been born. March was always a changeable month, unsettled, torn between winter and spring; no two birthdays of my life have yielded the same light. But on this one, the heavens wore a deep, convincing blue, sun sitting easily among white globules of cloud.

Alys and I were dressed in travelling garb: layered shifts and surcoats, riding boots and hooded mantles waxed against possible rainfall. Our things had been sent ahead of us, our goodbyes to the sisters of St. Brigid's spoken that morning. All that was left was to await my royal escort and make the long ride back to Tintagel.

A wide shaft of sun poured through the gateway, followed by a knot of snorting horses, gleaming under saddlecloths of white and gold.

Alys reached out and squeezed my hand. "Are you ready?"

"Of course," I replied calmly, though my pulse quickened in time with the approaching hoofbeats.

The cavalcade came towards us, tightly collected, drawing to a jangling halt several yards away. A pair of banners bearing Uther's snarling dragon snapped in the breeze. I looked for Sir Bretel, sure my mother would have sent him, but recognized nobody.

"Why have they stopped?" Alys whispered, but before I could wonder, I spotted their leader beyond, speaking to the gatekeeper from horseback. At length, the knight wheeled his gleaming bay courser around and cantered smoothly to the front of the group, easing to a perfect halt and jumping from the saddle in one elegant movement.

The rising sun was at his back, obscuring my vision, but if I had been struck blind in that very same moment, one glimpse would have been enough: the artless command of horse and self, the same careless grace I knew in one half beat of my heart.

I didn't need to see the loose-limbed stride, the confident way he wore his knightly silks, or hear the voice I had gone to sleep imagining for the past thousand nights. But it came anyway, that deep, melodic tone, as he stopped before me and offered a sweeping bow, throwing dark hair across his sculpted face.

He rose, pushing it back, and smiled.

"Lady Morgan," he said—*Morr-ganne*, just as before. "Sir Accolon of Gaul, at your service. I have come to take you home."

23

WE WERE A few miles down the Abbey High Road and more than an hour into a pervasive silence when Sir Accolon of Gaul turned his horse in a half circle and drew up alongside us.

Until then I had watched his silken back, shoulders mirroring the rise and fall of the horse's gait, body taller and broader than when I had left him but still lithe, long limbs sitting loose and easy. Despite my racing mind, it soothed me to watch him ride, his gold spurs flashing in the dappled light.

Then he was beside me, bowing briefly, face harder-boned, fully a man's, no less beautiful. His top lip curled pleasantly as he began to speak, flooding my senses with memories, bright as pinpricks of sun.

"My ladies, how are you finding the journey so far?" he asked with utmost courtesy.

"Very comfortable, Sir Accolon," I replied, glancing sidelong at Alys. I had told her of him one night when she saw the chess piece—the whole story, including his intention to leave Cornwall—but her serene face betrayed nothing. "Hopefully the weather will continue to favour us."

"You will not have to ride into the night, regardless. Lodgings have been arranged at a halfway inn." He gestured behind to where the others rode in a neat dovetail. "How do you find the guard? We are few, but there weren't many spare at Tintagel."

"They seem capable," I said archly. "Though I'm surprised to see you in command."

He looked amused. "Is that so, Lady Morgan?"

"I mean, when I left, you were yet to gain your spurs. Nor did you know where you'd serve." The inference hung between us, frank as it could be—the fact that he was riding back to Cornwall rather than seeking his future on a far-flung shore. "When were you knighted?"

"On my majority day." He sat taller in unconscious pride.

"Just as Sir Bretel predicted. A rare accolade. You are to be congratulated." I was happy for his success, but his chest bore a roaring gold dragon, and it dimmed my pleasure to see him so marked. "Then you swore fealty to Uther Pendragon?"

"I ride under his banner as one of Tintagel's house knights. But it was Sir Bretel who knighted me, and I swore my oath of loyalty directly to him. He is my lord."

"Did that please you?" I was certainly relieved to hear it; the image of Accolon kneeling at the feet of Uther Pendragon was too much to bear.

"Very much. Sir Bretel has been better than a father to me, and I love no man dearer." He gave a small, contented shrug. "It was the proudest moment of my life."

Our eyes met, and my instinct was to reach out, lay a hand over his. I straightened in the saddle, making myself formal. "I'm very glad for you. Sir Bretel is the finest knight I know. There is no higher commendation than his regard."

"Thank you, my lady." He cast a furtive glance at Alys, who was looking everywhere but in our direction. "Sir Bretel would have been leading this company, but as Queen's Knight, he is in Carduel with your lady mother."

"The Royal Household is not at Tintagel?" I exclaimed.

Accolon regarded me with a startled expression, as if I should have known. "No, my lady. They were delayed in the north, due in three weeks or so. We could bring only this small company because, aside from a bare staff and twelve knights to guard her, Tintagel Castle is quite deserted."

In the distance, a lone rider had appeared on the road—likely a merchant or messenger, but Accolon looked up, alert. "I should retake my position," he said, signalling for his men to catch up to our flank. "If everything is to your satisfaction, Lady Morgan?"

"Of course," I said faintly, but he had already trotted off, and my words drifted away on the wind.

*

I CAUGHT THE scent of it first, the faint whisper of sweetgrass edged with tingling salt, swirling towards us through the Duchess Wood. Then came gull screams, swooping and harsh, relayed over something deeper, a primal roar drawn from the earth itself.

Sooner than I expected, it appeared—vast, deep blue, scudded with foam—and though I had seen it thousands of times, had learned every one of its moods, sounds and dangers, the sight of it took my breath away. The sea that bore me, risen up before us like another sky, ferocious and eternal.

And there, safe within its turbulent embrace, was Tintagel, shining silver under pale spring light.

*

THERE WERE TOO few people at the castle for any kind of welcome, though some curious heads popped over Tintagel's battlements as we rode past the barracks and across the high-walled corridor to the island. Halting in front of the main keep, I gazed up at the castle's imperious beauty, the high towers and latticed windows, every chamber and passage still clear in my mind. Even Uther Pendragon's flags could not dilute my feeling of homecoming.

Accolon appeared beside me, holding out a gloved hand, and my heart tripped over its beats.

He gestured briskly towards the entrance. "Shall we?"

I dismounted and ensured Alys was following, then fell into step beside him, our footfalls echoing around the long entranceway. All was quiet, the only movement the dust motes glittering in the slanting sunlight from the stairway windows; no shouts, no dogs barking, no hoarse sea shanties sung in the language of Cornwall.

"I've never known it so deserted," I said, too loud. "How many are left?"

"Not many," Accolon replied. "Three cooks, several pages. Generally, we fetch our own wine, but I can arrange for a boy to be your cupbearer. Village women have been called in to attend your chambers."

"Is Gwennol here?"

"No, my lady. She went with your mother's train."

"Oh, of course." I swallowed a surge of apprehension. It had been one of my fortifying thoughts, that Gwennol would be there to soothe me regardless of what else I might face. "Go on."

"The rest of us are outside for most of the day, guarding, overseeing, maintaining," he said. "Knights have squires and a few local boys to help with the mews and stables. We gather in the Great Hall to eat and discuss necessary work. Father Felix went with the household, so communal prayer is at sunrise and sunset. Some say you'll want to lead Mass, given . . ." He gestured vaguely, leaving the thought unfinished.

Inexplicably, I blushed. "I may intend on taking the veil, but I haven't done so yet." Alys, roving about in her inquisitive way, came to rest just behind me. I pulled her to my side. "Nevertheless, Lady Alys and I will be happy to say our prayers with whoever is in attendance."

Accolon cast his eyes about the room. "*Alors*, what else? Your things came ahead of you, but we had no orders for where to put them. They went to your old quarters."

"I think you'll agree, Sir Accolon, that I no longer belong in a nursery." My attempt at lightening the tone only left him looking abashed. "Have our trunks conveyed to the former ducal chambers in the South Tower. We will await their readiness in the Great Hall."

"Very well, my lady," he said with a bow. Nodding formally, I slipped my arm through Alys's and swept past him, dragging her with me.

"There is one more thing," he called from behind us.

I looked back to see Accolon idly pulling off his gloves. Once done, he rested an elegant hand against the pommel of his greatsword and smiled, in that charming way of his, but softer, contemplative. An involuntary thrill skittered up the back of my neck.

"Welcome back, Morgan of Cornwall," he said, then turned and strode away.

24

ALYS AND I kept to our chambers for the first few days, served competently enough by a kitchen page. The rest of our needs were attended by Tressa, a timid nineteen-year-old milkmaid come up from Tintagel village. Alys oversaw the tow-headed girl, coaxing her from her shell with kindness and guiding her duties as if she had been a lady-in-waiting her entire life.

Though I preferred sharing a room, Alys was so thrilled at the sight of Constance's generous former chamber that I did not have the heart to deny her. I found the nights strange, lying alone and wakeful in my mother's enormous old bed, the sea breeze and musical swash of waves failing to lull me as they used to.

Eventually, I gave in to Alys's nagging and took her on a full tour of the castle: mainland and island; every room, tower and dungeon; gardens—kitchen and formal; the tiltyard and mews. Last of all, we ventured onto the headland, to the chapel, where I was astonished to find my father's candle freshly lit, despite the absence of Father Felix. I wondered who he had entrusted with my mother's secret rite.

I said a prayer over my father's tomb, then we tried the door of the sacristy to no avail. "Father Felix must have taken the key," I said. "That means, apart from my *Ars Physica*, we have nothing to read."

"We'll have to find entertainment elsewhere," Alys said.

I had ordered my mother's former solar opened, so we went there next. The yellow room was still bright and pleasant, though the walls needed a coat of paint and the roses outside overgrew the window-panes. A faded Penelope frowned down from her tapestry, intent upon her loom.

"There must be something here to occupy us," I said, opening a cabinet.

My searching uncovered only a cushion in need of repair, a cracked leather falcon hood and a white linen sleeve. I turned it over and saw my father's ducal arms, minutely embroidered in midnight-blue thread—sewn long ago by my mother's skilful hands.

I flung it back in the cupboard and went to a window, perching on the stone sill, watching the sun fight through tumbling clouds.

Alys flopped into an overstuffed chair. "There is one thing I'd like to do: have dinner in the Great Hall."

"There's hardly anyone here."

"I know, but I've never dined in a grand castle before. Oh, say yes, *cariad*. Please."

I could hardly refuse such a heartfelt plea, hence we found our-selves that same evening sitting at a quickly assembled High Table, eating roast spring lamb with Tintagel's tiny household. Three sparsely occupied tables stood below: one for the knights and another for their squires, and a third for servants not cooking or serving. Afterwards, the knights introduced themselves, explaining their various fealties and pedigrees somewhat like a livestock fair. Accolon came last, handsomely dressed in a long tunic of dark blue over pristine white linen, belted with silver-tipped brown leather.

"My ladies," he said. "I'm glad—I mean, *the household* is glad you've joined us."

"And you speak for them, do you, Sir Accolon?" I asked. "As Tintagel's ranking authority?"

He gave an uncertain laugh. "Not quite, Lady Morgan, though Sir Bretel did lend me his proxy in some matters. Of course, the person truly in authority here is you."

Alys threw me an impish look. "What fun! Go on, command someone."

I drew a tight breath, letting it anchor me as I prepared to dismiss her mischief. But when I released it, so went my resolve, leaving a sudden lightness in my bones. "Very well. Sir Accolon, I heard that you play lute and sing every evening for the household, but your instrument hasn't made an appearance tonight."

"No," he replied. "The songs can be . . . what's the word . . . earthy? Inappropriate in the presence of ladies."

"I was told you sing mostly in French."

"I do, my lady. But you speak it."

"Still, you should play, for the sake of the others. Lady Alys and I will bear it." I smiled widely at him, the first time I had allowed myself to do so. It caught him unawares, and his guard—feather-light and courteous, but a guard nonetheless—wavered in the candle-light. "In fact, I believe I command it," I added.

He tilted his head in acknowledgement. "If you insist, Lady Morgan, I can only oblige."

Accolon gestured for a page to fetch his long-necked lute, then sat atop the knight's table, plucking out the opening bars of a jaunty, popular tune. The first few songs were bawdy and comedic, more suited to a dockside tavern than a royal residence, which made it all the better. Accolon's deep voice—quite as musical as I thought it would be—danced across clever rhythms and complex wordplay as artlessly as he rode at tilt. His small but appreciative audience cheered and clapped, requesting verses ever more ribald; he winked and grinned in return, laughing through some of the lines.

"This is wonderful!" Alys said, gasping in mirth. "I assume you knew he possessed such troubadour skills?"

"Actually, no," I said. "I heard about this from Tressa."

"Ah, so you had to see him do it."

I eyed her sharply, then relented. "I admit I was curious."

She smiled and put her hand on my arm, but quickly withdrew it to smother a series of violent coughs.

"Goodness, are you all right?" I waved the wine page over to refill her cup.

She took a long sip. "Yes, just a tickle of dust." She gestured towards the knights' table. "Hark, he has changed speeds."

I looked back to Accolon, his head now bent over his strings for a song quite different—a spare, bittersweet melody that brought the room to a reverent hush.

We all knew it, a ballad famous as it was ancient, a moving recollection of yearning, love and loss, told through a single encounter across a crowded room. But he sang it in his own tongue, and I heard every change he made, fitting the rhythms of his dialect to the music flowing from his hands.

Then, as he gave pause to his voice after the first refrain, Accolon raised his dark head, caught my stare and held it. And I could not tear my eyes away, much as I should have, much as he had probably sung this song many times and it wasn't for me, about me, or the loss we had learned to live with.

Except that it was. Every word and long, aching note spoke to where we had been and where we were now, and just then, locked within our mutual gaze, it was as if there had been no absence.

Suddenly, he dropped his eyes, abandoning our bond as abruptly as it had formed, leaving the breath caught painfully in my chest.

I turned to Alys—the constant salve to my lesser nature—but she sat slumped, lightly sheened with sweat, breastbone pulsing up and down in swift, irregular movements.

"Alys! What's wrong?"

She tried to wave me away, but her hand fell limp. Her wheezing recalled the same deathly rattle of the nunnery fever, which I thought I had banished for good. I pressed my palm to her forehead; to my relief, it came away cool.

"Thank God, you're not feverish. But we must get you to bed."

"No need . . . a . . . silly turn."

"I'll decide what's silly or not," I retorted. "Come on."

I slipped my arm through hers and helped her up, our chairs scraping discordantly on the stone floor. All eyes turned towards us as I guided her swiftly from the room, including the blue-black Gaulish ones, though his song only wavered for a heartbeat.

*

I KEPT TO Alys's bedside for two days and nights to ensure she did not worsen. It was not as before, nor was it a new affliction; she was simply exhausted. Despite my healing, the savage illness and long ride had taken a toll on her lungs that required a steady regimen of good food and bed rest.

"You are fine to leave me," she said on the third day, as I sat down. "Watching me rest must be very dull."

I picked up a folded piece of muslin, upon which I had been practising the Prioress's herringbone wound-stitching method. "I have my skills to keep sharp."

Tressa crept in, dipping a neat curtsey. Alys beamed; before her collapse, she had been teaching our new companion the correct form for days.

"If you please, Lady Morgan," Tressa said. "There's a knight below who asks me to bring a message."

Something inside of me fluttered. "Which knight?"

"Sir Accolon of Gaul, my lady. He wishes to ask after Lady Alys's health, and if she wants anything sent up."

"Was that all he said?"

"Yes, my lady. He's waiting for a reply."

"I see." The flutter stilled, turned cool. "Tell him she fares better, and if *we* need something then *I* will send for it. Thank you, Tressa."

Tressa scuttled off, and I turned back to meet the frank amber gaze of my patient.

"That was a little abrupt," Alys said. "Sir Accolon was only being polite."

"Oh yes, he's very *polite*," I replied. "Next time I will let you send the response, since it is you he asks after."

Alys leaned back against the stacked feather pillows. "What's wrong, Morgan?"

"Don't be absurd; nothing's wrong." I rose and stalked to the fireplace, tossing a fresh log into the grate.

"If you feel like there are things to address," Alys said, "perhaps you should ask Sir Accolon for a meeting. Converse with him directly?"

I rounded on her like a gust of wind. "To what end? So we can fill in the gaps of our years spent apart? I can't—I wouldn't know what to say."

"I've never known words to fail you," she said, eyelids fluttering as the need for sleep crept over her again. "You say you want to move beyond the past—new cordiality, peace of mind, is the answer."

"But I'm needed here," I protested.

"Indeed you're not," she replied. "Go—Tressa will sit with me. She knows all about sea plants, Cornish foliage, local remedies they use in the villages. Learning from her is giving me strength." She shuffled down into the pillows, tugging the coverlet up to her chin. "Talk to him, Morgan. It will do you good."

I sat quietly as Alys fell asleep, gazing at the bright window without seeing much at all. After a while, Tressa tiptoed back in, busying herself at the fire. A prickle of irritation ran over my skin: no return message from him.

"Tressa," I said.

"Yes, my lady?"

"You will sit with Lady Alys this afternoon, in case she requires anything. But first, I need you to carry a message for me. Tell Sir Accolon I wish to speak with him."

25

I WAS CURLED up in the window of the solar, considering calling it off, when he appeared shortly after the midday bell.

"Lady Morgan?"

I whipped around to see his lithe frame hovering in the open doorway. I dropped my feet from the sill, batting at the disorderly folds of my gown. "Sir Accolon! My woman said you were busy in the bird mews—I didn't expect you so soon."

He bowed, looking abashed. "I apologize, my lady. I thought I should attend you in all haste."

His apprehension took the edges off my nerves somewhat. "Come in. You are most welcome. Will you have some wine?"

"Please. If you will permit me to pour."

It was a relief to watch him move, the long-legged steps as he went to the table and poured one gobletful, then another, with unconscious flair. "What shall we drink to?" he asked, handing me my cup.

"To cordiality," I said quickly.

"And to Tintagel," he added. "Regaining its fondest daughter. À votre santé."

I touched his goblet with mine. The wine was brisk on my tongue, washing through me with refreshing ease. "Though of course," I said, "I am called to Tintagel for only a short while."

He paused, taking another swig. Still we had not moved to sit down. "How so?"

"I was summoned. Some legal formality, I'm told. After that is discharged, Lady Alys and I will return to St. Brigid's. Shall we sit?"

We sat either side of a small table between the fireplace and the white spring gleam of the windows. I watched Accolon settle his frame into a curved-back sewing chair, which fit him not at all. He propped one leg atop the other and pushed a hand through his hair, shirt sleeve riding up to reveal a bandage around his forearm, knotted tightly and speckled with blood.

"You're hurt!" I exclaimed. "What happened?"

"That's why I was in the bird mews. One of the goshawks escaped into the rafters, and I was the only one tall enough to reach it from the ladder. The godforsaken thing bated up my arm." He tugged the sleeve back down. "It's just a scratch."

"From a goshawk? I doubt it."

"Truly, it's nothing." He shifted upright in his seat and levelled his gaze at me. "Lady Morgan, may I enquire why you asked to see me?"

"I wanted to thank you for your kind offer of help regarding Lady Alys. Happily, her health will mend with little intervention now, provided she keeps to her bed."

"Your reputation for healing is great." His dark eyes held mine for a long moment. "Lady Alys said you saved her from certain death."

I snatched up my wine and wondered when in God's name Alys had managed to impart that information. "I suppose I did."

"That makes two of us," he said softly. "Revived by you."

"I'd do the same for anyone," I lied, putting bravura into my voice. "I must say, Sir Accolon, I'm surprised to see you here, given you intended to leave after getting your spurs."

"Yes, somehow I remain." He leaned forwards, slinging crossed wrists over his knees. "The day I was knighted, I swore my oaths, walked onto the headland and realized I had grown fond of Cornwall. So when Sir Bretel asked me to take up the role of house knight at Tintagel, I found myself agreeing."

"Despite the weather?"

"Despite the weather." He smiled softly, inwardly.

A slight ease rippled between us, but before it could settle, Accolon said, "And what of you, my lady, these past few years?" His mouth dropped open. "I mean . . . I know you didn't choose . . . but . . . *non*." He swung up out of his chair, vehemently shaking his head. "Forgive me—I cannot believe my tactlessness. It's not until now that I . . ." He looked back at me, eyes bright with guilt. "My first words upon seeing you should have been to apologize."

I froze. "There is nothing to apologize for. I—"

"You were sent from your home because of me!" he cried. "And you went, never saying a word to accuse me, or save yourself. I finished my training, let Sir Bretel fix the spurs to my heels, when all the while you sat confined for the wrongs I committed. Then I dare ask how you fare? *Sacredieu*, what a knight I am." He put a palm to his forehead and turned away. "I'm sorry, I should go."

I flew from my chair even faster than he had and caught hold of his trailing hand.

"Don't," I said.

He looked down at my hand, burning in his, then back at me in question. We hadn't been this close since our last embrace years ago, and I should have been moving away but could not. Three small lines formed between his brows, beloved, painfully familiar.

"I haven't asked you to go," I said. "I haven't said you *can* go."

He contemplated me, but I held firm, fingers clamped over the back of his hand.

"Then send me away," he said.

"No, not like this. What you speak of—they were not wrongs, and I was in it just as deeply. But your knighthood is not in doubt. I wanted that for you. You deserve your spurs, Sir Bretel's regard, everything. I wouldn't change not naming you for the entire world." I paused, wondering how much truth was too much. "I wouldn't change any of it."

A look of quiet emotion lit up his face. Slowly, so slowly, he turned his hand over in mine until we were palm to palm.

"Morgan . . ." he murmured. He let his touch linger for a moment, then quietly slipped himself free.

I retreated to the window, laying my palm on the cool stone sill. A budding rose vine trailed across the embrasure; I counted twenty-seven thorns before he spoke again.

"You've spent years caged because I could not find my honour. There is no atonement great enough."

Turning, I saw on his anguished face that he believed it, had tortured himself for years for the night I sent him from the kitchen garden, and he had gone.

"Accolon, no. What happened wasn't your fault, or mine. And the abbey has been incredibly good for me. I've learned things I never could have dreamed of."

He was already shaking his head, and his refusal to listen, his insistence on punishing himself, inflamed me.

"Damn it all!" I said. "Come here—I'll show you what I'm capable of now."

I took his arm, pushing the sleeve back to reveal the bloodied bandage. "Do you trust me?"

He stood stiff as a statue but held my gaze. "You know I do."

Gently, I peeled the muslin from the congealing wound. He had cleaned it, at least, but the slash was dark and ragged, certainly worthy of pause.

"This is in no way a mere scratch," I scolded, but he only kept looking at me intently. Catching my breath, I braced my fingertips against the cut's edges, aligning the torn sides. It must have hurt at first, but he did not flinch, or grimace, or take his eyes from my face.

A quick bolt of warmth flared between my skin and his, and it was done. "There."

Accolon regarded his arm with a sharp intake of air. "Mother of God. How have you done this?"

I ran my thumb over the wound, now a neat and bloodless red line, body thrilling with success as always. "Some knowledge, a little concentration."

"But it's completely healed."

"That is what St. Brigid's has given me." I took my hands from him; he kept staring at the sealed cut. "Now do you understand?"

Accolon staggered across to the fireplace, steadying himself against the mantel. The fire had burned low, emitting a sweet charcoal scent from the seasoned apple wood.

"I do," he said eventually. "All those hours I spent watching you read . . . I already knew you were brilliant. Now this . . . incredible skill." He sighed into the flames. "It is your calling."

"Yes." I took in his image, sketching the lines of his profile into my mind as he gazed into the hearth, dark hair falling unchecked over his high forehead. An ache took up warm and deep in my abdomen.

I took a turn around the chairs, needing to move, away from the impulse to touch him again. "And what will you do, in the future?" I asked.

He pushed himself upright, facing me. "I think my time at Tintagel will soon be at an end, if Sir Bretel will release me. My close cousin whom I told you of—he is also knighted and intends to sail for the Continent. There are many opportunities there for a free lance, he says."

The air in the room had settled back to a cool formality, the way it should have been between us.

"I'm sure your endeavours will bring great fortune, Sir Accolon. Clearly you are a skilled and worthy knight, as I knew you would be. Which reminds me . . ." I reached into the purse at my belt. "I have something of yours."

The ebony chess knight looked strange in daylight, conjuring as it did the sound of my breaths in the dark. I offered it up and he came closer, saying nothing.

"Thank you for giving it to me," I said. "I was grateful—and always will be—but I no longer need it. However, there is a chess set that does. If you still have it, that is."

"I do, my lady." Accolon plucked the knight out of my hand and held it before him, smiling faintly at the curling *A* carved on the base. "I'm sure the *chevalier* will be very pleased to be back where he belongs." Then, in a flash of his artful hand, he snatched it out of the air and it was gone.

He tilted his head towards the door. "*Alors*, I should take my leave, if you will grant it. But please, if there's ever anything you require, do not hesitate to send for me." Bowing, he walked away, his stride halting, doubtful.

"I did wonder if . . ." My calling out took us both by surprise. Accolon turned in question.

"Lady Alys tires of me looming by her bedside," I said hesitantly. "I . . . I'd like to ride the countryside, but would require a knightly escort. You."

An escort: the word from our past evoked far too much. I saw it reach him at the same time as it thudded into my own chest.

He glanced at the door, inhaling deeply. "It's my duty if my lady requires, but—"

I held up my hands. "It's all right. It wasn't a command. Just a sentimental wish to see Cornwall before I must leave it again. I don't know why—I've seen it before." I gave a small laugh, seeking levity but not quite finding it. "You are busy. Forget I asked."

Accolon frowned, taking me in so intently I half expected his gold coin to appear, spinning across the top of his knuckles. His chest rose and fell in a barely audible sigh.

"Of course I will ride with you, Lady Morgan," he said. "It would be my honour."

26

THE FIRST THING Accolon and I did, the very next day, was ride along the coast to the neighbouring cove, a short trip under the midday sun. The weather of late had been warm, and the cliff edge was carpeted with early spring squill and ox-eye daisies, shining sea-grasses already up past the horses' hocks.

We rode most of the way in a companionable silence. As soon as Tintagel fell out of sight, I leaned forwards and urged my horse into a gallop, pulling to a halt just above a curving bay. I looked back to see my knightly escort thundering up, out of breath.

"My lady, please, give me fair warning!" he exclaimed, walking his prancing bay stallion in a circle to calm it.

"I like to ride fast—you must remember that."

He gave me a handsome look of disapproval and shaded his eyes with the back of his hand, watching a flock of sharp-winged sea swallows gliding by. The horses grumbled to one another, tugging to get at the sweet spring grass. Below, the golden sands glittered like sun-bleached silk, cobalt waves lapping the shore, playing the gentle music of water on sand.

"Why would you ever want to leave here?" I asked.

His gaze returned to me, his expression unreadable. "I don't," he said. "And neither do you. Yet we must, and soon."

And though he turned his face back to the sea, I caught the

whisper of his sigh on the wind, soft and persistent like the beating of a kingfisher's wings.

*

APRIL RAINS KEPT me indoors with Alys, but as soon as the ground dried, Accolon and I rode out again, into a world dazzling with colour, air drenched with the aroma of dew and fresh petals. Striped bees, furry as bears, buzzed industriously through the long grass among an abundance of wildflowers.

We struck out for the forest due northeast, known locally as the Saintswood, a tangle of trees and rocky outcroppings nestled in a steep-sided valley. Some distance in, we came to a small bridge over the stream we'd been following, and though Accolon said, "Wait," in a voice about to suggest we turn back, I pushed on, overcome by an unexplainable urge to keep going.

"Do you know where we are?" Accolon asked.

"No, I've never been this deep, just—" *I know it*, I wanted to say; *I feel it, pulling at my bones, an elemental siren song calling me on.*

But I could not find the words, so instead I followed what I soon realized was the sound of water echoing through the bent willows and silver birches. Not the trickling stream beside us, or even the confident rush of a river, but something much greater—a steady, muffled roar reverberating through the air as if originating from within the earth itself.

"Come on," I said. "I think I know what we've found."

We emerged into an airy clearing before an astonishing sight. In front of us stood a great rock face, velvety with moss, cleaved by a powerful stream cascading over the ancient stone and into a wide pool at the foot of the woodland cliff. The narrow falls crashed into the water, white and furious, but near the edge the pool barely moved, reflecting the sky like a looking glass. Spray glittered on the breeze, filling my airways with the scents of earth and renewal.

Dismounting, I went to the water's edge, trailing my fingertips across the chill, lustrous surface. It quivered, alive, brimming with whatever it held within.

"What is this place?" Accolon's voice sounded as if from miles away.

"Senuna's Glynn—it has to be." I sucked the sweet droplets from my fingers. "Gwennol spoke endlessly of this place when I was a child, though it's meant to be impossible to find. Legend has it the falls can be discovered only by those who truly need them. The waters are blessed, they say, imbued with healing properties."

Accolon followed me to the edge of the pool. "Is that true?"

"Didn't you feel the change in the air when we rounded the corner? It's different here, protected, teeming with divinity."

"It's peaceful, yes, and beautiful. But I cannot feel anything but the breeze."

I rolled my eyes, impatient with his pragmatism in the face of the natural force all around us, the winnowing light darting lucid in my veins, like when I laid on my hands to heal.

An idea struck me. "I must take some of this water back for Alys. It will speed her recovery. That must be the reason the glen revealed itself."

I unhooked the waterskin from my palfrey's saddle and unlaced my boots. I was barefoot and several yards into the water with my skirts bunched above my knees before Accolon realized my intentions.

"What in God's name are you doing?" he called after me.

"Logically, the most potent water will be nearest the cascade itself," I replied over my shoulder.

"Come out. It could be dangerous. You can't swim."

I laughed, small waves tingling at my shins. "Don't be ridiculous; it's barely knee-deep."

"And what if you take a chill? You'll be soaked through if you get much closer to that waterfall." He secured our horses to a nearby branch and kicked off his boots. "Come back. I'll do it for you."

"It won't take a moment." I waded a few steps closer to the bubbling water. "Since I'm already wet."

"Morgan! *Arrête.*"

In a few sloshing strides he had almost reached me, but I dashed away, laughing, water flying up around us, casting rainbows in the air. I was almost out of his reach when he swooped forwards and grabbed my elbow, pulling us together to stop me slipping away. His fingers slid around my wrist like a silken cuff.

"There," he said, his voice low and soft, "now we're both wet."

"And whose fault is that?" I replied, just as low.

I couldn't hear our breaths above the pounding waterfall, but their rhythms seemed to be one and the same. Accolon released my wrist and held out his hand for the waterskin. I shook my head.

"Let me," he insisted. "I'm here now."

And so he was. He was there, with me, up to his calves in water in this place of wonder and concealment, this ancient secret appearing only to us.

He gestured again for the waterskin. In one incautious move I threw it aside, holding his gaze, daring him. His eyes widened, bluer than usual in the reflected light of the pool.

"*L'enfer,*" he said helplessly, and in one swift movement took my face in two hands, bringing my lips to his for the kiss I had lived so many times: under deep night, holding the chess piece, my thumb on his carved initial; in the classroom's quill-scratching lulls; every moment in Tintagel, whether he was in my view or without it, long hours spent counting the walls that stood between my body and his.

I wrapped my arms about his neck; he paused for breath, then laid his mouth on mine again, harder, better, hungrier than before, his hands roving across my back. My skirts swirled and sank, adrift in the crystalline pool, water rising up my body and anchoring me to him, drawing me deeper into the harbour of his arms.

At length, we parted, and he smiled, top lip curling in its particular way. "Look at us. Always in chaos."

A ripple of yearning shuddered through my limbs. I put a water-streaked hand to the sleek bones of his face. "I don't care."

He held me tighter. "You're shivering. We need to get out."

A chill dread fluttered in my chest. If we went from this enchanted, blessed grove, what awaited us? Tintagel, daily life, sworn vows and duty; his knighthood and my life in St. Brigid's. Our respective futures, lived apart. "I'd just as soon stay," I said.

"Morgan," he said, both reproachful and a comfort, the sweet, familiar music of my name in his mouth. He released me, picking up the discarded waterskin so I could complete the task I had come for and return everything to the way it was before.

But as I corked the skin and turned to go back, Accolon caught me by the waist, sweeping me up in his arms and carrying me back to shore with my skirts pouring like a mermaid's tail.

"Quite unnecessary," I said, laughing. "But kiss me, all the same."

He obliged, and afterwards I pressed my face to his neck, inhaling the scent of his skin and hair, warm and fresh like summer rain. He lowered me to the ground, easing my resisting arms to my sides, fingertips lingering along the edge of my palms.

"That was . . . unexpected," he said.

"I've wanted that since I saw you at the abbey gatehouse."

Accolon took a step back, allowing cool air to stream between us. The cords in his neck stiffened, as if withstanding a sudden physical ache.

"This is impossible," he said. "You know that."

I did, but it hurt to hear it so soon, in this place, with the heat of his embrace still imprinted on my skin. The sun slipped below the rock face, taking what remained of his warmth, leaving only the clamminess of the water splashed across my bodice and the dragging chill of my skirts against my trembling legs.

"You *are* cold." Accolon pulled my mantle from the saddle and threw it around my shoulders. I watched his clever hands fasten the silver chain across my collarbones with a sad pleasure, all the while knowing he was right, that our situation was untenable and I should accept it, go back to how it was when the sun came up that morning.

But in truth, nothing had changed, and earlier I had watched the sun rise above the rebellious sea and thought only of him, as I always had. The fact that we had kissed made no real difference; the true battle in my heart had been fought long ago.

His hands left me and he walked off, pulling on his boots and busying himself with the horses. He fastened the waterskin to my palfrey's saddle, then swiped up my boots and held them out to me.

Reluctantly, I took them. "Tell me why it's impossible. Pretend I don't know."

"It just is," he said. "When we were younger, fool as I was, I didn't believe in the risks, the restrictions. I thought nothing could harm us. I know better now. Your mother, the King, they would never allow—"

I opened my mouth to protest, and he raised a halting hand. "Aside from that, look what you can do now. Your skill—it's remarkable. You have a future, a chance to be the great lady you deserve to become." He put his hand to my face, warm again, tender, telling a story his words would not. I leaned into it, closing my eyes. "The abbey is the one place you can answer your calling, and if you can't go back there because of this . . . weakness we have for one another, it will be the great regret of your life."

Every part of me wanted to argue with him, to say it wasn't a weakness, that we would find a way, that nothing could be better than him and me, as one. But it felt unfair to contradict him when I had acted on impulse, giving no mind to anything other than the fierce need to touch him again.

So I stayed silent, and he took it as agreement, looking up to the sky, starbursts of dying sunlight catching in his eyes. His obscure beauty in the tilting shade sent a pain through my chest so profound it was as if I would never unfeel it, and when he turned to gather the horses, I felt a searing rush of urgency—the innate, desperate sense of something left unsaid. I reached out, as if to stop him walking away, but my fingers missed and he did not see.

27

BY THE TIME I arrived at Alys's chamber, I had hidden my damp gown in the laundry pile, sat in a steaming, lavender-scented bath until my bones felt loose and dressed myself simply in a bliaut of sky-blue linen. My hair, I had gathered in a coil, pinned loosely at the nape of my neck.

I emptied the spring's water into a filigreed silver ewer and carried it in, surprised to see Alys out of bed, sitting next to Tressa before the fire. Their heads were inclined in deep conversation.

Tressa jumped up, swiftly pouring me a goblet of apple wine, then handed another to Alys, who took it with a fond smile. Tressa smiled shyly back, then dipped a curtsey to me and left.

I placed the ewer next to Alys's bedside and sat in the vacated chair. "How long have you been sitting up?" I asked, considering her pallid complexion. "You shouldn't strain yourself."

"Tressa and I were just talking," she said. "We've been exchanging life stories, and time got away from us."

"Clearly I've been too much abroad."

"Nonsense," she retorted. "It's been good for you, and I've enjoyed getting to know Tressa. I will miss her, when we go back to St. Brigid's. You were out for a long time. Where did you go?"

I looked down, smoothing a crease from my skirts. "There's a glen a few miles from here, with a cascade and a beautiful spring. It's hidden deep in the Saintswood, and somehow we found it."

"And?"

I didn't look up. "And what?"

"Your avoidance of my gaze isn't enough to conceal the brightness in your eyes. You're hiding something."

"Lady Alys, what impertinence! I . . . How did you know?"

She gave a weary smile. "My whole life, I've had very little to do but observe, though it has given me a keen eye for people's ways. Most of all, Lady Morgan, I know *you*." Leaning back in her chair, she steepled her fingers, my eternal confessor. "What happened?"

I took a long sip of apple wine, its cloying sweetness recalling the generous Summerland orchards of St. Brigid's. It felt so far away now.

"Sir Accolon and I . . ." I began, hoping Alys would finish the sentence. She only waited. "We kissed," I said hurriedly. "I shouldn't have, but I wanted to, so we did."

Her eyes flashed briefly, but she didn't otherwise stir. "Hardly surprising. Even a convent-raised maiden like me could see something still lay between you."

"It's *nothing*. Reawakened memories, that's all."

"You slept with that chess piece in your hand every night for three years," she said gently. "You never forgot. There were only ever two possibilities upon seeing him again: either you had both changed too much, or—"

"Don't say it!" I pushed myself out of the chair and went to the window, contemplating the receding afternoon through the diamond-leaded panes.

Alys followed, sharing my view through the lightly warped glass. "Or, despite your time apart, your affinity endures. Perhaps grown even stronger."

I stared at her in disbelief; she remained impassive. "You're obviously exhausted," I scolded. "Come, I have something for you."

I ushered her into bed and picked up the silver ewer, pouring a cupful of the glittering spring water. "Drink this and you'll soon be well. We'll be together again, thinking about our plans."

Alys sipped, savouring the water at first, then swallowing the rest in three gulps. "Delicious. Quite extraordinary. My limbs feel lighter and my insides becalmed. Is this a tincture?"

I poured another. "No, it's water from the glen—the spring is said to have healing properties. It should help restore the last of your missing strength."

"I think Tressa told me of this place, a local legend."

"Yes. I've known of it from childhood, Gwennol's stories. It's meant to be a secret place, enchanted so ordinary travellers can't find it. It's hard to explain, but as soon as I got there I knew exactly where I was. The air around it was special." I felt it all over again, the gossamer veil of protection across the treetops, air and water shimmering with pure life. "When I touched the water, it went across my body like a comet's tail."

Alys picked at the edges of the coverlet. "You don't need the abbey, you know. It may even be holding you back. I regret having that book burned."

"Perhaps you were right. It was too great a risk."

"If you hadn't taken that risk, I'd be dead." Tears formed in her great brown eyes. "They're wrong, Morgan. Imagine the good you could do with *all* knowledge, not just what the abbey deems correct."

"It's strict, yes, but we knew that. We've made plans to go back regardless."

She drained the cup and placed it beside the ewer. "And I will. I'll go back to my life of observation and take the veil. But you found an enchanted glen today."

"That's just part of an old story."

"What if it's not? Tressa says many have searched the Saintswood to no avail. You said yourself that you felt its healing power. That instinct, that intelligence, what you can do with your own two hands—it's rare, preternatural. Denying it feels like a waste of something miraculous. And then there's Accolon . . ."

"No," I said sharply. "I cannot think of him."

Exhaling, I took her hand, laying my fingers across hers. Her upturned palm was unmarked, whereas I bore the thin silver crescent of my self-inflicted scar. "There's nothing to be done, about any of it."

"Do you love him?" she said.

The question raised my head, though I averted my eyes not to betray myself. But the truth sat between us clear as a summer morning; I could never have hidden it enough to fool her.

"Yes. I love him. Again. Still."

"And he loves you," she said. "One only has to look at you both, beholding one another."

"I cannot speak for him. What happened today . . . he called it impossible, and perhaps he's right." I sighed, so deeply it left me hollow. "All I know is how it feels to be together again. Like I am whole."

Alys regarded me sadly; I had exhausted her wisdom. "What will you do?" she asked.

For once, I had no answer for her.

*

I TOOK THE long way to the chapel, walking the edge of the headland as the day eased towards evening. Inside, sunset prayer had long finished, leaving the empty nave full of its age-old peace, the same soothing scents of candle wax, ancient stone and solitude.

Only I wasn't alone. Soft footsteps sounded from the altar end, and a tall figure appeared, striding towards me, his edges blurred with burnished light.

"*Dieu!*" Accolon stopped as if caught in a trap. "What are you doing here?"

I gestured mildly to our surroundings. "Praying, perhaps?"

He smiled with soft reluctance, half-amused, half-exasperated, and it sent a rush of love through my body so strong that I was suddenly unwilling to endure another moment of pretence between us.

"Accolon—"

"I should leave you in peace," he said quickly, heading for the chapel door.

Accepting his retreat, I walked away, to the blue-shadowed alcove of my father's tomb. The ever-burning candle was lit as usual, my mother's secret rite diligently kept by an unknown soul. The candle stood tall, wax barely melted. Its newness struck me like an arrow to the chest.

I dashed back up the aisle and out onto the headland.

The sun-bronzed path between chapel and castle was deserted; there hadn't been enough time for him to reach the courtyard. I glanced right, just as a shadow vanished behind the chapel's back wall.

He stood at the cliff's edge with his arms folded, a sleek silhouette staring out to sea. The sky before him was streaked gold in the wake of the falling sun, glimmering palely with early stars. I came to a halt beside him and looked at the waves below, undulating between the wind and the tides—part war, part harmony.

"I didn't plan or intend any of this," I said. "The bond between us, the intimacy we've shared, the glen . . . Our lives were set—me taking the veil, you leaving these shores."

He sighed. "And set they still are. Earlier, in the forest, it was regrettable, but—"

"I don't regret it," I cut in. "Whatever we have to pretend hereafter, I don't regret kissing you. I never will."

Unwilling to speak my truth to the side of his head, I pulled him around to face me. He turned with such resistance it took every last shred of my bravery not to abandon it all. "I still love you, Accolon. Now, as I did then. More, even."

He stood motionless, brow pinched.

"You do not feel the same," I concluded. "I was a fool to think otherwise."

"Do not say that. You could never be a fool."

I frowned, and he squinted away from my gaze. "You've been keeping my father's candle lit," I said softly. "All along."

He exhaled deeply. "Yes."

"Why? You never met him."

"It felt . . . an important rite to keep."

But he was lying, and I didn't know whether to strike him for it, or fall into his arms, or both.

"You *do* love me," I said. "Admit it or be a knave, Sir Accolon of Gaul—you are still in love with me, as I am with you."

He looked down, jaw tensing, about to deny it; then his voice came, low and forceful against the echoing waves.

"So then you know," he said. "I love you and I never stopped. I've thought of nothing but you since you returned—and before that. Since ever I saw you." He met my eyes with a fierce, needful expression I had not seen before. "In truth, Morgan, I can no longer remember when I haven't thought of you. It's as if you've been my whole life."

The thrill that went through my bones near turned me to ashes. I reached for him, lacing my fingers through his, as I had done so many times, there, in our place of youthful love and concealment between sea and chapel. His hands tightened around mine.

"Why didn't you tell me?" I asked.

"What good does it do? We cannot be together, or act on the love we feel. I am a house knight with nothing, and you're still a Princess."

"Don't call me that," I said. "You've never done so. That title was thrust upon me—it's meaningless."

"To you, maybe. That doesn't make it any less true. No connection between us would ever be permitted."

"Then . . . we could run away. We don't need a king's damned permission for that." I pulled him closer, wishing only to feel him against me, but he stopped just short.

"That's no sort of life for you," he said. "Toiling the roads with a sword-for-hire, not knowing where our next meal or roof is coming from. You deserve someone who can dress you in sea silk, give you a worthy home, fill it with books and falcons and anything your quicksilver mind could want."

Reaching into his tunic, he drew out the Gaulish coin, Apollo's head reflecting the light like a miniature sun. He pressed it into my palm. "This is all the gold I have. It's yours, everything I possess. But it isn't enough."

"I can't take this," I protested.

He closed my fingers around the coin. "I want you to have it. If nothing else, you can look at it and remember it wasn't for lack of love. I would do anything to be all that you need. But alas, I am not."

He kissed my hands and tried to relinquish them, but I held on. "Why are you still here, truly?" I asked. "In Cornwall, at Tintagel?"

He sighed, a confession. "For you, Morgan. The thought I might see you, just one more time. *La folie*, I know, madness. But I could not make myself leave."

"And here I am, once more, offering my own truth. Accolon, I have never wanted or needed any more than you. You've always been enough."

Strong arms went around my body like a rope, pulling us tight, his heat against me just as exquisite as I knew it would be.

"*Mon coeur*," he said, as if it were a prayer.

Then he kissed me, and I kissed him, deeply, fervently, endless, until we were all there was.

28

LATER, WHEN THE star-hung sky was full dark, I listened for the final bell and the distant sounds of the household retiring. On the headland, it had been another bell that cast Accolon and me asunder, tolling for the evening meal, driving us back to the castle breathless, guilty and separate.

I had to resist the urge to seek him again. Alone in my chamber, I slipped on my bed robe and brushed my hair, then busied myself with the Gaulish coin, pushing an old medallion of St. Christopher from its setting and replacing it with Apollo's head. It hung low on a fine chain of gold, concealed next to my skin.

I hardly heard the soft rap on my chamber door, heart jolting at the sight of Accolon hesitating at the threshold, fine face unreadable in the low-lit corridor.

"Come in," I said, trying to mask the catch in my breath.

He entered, watchful as a cat. In the low-ceilinged room he seemed taller than ever, and it occurred to me I had only ever seen him under great high arches, or beneath towering skies. His long shadow split in the candlelight, casting him in darkening shades.

"I shouldn't be here," was the first thing he said.

"I'm happy you are," I replied, half-bold, half-tremulous.

He moved closer, brushing a lock of hair from my face. "Truly?"

"I suppose that depends," I said, leaning towards his touch, "on why you came."

"I came," he said, "because it is where you are. Because I've been walking these halls for hours, forcing myself in the opposite direction, yet here I am." His hand opened like a flower, curving under my jaw. "I came because all the holy words in Christendom couldn't keep me away. I know: I tried them."

I smiled. "Then stay. With me. I want you to."

He became very still, the only movement his thumb tracing my cheekbone. Slowly, he looped his fingers around my wrist, studying me closely, as if seeking his next action in the rhythm of my pulse.

"You astonish me, Morgan," he murmured. "I am unmade by you. You are not for me; you cannot be."

"If I am not for you, then I am for no one," I said, and watched the last shred of doubt leave his eyes.

He leaned down and put his lips to mine, not lingering but moving lower, trailing along my throat. Gradually, definitively, he came to a halt, pressing his mouth against the soft hollow between my collarbones. Buckling, I slid my arms around his neck, and he caught me, wrapping his arms about my body, gathering me up and away, across to the bed, where at last he laid us down.

With one hand, he parted the edges of my robe, fingers grazing the Gaulish coin. Sliding his palm beneath it, he considered its presence in the fluttering light, then looked up at me and smiled, unhurried, all-consuming, setting my every nerve afire with the arch of his lip. I lifted my face to kiss him, and we met there, beginning.

We were water then, fluent, indivisible; a lake in a rainstorm, rippling with life; a waterfall colliding with itself in tumult and thrill; a river in spring thaw, wild and unceasing, rushing to meet the salt embrace of the sea.

*

I AWOKE TO find him looking at me, dark eyes reflecting my image. Bare dawn edged through the open window with the cool coastal breeze, no sound but the distant rustle of the tide. Accolon smiled softly, sleepily.

I stretched up to kiss him. "You're still here."

"Where else would I be?" he said. "I didn't think you would wake this early."

"Ecclesiastical habits. Far stricter than knightly training." I ran my fingers through his silky ash-dark locks. "I'm glad you stayed."

He frowned through his haze of relaxation. "And how do you feel, now we've . . . ?"

"Well, I must confess to being a little surprised. After everything I was warned about as a girl, I never imagined my own ruin would feel quite so miraculous."

"*Pardieu*, Morgan," he said, failing to conceal a smile. "The things you say."

I laughed, kissing him again, and as I lay along the length of him, it struck me how natural it felt for our bodies to be this close—chest to chest, thigh against thigh, limbs entwined. The same thought had occurred the night before as we lay down together for the very first time: the rightness of it, the sheer absence of doubt or fear; self-assurance where there should have been timidity, and pleasure where I had been told there would be pain. It was as easy to love him in body as it was in heart and mind, and so we had loved, time and again, until we could do no more but sleep.

Eventually, Accolon drew away, face fading to seriousness. "They are coming, you know. A messenger arrived as we supped last night. The High King raised the pavilions near St. Juliot's to hunt, but not for long. The Royal Household will be here in three days."

I sighed. "They had to come eventually."

His hand cupped my face, tender fingers tracing the curve of my ear. "Whatever happens, I love you. Do not forget that."

"And I love you," I replied, reaching for him again. Almost immediately as I did, Prime bell rang, echoing, insistent.

Accolon looked up, cursing mildly at the sound. "I should go, before too many are stirring. By God, I wish it wasn't so."

"But you must," I concluded. "I know."

Reluctantly, I released him, his heat lingering on my skin as I watched him dress. His clothes—strewn across the chamber floor all night—cleaved to him exquisitely, as if they had just been fitted by an expensive tailor. I took in his concentrated profile, focused on fastening his belt, his hands stirring me with their casual grace.

"I want you here," I said urgently. "Tonight and every night while we still can. Will you come?"

At first he seemed to consider it, but once his belt was fixed and his sword neatly sheathed, he glanced up sideways and smiled in the way that had always made me ache.

"Yes," he said. "I couldn't bear to be elsewhere."

Three nights was all we had. It wasn't enough; not nearly enough.

29

WITH THE ROYAL Household's arrival imminent, the castle flew into motion: airing chambers, scrubbing floors and furniture, kitchen courtyards a flurry of laundered sheets. The outer gates stood open, admitting farmers bringing sacks of grain, strung game and livestock, and the fishing boats stayed out longer, hauling in crab traps and bulging nets. Squires rushed around, ensuring the stables and barracks were orderly and prepared for full capacity. Aside from our stolen nights, Accolon ceased to have time for anything other than official business.

In good news, Alys had sat up all day after drinking the spring's water, talking to Tressa and me, her breath and wit restored as if she had never missed a thing. The day after that, she was well enough to take an afternoon turn around the solar garden.

The morning the household was expected, I rose late—Accolon had long left me, but I had lain there awhile, thinking of him—and was busy at the fire, tending a delicately bubbling pot, when Alys pulled open the door connecting our two chambers and marched in with sprightly purpose.

"You're up!" I exclaimed, hastening to my feet.

"I have been for a while," she replied. "The first time I've risen without being roused since I fell ill. I think we can declare me officially restored."

"That's wonderful. What hour did you wake?" I thought of Accolon, throwing on his clothes and slipping from my arms, how easily he could have been seen by an early-rising Alys, or indeed Tressa, who slept on a cot at the foot of Alys's bed.

"Full dawn, near enough. I tried your door, but it was locked." She leaned forwards to look over my shoulder. "What's that you're brewing?"

"Nothing!"

She slipped past me anyway and stooped at the fireplace, taking the spoon out and sniffing at it. "Pennyroyal tea? At this potency . . . Morgan, why do you need this?" One glance at my stillness was enough; she dropped the spoon with a clatter. "My God. Are you guarding against *pregnancy*?"

"Alys, listen," I began. Then she stood with her hands on her hips to do just that, and I realized there was no tempering it. "All right, yes. Accolon has been here with me, these past few nights. The tea is . . . necessary good sense."

Her eyes widened in shock, mouth falling open, and I braced myself for her castigation, or worse, her disappointment. Instead, she glanced briefly over her shoulder, towards her own chamber, then dropped her arms and sighed.

"You love one another," she said. "There is no helping the heart—we love who we love."

She spooned out a cupful of the tea and handed it to me. "*Si non caste, tamen caute*," she said drily: *If not chastely, at least cautiously*—a singsong phrase thrown around by the abbey widows, supposedly irrelevant to us. "Where does it stand now, between you both?"

I could not reply. We hadn't discussed it, he and I. We had been too preoccupied, too fascinated with one another, with our pleasure and this powerful new intimacy, to think beyond the moment. Our hushed twilight words had been spent on exhortations of love and joy, regret for the time we had spent apart. We had not paused to wonder what it meant, or if we were changed now, beyond repair.

"I . . . don't know," I said. "All I know is that I love him, more than I thought possible." I sipped at the tea; it was strong and bitter, sure to be effective. If only there were a tincture or incantation for the rest of it.

A soft knock came at the interior doorway, and Tressa entered, curtseying to me and smiling at Alys. "If you please, Lady Morgan. The Royal Household has arrived."

*

THE ROYAL PARTY trotted into the courtyard in a din of snorting horses and rattling bits, bringing all the formalized chaos I had not experienced since the weeks before Elaine's wedding. Uther and my mother rode first, Sir Bretel on her side and Sir Ulfin on his, along with an unknown knight resplendent in forest green with a golden boar on his chest.

Behind them trailed a varied company: more men wearing the unfamiliar boar standard; the lords of Uther's Royal Council; my mother's train of ladies among a band of flashy Pendragon knights. Last of all came the squires, the huntsmen and the falconers, carrying hooded birds lashed to gloved fists.

My mother saw me at once in the doorway. Abandoning all queenly bearing, she enveloped me in a rose-scented embrace and cried.

"Morgan, dearest daughter!" She put a hand to my face. "Such health, such beauty. Truly your womanhood becomes you." Astonishingly, she had little changed: hair the same May-morning gold, skin rosy and unblemished, figure not a hair's breadth wider or narrower. "How fared you at St. Brigid's, my child?"

"Very well, thank you, Mother. Abbess Honoria sends her most loving regards."

"She is a godly woman. I'm pleased she took such great care of you."
I kissed her cheek. "She was well instructed."

We moved deeper into the entrance hall as the rest of the household found their way in; I watched a laughing Sir Bretel cuff Accolon fondly on the shoulder before pulling him into a mail-ringing embrace.

"Where's Gwennol?" I asked. "I can't see her or Father Felix."

"Still at Caerleon both. Gwennol is unwell—her joints have troubled her in recent years. The physician advised her not to make the journey yet. Father Felix wishes to take a pilgrimage along the Welsh coast. They'll return to us in the autumn."

I looked up to see the knights arranging themselves into a guard of honour, Accolon among them. Our eyes met, and he gave me the slightest of smiles—tender, half-shy.

"Mother," I said hurriedly, "I need to speak with you."

"All in good time, daughter." She glanced up as if pricked with a needle. "But I must go. The King will expect me at his side."

I reached out to stay her, but a firm tug on my elbow pulled me into line. I turned, protesting, but Alys shook her head, keeping a tight hold on my arm as Uther Pendragon marched past, my mother's obedient hand atop his gauntlet. Sir Ulfin, Sir Bretel and the boar-blazoned knight followed in brisk, formal step.

I stared defiantly at Uther's ruddy profile, teeth bared, but he did not look at me. It was only when he was gone that I tasted blood on my tongue and realized I'd bitten the inside of my lip clean away.

30

I HAD HOPED to speak to my mother at the evening meal, but Uther sat beside her like a guard dog, deep in conversation with the green-and-gold knight—a northerner, by the sound of his retinue—who remained unannounced but was nevertheless treated as though he was of great importance.

I slept little that night, my mind full of Accolon, our desires and complications, my bed empty without him in it. Only phantoms of our togetherness remained: a stray shirt-lace he had left behind; the secret, hungry looks we exchanged across the Great Hall; the Gaulish coin on its chain beneath my chemise—a talisman for all we could not do.

At the suggestion of dawn, I flung myself out of bed and into Alys's chamber. She was already up, leaning into the window embrasure beside Tressa, taking in the brightening seascape.

"I must know why I've been summoned," I said, pulling her into the dressing room. "My mother always prays this hour in her oratory alone, so it's my best chance. But with all that's happened, I may need your level head."

She regarded me gently. "Lead the way."

A combination of servant stairways and narrow corridors led us to my mother's north-side quarters, and a door at the back of her reception chamber. Every morning, after first prayers, she ate lightly at the long table, a solitary meal that—unbeknown to Uther Pendragon—she had once shared daily with my father.

I burst into the dim room. My mother stood beside the table, one hand clamped to the back of a chair as if interrupted in sitting down, only there was no food or drink set out.

She swung around. "Morgan! I haven't sent for you."

"I'm aware of that," I said. "But I must—"

"Not now," she cut in. "You should leave."

"Mother, please!"

"Let the girl *speak*, my lady, given it's all so urgent."

I hadn't seen him, and his rumbling drawl filled me with dread. With terrible slowness, Uther Pendragon emerged from the shadows, tinged with greenish dawn. "Greetings, Morgana. I hope the years have treated you well." The sentiment, such as it was, dragged across my skin like a razor. "Pray tell us of your great trouble."

I swallowed the ball of hatred in my gullet. "My lady-in-waiting is yet to be formally introduced. She should not sit at the Royal Table without receiving a queen's grace."

"Or a king's," he snapped, but gestured at my mother. "Go ahead, my lady. I'll have nothing but observance of convention in my household."

"Nay, my lord." Stiffly, my mother turned to me, fingering the high embroidered collar of her gown. "The King and I were busy, Morgan. Go, I will summon you presently."

"No need. I'm impressed Morgana even thought of it." The brightness in Uther's voice raised the hairs on my arms. His reptilian stare flickered to Alys. "Tell me, young woman, who is your father?"

Alys opened her mouth, but my mother cut her off. "This can wait, my lord. It is important we continue our discussion."

"I think we were concluded. In fact—" Uther brought two hard hands together with a resounding crack. "We may as well tell Morgana now, since it was her we were discussing."

"My lord, not yet," my mother implored him, but it was a feeble protest, one she clearly had no faith in.

"Why were you talking of me?" I demanded.

She sighed, pointing at Alys. "Is she sworn to you? Has she taken her oath of loyalty, promised to keep your secrets close, on pain of death?"

I grasped Alys's wrist. "No, but I trust her, I—"

"Then it is no good." My mother gave Alys a cool, queenly look. "I'm sorry, but you must leave us."

I protested, but Alys shook her head. "No, *cariad*. I must go. I'll await you in your chamber." She curtseyed to my mother. "My lady Queen."

I watched her leave by the main door, gathering my wits. "Very well," I said. "Why was I summoned to Tintagel? Some legality, they said."

My mother drifted sideways, coming to rest before a long, bleak window. Whatever this was, she wasn't part of it. Nor, as ever, could she stop it. An ominous prickle crept between my shoulder blades and up into my hair.

"It *is* a legal issue of sorts," Uther said. "Did you notice you are not the only person who's been summoned? You've seen him at table, next to me. King Urien of Gore."

"Another of your scraping tribal Kings," I said scornfully. "That's nothing new."

Uther's lips twitched in irritation. "I see your time at the nunnery hasn't blunted your edges, Morgana. You'll do well to get your manners intact before meeting King Urien."

I frowned. "This stranger will find me however I am. I care nothing for his opinion."

"Oh, but you should." Uther's eyes lit up with a horrible glee. "You should care very much, since he is to be your lord husband."

I ought to have seen it coming: Uther's gloating calm, my mother's silent agitation, the same fervent preparations. The castle's bustling mood had even reminded me of Elaine's turn to be wed, and now, of course, it was mine. The fact that it hit me like a crossbow bolt shamed my intelligence.

I steadied myself against a chair, rage rising to bolster me. "He will not be my husband," I snapped. "I absolutely refuse."

"You will absolutely accept," Uther replied. "Legally, the betrothal is already done."

I flew at him, hands like claws, ready to scratch him blind, and I had never known my mother to move so fast. She caught my flailing body in her arms, holding firm across my torso, a jousting boundary between me and her grinning husband.

I braced against her, spitting like a cobra. "You mistake me for someone of lesser intelligence. I know betrothal cannot be legal without me swearing an oath before witnesses."

Uther laughed; my mother's arm hardened. "Regardless, Morgana," he said lazily, "you will obey. Tonight, you will be presented to King Urien, sit beside him at table and let him appraise what he intends taking back to Gore."

"I will do no such thing!"

How many times did I have to say it? How old, how angry, how mutinous did I have to be before he realized I would always defy him, no matter the punishment; that with the last breath in my body, I would fight, and refuse to obey any word that came from his lying, murderer's mouth?

"King Urien will take good care of you, dear daughter." My mother's voice came as a surprise amid the roaring in my skull: calming, maternal, coaxing me like I was six again, after a tussle with my sisters. "He is handsome and his kingdom is prosperous. He has delighted in your beauty."

I pushed away from her in disgust. "What do I care if my face pleases him?"

"Let her protest," Uther said in a bored voice. "She will marry him, like it or not. In fact, I'll have the betrothal contract brought to us now, bring this nonsense to an end."

"I'm signing *nothing*."

"He will give you all you could ever want," my mother went on. "Your sons will be Princes."

"My children will not be his!"

I stepped backwards, veering away. There seemed no way to escape this nightmare for which, inexplicably, they both stood on the same side. All that was left in my weaponry, in its stark, dangerous glory, was one final truth that—until now—I would never have dreamed of speaking. I took a shuddering breath.

"I won't marry any king. Indeed, I cannot. I . . . I love another, and have given myself to him."

Uther gaped like a landed fish, the most genuine expression of emotion I had ever seen on his face. At last I had broken him, and as I tasted my victory, bleak and bitter, I knew that, in turn, he would have to break me.

My mother grabbed me before he regained mastery of himself. "Morgan, what are you saying? You've fallen in love, is that it? An attachment of the heart?"

"No, Mother." My voice felt crisp in my mouth, measured, quite unlike myself. "Far more than that. There is no undoing it, and I certainly cannot marry." I gave Uther a cold, unyielding stare. "You could say, I suppose, that I am already married in the eyes of God."

Uther Pendragon stiffened like I had struck him across the face, turning puce. Perhaps he would simply keel over, some savage, overworked vessel bursting in his black heart and setting us all free. I watched with interest as he convulsed, for once desperate to contain himself, not to allow me the satisfaction of his shock.

But I *was* satisfied; nothing could take that away. I barely noticed my mother's fingers gripping ever tighter: afterwards I would discover yellow-brown bruises circling my upper arms like fairy rings.

Uther did not collapse, but took a few ragged steps towards us. "What did you say? You foul, demon-born slut, *what did you say?*"

"You heard me," I retorted. "You'll have to find some other fool to buy you King Urien's men. How many swords is it this time— ten . . . twenty thousand? A crypt full of gold? No matter—I am not for sale."

Wrenching away from my mother, I marched towards the door, crossing Uther's path with my head held high. I was barely three feet beyond him when he lunged, snatching me up like a doll. I struggled madly, but he was both stonelike and rabid, spittle settling on my cheeks as he roared from a distance of inches.

"You spoiled, arrogant *whore*. I am sick to my marrow of you believing you can defy me!" He shook me hard, rattling my teeth and sending lightning bolts across my vision. "Whoever he is, this devil you have let cover you like a kennel bitch, he will be headless before sunrise tomorrow. I swear it on the shards of the Cross. Without him, there is no compromised body, no marriage made by sin. Who is he, this bold knave of yours?"

He slung me at the floor in disgust, but I grabbed a side table and stayed upright. "You may do your worst to me, but I will never speak his name."

"Confess to it now, Morgana, or I will have every gold-spur in this castle tortured until I find him myself."

"You have no control over my words," I shot back, "and you won't torture your men for my sake."

"Perhaps not," Uther said. "But what about your woman, with you today? I'm sure she knows your secrets. She isn't sworn to you, and she will crack. I have men that could force the knowledge from her and have it in my hands by noon."

The threat made me feel faint, my last shred of power flying away at the thought of Alys in danger. Quick as I had prevailed, I was once again felled, torn down by a world where, no matter how much I learned, or raged, or fought to the end of my wits, I would never be allowed victory. The King had only one move, but the entire chessboard was his.

"You can't do that."

"I can, and I will," Uther said. "Unless you tell me yourself, now. *Who is he?*"

"It's . . . it's . . ." I put a hand to my spinning head. "It's no one."

"Don't take me for a fool, girl. Others will suffer because of you."

"There is no one, I swear it."

"I think what my daughter is saying, my lord, is that she *is* sinful, but not in the way she first claimed." My mother glided over to her husband, a pale column of composure. "Her true sin is lying, and blasphemy, isn't it, Morgan? You know how she is—stubborn, quick with her tongue, desperate to disobey you. But look at her—she cannot even invent a name fast enough. There is no lover, no ruin."

Uther regarded her with disbelief; she looked at me in expectation. I stared dazedly between them, my eyes resting on a tapestry beyond—one of Uther's, not ours—yet another scene of slavering dogs and relentless hunters, running down a beleaguered white hart, half torn to shreds. The violence of it made me nauseous.

"Mother's right," I said. "I lied, to force my own will in place of yours. There is no love affair, no bodily sin. I recant every word."

"And why should I believe this now?" Uther snarled.

"My lord, she has been raised to womanhood in a nunnery, as per your own wish," my mother said calmly. "What does she know of these things, outside of lurid ballads and gossiping servant women? Does it ring true, this convenient tale? Surely there's not a man in the country who would dare show you such disregard."

Her appeal to his overstuffed pride was effective, but it stuck in my craw to see it work—Uther's belief that no action, no life, went on outside his say-so.

"Bring me a priest if you don't believe me," I said. "I will swear before God Himself that I have done *nothing* I regret."

Uther's brow darkened and I wondered if I had gone too far, undoing all that my mother had managed to tie up. He raised a hand, as if about to pronounce a sentence in judicial court. Only there was no justice about it; I could not take up a sword and fight for my freedom, as men could. Even Accolon could have defended his innocence, or mine, but I could not argue for myself.

My heart jolted at the thought of him—Accolon, my love, my lover, my fated one. What were we to do now, with the eyes of the world upon me and disaster looming in the shape of a boar-headed King?

But if Uther Pendragon chose not to believe me or my mother, then the future was sealed anyway, and it was deadly. In slow motion, the royal hand came down in a hard fist, as if to slam onto a surface that wasn't there.

"*Get out of my sight,*" he said, and I ran.

31

ALYS WAS PACING my chamber in front of an agitated Tressa when I flew in.

"Tressa," I gasped. "Get a page. Tell them to find Sir Bretel and send him urgently to Lady Morgan's chambers."

"Of course, my lady." Sure-footed, she fled.

Alys slipped an arm around my shuddering shoulders. "What on earth's happened?"

"Uther . . . he's betrothed me to someone, sold me for men, swords."

"Betrothed!" she exclaimed. "To whom?"

"The knight with the boar standard. Yet another northern King, negotiating an alliance to avoid war."

"It cannot be legal. You haven't consented."

"Consent is the least of his concerns." The thought spoken aloud made my senses spin. "It gets worse. I told them about Accolon—not who he is, but that I love someone and I'm compromised. I thought it would stop this so-called marriage, but Uther said he'd kill him. Then he said *you're* not sworn to me, that he'd make you tell him who it was by force. I'd rather die than let him threaten you. So I took it all back; I had to. But I know he'll act in some way, soon."

Alys tightened her arm around me. "And Sir Bretel?"

Before I could respond, there was a knock at the door, and the man himself appeared. He dipped his sandy-blond head. "Lady Morgan, I am at your service."

"Sir Bretel, thank goodness." I beckoned him in. "I want you to make arrangements for Lady Alys to return to St. Brigid's Abbey. Leaving today, if you can. It is imperative she reach there in safety and comfort, so she will need a band of your most trusted knights."

"Of course, my lady. I will arrange it personally."

"*Iesu mawr!*" Alys rushed forwards, putting herself between us. "I apologize, good Sir Knight, but there's been a mistake." She glared at me. "I'm not *going*."

I glanced at Sir Bretel, but he had politely withdrawn to the doorway. "You must, dear heart," I said in a low voice. "Uther has already promised you harm."

"Let him do his worst. I'm not leaving you alone in this."

"But Alys—"

"I'm *not* going." Suddenly, her shoulders dropped and her stubborn brow cleared. "I . . . in truth, I'm not sure I even want to go back. For reasons far beyond all this. I know you might have a different future, where I don't fit. But I will stand beside you for as long as I can. Will you let me?"

Stunned, I put my arms around her. "Of course, you mad Welsh heathen. And you will always have a place by my side, if you wish it. But I can't guarantee us any kind of life."

"You don't need to. Whatever happens, wherever it takes us, we should forge our own path." She held me tighter, then called out to the doorway. "Sir Bretel, if you'd be so kind."

Sir Bretel strode back over to us. "My ladies?"

"Witness something, if you will." Alys took up my hands and turned us to face one another, as if we were about to be wed. "I wish to swear an oath of loyalty to Lady Morgan of Cornwall, so I will truly be a woman of her household."

"Very well," said Sir Bretel. "I have borne witness to a few oath-swearings in my time. It'd be an honour."

"Alys, no," I protested. "How can you swear to be my servant?"

She smiled in her wise, enigmatic way. "Not your servant. Your woman. In loyalty and faith."

And there, in the soft peace of the room, with the tide roaring gently outside, Alys knelt before me and spoke her oath of loyalty, first in our shared tongue and then in her own. As soon as she finished, I accepted, raising her up to embrace her, knowing she deserved so much better.

Sir Bretel bowed. "It is done, and well spoken too. You have a great and true-hearted lady at your side."

"I know," we said in unison, and barely had enough time to laugh at ourselves before the heavy echo of footsteps sounded outside my door.

Sir Bretel stepped into the corridor. The marching feet skidded to a halt, a knot of Pendragon guards filling my doorway. "Well met, gentlemen," he said. "Is it me you seek?"

The head guard came stiffly to attention. "No, my lord. We've been sent by King Uther to guard the Princess, as befits her status."

"I see. So many of you?"

"Six for the Princess and six for her companion. We're under orders to ready the Welsh girl to go back where she came from."

I charged to the doorway, bristling. "*Lady Alys* is not going anywhere. She is my sworn woman and under my care, by the laws of this land and God Himself."

The guard shifted beneath his armour. "His Highness told us she was not sworn."

"Lady Morgan speaks the truth," Sir Bretel said sternly. "The daughter of *our Queen* would not lie. Lady Alys is sworn to Lady Morgan;

I witnessed the oath of loyalty myself. All protocol was correct—she cannot be removed from her service. I will apprise the King and Queen of this, but your men are not required. And I hope to God your manners are better next time you see fit to address a lady, of this—or any—house."

"Yes, Sir Bretel, of course." Chastened, the guard dismissed the farthest five men and followed them down the corridor. The other six remained, arranging themselves outside my door.

"They lack delicacy, and training," muttered Sir Bretel, ushering me back inside. "Don't worry, Lady Morgan. I will go to the King at once and make clear Lady Alys's circumstances. And if the guards are not to your liking, send word and I will have them changed."

I smiled weakly, trying to appear soothed. One set of Pendragon dogs over another made little difference. Good as he was, Sir Bretel would never know the truth: I was not being protected, I was being watched, and I would not see freedom until I submitted to the King's malevolent will.

*

I WAS, HOWEVER, summoned to attend that evening's banquet, to sit next to some crowned stranger and act the agreeable woman while the love of my life looked on.

"I won't go," I said to Alys, as the bell rang. "I refuse to participate in this great spectacle of Uther's. My only concern is that Accolon might worry at my absence. If he does so much as ask after me, it could be catastrophic."

"I'll go to the Great Hall to sup with the ladies, and say you're unwell," Alys said. "When the dancing takes up, I'll speak with Sir Accolon secretly and bring you his response."

"Are you sure you're safe? What if Uther does something?"

"He won't," she said. "Sir Bretel's intervention must have done the trick or I'd be halfway up the Summerland road by now. Or else in a ditch, I suppose."

"Alys, don't! I feel sick just thinking about it."

"I'll be fine, I promise," she assured me. "Any particular message?"

I sighed. "Tell Accolon I love him. And that I am only ever his, come what may."

We embraced briefly and she left, offering the guards a disdainful look as she passed.

Thus I waited, sat at the window, or by the fire, or roving past the door, ears straining for banquet sounds against the constant cry of the sea. Latterly, I listened only for Alys's long stride in the stone corridor.

Eventually, she dashed through the connecting door, eyes wide like a beaten dog. My stomach turned over.

"What's the matter?" I said. "What did Accolon say?"

"I didn't speak to him. I caught his eye, but before Uther even said grace . . ." She put her head in her hands and groaned. "Oh, Morgan, I'm sorry. I'm so sorry."

Panic rising, I ran to her and pulled the hands from her face. "God's blood, are we discovered? Is Accolon in chains?"

"No, but . . ."

I almost stopped listening; nothing else mattered now I knew we were all safe. Accolon could live with the mystery of my absence for another day. But somehow Alys was still talking, stumbling over words, entirely unlike herself.

"Before we ate," she continued, "Uther stood up, silenced the whole hall and asked them to raise their goblets to King Urien of Gore, and the *happy* occasion. He announced it, Morgan, your official betrothal and imminent marriage, to the whole household. I looked for Accolon, to give him some reassuring sign, but there was so much clamour, people standing, the applause. When I finally caught sight of his seat, he had vanished."

32

I SPENT THE night staring into darkness, trying to order the chaos in my mind.

"You don't think Accolon would believe the announcement?" Alys had said.

"No," I said quickly. "I trust him. He knows my true feelings."

But our predicament had changed; Accolon and I urgently needed to talk, make plans for our life together. Perhaps we could run—elude my guards and ride as fast as we could until we found a boat that could carry us across the British Sea. Alys was another consideration; she had sworn to me, and our loyalty was mutual, but to enter a wild unknown with my lover was my choice, not hers. Her safety and happiness were on my shoulders.

I sighed, and it sounded unnaturally loud to my ears. My chamber was eerily silent, a contrast to the soft, rustling waves that had accompanied my rolling thoughts only moments before. Curious, I got to my feet, led to the open window by a path of high moonlight.

The headland was shrouded in mist, filling the cove and glowing blue white under the fullness of the moon. Just beyond, the sea had paused, quietened to the occasional splash against the rocks. Suddenly, two robed, hooded figures emerged at the top of the cliff-side path, one wielding a black, gnarled staff.

Merlin.

I gasped in horror. It was barely audible, but the other figure glanced up at once, hood sliding back to reveal a flash of copper hair. Ninianne, the mysterious red-headed girl—she who had both saved me from the sorcerer's clutches and helped him carry off the lost son my mother never spoke of. Since that day, Merlin had ceased to haunt Uther's courts—or so it had seemed. How many times had they come here, amid this unnatural fog, their presence and purpose concealed? What had they wrought?

I crouched, not to be seen, as a thick cloud extinguished the moon. By the time it passed, they had vanished, absorbed back into the halls of Tintagel.

*

"MY LADY, WAKE up." The voice was apologetic but insistent, distinctly Cornish. "Please, you'll be late."

I opened bleary eyes to see Tressa's anxious freckled face. "Sorry, Lady Morgan. I'd have left you sleep, but Lady Alys isn't here, and Sir Ulfin said he came directly from the King and Queen."

"Ulfin was here? Whatever for?"

"You're required in your solar by next bell for an important meeting."

I pushed myself upright, my mind fogged. Somehow, I had slept, a thin, scratchy slumber full of unsettling, formless dreams. Had my vision of Merlin even been real? Life seemed to be going on regardless.

I rubbed my eyes, grasping for focus. "Thank you, Tressa, it's all right. Though why a meeting with my mother and her godforsaken husband is so urgent . . ."

Tressa's nimble fingers began working at my night braids. "It's not with *our* King, my lady, but *your* one. Him that you're promised to."

I stared at her. "King Urien of Gore? I am meeting *him* in the solar?"

"Yes, my lady." Her happy tone recalled the betrothal announcement, the air of congratulation that had clearly enveloped the household.

I stood up, steadying myself on her forearm. Next to her warmth, I was cold to the bone. "Where's Lady Alys?"

"Gone for a walk, my lady. Said you'd know why."

I did: Alys had gone to find Accolon, to do what she couldn't the evening before. "I need you to find her, Tressa."

"But my lady, you're not dressed, and your hair, and—"

"I'll see to that myself," I said. "But I cannot meet King Urien alone, and I don't want anyone but her. Please."

With a determined nod, Tressa trotted off, and I went into the dressing room. My eyes alighted on a new green gown, skirts ornately stitched with gold flowers, laid out along a tabletop near the door. When Alys entered soon after, I was already standing half in it. Wordlessly, she reached for the dangling mess of fabric, lacing me up with a smooth, automatic rhythm.

"I've been ordered to meet with King Urien of Gore," I said. "If I refuse, they'll only march me there under guard. He obviously wishes to see how I am, so if I hold forth on my devotion to the abbey, my great desire to become a nun, marrying me may not appeal to him."

"Will that work?"

"It's the only way. Even if it doesn't put him off altogether, it might buy us time."

"Perhaps." She frowned. "I haven't seen this gown before."

I considered myself in the glass. "My measurements were sent to the Royal Tailor while we were still in St. Brigid's. I assume Tressa took delivery of it."

Alys sighed, picking up the Gaulish coin pendant from where it glittered against my bodice. "You should hide this."

I closed my fingers around it. "Did you get a message to him?"

"No." Alys moved behind me and began swiftly plaiting my hair. "He was leading drills in the tiltyard with a crowd of knights. Practising for your wedding tournament, of all things."

"Oh God. How did he look?"

"Like he was concentrating on staying ahorse. I got as close as I could, but he didn't see me." Her eyes met my tired reflection. "I'll get word to him, I promise."

She picked up the braids she'd woven with gold thread and pinned them around my head, arranging the loose tresses down my back. "I think you're ready."

"I'll never be ready." Opening my hand, I kissed Apollo's head, then dropped the cool disc down into my chemise, where it settled, as it always did, beside my heart. "But I'll endure it. Let's go."

*

KING URIEN OF Gore was a man like many others, built from pleasant generalities. Our meeting began inauspiciously—he arrived early, running into us abruptly where the corridors intersected outside the solar. Alys and his guiding page hurried inside to ensure it was suitable to receive a king's company, leaving us idling in the empty passageway.

"My lady Princess." He bowed deeply and offered a broad, unflustered smile. I said nothing, which he took as lack of recognition. "Apologies for my familiarity. I am King Urien of Gore."

"King Urien," I said. "Of course."

Tall and well built, with a figure cut for lance and sword, he was certainly handsome, possessing strong, even features and an impressive, proud-chested carriage, along with a natural confidence and quick attentiveness that was in no way intimate but nonetheless proved absorbing.

"It appears we had the same thought." He gestured to himself, expensively dressed in green-and-gold silk of the exact shades I was draped in. His colours, I realized, too late—of his house, the boar's head standard. "We make quite the pair, do we not?"

I stiffened, and he smiled in apology. "The error is entirely mine, my lady. I should have checked beforehand. What you must think of me—we have barely met and already I must ask your forgiveness."

It was the kind of brisk charm only knowledge of rank could bestow, but rare in the typically dour men of his station, which softened the tension in me a little. "Think nothing of it, King Urien," I conceded. "Though you *are* early. It is usual that I should be waiting to receive my audience."

He flushed slightly under his chestnut-coloured beard, clipped so neatly along his impressive slab of jaw it put my teeth on edge. His thick tawny hair was cut above the collar, arranged in carefully tossed waves; all knights of a certain age seemed to wear it this way, which put him near thirty years old. A thin white scar curved across the bridge of his nose between large, lively eyes, blue green like the feathers of a peacock.

"I know, my lady. In truth, my enthusiasm to meet you overcame me. At least introductions can be done while we wait. If I may?" He gestured for my hand. Hesitantly, I gave it, and he lifted my arm high, bestowing a theatrical kiss on my knuckles.

"There, now that's over with," he said rakishly, and it raised a smile from me, even a small chuckle. He laughed softly back, holding my gaze, just as Alys appeared in the doorway. The bell rang, announcing the meeting's beginning.

I turned again to King Urien; he was still smiling at me, eyes glowing like coals in a brazier.

"Shall we?" he said. The distance was mere yards, but the King of Gore held out his arm in expectation and, still tired, still half-clouded and not myself, I took it.

*

MY AUDIENCE WITH King Urien went surprisingly well, between Alys's supportive presence and the northern King's careful manners. I learned a great deal of him: his upbringing, his kingdom and the battles he'd fought on its behalf—mostly with Uther Pendragon— though there was now the opportunity for a prosperous peace. And he learned something of me: an abridged account of my childhood in Cornwall, then much more of my years at St. Brigid's. I talked at length of my devotion not only to learning, but to my prayers, God and the abbey itself, emphasizing my ambitions towards holy work.

King Urien took all of this in, responding with politely impressed surprise. There was no mention of the betrothal, and the King of Gore left Alys and me as he had arrived: smiling, urbane, sooner than expected.

"That was strange," Alys said, the moment he had quit the room. "No mention of the announcement, despite the whole household talking of weddings."

"Hopefully, my plan is working," I replied. "Upon meeting my pious self, King Urien now finds me completely undesirable."

Alys laughed. "I wouldn't quite say that. His eyes rarely strayed from your face. I think he was rather taken."

I elbowed her in jest. "Then it's a shame for him I will never be his wife."

I was surprised by the mirth in us, as if the air carried a strange lightness. Even my guards were yet to come, sent away, no doubt, by Uther's command, to ensure King Urien didn't see my imprisonment for what it truly was. I was free to go anywhere I wished just then, and was about to point this out to Alys when Tressa appeared in the open doorway.

"Thank goodness, you found one another," she said breathlessly. "I'm very sorry, Lady Morgan, but I couldn't find Lady Alys anywhere. I returned to your chambers, and you were already gone. I thought to tell you before your meeting, but I was waylaid just outside, and then the bell rang and—"

"It's all right, Tressa," I interrupted. "It seems Lady Alys simply came back. I apologize if you were running around without cause."

"Oh no, my lady. I'm just glad Lady Alys was there for your meeting. And you found the right gown, in any case. It looks very becoming. Sir Ulfin said it would. Did your gentleman like it on you?"

"*Ulfin* brought the gown?" Alys exclaimed, and everything clattered into place. Of course the green and gold was not a coincidence: Uther Pendragon had arranged that I would look as compliant as possible in front of my supposed husband-to-be.

"Never mind, it's done now," I said wearily. "But you should know, Tressa, that this isn't what it seems."

She immediately looked aghast. "I'm sorry, my lady. I shouldn't comment. Your business is private, and I've hardly been here a six-week—you've no cause to trust me."

I shook my head. "I *do* trust you, Tressa. Lady Alys trusts you completely, and that's recommendation enough."

Tressa flushed and glanced at Alys, then turned wide eyes back to me. The weight of my secrets felt like a stone on my chest.

"I have a . . . different attachment, of the heart," I told her. "To Sir Accolon." My confession spoken aloud came with a strange exhilaration, as if reminding me it was real.

"Oh!" Tressa gasped. "Then *that's* why . . . Sir Accolon came to your chamber, asking for you, after you'd gone to the solar. It was him who waylaid me."

My heart skipped. "What did he want?"

"I don't know. He was halfway to the door, still in jousting garb, flustered. Said he needed to see you and it couldn't wait. The bell hadn't yet rung, so I told him you'd gone to the solar. He ran off, but obviously didn't catch you in time."

I knew nothing except that my blood was running hot and cold. "The bell hadn't rung when . . . I was greeting King Urien, let him kiss my hand, smiled at him. What if Accolon saw and, in the wake of the announcement . . . Oh God, I was *wearing his colours!*"

I tried to bolt, but Alys grabbed my arm. "Where are you going?"

"I have to find Accolon—it cannot wait. I'm unguarded; it's my only chance."

"What if you're seen? Let me go, or Tressa."

"No," I said. "He came to my chamber, risked his knighthood, his neck, everything, to talk to me. I must do the same."

"You told me last night that you trusted him," Alys said.

"I do. But things are different now, changing fast. I just need to look him in the eye before it's too late."

I pulled free, heading for the solar's garden exit. "Close the inner door and talk loudly to one another—if the guards come, it'll sound like we're still within. I'll be back as soon as I can."

33

FROM THE SOLAR garden, the best route to anywhere without being seen was to skirt the castle and courtyard wall, then track the slanted path to the chapel. It suited my purpose; if Accolon was brooding or waiting for me, most likely he would go to the headland.

I was about to check the chapel when a thin column of shadow caught the edge of my sight. I hastened to the back wall, expecting to see Accolon's long figure in our usual place.

He wasn't there, but neither was I alone. A wide trail of mist bloomed from my feet to the cliff's rocky edge, culminating at the hems of a tall female figure. She was robed in violet and gazing out to sea, copper hair blazing down her back like liquid fire.

"Lady Morgan," Ninianne said, without turning around. "I wondered when you would come."

Her voice was different from when I had first heard it, the soft, girlish tone she had used to coax Merlin's attention now deep and smooth, instantly alluring. I followed the low, silky sound until I reached her side.

"I didn't come for you," I managed, though I could no longer quite remember why I *had* come.

She turned to me slowly. "Indeed you did not. But in times of trouble, it is only natural you should seek the sea."

I had forgotten how she glowed, her shimmering light flaring forth in the afternoon sun like a blanket of woven gold. To my confusion, she had barely aged, looking the same in years as I was, which made no sense given that, on my childhood encounter, she had appeared almost a decade older.

"Who *are* you?" I asked. "*What* are you?"

She pursed her lips, casting her eyes back to the waves as if averse to questions. Then, at length, she sighed.

"I am Ninianne," she said. "Of the Lake. A water fairy, some call it, though mortal understanding is limited. But I am a woman too, and not altogether unlike you."

"What did you mean, I seek the sea? I'm not—"

"No," she cut in. "You are not like me in that way, born bound by magic, belonging to a different realm. You are a flesh-and-blood woman in your entirety, with all that entails. But we share an . . . elemental affinity, if you like. This sea brought you forth to life—I can hear it roaring in your veins. It brings you strength, is felt in the tidal shift of your moods."

She looked back, considering my face with interest, as if something were written there. "The connection runs deep—a Celtic nymph, perhaps, tangled up in your ancient bloodline. No doubt you derive some thrill from any water."

It made a certain sense, and very little at the same time. "That's all very interesting," I said, tearing myself away from her dazzling green gaze. "But you did not come to Tintagel to talk to me about the sea. Merlin is here too. Why? He hasn't attended Uther in years."

"Do not worry," she said. "We'll be gone before the sun sets, and only the High King will know. But it's worth remembering, Morgan, that what you have or haven't seen isn't always the truth."

She paused, sparking a sudden memory.

"What really happened that day?" I asked. "When you delivered my mother's son."

All at once, her face closed and she turned purposefully back to the sea, silent as though I had ceased to be there at all.

"Of course," I snapped. "I expected as much, given you belong to that demon Merlin."

Ninianne rounded on me, eyes like Greek fire. "I belong to *no one*," she said vehemently. "I am his student, a scholar of his arts, nothing more."

"And yet you keep his secrets, conceal what was done. He claimed the child was written in the stars, yet supposedly it was lost."

"What you were told was true," she insisted. "The stars speak their wisdom, but how we interpret them is imperfect. I failed that day; that is the simple truth. Trust me or do not, but I will justify it no further."

Her voice was forceful, assured, underscored by something else— tiredness, perhaps. A student of Merlin's she might be, but she had saved me from him when I was a child. What reason did I have to disbelieve her? Did it even matter, after all these years?

I glanced behind me at the chapel; I'd had a different purpose for coming here, and Ninianne, Merlin, their unknowable mysteries, held no importance for me.

"Lies, truth, it's all the same," I said. "I have no part in this."

"How do you know?" Ninianne said.

"Because I don't *care* about kings, sorcerers, the plots they weave. I am only seeking my own future."

Turning on my heel, I walked away, parting the mist, leaving the past in its opacity.

"He's gone," she called after me.

I halted, swinging around.

Ninianne turned, sea and sky blurring together at her back. "The one you are looking for."

"How do you—?"

"I saw him," she said simply. "Tall, dark, graceful. A French knight, greatly skilled, much respected, though his uncertainty runs deep. And undeniably yours—your presence came off him in waves."

I stiffened, holding myself steady. "And?"

"I watched him go into the chapel and felt him all the while—his pain, his fury, his love and doubt—vibrating in the air even through those stone walls." Ninianne moved towards me, her hands spread wide. "Then I felt something break, and his decision was made. He laid his heart on the altar and left. Left the chapel, Tintagel and, soon enough, Cornwall. Left . . . you."

"You lie," I said tremulously. "He would never . . . Not him."

The sun tracked her approach, combining with her glow until she shone white gold, so bright I had to look away. Her presence reached out to my shivering body, warm, enveloping, a comfort despite my resistance.

"I am not here to cause you hurt, Morgan," she said. "Though the truth is sometimes painful. The man you love, the one you came to find, is gone. But perhaps it is a good thing."

I stared at her, speechless; she was within arm's length now, her aspect so soft and soothing I could have basked in it but for the cold, hopeless pain seeping through my insides.

"Love," she continued, "is potent and powerful—it gives pleasure, meaning. But it also dominates, weakens, is a beast greedy and selfish, requiring constant sacrifice. To love is to cede our own power, an act of surrender we cannot guarantee will be returned. Perhaps in leaving you, your lover has bestowed a great favour. Isn't it far better to choose a fate entirely on your own terms, in service of your deeper talents and wants of the mind, rather than be led by the weakness of the heart?"

"It isn't weakness," I protested. "Love clarifies, not destroys. It brings strength, fulfilment to our hopes and wants. My love for Accolon, I chose it. He is my fate—one *I* decided upon."

"How can that be true when it can so easily be made to go wrong?" she asked. "The slightest force beyond your control, and this great love shattered, taking your fate with it."

I drew a deep breath, mind fogged with her oblique words and low, persuasive voice. "What 'force'?" I managed.

"It need not be specific, or even that powerful." Unexpectedly, she reached out and ran a hand down my arm, along the trailing green and gold of my sleeve. "No more complex than a gown, say, that makes the wearer feel charmed when it's next to the skin, encouraging a pleasant exchange between two disparate people, forming an effective image. Or a notion that strikes a man to seek his beloved at the precise moment this image is at its most potent."

I glanced down at my body; the silk looked and felt completely usual. "This gown has been tampered with? It made me . . . what? Good-natured? Smile at King Urien? And somehow Accolon was *made* to see? Who would—?"

I stopped, arrested by Ninianne's cool, pointed look. She did not have to say the name *Merlin*—the air between us was full of him.

"That's absurd," I scoffed. "Merlin has no interest in me. He wouldn't come here to interfere with such trivialities."

"It's not about *you*, Morgan," Ninianne said. "It's about *them*—men, their power, their battles, their pride. Everything they do is to provide them with what they need, no matter the cost."

"Are you truly saying—"

She shook her head, cutting me off. "What *I* am saying is, whatever the possibilities of the situation, *love* had to fail you for it to happen. You call this man your fate, your strength, but this love, this great act of faith, could not withstand the slightest whisper from the outside world. The man who claimed to love you above all else abandoned your bond the first moment it was challenged. Is that what you wish to stake your life, your potential, your future upon?"

I put a hand to my forehead; I was so very tired, and all I wished to do was curl up on the grass within Ninianne's light. She was wise, I accepted that, and knew more than I could ever hope to learn.

But what she didn't know was me, or Accolon, or a single thing about our love. Even if he had left Tintagel, it did not mean he had left me, or abandoned the notion of us. There would be an explanation, a plan. I felt it as keenly as she had felt my presence radiating from him; whatever he had done in the chapel would tell me where we stood.

I shook Ninianne's hand from my arm. "You're wrong," I said defiantly. "He loves me, and that's all there is."

Breaking away from her warmth, I grabbed my skirts and ran to the chapel. From the porch, I saw several figures on the castle path: Alys and Tressa, backed by my half-dozen guards. I turned back, seeking Ninianne, but she had vanished, taking the mist with her.

My hurried footsteps echoed along the nave. I glanced down to my father's tomb, half expecting to find Accolon still there, sat on the steps and smiling as in our earliest days, but the chapel was empty, not a movement except the flicker of the remembrance candles.

A shadow caught my eye against the pale marble of the altar, a dark shape both incongruous and familiar. Cautiously, I approached, revealing a sleek rectangle wrapped in rough grey muslin.

I picked the object up, cringing when I heard the hollow rattle from within. With shaking fingers, I unravelled the fabric to reveal the unmistakable checkered surface of the chess set. The squares caught the filtered sunlight, glinting and repeating, light and dark, our rejected past.

In desperate hope, I flicked the hook, heart leaping into my throat as it opened. There, sitting atop the carved pieces, was a square of parchment, folded tight—a message from Accolon; our future.

Quivering in relief, I drew out the note, but the parchment slipped away from my grip, fanning into several pieces on the altar.

Barely breathing, I aligned the jagged sides, falling to my knees when I saw the words in stark black.

Protect the chevalier, it said, in my own hand. Once a plea of love and wilful sacrifice, now discarded and torn to shreds.

"Morgan?" said a worried voice. I looked up to see Alys halfway along the nave.

"It's Accolon," I said, staring back at the mutilated note. "I have to find him, I—"

"You can't, *cariad*," she said. "Tressa and I went to the barracks, spoke to the knight he bunks with. He told us he found Accolon throwing things into a pack and—"

"Where is he?" I demanded, unable to bear any more. "Where is Accolon?"

"Gone," Alys said. "Took his arms, his horse, his hunting hound, and rode out. He's taken to the road and isn't coming back."

34

RUMOURS ABOUNDED, THOSE Alys and Tressa could gather: Accolon was sailing to Ireland to joust for gold; or in Westminster guarding the Archbishop's relics; off to Paris in pursuit of a countess; or on his way to Rome to sell his sword to the Pope.

"How could he?" Alys hissed at intervals. "If I ever set eyes on him again, God only knows what I'll do."

In my grief, Alys's anger was a comfort. She was loath to leave me, sleeping some nights by my side; on others, I preferred to be alone, staring at the place where Accolon had lain. After a week, word circulated that Sir Bretel had released his former squire from his service in a completely usual fashion, and the small tempest of gossip died down, leaving only my memories, shattered and distorted.

"You know me, to my core," Accolon had said once, fingers tracing my cheek in the blue moonlight. "My troubles, my failings, my weaknesses. Yet still you want me here, still you keep opening that door."

What I once heard as proof of a love unbreakable I now reckoned with as something entirely other. Not lies, perhaps, but a warning, a confirmation that Ninianne's wisdom held true; that love could not conquer all, as the poets claimed, but held its own against very little when faced with the forces of reality. That all along, Accolon was telling me who he was, what he would do, and I was too enthralled, too raw with love, to know it.

Meanwhile, still under guard, I was summoned daily to meet with King Urien of Gore. I sat distracted, Alys answering more of his questions than I did. King Urien remained genial, patient with my reticence and unfailingly courteous, though he still hadn't mentioned the betrothal, or expressed any feeling above polite regard.

However, one day, after several meetings before my wan face, he enquired if I was well, and when Alys cut in to make some excuse, he shook his head and regarded me directly.

"I beg your pardon, Lady Morgan," he said frankly. "But your place in this household does not seem to be an entirely happy one. Please know that if there's something that will bring you ease, say the word and I will do it."

It surprised me, the way he spoke—genuine, without expectation—and for once the retort that he should return to the wilds of Gore did not occur. After that, I began to anticipate our meetings. They gave form to my days, a reason to rise from my bed and walk to the solar, to sit opposite someone not part of my pain or failure.

So it went, day after day, though it barely occurred that time was moving on, that the goods and guests were trundling in, the white-and-gold banners were being unrolled, and the household grew impatient for a wedding day to be named.

I was soon summoned to face Uther Pendragon again in my father's Great Chamber. When I arrived, he was sitting in a chair casually pulled out from the council table, and I was reminded of the day he first came to Tintagel, to this same room, fighting for supremacy over a grieving and furious widow while I listened, understanding little, cowering every time the sorcerer's staff thumped past my hiding place.

"Morgana," Uther said. "How have you fared since we last spoke?"

I realized with a jolt that we were completely alone. "Where's my mother?" I demanded.

"This is between you and me. Though hopefully for the last time. You are King Urien's concern now."

"Not this again," I retorted. "I will not hear it. The whole thing is repulsive."

Uther laughed, and I instantly despised myself for not cleaving to silence. "The man himself does not repulse you, however. He is handsome, healthful, reasonable enough. And you've seen him daily going on a fortnight now."

"I've had no choice but to meet with him. Aside from that, I have no opinion."

"Never mind *your* opinion," Uther said. "It's his that matters. And by some miracle, Morgana, King Urien has deemed you suitable to wed. Seems you are young enough, and pleasing enough on the eye, that he doesn't mind getting his children on you."

"*I don't care.* As if the world needs yet another meaningless queen, sold into submission."

"Quiet," he snapped. "Not another word. For courtesy's sake, the man himself still wishes to propose privately. You will receive him and accept it, much as it's irrelevant to the betrothal already agreed upon."

He was still weak on this point, despite his attempts at breezing past it. We both knew if I continued to refuse, there was no argument Uther Pendragon could make. Ultimately, I had signed nothing.

Yet something gave me pause. The precariousness of his situation should have enraged him, but his demeanour was too smooth, grim but unconcerned.

"What makes you think I will accept?" I asked.

"You will, Morgana," he said. "After all, where else would you go? Your nunnery would not be so kindly disposed without the Crown's

gold. Or would you prefer to stay here, under my watchful eye as
your lord father?"

The thought of seeing Uther Pendragon's sneering face every day
left me cold. True, there were other nunneries, the laws of sanctuary,
new names—but those places weren't St. Brigid's.

"Aside from that," Uther went on, "there is the tale of a particular
house knight, who left on urgent business. You see, unlike your lady
mother's misplaced faith, I believe you *didn't* lie when you claimed
you let a man have you, and the haste of this knight's departure
caught even the noble Sir Bretel by surprise. An entanglement with
a betrothed Princess seems a powerful reason to flee."

He is long gone, I wanted to shout, *free from your clutches, and for
that I am glad.*

But Accolon hadn't been gone long enough to get as far from Uther
Pendragon as he needed to be, if there even was such a place. And for
all he had done, I still loved him. It was innate, inescapable; I could not
wish him harm. So I kept silent, cool, stone like the walls all around me.

"Men don't *stay*, you understand, not for women like you," Uther
said. "So he won't be back. Unless I find him, of course. And I could,
very quickly. I have eyes and swords everywhere. No doubt it would
displease you to wake up one morning and find your paramour's
head on a spike."

My mind supplied the image, and I closed my eyes against it.

"Nothing is ever truly hidden, Morgana, not from me."

I forced my eyes open and stared Uther down. "It's not true. None
of it's true."

Uther leaned back, regarding me like a snake—poised, dead-
eyed—before it devours its prey whole.

"Maybe not," he said. "Only you know the truth, just as only you
know what paths you believe lie before you. I wonder, Morgana the
Wise, which will you choose?"

35

THE MEETING WITH my fate was set for mid-morning the following day. I went to the solar alone and circled the room until
there was a brief knock at the door and a page announced King
Urien of Gore.

Yet again I admitted to myself he was handsome. He wore a rich
combination of samite and summer linen in green and gold, a com-
plement to his glossy, sun-burnished aspect. Encircling his newly
barbered hair was a small coronet of knotty gold, his first acknowledgement of kingly status. To all appearances he was the most regal
he'd ever been, but his eyes were darting, unsure, marbles of ocean
jasper in the thin sunlight.

"My lady Princess." His fingers closed around mine, and I caught
the exotic scent of cinnamon and clove as he kissed my hand. Each
day his lips had travelled farther from my knuckles, landing softly
now near the ridge of my wrist. "You look very beautiful, as always.
Shall we sit?"

I took my usual seat opposite him, missing Alys's comforting
presence. He cleared his throat, then adjusted his towering frame to
face me more squarely.

"I know we haven't spoken of it, my lady," he began, "but I can
only assume you know of the . . . connection between us."

"I've heard rumours," I said.

He gave a rueful smile. "It is not how I wished it to happen, a courtship assumed. In case—"

Abruptly, he rose and stepped away, as if gathering himself. I followed, thrown off guard by his inarticulateness, the lack of confidence that was so far removed from our previous meetings.

"Please, my lord, speak freely," I said.

"In case it did not suit you, my lady." He swung around with a sigh, hands on his hips. "I know you have been given to me—betrothed—and I have promised men, gold and fealty in exchange for your hand. I did not anticipate our meetings would be more than mere formality, or that I would care how you regarded me. Yet I do care—I find myself in unusual need of your good opinion."

I had not expected such vulnerability, and my vain heart fluttered a little at the thought of his weakness before me. But I could not form words to appease him; it was not in me to speak of affection that wasn't there, nor could I tell the truth in the face of his heartfelt declaration.

King Urien reached out and took my wringing hands, holding them against the steady beating in his chest. "I know you will not believe me if I speak of love. It is too sudden. Nevertheless, my lady, you have me bewitched."

Stunned, somehow unable to pull away, I said nothing.

"I see it is not the same for you," he said. "A woman's sensibilities are delicate; she must be careful where she bestows her heart. But I hope, if nothing else, that my conduct in our meetings has at least been pleasant for you. Pray tell me it is so."

"Of course it has," I said quickly. "I've appreciated your courtesy very much."

"Then I must ask. Is it possible you could condescend to my rash, ill-expressed feelings and accept me as your lord husband? I truly want for no other Queen than you."

"King Urien, this is all so difficult." I drew my hands out of his grip, escaping back into the centre of the room, head spinning. What was the matter with me? It wasn't as if the question came as a shock; indeed, it was why I was in this room with this man at all, only a sliver of legal doubt and my own fortitude keeping my engagement from certainty.

But King Urien knew nothing of that, and seemed to have forgotten the supremacy of his status, putting his happiness at my mercy as if I'd ever had the prize to bestow or snatch away. The softest flutter of power whispered up the back of my neck.

"Flattering as it is, my lord," I said carefully, "my life's path is planned. I am returning to the nunnery, in service of learning and God."

He stood gazing at me, peacock eyes gleaming, forlorn and intense, wracked with what I quickly recognized as desire. The whisper of power became a pulse—disinterested, bodily, distinctly female—something I had never felt in the presence of a man.

"My lady, I know marriage is hard to imagine, and far from your intentions, but I assure you I want only your comfort and happiness."

Jewels, I supposed he would offer—furs, silks, the finest palfreys and hawks, gowns threaded with pearls, exotic perfumes like those he wore. And a crown, of course, gold and weighty with the promise of reflected respect. Little did he know, none of those things would ever compel me.

I inched closer with a detached, almost animal interest. His back straightened, as if I were a dangerous creature, worthy of caution.

"I know of your dedication to the abbey," he said, "and I wouldn't ask you to be without that which feeds you. Gore is a small kingdom, and unrefined, but it is prosperous. If you were its Queen, I would implore you to build yourself a library and procure all the books you wish. Call it a wedding gift, if I am not too forward in saying so."

This I had not foreseen, my body instantly drained of the cynical confidence that had filled me moments before. King Urien moved to within arm's reach.

"I may not have your book knowledge," he continued, "but I can read rooms and men, and it has not escaped my notice that you have been little better than confined these past few weeks. The High King's conduct—to put it politely—has not pleased me. In truth, the only thing that has pleased me in his court is you." He lifted his hand as if feeling the need to touch me again, but resisting the impulse. "In Gore, as my Queen, you would be safe, you would be valued, you would be *loved.*"

"But I do not love you." Finally it was out of me, the truth, hanging between us like damnation.

King Urien flinched, but barely, raising a brave smile. "I know, my lady. But perhaps one day you could. If nothing else, I will love you, and make it so you are pleased with me."

I sank back into my seat, where the whole thing had begun. Or maybe it didn't begin there at all and this course had been set for years, my fate sealed in the scribe's closet, hearing my mother resist the machinations of Uther Pendragon only to learn she had already succumbed. It didn't matter *who* stood before me like this; the fact was, it would always have been somebody not of my own choosing.

And it could have been worse. King Urien of Gore at least understood my dilemma, and saw me as a person, complex and whole. With him, I would be out from under Uther Pendragon, safe and cared for by a man whose only fault seemed to be that he was not the faithless knave I had fallen in love with.

Put next to my mother's existence with her bleak, marble passivity, the prospect of a new life in another place, with Alys by my side and our interests restored to us, seemed far from submission, or accepting a fate handed down. It felt like taking control.

"I have a woman to bring, possibly two." My voice rang like a high note from a lyre, in opposition to the floating sensation I felt. "And I won't marry in Tintagel, or any of Uther Pendragon's courts. These are my conditions."

A wide, handsome smile spread across King Urien's face. "My lady, does that mean . . . you accept?"

I put a hand to my neck, fingertips grazing the fine chain that held Accolon's coin next to my skin, affording me a bolt of doubt. But he was gone, and I was still here, and maybe I was saving us both. If Accolon would not die for me, then he could live for me instead.

"Yes, King Urien," I said. "I will be your wife."

36

WITH KING URIEN devoted to pleasing me, I secured his promise of the swiftest possible departure, arranged for the trunks to be packed, informed my mother that not a soul from the Royal Household was welcome at my wedding, then made myself numb. Within days, Gore's retinue was ready to leave Cornwall and so was I, along with Tressa, who surprised me and overjoyed Alys by agreeing to come with us.

One clear blue morning, I lit one last candle over my father's tomb, then rode away from Tintagel without a backwards glance.

The Kingdom of Gore lay in the far northeast, pushed against a rugged coastline once ravaged by Norse invaders. The road was hot and slow, air swampy with summer, smelling like rotting grass.

I saw him in every landscape—Accolon, my Gaul—amid rolling meadows, reclining on a riverbank, around corners in the manors where I laid my head. I sought his lithe form on the horizon, imagining his intention had always been to escape and spring upon me from the roadside, carrying us off so we could be together on our own terms.

"What are you looking at?" Alys demanded one day. "You're watching for *him*, aren't you?"

"Hush!" I hissed, though she spoke in Welsh and only Tressa was near enough to hear. I glanced guiltily ahead to where my future husband sat proud on his snow-white courser, chatting with his men. "What does it matter?"

She reached out for my wrist, as if holding me firm in the saddle. "It is no sin to wish yourself free of this marriage, but that coward wouldn't have vanished only to rescue you on some indeterminate road—he would have stayed."

"I know that," I said quietly. "But what can I do? I am not simply cured of it all."

"You can stop believing. What he did was unforgivable."

She was right, though it would not change me. How could I stop looking for someone I had never ceased seeking since I had first laid eyes on him?

*

A FEW DAYS short of Gore's southwestern border, the men raised the pavilions beside a lush oak wood, in the shadow of a ruined abbey. The huntsman soon discovered brown hare running abundant in the meadows, so Urien and his knights took off with their dogs to seek sport. Alys, Tressa and I were left to our own devices.

My two companions immediately took to the hedgerows to examine the plants of the northeast, kneeling side by side, murmuring contentedly to one another. Neither saw me slip into the trees.

I kept walking until the leafy branches receded, emerging onto a grassy stretch of riverbank. The water was low but clear, trickling over a flat bed of stones. I was watching it glitter in the still of the afternoon when there came a sudden disturbance from the opposite bank, the soft rustle of feet against a woodland floor. I glanced up to see a flash of shadow disappear between the trees: the hem of a flapping tunic, perhaps, or the sweep of a dark, long-haired head.

"Is someone there?" I crept forwards to the water's edge. "Accolon?"

I waited, listening. Hoping. From the trees, only silence.

Alys was right—believing in him was folly, a useless fantasy grow-ing ever more futile as we trekked upcountry. Standing there, waiting for Accolon's face to appear across the river, had thrilled me for the shortest moment before it hurt, only hurt, filling me again with the bone-deep ache of loving so much while being utterly betrayed.

It was time to stop this. The Gaul was not coming, and never had been.

"My lady, there you are!"

I whipped around to behold King Urien of Gore. He smiled, as if genuinely pleased to look upon my face. "Your women were alarmed to discover they'd lost you."

I shied away from the water, steadying myself against an enormous oak tree. "King Urien, you surprised me. I thought you were hunting?"

"The hares are too numerous," he replied. "I prefer a greater sport-ing challenge. I returned to ask if we might take a walk together. What brings you all the way out here?"

"I didn't realize I'd come so far. Though Lady Alys would have found me soon enough."

"I know, my lady, but I confess I felt compelled to seek you myself." He glanced down at me, eyes dappled with sun. "It is my duty, after all."

"And so you did," I murmured. "You came, and you found me."

King Urien stepped closer, head slightly tilted. "I will always find you; have no fear of that." He lifted his forearm, shirt sleeve folded crisply back against tanned, gold-haired skin. "Shall we take that walk?"

I took his arm, feeling it warm under my hand, tangible, and saw how I had been—aloof, distracted, chasing phantoms—when in the end, it was he who felt my absence, he who hadn't hesitated. I did not love him—it likely wasn't in me to ever love again—but just then, there was something else: a sudden want, shadowy yet undeniable, stoked by his great, immutable presence; or a need, darker still, to have him want me.

So instead, I drew him to me and kissed him on the mouth, deeply, forcefully, in a way I thought he would resist, given there had been no more than a peck on the hand between us. But he didn't shy away, returning the kiss with vigour, like he had been lying in wait for a long time. Large hands went quickly to my waist, gripping, pushing, driving me against the knotted whorls of the oak tree.

And I welcomed it: his physicality, the weight of his desire against me, this bold, instinctual connection we had so abruptly uncovered. King Urien's vehement embrace brought a sense of destruction that I suddenly craved more than anything, wanting only to vanish beneath him, every thought in my tired mind crushed into dust. If only he would go further, push harder, splinter the bark at my back so I could slip inside the ancient tree, absorbed into the soil with the burrowing roots. Then I too could dissipate into the wilderness, with nothing to feel but my essence in the wind.

I pulled him closer, and it was enough to give him pause. He drew his face away, staring as if shaken from a fever dream, and in his eyes, I saw it, beyond the hunger: the quick calculation, the sudden suspicion I was not a chilly, convent-raised maiden, needing gentle guidance into the ways of wives, that this woman he wanted—maybe even needed now—was nothing like he had imagined her to be.

And perhaps that was what I wished: for him to see me clearly, that I had chosen this life for reasons far beyond his understanding, and however he had bought me, he did not have mastery here.

"Well, my lord?" I said.

"You are not what I expected," he said. "Not at all."

"Does it please you?" I held his stare, daring him to choose what he believed, and decide at what cost he must have me.

His eyes flashed, and he leaned in to kiss me again. Short bristles of beard pricked the sides of my mouth, leaving it tenderized. Eventually, he stopped, grinning long and lazy, satiated. "You and I will do very well together, I'm sure. But not here, not like this."

He shifted off me, returning my breath. I peeled my back from the gnarly ridges of the oak and took one last glance at the river. It seemed farther away now, quiet trees blurring into shadow. King Urien of Gore stood nearby, fastidiously brushing himself down, then returned his blue-green gaze to me and bowed.

"My future Queen," he said, and smiled, sharp and knowing, like a fox might.

I decided I enjoyed it.

*

URIEN AND I said our vows almost immediately after our arrival in Gore, in his freshly painted ancestral chapel, followed by my coronation and a raucous week-long feast in the adjoining Castle Chariot.

The sprawling brownstone fortress sat atop a windblown hill, moated by a pair of ferocious rivers and accessed by two narrow bridges, so battered by the frothing torrents they were under near-constant repair. Beyond the outer walls lay nothing but moorland thick with heather, hardy amethyst beauty stretching for miles between rocky mountainsides and the occasional jutting tor.

This impressive but difficult location was where Urien preferred to keep his main court and residence. Travelling there held his liege-men in check, he explained; Chariot could be seen long before one reached it, and the hard, uneven ride always left men wind-chilled and tired. So grateful were they for a hot meal and soft bed that they tended to be amenable to anything he asked of them, and often forgot their own complaints.

It was a clever strategy, though at first it did not seem possible one could be anything but cheerful at Urien's court. His geniality was disarming from a King, his pride in presenting me as Queen flattering in particular. In public, his jovial demeanour both surprised and appealed to me; privately, it carried us quite easily into greater intimacies.

Our wedding night passed successfully and without suspicion. I made myself coy and let him guide my way, just as Morgause had once advised Elaine. And he was an excellent lover, more than handsome enough in face and body to warm the required senses, with an excess of charm and skill that ensured my enthusiasm was genuine.

Thereafter, when he rolled away to pour us wine, a few furtive pinpricks inside my thigh produced the blood required to convince the royal sheet-checkers that the marital bed was a righteous one. The widows of St. Brigid's told it true: there is nothing simpler than convincing a man of what he believes he already knows.

"Now you are truly mine," he said, with no concept of how wrong he was. But regardless of who had lain where before, in the view of the law and the Crown it was done. I was another man's wife.

Once the wedding celebrations were over, I had just enough time to settle in my new Queen's Chambers before my husband swept us off on a pleasure tour, stopping at the numerous well-kept manors of our estate and those of his liegemen, entertained with rich banquets, endless wine and good music. We spent long summer weeks deep in his Kingswood, under pavilions of green and gold, where we hunted by day, then feasted and danced the evenings away.

One night, as I joined the round with the ladies under a sultry twilight, I caught my husband looking at me, intent, half smiling, distracted from the group of knights he had been conversing with. At my glance, he left them, reaching into the whirling dance and pulling me against his chest as if nothing in Heaven could have prevented him.

I smiled, catching hold of his wandering hands. "Gracious, my lord, we are in company!"

"Let them look. They see your beauty, how impressive you are, how you become our Crown." He leaned in to kiss me, tasting of hippocras.

I put my fingertips to his torchlit face. "When I assemble my library, I will learn your laws, help you rule and make you an even more impressive Queen."

Urien grinned, wide and wolfish. "Whatever you say," he murmured against my earlobe. "But dare not keep me from taking you to bed a moment longer. I cannot bear it."

I laughed, liking that he could not bear it, so I took him away from the others to where we were best, falling asleep under silk, bareskinned and close, with the forest-scented breeze warm across us.

Eventually, autumn approached, and we circled back towards Castle Chariot for Michaelmas. For our last stop, Urien led us into the cleft of a green valley to a neat, solitary castle, built in dove-grey stone and wrapped in ivy. Deep woodland stood at its back, enclosing the estate in leafy peace; at its front, a yellow strand of beach stretched from one end of the sky to the other. Beyond, a brownish sea lurched in the wind—not wild and blue as I knew it, but still it was there to greet me each morning. Called Arrow Castle for its dark, pointed turrets, the place lodged itself within me as swiftly as its sharp-headed namesake.

Upon our arrival, Urien led me up onto the narrow outer wall to see the shivering high tide. "We don't have the coves and cliffs of Cornwall, but I thought Arrow, of all places, might bring you happiness."

"It's beautiful," I said. "And it does—make me happy." Such a feeling had not seemed possible months ago, sat opposite him in Tintagel's solar, hollow and devastated, but for one bright lacuna in time, it felt true.

From then on, as we travelled west along the coast road, I kept my gaze fixed on the fox trim of my husband's mantle and searched the horizon no more. Back in Castle Chariot, as the court rode in to inspect my worthiness, I looked out of the windows less and told myself it was all for the best.

Only in the depths of the violet-black nights, once my husband's weight had lifted from me and taken itself away, did I succumb to thoughts of him—Accolon: my heart, my lover, my betrayer—of all we had been to one another, and what we should be still. Alone, with my skin cooling from another man's touch, I slipped his Gaulish coin from my pillowcase and looped it around my neck, watching the golden god's head shuddering against the thunder of my heartbeat, scorched by his absence and the intensity of his memory, knowing I should have forgotten.

37

IT TURNED COLDER in Gore far faster than in Cornwall's easy climes. Darkness fell quick and profound, giving way to bleak, misty dawns and frost on the heathland, fires banked high with hardwood, furs thrown across shoulders and beds before the harvest moon had waned.

Public life was also not as I expected. Unlike the draped silks and gilded obedience of Uther's courts, Gore was a place of hard men and expensive wool—its pedigree old and prosperous, its court demanding and proudly informal. We sat to dinner at tables all on one level, and the minstrels played loud and bawdy into the night, mead and laughter flowing like the rivers outside.

The ladies put in my service were similarly confident, crowding into my low-ceilinged solar—rosy-cheeked, well-fed noblewomen in gowns the colours of two years ago, hair tucked into cauls in determined uniformity. They were covetous of their King—particularly the unmarried cohort, those Urien could have had—suspicious of my southern pedigree and, to a woman, named for flowers.

"Has my lady been praying for a son?" asked one, within a week of our introduction. They were enquiries I would quickly become used to—innocent in tone, bordering on intrusive.

"What a foolish question!" The snap came from Lady Flora, wife of Sir Aron—Urien's trusted Seneschal—and self-appointed leader of my womanly cabal. She was pert and yellow-haired, with huge blue eyes in a kittenish face, which in Gore passed for great beauty. "What else would the Queen be praying for?"

I glanced at Alys; she raised baffled eyebrows. "His Highness and I hope for many sons. Daughters too," I said diplomatically, and thought I had done well until that evening, when my husband leaned in at table, asking, "Did you tell the world and his dog that you wish to birth only girl-children?"

I stared at him, incredulous. He wasn't annoyed; in fact, he looked rather amused, as if I had predictably failed some Goreish test. "I said nothing of the sort, I—"

He waved it away. "Women's talk; it matters not. It's only natural they envy you."

"I don't want them to envy me. If I am to spend so much time in their company, it should at least be pleasing to us all."

"Then it's a lesson in ensuring their loyalty," he said. "Show them why they serve you. Let them know who you are."

The opportunity to take my husband's advice soon presented itself. Lady Flora had been complaining of cold in her bones for weeks, limping into the solar like a woman in her dotage rather than one still mired in her childbearing years.

"It was the fourth child," one of the flowers whispered. "Her poor ankles have never recovered."

"I *think* you'll find," Lady Flora said imperiously, "the damp in this castle is to blame, those rivers coursing so high. I have often told His Highness that holding court here is *most* inadvisable."

Several pairs of horrified eyes swivelled towards me, to see whether I was a Queen inclined to defend her castle.

"I can help you, Lady Flora," I said evenly, "if you would allow me to see."

The Seneschal's wife hesitated; evidently there had been specula-tion on my nunnery past. "Of course, my lady, if it isn't too much trouble." She propped her strained red ankles up on a footstool. One glance told me it was pressure from trapped fluid—in her case from pregnancy, but I'd seen it in the knees of St. Brigid's sworn sisters often.

"Happily, I have the perfect tincture for this," I said. "Some dried parsley, a little juniper and a prayer to St. Servatius. I'll have a vial sent to your chambers."

Lady Flora looked mildly surprised, but nodded and thanked me amid impressed murmurs from the other women. I heard little else thereafter, only brief confirmation that her feet had returned to their pain-free, milk-white delicacy.

Soon after, I was drawn aside at the evening meal by my husband, who guided me into a panelled window alcove instead of to dance as expected.

"There's something I must address," he said. "I heard you helped Lady Flora with some female-type trouble."

It threw me slightly, how he kept learning of these things. "Yes, my lord. I took your advice and showed them something of myself."

"That's *not* what I meant."

I frowned at his tone, and he softened, taking up my hands. "I meant letting them know you as Princess of Britain, now Queen of Gore. Set apart, deserving respect. This strange behaviour, claims of curing petty women's ailments—it is beneath you."

"These are skills I learned under godly teaching."

"Maybe so, my lady, but this is not a spinsterish nunnery. It is a royal court."

"Yes," I said tersely. "And I lived in a royal court for many years. They are my sworn women, and Lady Flora consented. There is no wrongdoing here."

"Not *wrongdoing*, my sweet. A mistake, that's all." He lifted my hands and kissed my fingers, face earnest. "You are learned, but dabbling with sickness, herbs, chants and suspicious elixirs? At best, it looks odd for a queen."

He was trying not to offend, but clearly he had no concept of the depth of my skills or their potential value to his kingdom. However, it was not entirely his fault: we had not known one another very long, we kept different chambers, and there had been precious little chance for private conversation. There would be time to enlighten him yet.

I nodded noncommittally. "I thought only to improve relations with my women, my lord."

My husband smiled in his wide, handsome way, as if satisfied we had come to marital accord with such ease. "My darling wife," he said indulgently. "I absolutely forbid you to waste time trying to please the likes of Lady Flora. Sir Aron can barely manage to do so himself." He hooked a finger under my chin, kissing me hard and deep, and for a moment I basked in it, letting myself smile. "You are the Queen, *my* Queen. That is all anyone needs to know."

*

INDEED, I WAS a Queen, and for the first year of our marriage I never had a moment to forget it. When one court left, we rode to another castle, our wedding tour of pleasure replaced by an endless trek of administration, formal appearances and political introductions. We spent Christmastide to Candlemas in Gore's capital city of Sorhaut, hosting feast after feast for various lords and clergy.

A round of spring hunts followed, where I rode part of the chase with a bird on my fist to impress the great and good of Gore. I was allotted a small hobby falcon, fit only for hunting dragonflies, and never given the opportunity to untie its leash.

Thereafter, it was back to Castle Chariot for Easter court, where I was awoken every morning by a chamber-mistress lunging at my head, untangling my night braids with one hand, a soaked piece of linen in the other to scrub my sleepy face. Once clean, I was bundled into my robe and escorted to a dressing room, where several flower-women awaited to dress me in whatever gown was deemed appropriate, only to do it all over again for the evening banquet.

It was not unknown to me, being handled in this way: I had been assisted with dress and hair my entire life without giving it too much thought. But since becoming a Queen I had been subjected to more chamber-women, more intimacies, more skin scrubbing, hair plucking and limb oiling than ever before. At the peak of my inaugural year, three or four gowns a day were draped or stitched around me, sleeves arranged to trail just so, hair tightly woven and coronets pinned, jewels clasped around my throat and wrists. For my wedding, the women had even pierced holes in my ears so they might dangle with Urien's golden boar heads.

When summer arrived, late and humid, bringing our first wedding anniversary and a tournament to mark it, I was exhausted in every way, so I made my first regal decision and proclaimed that only Tressa and Alys were permitted to attend my innermost chambers.

This authoritative act weighted the air in the solar, and Urien heard it as gossip, though he merely laughed at my boldness and drew me into his arms. At our tournament, he rode displaying my favour and won the joust, laying his sword and victory at my feet, an ostentatious show of husbandly devotion that amused me, made Alys roll her eyes and set the court whispering.

But by then, the only thing they whispered about was how I had not yet borne him a child.

38

LIFE DID NOT assume an easier pace until my second Michaelmas, when the court departed from Chariot without the Royal Household. Urien rode off for a fortnight's boar hunting, leaving his administrative proxy with Sir Aron and peaceful, unfettered time to me.

We were deep in autumnal chill, so Alys and I layered ourselves in wool and took to the heathland, where she delved into riverside gorse bushes and marshy tor ponds, happily slicing at roots and leaves, and I returned to one of my oldest loves—tracking through the sweet-scented heather in the wake of a flying bird.

We were accompanied by Kit, the deputy falconer—a shy, red-haired youth who had been plucked from Chariot's village due to his affinity with birds of prey. I did not yet have my own bird, but he chose for me a white-throated saker falcon, a large, proud creature of excellent accuracy, raised by Kit and, somewhat prosaically, named Joan.

One day, we were awarded rare clear skies, and Joan performed better than ever in the sharp light, flying low with flat precision, seeking the darting grey of partridge in the long grass. She was so close to the ground the heather blossoms looked like they would catch her breast feathers and throw her off balance, but she knew her surroundings to a hair's breadth. Suddenly, her head twitched and she thrust her talons out and struck, crushing something unseen into the grass. Her brown-and-white-flecked wings arced outwards, jealously guarding her conquered prey.

"Kit, did you see that?" I exclaimed. "The way she chooses her moment! The trust she must have in herself to strike from so little height. She is a marvel!"

To my surprise, he made no response. Usually, he was attuned to the bird's every move—her speed, her focus, whether her recall was too sharp or too sluggish—but now he stood a few feet away, gazing at the far-off rocky slopes.

The saker gave another jolting leap to secure her quarry, so I hastened across, calling her to glove. She had already begun impatiently plucking the partridge's feathers, and it took three firm whistles before she flew to my fist.

"Kit?" I called again. "Quickly, I need meat for her."

It stirred him, and he rushed over, handing me a scrap of rabbit from his pouch. The saker tore it from my fingers, inconvenienced.

"I'm sorry, Lady Morgan," Kit said. "My mind was twenty leagues away."

"You missed the strike. That's not like you. What's wrong?"

He sighed, eyes turning watery. "My sister, Elisabeth. She's been unwell for a while, but this past fortnight has grown much worse. Her back hurts, she's unsteady, short of breath, and has taken to her bed. She eats and drinks but cannot pass water. Lately her nose bleeds, many times a day."

"Has anyone seen her—a physician?"

"There's a wise woman two villages across. I rode miles last Sunday and brought her back, but Elisa refused to speak to her. The woman burned some blackthorn and said Elisa is being called to the Lord. Perhaps I should find it comforting she'll be in God's arms with my mother and father, but—" He cut himself off with a shuddering breath.

"You don't want to lose her," I said. "It's not a sin to say so."

"What isn't a sin?" Alys trotted up, sheathing her pruning knife.

Kit merely shook his head and eased the falcon from my glove, running a shaky hand across her wings. "The wind's getting up, Your Highness. I'll fetch the horses and take you back."

"Kit, wait," I called, but his gangling stride carried him out of earshot.

"Is everything all right?" Alys asked.

"Kit's sister is sick," I replied, pulling off my bird glove. "Have you anything left of your medical supplies?"

"Some unguents I made, loose herbs and several powders. But you cannot stride into the village and heal some unfortunate girl."

"Why not, if I'm able?"

Alys sighed. "You're the *Queen*. I'll go in your stead."

It wasn't a bad idea, but inside I flared, as instinctively protective of my plan as the falcon shielding her kill. "Her condition sounds mortally serious. What if Kit's sister dies and my hands could have saved her? I'd never forgive myself."

"I know," Alys conceded. "And if it's life or death, then you are the difference, not me. But what would the King say? He told you in no uncertain terms not to heal, even in your own solar."

"That was a long time ago," I said vaguely, though we both knew I hadn't sought to readdress the subject with my husband. "Anyway, Urien isn't here, is he? And there are greater things at stake than his opinion."

I glanced over my shoulder; generally, I refused the clanking presence of a guard, so aside from Kit's lad from the mews and our accompanying page, we were quite unsupervised. "Send the page to Tressa," I told Alys. "We need your medicinal supplies and two plain hooded cloaks to conceal ourselves. No one need know at all."

Alys's rueful smile was agreement enough. I beckoned to Kit, his shoulders sagging but his bird arm strong. The saker falcon sat poised, ignoring us, watching the skies.

"Kit," I said. "Take me to your sister."

*

CHARIOT'S VILLAGE STOOD beside the river, protected from the wind by a swath of evergreen forest and the castle's south-facing wall. Stone buildings dotted the hillside, leading down to a square of flattened earth with a central well, flanked by a smoking blacksmith's forge, a brewhouse and a gabled hut with a rough cross nailed above the door.

The home Kit shared with his sister was the topmost building, a squat stone-and-thatch cottage with a chicken coop and vegetable garden on one side. On the other was a fenced animal pen, empty and overgrown with weeds.

"My father kept sheep," Kit explained. "Grazed them up on the moor. Elisa has a lad she's fond of—he wants to take it up again, when he has enough for a wedding token and a flock. But with her as she is now . . ."

He pushed open the door, letting Alys and I pass into a single room, sparsely furnished but laid with flagstones and scrupulously clean. A ladder led to a galleried upper floor, and a decent fire burned in the hearth. A cot had been pulled close to the warmth, containing a young woman beneath a bundle of blankets.

"Elisa," Kit said softly. Her eyes fluttered wide, pale green like her brother's, her hair the same strawberry fair. "I've brought some ladies to see you—Lady Alys, and . . ."

"Lady Joan," I supplied. "We want to help you, Elisa. We're from an abbey in the south and know about healing."

Kit's sister groaned, shaking her head. Amid her protest, a gush of blood sprung from her nostrils, splashing onto the blanket. Alys rushed across, pressing her kerchief to the girl's face, murmuring comfort. Surprisingly, she didn't resist.

Alys began untangling the nest of blankets, flashing me a significant look.

I shook off the brown cape Tressa had borrowed from the hunts-man. "There, she has settled," I said to Kit. "What we need now is fresh water, if you'd be so good."

"I'll go to the well, my lady." Kit unhooked the boiling pot from the fire and left.

As soon as the door shut, Alys hurried over, fingers worrying the end of her braid. "There's a problem. It's more complicated than we thought."

I looked at the girl, huddled in her neater bed. "She's weak, granted. But I'll soon halt that bleeding, then lay hands against her back and help her pass water."

"You can't," Alys said. "She is with child. I'd guess about half-way gone."

"Sweet Lord! So that's why she rejected the wise woman."

"Most likely. And you can't simply lay on hands when she's with child. Who knows the possible effects, with another body in her body, another set of humours to account for."

I considered the fact with unease. "You're right—it's too great a risk. Logic also suggests that if her affliction is caused by pregnancy, it would recur until the child is born in any case."

"Or until they both die," Alys said. The door creaked open, and Kit came in with the pot full of water, which he took directly to the hearth. "What will you tell him?"

"Nothing yet." I pointed at Elisa. "Examine her—pulse, reflexes, listen to her chest. See if she will answer questions on her pain, appe-tite and so forth."

Alys returned to the bedside as Kit approached, a look on his face of such innocent optimism it pained me.

"I'm happy she's letting you tend to her," he said. "Have you found the ailment?"

I swallowed hard. "We will, given time. Now she's content, you must return to your post, so you're not missed. Come back at dusk."

"My lady, there are no words for how grateful I am." He bowed and left.

The guilt of his hope and my limitations burned in my gullet like bad wine. I walked unsteadily to the bedside.

"Clear-headed, and stronger than she looks," Alys murmured. "She's eating and drinking, despite not passing water, and her pulse is steady. However, her sleep is broken, and twice in the past few days her eyes have blurred. Elisa?" she said to the girl. "Lady M—Joan will speak with you now."

I took up the stool beside her. "I know this is difficult, Elisa," I said kindly. "Be assured, everything you say is private. You knew you were with child?"

Her eyes widened, then she deflated and gave a resigned nod.

"Was it . . . lawful?" I asked. "Did you wish it so?"

"Yes," she croaked. "I went to Thomas willingly . . . for love. We want to marry, but he doesn't know of this."

"Then married you are, by virtue of this child," Alys said.

If she survives, I thought grimly. "When did you last have your courses?"

"Midsummer, just before."

Alys's timings were correct, then. I put my palm to Elisa's forehead: no fever. The nosebleed had stopped for now, but she winced, shifting to ease her lower back. My hands tingled with the desire to banish the pain.

"Therefore, there's your inability to pass water, a deeply aching back, disturbances in your eyes and bleeding from the nose," I recounted. "Anything else?"

Elisa shook her head, then paused. "Nosebleed first, before my water stopped. But I'm not sure how long."

"It matters little," I said, rising. "Thank you, Elisa."

I took Alys by the elbow and led her into the shadows. "I can't recall anything that combines those symptoms."

"Nor I. But if she doesn't pass water soon, it'll poison her from the inside."

I felt a sharp pang of regret at my lack of childbearing knowledge. "Damn my bones! We are better than this—I know it."

I looked at Elisa, one arm cradling her belly and Alys's kerchief back at her face, stemming the resurgent blood. "She said the nose-bleeds came before her urine stopped. Irrelevant, I thought, but . . ." My mind sparked, thoughts cascading into place. "What if they aren't simultaneous occurrences indicating one illness, but a *progression*? Taken separately, they are simple to treat. The backache is from not passing water. What causes bleeding from the head?"

"An excess of blood within, creating pressure." Alys snapped her fingers. "Which would account for the blurring vision. Willow bark will treat it *and* ease the back pain."

"It'll recur unless she passes water. There's a patch of dandelions in the sheep pen. Dandelion tea should release the bladder and ward off infection. And if the willow bark halts the nosebleeds, any link between them should cease."

Alys's face brightened. "Then, if our theory is correct, the birth of the child will see it off altogether." She gave me a brief, exuberant embrace.

After a few hours, two doses of willow and a large quantity of dandelion tea, Elisa passed water several times, bravely and in great relief. Her nose stopped bleeding, and by the time Kit arrived, his sister was sitting up in bed, much restored, and I watched with joy as she told him he would soon become an uncle.

I glanced at Alys, who beamed with the same satisfaction. A soft, exhilarating flutter took up in my chest, like a small bird of memory awakening once more, whispering of possibility and new determination.

*

THE NEXT MORNING, I guided Alys deep into the East Wing, a little-used section of the castle belonging to the original fortress. Eventually, we came to a heavy door in a deserted passageway, which I pushed open to reveal a tall, chapelesque room with a row of narrow windows running down one side. The remaining walls were made of shelves, on ground level and along a large upper gallery. Dust swirled in the filtered light, not a sound to be heard apart from the far-off pounding of the rivers.

"What is this place?" Alys asked, gazing around.

"I found it over a year ago," I said. "But things have been so busy it slipped my mind. Urien's great-grandfather was a prominent warlord. Chariot was his battle fortress, and this his map room."

I could see it suddenly: manuscripts neatly stacked, reading before the fire on a cold day. "It's perfect for—"

"Your library," Alys said, smiling.

"*Our* library," I corrected, counting the shelves above our heads, imagining them swept free of dust, lit by large hanging lights, fresh parchment on the table alongside swan-feather quills and ink bottles of every colour. "Urien promised to build me one, and now is the time."

39

WE VISITED THE map room several times, taking Tressa with us and spending pleasant, peaceful days sorting cartographic scrolls, clearing shelves and inspecting if there was anything worth preserving. Most exciting was the discovery of an entire manuscript of blank pages bound with dark-blue leather, which we brought to my chambers for safekeeping, along with any other usable parchment. I sat at the long table, making a list of written works to acquire, listening to Tressa's soothing vowels as she sang old Cornish ballads I had not heard since Gwennol's time.

One evening, I left Alys peacefully teaching Tressa to write, and went directly to my husband's reception chamber. It would be the first I'd seen Urien in weeks; his hunt had dragged on, the quarry ferocious and elusive. I knocked, then entered without waiting for an answer.

He was standing before the fire with Sir Aron, presumably hearing what little news there was. Upon seeing me, Urien grinned and dismissed his liegeman at once, to Sir Aron's obvious vexation. They were close as brothers and always had been, but the Seneschal treated me with the same chilly, unconvincing deference that Alys used with my husband.

"My darling wife." Urien swooped over me, kissing me heartily on the mouth. I was used to him like this—warm, cheerful, charm unwavering despite the fact that he had me by law. "I've missed you. Are you well?"

"I am, my lord, and have too felt your absence. I was wondering if we—"

"Wine?" Abruptly he drew away, pouring for us both. I took a long draft; it was rich and deeply sweet, better than we generally drank. Urien warmed his cup against a candle. "Good, isn't it? Sent up from your father's buttery in London."

It threw me for a moment, then I realized he was referring to Uther Pendragon, and the smooth taste turned bitter in my mouth. I placed my goblet decisively on the table. "As I was saying, my lord. I wish to discuss something—my library. I've decided to have it here in Chariot."

A faint shadow crossed his brow. "But you already have one. I ordered the manuscripts sent from our other manors and put in the closet off your solar."

"And that was very generous. But there weren't many, and nothing relevant to my particular interests. I imagined a room much—"

A brisk knock at the door cut me off, and he swivelled towards it. "Come in!"

A page entered. "I beg your pardon, sire. A messenger has come urgently from Carduel. Sir Aron bade me bring him straight to you."

"Very well." Urien sighed and strode to the doorway as the messenger appeared, pink with cold and dressed in muddy Pendragon livery.

I moved towards the fire, out of earshot; I had no desire to become entangled with business from Uther's court.

Urien bent his head to the breathless rider, saying a few clipped words now and then. At length, he dismissed him with a sharp nod, then returned directly to the wine jug. He didn't offer me any this time; indeed, as he gulped it, he seemed to have forgotten my presence altogether.

"What did he want?" I asked.

My voice made him jump. He put the cup down with an exasperated sigh. "Uther Pendragon asks for another thousand men, barely two months after the last."

"Is that outside of the agreement you made?"

"Not entirely. The finer points were never negotiated." He paused, regarding me. "But *you* could send a note, suggesting delay. An entreaty from a daughter to—"

"I am *not* his daughter."

"Well, as good as."

"No, not 'as good as.' Besides, an entreaty from me wouldn't alter Uther Pendragon's mind. It might well make him ask for *two* thousand men."

He frowned, as if I'd just confessed to growing a serpent's tail. "You have no sway in his court? In private, with his easier nature?"

"Uther Pendragon has no easier nature," I said. "Regardless, I wouldn't prostrate myself before that man if the Holy Mother asked me to. You know that—it's why I'd never go to his court, even if invited. You yourself condemned his treatment of me on the day you proposed."

He recoiled slightly, eyes blazing blue green. Under his well-oiled beard his jaw was tight as a drum. Then, abruptly, he exhaled. "Indeed. I quite understand. You were fixated on something—continue."

I hesitated; he had gone again to the wine table, and I could not see his face. "The library, my lord. I thought the old map room—"

"These 'particular interests' of yours," he interrupted. "They don't involve any of that nonsense from before—strange claims about sickness, elixirs made from God knows what?"

So he still held that narrow, suspicious view. "I merely wish to start seeking books, my lord," I replied through gritted teeth. "It is my wedding gift, and we've been married over a year. A note to the Treasury with your seal is all you need give me."

"The Treasury, of course. First Pendragon comes for my men, now you want the keys to Gore's dwindling vault. I suppose all the jewels, furs and palaces are not enough?" His tone felt sharp, but when he turned, he simply swigged at his goblet and smiled without teeth. "There's no money for it, my lady, not yet. There are the books already provided; you read my letters and keep an eye on the household ledgers. You must make do."

"It'll be done slowly, not the library at Alexandria recreated in a six-month," I said. "Indeed I *can* read the household ledgers—there is money enough."

"There won't be if I'm forced to keep sending men at this rate. Every week there's another messenger at my gate, demanding more swords. I'd have lost fewer soldiers if I'd gone to war with him myself, rather than exchanging Gore's power for peace and a legacy."

I was the legacy, of course, bringing a royal pedigree higher than his—by status, if not by blood—to his rocky, wind-bruised kingdom. Back at Tintagel, I was the future he had wanted for his country. Now, the court chattered about our childlessness and questioned my worth.

"I see," I said curtly. "I apologize that my lord traded his men-at-arms for so little."

"No, by the saints, my darling wife." Urien threw his cup down and took hold of me, clutching me to his chest as if I might flee. "I didn't mean you were a mistake, or I regret for a moment that I married you." He spoke quickly, in the same faltering tones that had disarmed me on the day he proposed. "But if you have no way of reasoning with Uther Pendragon, then I cannot spare the gold."

I shifted in his tight embrace. "Didn't you consider Gore rich enough when you said it? You promised I could build a library, not merely reshelve the volumes you already had."

"A promise I thought fulfilled." He sighed, releasing me. "But even if there was gold—for books, all the work that desolate map room would need—why begin such a lengthy, expensive endeavour when it might not be of importance once we are blessed with a child? Instructing nurses, teaching our offspring the ways of court—there'll be much to consume your time. And how far away can God's grace be? Surely we must keep our prayers, and our focus, on Gore's heir, its future?"

I looked up at my husband's face—certain, persuasive, urging agreement—he of generous hospitality and good nature; a man I had not once minded lying down with, even if there were times in the deepest dark when I pretended it was not him. To his mind, this was not a broken promise, but a righteous question in need of a convincing answer: how could he be expected to give to me, when I had not yet given to him?

And in terms of my purpose in the eyes of kings and men, what argument could I possibly make?

40

WINTER PASSED IN a particularly dense cluster of court duties and feast days, narrow light and whirling flurries eventually giving way to slowly brightening skies and the scent of spring on the wind.

In the weeks before Lady's Day, the court had departed, and my husband had been called to the capital. The day before he was due to leave, I rose to a silver, wind-tossed morning, and wandered into Alys's antechamber, a cozy, blue-painted room connecting her and Tressa's quarters to mine. Three comfortable chairs were arranged around the fire, Alys's loom tucked away in the corner. A table stood under the window, Tressa's and Alys's wine goblets still on it from the night before, a small ritual they always shared before retiring to bed.

I smiled at the sight. They had been lovers for a long while, sleeping in one another's arms and going about their days in undeclared bliss. I didn't know when their courtship began—in Tintagel, I guessed, out of endless hours spent talking—and I often forgot how it was between them until reminded by some casual, intimate gesture, or two cups nestled together. Nevertheless, their quiet, natural bond had always bolstered me, knowing Alys had found her happiness despite the restricted life I had let her follow me into.

A squat door beside the table stood ajar, leading to a circular oratory lined with windows, capturing the indifferent northern sun like nowhere else in Chariot. Alys had sensed not only its potential, but an idle opportunity to defy my husband, securing pots, soil and cuttings with Tressa's help to create a flourishing indoor herb garden. I pulled the door open, filling the air with scents savoury and medicinal, evoking the courtyard garden in St. Brigid's.

I was deep in abbey memories when Alys rushed in. "Kit sent word," she said excitedly. "Elisa has been in labour since the early hours. She's hoping we'll go and help deliver the child."

She and I had visited a now-married Elisa several times in the past few months. I had confessed to my true identity on our second visit, which Elisa refused to believe until Alys produced a rosary and I swore upon it.

"Curses," I said. "Urien hasn't left yet. I can't."

Alys frowned. "You love this work, and it saved Elisa's life. You should be there. That the King still refuses to acknowledge your skills—"

"He will understand, in time," I insisted, though it rang hollower every time I said it.

"I'm not so certain. Remember Christmastide, when you offered to look at his shoulder strain? He preferred to go to his surgeon and wear a sling for a month."

Indeed he had, referring to even my wifely interest in his health as "improper for a queen." His assertions were gaining a significance I could little deny.

I sighed. "You must go. Take Tressa—she'll be a great help. Tell Elisa I'm sorry, and I assure her she could not want for more than you."

Alys looked suddenly apprehensive. "What if it goes wrong? I've never done this before, and without you . . ."

I pulled her into a brisk embrace. "You'll be wonderful, dear heart. Go, Elisa needs you."

"All right." She smiled nervously, heading back towards her bedchamber.

The sting of regret was almost unbearable. "Alys," I called, and she turned. "If it's life or death . . . send for me."

She nodded and disappeared, then I attempted to go about my day in patience. I walked the castle gardens, then Chariot's halls, watching the household close up the rooms one by one. Upon his return, Urien and I were riding directly to Arrow Castle with little company, for several restorative weeks without court business, councils or demands from Uther Pendragon.

Finally, I retrieved a jug of wine from the buttery and returned to the antechamber, drawn irresistibly to my old storage trunk. Beneath layers of summer linen and old mantles, I found it, well concealed: the *Ars Physica*.

I placed it on the table and eased open its cover, a shiver of possibility travelling over my skin. I had done no healing—except Elisa, months ago—and even then I had not felt the golden euphoria of laying on hands, though the thrill of thinking on a problem, using one's knowledge to bring forth a solution, had felt almost as powerful.

I was still reading in the afternoon's slanting light when I heard footsteps and animated chatter. The anteroom door opened, spilling in Alys and Tressa, high-coloured with spring chill and joy.

"I didn't think you'd return until nightfall," I said. "Did everything go as it should?"

"It went perfectly!" Alys replied. "Mother and child are doing well. The village midwife was glad of the help and taught us a great many things. Tressa was Heaven-sent. She talked Elisa through all her labour pains and was far calmer than I felt."

Tressa beamed. "It was a miracle, Lady Morgan. One moment just the four of us, then suddenly a new life in the world. I could hardly believe my eyes."

"I envy you both," I said. "What did she have?"

"A daughter, plump and beautiful." Alys glanced at Tressa, who nodded enthusiastically. "She named her Morgan."

My mouth dropped open. "But I wasn't even there."

Alys patted my arm. "You did more than enough. Elisa herself said, if you hadn't insisted Kit bring us to see her that day, she and *Morgan fach* wouldn't be here."

"Still, I didn't expect such a great honour as that. We should drink to them."

Tressa quickly filled three goblets with leftover wine.

"To Elisa, and little Morgan," I said. "May God bless them both."

Our cups met with a satisfying clink, and we took a deep, celebratory swig.

"I should get these capes back to the huntsman," Tressa said. "Show my face in the servants' hall." She reached across to unfasten Alys's cape, shifting her braid aside with a proprietary gentleness, and they shared a look of such deep affection I felt it, bittersweet in my chest.

After Tressa left, Alys drifted to the oratory to check on her herbs, and I returned to the *Ars Physica*, mulling over the day's reading: no words that could have saved Elisa from a complicated birth, or tell me why I had so far failed to beget a child.

I placed my hands over my empty abdomen, as I had many times before, feeling for the fault. Nothing—no damning blockage, or poison swirling in my womb, no discernible reason why it hadn't happened. And yet, even if I could sense something, what use if I didn't have the knowledge to understand what it meant, as I did with cuts and burns, or the lung fever? More importantly, *why* didn't I know what was so fundamental to life?

"What are you looking at?" Alys peered over my shoulder, smelling faintly of mint.

"This." I flicked past endless sketches of heads, limbs and organs in male figures. "One—*one* single diagram of a woman's body, displaying a child within, and little comment beyond basic anatomy. It's no wonder we were at a loss with Elisa. How could we have known what to do?"

I could hardly believe I had not seen it before, this flaw, this enormous crevasse in all I had worshipped for years. "Aren't we constantly told our bodies are troublesome, complicated, our insides a dangerous tangle compared to men's? Yet it is nowhere in this book, nor anything we've studied. We are half of this living world, and no one has ever seen fit to write us down."

"Perhaps there are manuscripts we've never seen with more detail?" Alys suggested.

"There should be a book just for that! I've read more words than I care to remember about men's peculiarities—why aren't there volumes dealing purely with the afflictions of women? God knows there are many ways for us to die." I stopped, nerves prickling, sparking with possibility. "We should do it, Alys—write the book on women's bodies. It could change the course of physic and healing for all time."

Alys regarded me with a peculiar, wide-eyed expression, hopeful and despairing all at once. "It's an incredible idea. But how could we? Without other manuscripts for reference, real cases? Your husband—"

I waved it away. "Forget about him. Urien says I can't heal in public or have gold to procure books. He didn't say I couldn't write down what I already know. We have the blank manuscript from the map room, our experiences with Elisa, enough knowledge from St. Brigid's to keep us busy for a while. In the meantime, I'll keep seeking a way to change my husband's view."

My mind surged ahead of us, to a future where lives were saved—lives like ours, Elisa's, countless women snatched from deaths the city leeches and court surgeons deemed inevitable. "Imagine it, Alys—our own book. A true purpose, a legacy. What do you say? Shall we do it?"

"Of course!" Alys said, then fixed me with a shrewd look. "On one condition. You're not to go cutting your hand again. Agreed?"

I laughed, turning up my left palm. The silver scar grinned at me, neat and reminiscent. I could have long ago healed it away, but it was not a blemish—it was a reminder, of what was possible if I had courage and kept faith with my intelligence. All we must do was begin.

4I

URIEN AND I went to Arrow Castle as planned, entering a cocoon of private calm and unexpectedly good weather. We hunted the woods, shot arrows in the walled garden and spent languorous nights together, often right through until morning. Our togetherness, the amity we rediscovered, once more had me believing that my husband could understand me, that I could bring him around to appreciating the woman I had always been.

But such ease was mere novelty. In truth, something in us was broken; our previous differences had formed an irreparable crack in our marital accord, which fractured with startling speed when we returned to Chariot and I had still not fallen pregnant.

My husband became suddenly impatient, disappointed, unexpectedly cold; his visits to my bed dwindled, robbing me of the brief oblivion his body had once brought to my own. He stayed away most of the summer and autumn—hunting, feasting, every snatched moment spent cantering through the trees in search of blood sport—while I was confined to court and castle, rejected, exposed to gossip, denied even the pretence of sitting as Regent. Sir Aron the Seneschal held more power of rule than I did.

By our third, then fourth, wedding anniversary—occasions we did not mark—I had seen Urien so little that getting with child would have been a miracle anyway. Our encounters were infrequent, mandated by God, efficient enough but laced with an air of lordly disappointment, ultimately ineffective. Eventually, I paid no heed to my cycles and told only Alys whether they aligned to the moon or not.

Marriage is like the wind, the widows had told us. *Husbands blow warm, then cold, gusting elsewhere, then sweep back in with a sensibility of their own. It is pointless to question the wind.*

But I was of the sea, turbulent and unceasing; it was not in me to accept platitudes and inconstancy.

Then came a February day when Urien summoned me to his chamber under the auspices of a private dinner. "Did you know there is a girl-child in the village named after you?" he demanded over stuffed capons.

"I am Queen of Gore," I replied offhand. "I'd imagine many children will be named for me."

"Maybe," Urien said. "But I heard a rumour of holy women in the village, dallying with herbs and chants, like you once did. You hardly need telling, I hope, how damaging it would be to my Crown for you to associate with those far beneath your status."

"I don't know, my lord," I said tersely. "Do *you* think I need telling? Or must I reassure you *yet again* I would never do something unworthy of me?"

He contemplated me for a moment; I made my eyes cool and still as a mountain lake. Eventually, he dropped his gaze and speared a sliver of meat with his knife. "Forget I said anything. Of course my own wife would not disobey me."

"Perish the thought," I retorted, and I knew then that there would never be any convincing him; that lying about Elisa and my endeavours came from a survival instinct, written deep into my bones. Any possibility of truth between Urien and me was over.

So instead, Alys, Tressa and I acted in secret, any way we could. The herb garden grew crowded and impressive, our notes and discussions gradually turning into pages of our manuscript. Alys's antechamber became our makeshift library, classroom and apothecary, full of ink bottles, scattered parchment and pouches of ingredients for mixing remedies.

We continued to go to the village whenever Urien abandoned me at Chariot for another of his jaunts. Elisa had far better luck with children than I did, producing twin sons, as predicted by Alys, whose keen ear had discerned two galloping heartbeats. Alys and Tressa were present for the birth, and Elisa graciously allowed us to record our observations.

One day, there was a knock on the farmhouse door, and a pregnant woman of similar age entered, asking for the "holy ladies," seeking help for bleeding gums and constant itching. Word travelled, and we diagnosed and treated widely, giving out tinctures, recipes and advice for various afflictions. I even laid on hands, secretly, mildly, when there was no childbearing involved. Whether they suspected my identity I never knew, but it didn't concern me; we were women bonded, complicit in troubles the world hardly acknowledged. We knew how to hold our secrets close.

But to truly move our work forwards, we still needed books. And for books, I needed money. Of all the things being Queen provided, coin was not one of them. Gore had contrived to stay rich, despite Uther Pendragon's war demands, but without my husband's note to the Treasury I would never see a mark. Every jewelled circlet, silk mantle or fur trim was ostensibly a gift, my gowns, horses and perfumes kept track of in a meticulous Royal Inventory. Even the needle and thread I used to stitch my husband's shirts were ordered directly through Urien's counting house.

The only gold I had at my disposal was the portion allowed each month for benevolences. The amount was checked in and out as closely as a cat watches a caged bird, but I knew, somehow, there lay my freedom.

After a few months' unsuccessful plotting, I was dividing up the amount among several indiscriminate holy houses and thinking of my mother—how her generosity to St. Brigid's had ensured my place and education—when I hit upon the answer. I was, in fact, buying *something* with my charity, the one thing more valuable than gold itself: favour, and influence, from the exact places I needed it.

I began to write letters, polite, veiled words that no messenger, husband or any of his solar spies could interpret as more than a generous, God-fearing queen, thinking fondly of her younger years among nuns. At length, I discovered what places had libraries and diverted greater donations there, soliciting lists of their books, lauding the virtue of holy education. I had enjoyed one myself, I wrote, and found it formative in becoming the good Queen I now was.

Two convents even had successful infirmaries, and to them I redoubled my praise, detailing how our physicians wished to study great healing works, and to bestow such a gift in the name of God would please me indeed. By then, these nunneries had reglazed their transepts with my gold, and soon enough the manuscripts began arriving—Galen, Aretaeus, Soranus of Ephesus—blazing torches on the path to enlightenment.

Tressa had charmed Chariot's gatehouse clerks, and they sent word directly to her when any delivery was made bearing my name, artfully avoiding Sir Aron's diligent record-keeping. And so the books kept coming—innocent, unasked for—tokens of respect from a holy house to a charitable and virtuous queen, well known for saying her prayers.

42

MY FIFTH WINTER in Gore took hold in its usual way, summoning hard frost and a wind like knives. Christmastide would be difficult: I had no child and an indifferent husband, my personal endeavours—however rewarding—were arduous secrets, and the year ahead looked no different. I would be twenty-five in March, but felt I had lived for an entire century.

Afternoons in the solar had been dull but easygoing, Lady Flora having left Chariot for her own manor. One frozen, sluggish day, I excused the ladies and retired to my chambers in solitude; Alys had stayed with Tressa, who was in bed with minor stomach cramps. I would see how they fared, then take a long hot bath before dinner.

The skies were already darkening, and someone had been in to light the candles in my reception chamber, illuminating two large rectangular objects on a table by the door. Hand-cut pages peeked from between pristine covers of green leather, gold vines twining around the immortal name Hippocrates.

I almost cried out for joy: here was the greatest boon a holy house could have given me. I had been seeking, wanting, *dreaming* of these volumes since my earliest days of learning—pages on medicine, anatomy, illnesses, women's afflictions and healing from one of the greatest physicians of recorded time. The year ahead already felt brighter.

Before I could examine them, a soft movement sounded behind me, and I swung around to the unexpected sight of my husband in a chair, perusing a letter by the light of the blazing fire. My gut lurched; had he noticed the manuscripts?

Urien looked up. "My lady, there you are."

I moved sideways, obscuring his view of the books. "My lord, I did not expect you. Did you send word asking for an audience?"

He smiled, eyes back on his correspondence. "Need we be so formal as that?"

It was not the response I had anticipated, given that our private meetings had been largely formal for a while now. But something about his smile struck me—amused, half-sly—and it occurred to me his thoughts might be on quite another bent. His wind changing, perhaps, blowing again in my direction. My pulse quickened, which galled me no end.

"No, my lord. But should I guess at the purpose of this visit?"

He rose, flicking the letter into the flames, parchment curling in on itself until it became ash. The hearth was banked unusually high, heat roaring against the side of my face.

He stood over me, handsome and keen-eyed in the firelight. "Try," he suggested.

Taking him to bed would keep him away from the manuscripts, I reasoned; nothing but necessary distraction. I placed my hand on his belt. "Let's see—it's been weeks since we were last man and wife . . ."

"Oh God, *that's* what you thought?" he scoffed, stepping away from my touch. "No, my lady. I am not at liberty for such things."

Humiliation burned in my chest, quick like dry grass. "You are not at liberty to love me, you mean. All these years I've trusted in your regard."

It was for the books, I assured myself, to keep my secrets. But part of me was lying—in truth, he had pricked my vanity, denying me

the little power I thought I held over him. How shamed I felt to be
reduced to this, begging for the touch of a man I never truly chose,
base needs of the flesh destroying my last scrap of pride.

Urien sighed in irritation, turning away. "That sort of talk is not
becoming for a queen. Regardless, I cannot. I will soon be leaving
again and must prepare."

"I remember when a summons from Christ himself wouldn't have
stopped you from lying with me," I spat. "Perhaps you are far less the
man you were."

He rounded on me savagely, thrusting an accusing finger in my
face. "Or maybe I see little point in having dealings with you if you
cannot keep a child in your belly."

I had long suspected it, but hearing it aloud still hit me like a
horse kick to the ribs. I stared at him in haughty disbelief.

Urien put his hands on his hips, stalking back and forth like a
caged beast. "And why *is* that, I've been wondering?" he continued.
"You're fairly young still, healthful. In fact, I've never known you to
be unwell. Perhaps there's something . . . unnatural about you. When
added to odd tales of 'holy women' in the village, curing ills with
trickery, it all begins to seem very peculiar."

He paused, no doubt waiting for me to fall on my knees and
confess. I tilted my chin up, curling my lip as if he was ridiculous.

"Then today," he went on, "I was in my council chamber, when
what is brought . . . ?"

In a few long strides he was around me. I watched with horror as
he went directly to the side table and picked up both manuscripts,
holding them away from his body as if they might bite.

"*You* brought those here?" The exclamation was out of my mouth
before I could stop it. "How . . . ?" But of course: lying on her sick-
bed, Tressa would not have received word from the gatehouse clerks.

"Ah, so you *do* know what they are."

I folded my arms. I hadn't bought them; there was nothing to damn me if I didn't reveal it. "They are a gift from a holy house, thanks for my benevolence. I can hardly control what they send."

"Maybe," he sneered. "But quite a coincidence, is it not, that the pages contain precisely your former area of interest? I wonder now if this unhealthy obsession with knowledge, libraries, the stuff of child-less nuns, has subverted a wife's natural purpose and prevented you from giving me an heir all along."

How I didn't strike him I'll never know. But there was more at stake than my pride or his ignorance; there was Elisa, Alys and Tressa, our manuscript and all the antechamber held. I could keep our secrets as long as was needed.

I managed a shrug. "Then it is a coincidence."

Urien looked down at the books as if the bindings would reveal my lie. "If that's the case, my lady," he said slowly, "then you have no need of them."

Before I could blink, he strode past me and with one violent thrust threw both manuscripts into the fire.

"*No!*" I screamed. I flung myself towards the flames, ready to pull them out, even if my hair burned, my skin, my whole self.

Urien snatched up my wrist, holding me back as I struggled and protested. "Careful." His voice was rich with mockery. "You wouldn't want to come to harm over something so *inconsequential.*"

I glared up at him. There was no pleasure in his face, only grim determination in his clenched jaw, and a lack of anything at all in his eyes. I tried again to pull free, but he gripped me firm to his side. He wanted me to watch, to see the pages ignite and blacken, and under-stand his power once and for all.

"Lord knows I have *tried* to be reasonable, *tried* to guide you to the right path," he said. "But if you are determined not to see sense, let me be absolutely clear. From now on, any of *this*—secret books, seeking knowledge, toying with the unnatural like some ragged crone—is completely forbidden. If you deviate from these commands, as your King and lord, I will have no choice but to view it as an act of treason."

"Treason!" I exclaimed. "What will you do? Lock me in a high tower? I am already your prisoner."

His fingers tightened around my wrist. I refused to cry out.

"You ungrateful harpy," he snarled. "After all I've given you . . . How dare you!" He threw down my arm in disgust. "I don't have time for dramatics. You are my wife and will obey my word. There is nothing else." With a jerk of his shoulder, he spun on his heel and stalked towards the door.

"Don't walk away from me, Urien," I warned. "If you do, I'll—"

He stopped and looked back, face glowing with contempt. "You'll *what?*"

I froze, teeth bared.

He pulled the door open so hard it slammed against the wall. "I thought so. All fire and no substance. If you're not careful, my Queen, one day you too will burn yourself out."

43

WHEN HE HAD gone, I fell to my knees and watched my manuscripts turning to leather-scented ashes, the wisdom of ancient worlds charred and smoking, disappearing up the chimney into the Goreish wind.

I might have sat for hours, staring at the dazzling flames, but for my wrist finding its throbbing voice, swelling and red with his fingermarks. I looped my hand around the injury, circling the bones. The damage was delicate, a petal-thin heat under my touch; there, bruises would come. Then, beneath, something worse—a pair of slim fissures Urien's hard hands had left behind. My husband had broken my wrist.

Fury rushed up from my chest, bursting comet-like into my head. How dare he mark me in such a way—or any way! I got to my feet and paced, trying to control the hot need to react, to avenge, channelling my concentration to the place I most needed it: fixing myself.

The warmth gathered and the twin fractures knitted together in a golden surge. I rotated my newly painless wrist, savouring the pleasure coursing over my fears, leaving determination in my hard-beating heart. Preservation was my task now: Alys, Tressa, our makeshift library, our manuscript and my own sanity.

I ran through to the antechamber. The door to the herb garden stood open, letting in the faint yellow glow of torches below. On

the table sat our blue-bound manuscript, the only copy of years
of work, which my husband would have no compunction about
burning.

I was shoving the manuscript right to the bottom of a storage
trunk when Alys appeared, stopping dead.

"Urien found out about the manuscript deliveries," I said breathlessly, piling an armful of fabric on top of the *Ars Physica*. "Two
Hippocrates went to him by mistake. He threw them in the fire,
threatened me. Physic, healing, books, any of it—he's decided it's
treason. We must hide all this."

I slammed the trunk shut, locking it tight, then turned to Alys.
Her face twisted in sudden despair.

"My God, Alys! What's wrong?"

"It's Tressa. Her stomach pain's worsening. I've tried everything I
know, pain drafts, begging the saints. Nothing works. She's shivering,
gasping, starting to take fever."

"Why didn't you call for me?"

"They said you were with the King. And now he's forbidden you
to heal, and—" An anguished cry from the next room cut her off.
She swung around. "I must go to her."

Urien could come back, my mind warned. *If he catches you defying
him, you'll be on trial by morning. Or worse.*

"I'm coming with you," I said.

"But the King—"

"I don't care about him."

"It's *treason*, Morgan. You can't . . ." Her breath shortened, coming
hard and jagged.

I took her panicked face in my hands. "Tressa's in my household.
I can lay eyes on her, can't I? Come on."

When we entered the bedchamber, I was alarmed to see Tressa's
state. She reared from the bed, vomiting into a bowl so violently it

came up streaked with blood. Purged, she collapsed onto the pillows, eyes rolling back in her head.

Alys ran to her, frantically patting her cheek. "My love, can you hear me?" She stared at me across the bed. "I can't make her wake."

I picked up Tressa's limp wrist, feeling her racing pulse. Her forehead was hot as a hundred suns. "Tressa," I said calmly, "open your eyes, nod, anything. Show you're still with us." Nothing, not even a flicker of her eyelids.

Alys dropped to her knees. "Oh God, Morgan, she's dying. What will I do? I love her too much to lose her—she can't die." She slumped forwards, sobbing like a lost child against Tressa's unmoving shoulder.

I had never seen Alys this way—devastated, abandoned of hope, so unlike the wise, unshakeable woman I had always relied upon— and it frightened me more than I thought possible. It wasn't fair; they were good, and devoted, yet destruction had come for them anyway. Sickness was a force without justice, and often powerful, but it would not have its cruel way with them.

"You're not going to lose her," I said. "I'll save her, or the Devil take me."

I pressed my palm against Tressa's forehead, sending a brief surge of light into her clouded skull. Instantly she stirred, throwing an arm across her belly and moaning in Cornish, "It hurts . . . won't . . . stop."

Alys jumped to her feet, snatching up Tressa's hand. "I'm with you, my love. Just stay awake."

"Keep talking to her," I said. "Tressa, I'll stop the pain. Hold Alys's hand, and I will fix everything."

I pulled back her nightgown to expose her pulsing belly, skin oyster grey and sheened with sweat. As soon as I touched her, it hit me: wrongness, poison, seeping into Tressa's abdomen like a river burst free of its banks. Before long it would be in her blood proper, running too fast for me to catch it.

But not yet. Tensing my fingers, I caught the rippling badness by its slippery edges, holding fast and taking up my chant. For our new work, I had mastered the black book's formula using language alone, honing the incantation until it was sharp and potent, no longer needing belladonna ash or the onset of twilight.

The poison yielded to me more easily than expected, pulling inwards at my word, shrinking under my fingertips until it was reduced to a sphere of darkness at each hip.

"Alys," I commanded, "take the knife from my belt and prick her beneath my thumbs."

Alys's hands shook as she unsheathed my father's falcon-shaped knife and held the point to a candle flame. By the time she made the incisions, she was steady as a rock. Thick black spots erupted from the cuts in Tressa's sides, pouring into the air and dissipating until they were nothing but wisps of smoke. I waited until there were no more, then chanted the small slits closed.

Tressa's eyes flickered wide.

"She's awake!" Alys cried. "She's cured, she's—"

"No," I muttered. "The poison came from somewhere. I need to find the source or it's not done."

I passed my hands over her abdomen again, hovering, seeking. "There! A tiny rupture, deflated. It must have expanded and burst, spilling waste forth."

"Is that bad?" Tressa croaked.

"Not now it's found." With a flourish of my fingers, I willed the rupture closed, layers of light climbing my spine. One more breath was all it took.

"It's done," I said.

"I . . . know," Tressa replied. "I can feel it, somehow."

"Mother of God, I thought you were gone from me!" Alys threw her arms about her beloved's neck, renewing her sobs, for happiness this time.

And I stood, coursing with joy, knowing that this—good healing, my purpose fulfilled—was the only existence worth having.

Treason be damned.

*

TRESSA SOON FELL asleep, and I sat with Alys as the candles burned low, sounds of mealtime echoing faintly up from the Great Hall.

"Thank you," Alys said suddenly. "I know what you risked by saving her."

"I've risked nothing I wouldn't give a thousand times over," I said. "I love her too, as I love you. I will never hesitate where you are concerned."

"I owe all of my happiness to your bravery. Both of you." Alys returned her gaze to Tressa, kissing her hand. "Do you know how she and I truly began? When she was learning her letters, I used to recite poetry to her. There's one about a love that grew in springtime, which became strong enough to bloom all year round, and she always asked for it in particular. One day, she came to the herb garden, handed me a tiny scroll and said, 'This is for you. Every word of it is true.' She'd copied out the verse—it must have taken her an age—and for once in my life I didn't have a wise word to say, or dare hope at its meaning. But she dared for the both of us and kissed me, there and then."

She brushed a lock of hair from Tressa's serene face. "I can't say if I ever would have done the same. Every time I enjoyed our closeness, or imagined she felt as I did, I thought only of the obstacles—that we were women, the gulf in our status, that acting on it might be taking advantage. My supposed sense could have prevented it all."

"Tressa left Cornwall to follow you to the cold wilds of the northeast," I said. "You would have found your way. Anything is possible where there is great love."

Alys gave a sad smile. "I don't think I truly understood how you felt losing Accolon until I stood here watching Tressa almost torn away from me. You have withstood so much."

A strange pressure formed in my throat. "I didn't lose him; he left me. You and Tressa have a true marriage—trust, loyalty, a bond that cannot be broken. There's no comparison."

"And what of your marriage? By your husband's decree, you have just committed treason. Can he really threaten such a thing?"

"He can threaten anything he wishes, and the law would doubtless side with him. The easiest way for me now would be to simply obey. But when I imagine giving up physic or seeking knowledge, I . . . cannot fathom it."

"What are you saying?"

"I'm not sure yet," I said. "Contemplating it feels impossible. But as it stands, I don't see how I can stay in Gore."

44

ONCE IN MY bedchamber, I found myself in possession of a profound and eerie calm as I slipped beneath the mink-lined coverlet. The cool weight of the Gaulish coin stirred up thoughts of Accolon as it often did, but my mind slid pleasantly past them, and I fell into a dreamless slumber. How my marriage—and indeed my entire life—would proceed from here I did not know, but Tressa was saved, and my conscience was clear.

I awoke at dawn, body still light from the aftermath of healing, my mind tenacious. Was it possible to leave Gore without Urien hearing of it? And if so, where could I get to safely on a winter road? The nearest nunnery was weeks away.

Then there was my family: my mother was an impossibility while Uther drew breath; my sisters I had not heard of beyond gossip. Elaine had always been better disposed towards me than Morgause, but Garlot was small and peaceful, priding itself on alliances. Elaine's great pragmatism would rightfully balk at the idea of Gore's army hunting me down, and I would never bring such trouble to her gates.

I had just left Tressa—sitting up and breakfasting well under Alys's relieved supervision—when a page knocked, bringing the message that "your husband, the King" had summoned me to a private audience.

"Tell him he may come to my solar," I replied, and went directly there, circling the long table and biting the skin around my thumbnail until it bled. Eventually, there was a soft tap on the door, and Urien entered.

That he had knocked was something of a surprise, the way he edged in even stranger—eyes downcast, shoulders drooping, hovering far away from where I stood beside the hearth. He was dressed in the green and gold of his house, which usually became him, but today his ashy pallor fought with it, affording him a sickly look. His sunken eyes struck a small chord of satisfaction in me at the idea he hadn't slept.

"My lady, many thanks for receiving me."

"I cannot prevent it, my lord."

He slunk across the room with an air of contrition I had never seen, and for a perverse moment I felt sorry for him. In my benumbed state it did not feel like he was my husband at all, merely a handsome stranger sent to account for some infraction of manners.

"I wish to apologize for my words last evening," he said. "They were in no way how a king should speak to his queen."

Still I felt nothing. "Very well," I said, for I could think of nothing else.

"Do not hold it against me," he pleaded. "It is not what I feel, not truly." He sighed with unlikely anguish. "I know you will give me a healthy son one day, and a houseful more. My own mother had her struggles—six years before she birthed me. Gore's heirs take time, so do not think I harbour a grudge."

Childbearing was to be the basis of his atonement, then—no mention of the burned manuscripts, or my wrist. Perhaps those were lessons he believed I must learn.

"And treason?" I asked.

"I was angry. How could I—my own wife?" He held his hands out, imploring. "It's never been right, with the way we began. The High King's endless demands, while Gore wasted away. I let you drift from me, blamed our marriage for it all, when perhaps it was Uther Pendragon, the circumstances we were forced to live under. It will be different now—*I* will be different. But I must be forgiven."

I did not see Uther's relevance, but further argument was futile. "I am bound over to do so, as any wife must forgive her husband."

His expression was one of utter perplexity; he had clearly expected far worse. He would ask if he could come to me next, I supposed, reaffirm my forgiveness in the bedchamber, as we always had in the wake of disagreement. But the plea never came; he turned towards the fireplace, rubbing the scar on the bridge of his nose.

"I have something to tell you," he said uneasily. "Uther Pendragon is dead."

I fell forwards at once, and to his credit he caught me, swooping underneath my stumbling form. It wasn't a full faint, just enough blackness to set me falling, followed by an instant return to reality that left me nauseous and shuddering.

Urien draped me into a chair, crouching down. "Darling, are you all right? I know you and the High King weren't on the closest terms, but it must be terrible to hear."

My instinct was to retort that Uther and I weren't on any terms but hatred, given he murdered my father and forced himself on my mother, but instead I asked, "How do you know he's dead?"

"A herald came from Carduel just before dawn, bringing a letter with the High Priest's seal. The King was very ill, robbed of the use of his limbs and unable to ride into his next battle. His seer said the army was certain to lose if he did not show his face—"

Cold rushed up into my scalp. "His seer? The sorcerer Merlin?"

"Yes, so the letter says." Urien regarded me in amazement. "By God, do you know him? His legend is so great I was never sure if he existed or not."

I shielded my mouth against another hitch of nausea. "Oh, he exists. But recently it's been widely assumed he was dead." Indeed, I had hoped it was true almost as much as I had prayed for the death of Uther himself.

"Only men die," Urien said grimly. "Rumour has it the great and powerful Merlin was sprung from the loins of a demon."

I shivered and my husband moved closer, rubbing my arms in a firm, soothing rhythm. "Do you see now, my sweet? When I spoke of things being different—it is a new beginning for Gore, for us."

"Tell me how Uther died," I said.

"The famed Merlin convinced the King to go to battle on a litter to command his men, and his army was victorious. They got him back to Carduel unharmed, but he died later that evening. A great warrior to the end."

Sour tears rose in me like floodwater. A hero's death it had been after all: no reckoning, no life cut short, his abuses forgotten. It would have been painful, probably, but with the best of care, surrounded by his fawning acolytes as he stomped off to meet his maker. I wasn't even certain God would deal with Uther Pendragon justly.

"Did the herald speak of my mother?" She was free of him at last; I could go to her, use Uther's death as a reason, then never return. She had armed men, more than my husband did.

"Briefly. The Queen has gone into seclusion to mourn. They didn't say where. She will retain the style of Queen and some of her household, but she will not rule."

So she had no army and had gone into hiding—wise, but it was no help to me. "Who *will* rule?"

"That remains to be seen. The High King named no successor and has no known issue." Urien stood, stretching his limbs. "The tribal Kings will be rattling their swords, no doubt. Neutres of Garlot will join the best prospect, but others will be lusting after their sovereignty. Warlike Lothian, Northgales, the Cymri—"

"Gore? Are you not a 'tribal King'?"

He gave me a sharp look, fondling his jaw with musing fingers. "I will wait and see. I am already hearing news of unrest. Garlot immediately closed all its borders, and others will follow. This morning I sent men to secure our own boundaries. There will be no free passage into or out of Gore for the time being."

Any wind I still had left my sails. "And us?"

"Naturally, we'll keep to Chariot, increase the house guard, double the watch on the battlements, keep the gates shut. You will stay safe within the palace and innermost gardens." He was full of his old vigour now, empty of the shame that had brought him to me stooped and repentant. "Don't try your nerves, my lady. You are in mourning. Your women should be brought to comfort you."

"But—" I rose imperiously, to show him my nerves were entirely in order.

He merely patted me on the shoulder. "I must go, make sure Sir Aron has everything in hand for Gore's show of sorrow. We will throw a banquet for the late, great Uther Pendragon."

I rolled my eyes—at my husband's hypocrisy, at the thought of celebrating Uther's life at all—though Urien was already gone.

I was still mulling my confinement within castle walls when the door flew open and Alys rushed in.

"Morgan! I heard he summoned you . . . I came as quickly as I could. Are you all right? You look like you've seen a ghost."

Her voice brought me back to myself. "I'm fine. Urien apologized, took back the threats of treason, and then . . ."

Suddenly, the true news hit, shock and relief crashing over me like an almighty wave. I hardly knew I was crying until I tried to speak. "Uther Pendragon is dead. After all this time . . . it is done."

Without words, Alys pulled me into a swift, all-encompassing embrace.

"But . . . Britain is in uproar," I continued. "Urien has closed Gore's borders. I was thinking of ways to leave, and now we can't. But I won't give up, I—"

"I know, *cariad*. You'll find a way. You always do."

I wrapped my arms about her waist, feeling the weight of the past lifting, long shadows dissolving, years of darkness giving way to the possibility of light.

"So," Alys said at length. "What happens hereafter?"

I raised my head, eyes dry once again.

"We wait," I said.

45

IT CAME IN slivers at first, bare whispers swirling from one Great Hall to another, carried on the warm south wind. Within six months the tales began to coalesce: rumours of a boy-king, claiming the Crown of All Britain, gathering swords and support, riding into battle at the head of knights twice his age and pulverizing Saxons at will.

Seventeen years old, they said, but tall and strong as a man in his prime. He took to the charge like the Angel Gabriel, golden and gleaming—or a bright and bloodthirsty Lucifer, depending on who you asked.

His parentage was a mass of confusion: a knightly father, respected but of little note, living quietly in his forest castle; a loving lady mother of unremarkable breeding; a brother who was older but made no claims to the Crown himself. The family followed the younger man without question, along with Uther's southern bannermen, who flocked to the cause as fast as their destriers could carry them. The North, torn between natural suspicion and its own self-interest, had so far remained hesitant.

By all accounts they called him Arthur, and it was said he held court on the battlefield.

*

"I'LL HEAR NO more of this worn-out story!" Urien declared one evening near the end of Whitsuntide.

The air was close in Chariot's Great Hall, evening light soft pink as we sat, cheerful and wine-sleepy, hearing the same breathless battle report of three days earlier. My husband stretched, one hand aloft to have his goblet refilled, his other arm settling across my back. "Can no one bring news we haven't already heard? Some explanation for the wayward South?"

A rumble of laughter sounded over the pattering feet of cupbearers, pouring out more good wine than we had had in months. Urien and I were better—I had not forgotten my intentions, but we were cordial, sometimes much more than that. He seemed happy to assume I had forgiven his actions and, for now, I was content to let him believe it.

It had been brighter in Gore since Uther Pendragon's grip had released us. We were safe and had seen no unrest; even our surviving soldiers had returned home in a ragged procession. A new beginning, Urien had styled it; the bringing of hope.

But now this, from elsewhere.

"What I cannot fathom," Sir Aron put in, "is how a boy from the Forest of Nowhere—good warrior as he may be—makes this claim and stays alive, much less gains the support he has. They're soft down that way, but not that soft. What in God's name is compelling them?"

"It's the prophecy, surely? He pulled the sword from the stone."

A dozen heads turned to behold Sir Lucas, a newly made knight in the marshal's service, recently returned from accompanying a wool train to London.

Sir Aron scoffed. "We all know about that, lad. It's no less ridiculous now than it was months ago."

Indeed, not a soul had given the story any credit: the sword stuck in an anvil atop a stone, supposedly appearing from nowhere in a

MORGAN IS MY NAME

churchyard the day after Uther's death—the message engraved on its side claiming whoever removed the blade was the true High King of All Britain. But it was the first time we'd heard the boy-king linked to this so-called prophecy.

"That's just a washerwoman's tale," Urien said. "Not one man I've spoken to has laid eyes on this stone."

"But many did, sire. At the tournament."

The table quietened. Sir Lucas was so unworldly and inconsequential, no one had considered he might have pertinent information.

"I've heard nothing of any tournament," snapped Sir Aron.

The knight glanced nervously at his King.

Urien waved him on. "If there's more to this fantastical tale, we shall hear it. What tournament?"

"It was held a few months ago, when the stone first appeared. Hundreds of knights went to try to pull the sword and claim the Crown. The strongest men in Britain."

"Impossible!" Urien laughed, slapping his Seneschal heartily on the back. "Gore's finest weren't there, were we, Aron?"

A cheer rippled up and down the table. Sir Aron gave a reluctant smile.

"This Arthur, the boy-king," Sir Lucas continued, "he was squiring for his elder brother and drew the sword when no one was looking. Nobody believed it, so they made him put the blade back in. All of the knights tried to draw it again and failed, so he returned to the stone and did it over and over, until they had no choice but to accept it."

There were a few sniggers behind cups and hands.

"Where did you hear this?" asked my husband. "In a tavern somewhere, full of ale and song?"

"No, sire, though I did afterwards. It's all they speak of down there. But it came first from the priest of a church south of the river, where I went to hear Mass. There were two other knights praying—God-fearing men who had both witnessed the feat. One had attempted the sword himself. He still could not believe that a boy without spurs could hoist the sword out with such ease, when for him it moved not an inch. The priest comforted him and said there was no shame in failing in the presence of the true High King. Because that's what he is now, to them."

Urien leaned back in his chair, stroking his chin. "They believe it, from words carved into a stone?"

"Not just that. They said that the Archbishop of Canterbury was summoned to bear witness." The table fell silent, not a smirk or nudge between Gore's eminent knights. Sir Lucas drew a long breath. "His Holiness crowned the boy right there at the stone."

This we had not heard—news of a coronation quite different from tales of a young warrior winning battles and riding his luck. Every pair of eyes turned to my husband, who now sat quite still.

"God's bones," Urien said at length. "Can it be true?"

*

"IT'S STILL ONLY a story!" Sir Aron's hand landed on the table like a thunderclap.

There were six of us in Urien's private dining room: my husband, myself, Sir Aron and Lady Flora, and two serving pages. It had been a month since Sir Lucas's revelation, and our collective nerve was not what it had been.

"It gains traction by the day," Urien said. "What are you doing about it?"

"I sent more men out to seek the truth," Sir Aron replied. "Further reports came back this afternoon."

"And?"

"They . . . concur with Sir Lucas's version."

"Then how can you say it's only a story!" My husband gestured for the servants to leave, drumming his fingers on the tabletop. "I think it's time to see this sword and stone for ourselves. Not all the land's best men have tried their arm."

"The sword is gone," Sir Aron replied. "The boy-king took it with him and wields it in battle. The stone and anvil have vanished too."

"Vanished?" I said, interest pricked by the idea's strangeness. "How?"

Sir Aron regarded me with hooded eyes. "There one moment, my lady, and gone the next. Disappeared. Just as Merlin the Wise predicted it would."

"Merlin!" I exclaimed, coughing up a mouthful of wine.

"What's Uther Pendragon's seer got to do with this?" Urien demanded.

"He was at the stone, then rode off in the new King's train. He's been at the boy's right hand ever since. That's why the most powerful lords and knights flock to this Arthur. Merlin the Wise has three eyes, they say, and one is on the future."

I took another long draft of wine. He was certainly everywhere— Merlin, the sorcerer, this creature that Uther had trusted so completely—reappearing to look upon the death of one King before confirming the arrival of a new one.

"My lord." Lady Flora leaned towards my husband, whose chin now sat glumly in his hand. "He's what—seventeen? How much of a threat could he be to a man—or indeed a *King*—such as you?"

Urien straightened, allowing himself to smile. "Perhaps you are right, Lady Flora. Life in Gore must go on."

She beamed back at him. It baffled me that she was even there— indeed *I* had not made the invitation, but Lady Flora's ability to gain access to places that should have been denied her was an impressive skill.

My mind drifted back to the sorcerer, his curious affiliation. Merlin might be mad, I supposed—such things had often been claimed. But he could not be called wrong thus far. This unknighted, ferocious boy, with his undistinguished family and slender claim, was winning.

"My *lady*." Urien's insistent voice roused me, and I looked up to see Sir Aron and Lady Flora leaving. My husband had already risen, and was smiling, soothed out of his troubles by flattery.

"They're going?" I said distractedly.

"I took our leave. We've had enough talk, wouldn't you say?" He held out his arm, flexing taut as I took it. "Let's go to bed."

*

AFTERWARDS, I WAITED until he laid his head on my pillow and faced me, his aspect relaxed and pleased with itself in the candlelight.

"You should go to this Arthur and quickly," I said. "Speak with him one King to another."

Urien frowned, as if I had used a foreign tongue. "All in good time. Once he heads north, I'll invite him to dine. Then I will see how he is."

"That will be too late. When he turns north, it will be with a sword in his hand, to come and claim what is his."

He snorted, turning onto his back. "I see nothing inside or outside these walls that belongs to him."

"If you want to keep it that way, you'll ride to London and assure him of your loyalty before he is officially crowned."

"Are you mad?" Urien's laugh sent a bolt of irritation up my spine. He pushed himself into a sitting position, hooking a bare leg over the sheets. "What loyalty? The northern Kings are in council in less than a month—we may not be offering this boy-king anything but war."

I would never get free of Gore if it got into a conflict with half the nation.

"If you do, you will lose, all of you," I snapped. "Land, men, crowns. Your lives."

He stiffened at my tone; it was no way to bring him around.

Easing myself upright, I leaned close, tilting his jaw towards me. "Don't let's argue. Surely we have left one another far too contented for that."

He raised an idle hand to my face and slipped it under my dangling earring, garnets on twisted gold wire. He had selected them from a recently plundered Saxon hoard, though their bloody hue did not much suit my colouring. But it had pleased him to give them to me, so I wore them in his presence.

"Good stones," he murmured. "No woman wears my jewels as well as you."

Sensing I had him beguiled, I tried again. "My lord, can you not feel the way the wind is blowing? Trust me on this. I know of what I speak."

He inched closer, as if to kiss me on the mouth, then angled his face away at the last moment. "How can you? You know nothing of power, rule or politics. These are serious decisions to be made by ruling men."

I drew a hard breath to stop the curdling annoyance from rising. My words were in the best interest of the kingdom; could he not see it because it was me who said so?

Or perhaps he had simply become impatient—spent, satisfied and ready to be gone. Despite coming to me more frequently of late, he had been this way for all our encounters: full of fire and vigour when he was in the midst of it, but loath to linger more than a heartbeat afterwards.

I forced sweetness into my voice. "You are a man of your own mind, and it has served you well. But I *know* of Merlin from my youth. Uther Pendragon trusted him and let him steer his path for a long time."

He rolled his eyes, shifting around and reaching for his robe. "What of it?"

"Consider where he has chosen to put his faith. Merlin knows all about the northern rebellion, and still he stays with the boy-king. Go south; offer this Arthur your sword before he puts us to his. Think on it, I beg of you."

It was all I had—begging was the last gambit.

Urien stood up and fastened his robe, regarding me with infuriating pity. "Keep to your own affairs, my lady, and I will keep to mine. But I will not, for you or anyone, go to London."

46

WE WERE SUMMONED to the official coronation anyway, by a severely worded Royal Decree that Urien derided in public but could not find spine enough to refuse. The boy-king's herald was late getting to us, which—combined with Goreish stubbornness—left very little time to prepare, and we arrived at Westminster Abbey mere moments before the ceremony began.

We slipped into the cathedral's enormous nave at the back of an impressive crowd. The air was heady with incense and heat from so many bodies, draped in a rich array of patterned silks, luxurious furs and fine linens. Jewel-coloured light streamed in through rows of stained-glass windows, dazzling off gemstones and precious metals.

Eventually came the moment. "I crown you Arthur, High King of All Britain. In the name of the Father, the Son and the Holy Spirit." The voice of the Archbishop echoed around the leaping arches like a pronouncement from God Himself.

I craned my neck and saw only a glint of light, sharp on the edges of a plain golden crown. When the anointing was done, the new King left through a different door, and we followed, pushed forwards in a crush of bodies.

"Can you see him?" I asked my tall husband. "How does he look?"

"Hush, woman," Urien hissed. "What care you how he looks?"

I let him walk on, looking beyond the crowd to the crenelated White Palace, the boy-king's current stronghold, where his coronation feast would take place. Gold banners flew, devoid of device, reminding us of our new lord's lack of provenance, and his all-encompassing presence.

I fell into step with Alys. Lady Flora and my other women moved past us in a huddle, complaining about the fish smell from the river and the indignity of having to walk even a short distance.

"Have you seen anything interesting?" I asked. "Like a High King, perhaps?"

Alys smiled. "No. But Sir Aron has secured us lodgings at last, several miles north of the city proper."

"A late-night ride to sleep in a horse trough. I am tired at the very thought."

Her brow clouded. "Are you still feeling unwell?"

It had been an unsettled journey south, the threat of the royal summons dancing on my nerves. We left Gore after weeks of furious rain, riding through air soaked with scent—late fruit crushed into metallic soil, the rotting petals of summer—assaulting my skittish senses. Food and wine I could barely face, and my sleep was heavy and desperate. Alys worried at my every nauseated grimace, but I knew, somehow, that it would pass—that I was not ailing, but awaiting the future.

"It comes and goes," I replied. "Once we know Gore's fate, it'll settle."

"You know best," she said doubtfully. "There's more news—your lady mother is here."

My stomach made a different sort of lurch. "She is? Where?"

"Due to her status, she'll be near the front of the procession."

We passed under the portcullis, to the sound of exultant bells, into a sprawling, sunlit courtyard. The damasked crowd clotted into a wide line from the palace's main door, gradually admitted by heralds in gold silk.

"It *is* you." A gentle hand halted me. I turned to behold a composed hazel-eyed face, smiling out of the past.

"Elaine!" I threw my arms around my sister. "My God, how long has it been? I'm so pleased to see you!"

"Goodness, Morgan, such ado." Elaine disentangled herself and smoothed her sorrel-coloured gown. "Indeed, I am *surprised* to see you. Last we heard, Gore had half a foot in the northern rebellion."

I thought of Urien's wavering, his obstinacy, the meetings with prideful, glory-hunting lords. He had capitulated to the obvious at long last, but at what cost?

"Not us; hence, we are here," I said uneasily.

"Morgause isn't. I'm surprised she missed all this rich fuss."

"Lothian is very much part of the rebellion. She cannot come."

"It's not so simple," Elaine replied. "Apparently, she's been upriver, staying with the Duchess of Richmond, even met the new King when he stopped there. Rumour has it they came to a friendly accord. Awkward, given her husband's declaration of war."

"No doubt she knows what she's doing." Our elder sister's political intelligence was much talked-of, as was her reputation as a mother: protective, ambitious, hell-bent on ensuring the future greatness of her sons. "If Morgause has committed treason against her Crown, it will have been for her children."

Elaine nodded. "And how do you fare? With marriage, children?"

"Oh, you know, husbands are husbands," I said dismissively. "We have not yet been blessed with children. But I would rather hear of you. Are you contented, Elaine?"

She looked over to where King Neutres stood some yards away, conversing pleasantly with his guards. He was as indistinctive as ever—in fact, they were both broader in the face and waist, their mouse-hued hair taking on a greying sheen—but the fondness in Elaine's eyes made my heart grow.

"We are blessed indeed," she said. "We have a son and a daughter, both healthy. Neutres is a good man, devoted to his family and country. Garlot is peaceful, and he works tirelessly to keep trouble from our door. I never expected love from marriage, but as soon as we met, there was a . . . rightness. I was meant to be there, I think, with him."

I felt a rush of relief that the connection I had seen at their wedding was indeed a real one. "I'm happy for you. Garlot sounds like a true home."

"It is," she replied. "Indeed, my husband and I both hoped you would accept our invitations to visit."

"Invitations?"

"I sent four separate messengers. All returned, bearing official regrets. But royal life can be busy, I know." My mind twitched with questions, but Elaine's voice brought me back to her. "Dear Morgan, if I'd known you were coming, I'd have arranged this visit differently. I'm afraid we are leaving."

"But we've had mere moments! Won't the High King expect you?"

"My husband swore to King Arthur months ago and sought his blessing to take our leave after the abbey." She placed a hand over her heavily draped abdomen. "Our third, God-willing. By the time we return to Garlot, my lying-in will not be far away."

I could see it now; she was carrying wide and flat: a girl, Alys would have predicted. I embraced her again. "Congratulations. You are heroic to have travelled at all."

"Ah, these are the easy middle months, where one is all high spirits and full of doing. I could not have ridden the roads at the start— I am always so sickly, averse to every smell on the air, sleeping endlessly. Even wine holds no pleasure. You will know the joys soon, I'm sure." She kissed me deftly on the cheek, her quiet certitude comforting as ever. "And once Garlot's gates are open again, you must visit. Charming Aunt Morgan will be much loved by her nieces and nephews. Farewell, dear sister."

"Farewell," I said, and watched her steady retreat towards her husband's patient smile. She put a tender hand to his face, kissing him lightly, before they moved off and were gone.

I spotted Alys near the doorway and went to her, full of thought. "Do you have your almanac?" I asked, referring to the small volume she kept containing my Queen's calendar.

"Among my things," she replied. "Why?"

"I need you to check something for me."

47

THE GREAT HALL was teeming with people, stopping to marvel at the rich hangings, the gilded ceilings, the long, polished tables gleaming with gold and silver plate. Late-summer flowers cascaded from painted rafters, filling the air with the warm sweetness of a Babylonian garden. At the far end, three circular windows sat high up the wall, casting coronas of sunlight down onto where the dais—and the throne—would be.

"Incredible tapestries." Alys pointed to a vivid depiction of Salome doing her fateful dance. Beneath it stood Urien, huddled in tense discussion with his closest knights. I watched his hands swinging, exhorting his men, and wondered if my fate was contained in those indecisive gestures. I felt another internal quiver.

"Stay here," I told Alys. "I'm going to find my mother."

I made my elbows sharp and pushed through the crowds, the mass of bodies thinning out as guests gradually took up their seats. I ran my eyes up and down the long flower-and-silk-covered tables, seeking my mother's gold halo of hair.

I didn't get far before a great blast of trumpets brought the room to attention. People surged forwards, anxious for a better view of what I assumed was the newly crowned King's arrival.

But first came another. A door beside the dais opened, and through it came Merlin, slinking in like a winter wolf. Unease rippled through me—not the violent disgust I expected, but fear, needle-sharp and cold. I waited, expecting Ninianne and her comforting light, but no one followed. The sorcerer's gaze flickered across the room, noting me, just as the herald made his announcement, and Arthur, High King of All Britain, appeared on the dais to the sound of thunderous applause.

I watched him come, striding forth under ermine and crown, and saw at once why powerful lords threw their swords at his feet. It had only ever been folly to refer to him as boy-king. Tall and wiry with strength, shoulders broad enough to bear the nation he now carried, it was impossible to imagine he had ever been a child, much less born screaming and bloody like the rest of us.

But he had been, and in one stark, astounding moment, I understood.

My lord King has put a child in you, Lady Igraine, one you will bear alive.

I heard a baby cry . . .

The red-headed girl said he never drew breath.

There, beneath the true Crown of Britain, made masculine, were the silvery eyes, fine-boned face and pale-gold hair of my own mother. What I had seen and heard that bright March morning was not a dream-soaked trick: this regal, formidable figure was Queen Igraine of Britain's lost son, carried off in silk and mist by the sorcerer and his Lady of the Lake.

Ninianne had lied to me, barefaced, Merlin's servant all along. And I had believed her all these years—why? Because she had once saved me from Merlin, or seemed to understand aspects of my being, deep and unspoken?

I looked again at the High King, hoping myself mistaken, but to lay eyes on this Arthur was to be beyond all doubt. And somewhere in that room, my mother saw him too. I had to find her.

"King Urien of Gore and his lady Queen, come forth to the High King!"

The command came from the herald. There was a scuffling at the back of the room, and I watched Urien charging through the parting crowds. Spotting me, he bared his teeth and beckoned impatiently, as if I were the cause of whatever disaster this was.

"Where in all Hell have you been?" he snapped. "God's blood, I should have left you in Chariot."

His tone sent a flash of fire up my neck. "Is it true you kept me from my sister all these years?" I hissed. "Rejecting invitations from Garlot?"

"I don't know what you're talking about."

"For God's sake, don't *lie* to me, at least."

"Don't you think there are far more pressing things," he said through gritted teeth, "with the fate of my country at stake?"

"There'd be nothing *at* stake if you'd listened to my advice." We were two-thirds of the way to the throne, and the eyes of the room were upon us. "I told you to bend the knee as soon as we knew the sorcerer was involved. Now you might have killed us both."

We came to a halt beneath the looming figure of King Arthur. The fair face was no longer smiling, grey eyes radiant with intensity. My husband stood stiff, vibrating with righteousness, and I knew he would not save us.

Before his hubris saw us thrown in the dungeon, I sank to my knees, chin to my chest. After an endless, terrible pause, there was an exasperated thud beside me as Urien finally followed. I kept my eyes shut until I heard the clear, even tones of the High King.

"I welcome you, King and Queen of Gore. Please stand."

Urien stood without offering to assist me. Instead, King Arthur swooped forwards, extending his hand to ensure my graceful rise. I took it, surprised, and he smiled boyishly back, so much like her— my mother, his mother—that I almost stumbled. But his grip was warm and strong, fortifying me.

Then he was gone, withdrawing and returning to full height. "I am grateful for your courtesy, King Urien. Though I confess I am taken aback to receive it. It's a little late, don't you think, to kneel to my Crown now, when so many of your northern neighbours either swore fealty long ago, or chose to rebel against me?"

Urien wavered. "I . . . I do not know, my lord."

"Perhaps you were waiting for a sign from God? But still, your hesitation seems a great risk. Wouldn't you agree, Queen Morgan?" The High King's steely gaze switched to me, seemingly in expectation of an answer.

I glanced at my husband's florid profile. "I do agree, Your Highness," I heard myself say. "I advised my lord husband to swear to your Crown the moment we heard of your drawing the sword from the stone. Unfortunately, our council was doubtful, unused to acting quickly. Or indeed on good advice."

Urien stared at me, incredulous; it was the most I had been allowed to hold forth on Gore's political stance in the entirety of my reign. It would mean a fight between us later, but I had ceased to care.

"My lord, do not listen to her," Urien spluttered. "My wife knows nothing of rule."

The High King gave a loud, youthful laugh. "By God, I disagree, King Urien! You should have listened to your lady Queen. The men at your council table have ill-served you, and she is very wise."

A ripple of amusement travelled the room, turning Urien an even darker red. "My lord, Gore is here now," he protested. "We could not be sure if . . . if . . ."

"If *what*?" The High King shot forwards with quick aggression, like a striking cat. The ease in the air evaporated. "If I would fall in battle, because of my youth? If Britain's men would turn on me, rather than continuing to join me in their droves?" He stared down from his lofty height, expression contained but imperious, decades beyond its years. "Or is it that you believe *even still* that I am not the rightful King, and your heart too lies with the northern rebels?"

Urien's large frame seemed to shrink. "No, my lord . . . I . . . we . . ."

I took it all in with an abstract wonderment, fascinated at the ease with which this boy of seventeen had brought my obstinate and self-righteous husband to the brink of panic.

King Arthur waved a dismissive hand. "It matters not. If you wish to save your kingdom from bloodshed, you must prove yourself with a greater display of loyalty than this. I will expect to see you on the battlefield, fighting under my banner, when I ride north."

Urien bowed deeply. "If that is what Your Royal Highness requires."

"It is." He fixed my husband with a cold, shrewd gaze. "Let there be no more talk. Does the Kingdom of Gore swear its loyalty to this Crown, and to me, as High King of All Britain?"

Urien paused, even still. It was my turn to stare at him in disbelief.

"Gore swears, Your Highness," he said eventually, and I sank to my knees in sheer, collapsing relief.

The High King nodded and said a few more official words, none of which I heard, then must have bid us return to our place, as my husband's hand appeared, urging me to rise.

As soon as we were far enough away from the dais, he snarled into my ear, "How could you? Opening your mouth, betraying me. Do you realize the shame I will face back in Gore because of your loose tongue?"

"I only told the truth," I snapped, "as you well know."

"You don't know the first thing about how a kingdom is run. You cared only for being impressive, like a performing dog."

"If I hadn't knelt first, or spoken as I did, you'd be chained up in a dungeon by now. You ought to be ashamed of your stupidity."

I angled my face away from his next insult, and a flash of colour, sky blue and evocative, caught in the corner of my eye. Looking again, I saw the tall, sandy-haired figure of Sir Bretel, in the colours of my father's Cornwall. Beside him, wearing a gown of the same shade and speaking into his ear, was my mother. I knew from her calm demeanour she had seen the High King and suspected nothing.

I started towards them, but Urien pulled me back. "I won't forget this. We will discuss your conduct later, when this masquerade is finally over." He gave my arm a warning squeeze, almost to the bone.

I didn't flinch. "You'll be too hog-drunk by then to even stand," I spat. "Take your hands off me."

He daren't hold me any harder, lest we be seen, and I tore away without another word, sliding through the dense crowd.

"Morgan!" Beaming with joy, my mother held out her arms, enfolding me. She looked different in a way I could not quite discern: looser-limbed, lit from within; perhaps it was the colour I had not seen next to her skin for almost two decades, or the fact that she wore no crown over her gossamer-thin veil. Around her neck hung two ropes of gold, Welsh and Cornish entwined, given to her by my father on their wedding day.

"Mother." I leaned into her embrace, still rose-scented, smothering me in memories. I savoured her warm skin against my cheek, then prised myself free. "I thought you were in seclusion?"

"I was, until summoned here," she said. "Did you see Elaine?"

"Yes, I did, but—"

"I wish she had stayed longer, but she prefers to be in Garlot, and you know Elaine—quietly determined. And the first of Morgause's four boys will soon be taking knighthood. Can you believe how the time has passed?" She was in a state of happy distraction, pouring out sentiments she had been forced to hold in for years. "What of you, my dearest? Are you too blessed with motherhood?"

"No children yet. But I pray, and endure, as women do." I gestured to a window alcove just beyond. "On that subject, Mother, may we speak alone?"

She nodded and we moved off together.

A razor-sharp voice called out to our backs. "Igraine, formerly of Britain!"

Merlin stood in the centre of the dais, staring directly at us. Or rather, at her. He beckoned with a thin, authoritative hand. "Come before the High King."

King Arthur, until then sat sanguine upon his throne, looked up, his surprise mirroring my mother's in perfect time. Leaping to his feet, he rushed over to the sorcerer, whispering questioningly in his ear.

My mother sighed. "I knew there was a reason they demanded my presence."

"What reason?"

"He must want my lands, those I have left. Why else would the new King insist I come to this ceremony?" A look of disgust passed over her face. "I only wish it did not involve that . . . creature, Merlin. That he still presumes to command me, after all he—" She cut herself off, a reminder that I wasn't supposed to know about any of it. "But I will face him, one last time. If they want what's mine, they can wear their thievery and dishonour in full view."

"My lady," came the waspish drawl. "You keep the High King waiting."

She straightened her spine, hands neatly clasped before her. A quick glance brought Sir Bretel immediately to her side.

I blocked her path. "Don't go," I pleaded. "Not to him, not again. Please."

She put a hand to my face, smiling with a warmth I had not seen for so long—a look of maternal love and reassurance, without the dark pall of fear that Uther Pendragon had cast over her every breath.

"Morgan, do not fear," she said soothingly. "What more can they do to me?"

Just then I believed her, and she walked away in long, defiant strides, halting before the dais with Sir Bretel at her right shoulder.

Merlin's shadow slanted across her in the late-afternoon sun. "It was good of you to come, Lady Igraine."

"Queen Igraine," she corrected. "And I was told I had no choice, or I would not be here."

Merlin's mouth curled into what once might have passed for a smile, light catching on the edges of his teeth. "That would have been a shame, *Queen* Igraine. You are integral to the day's proceedings, as you have been to so many important events since our worthy King Uther first came to you at Tintagel."

The brazen reference to her violation caught her off guard, a barbed arrow shuddering through her frame. This, I realized—putting her shame and horror on display—*this* was what they could do to her.

"No, no, *no!*" I charged forwards, staring down the inquisitive sneer of the sorcerer.

"My lady Queen of Gore," Merlin said. "This doesn't involve you."

"I'm not going anywhere," I snapped.

"My daughter can stay where she is." My mother's voice rang in the stillness. She tilted her head and addressed the High King. "If you wish to take my lands, King Arthur, please declare it quickly, and show me the courtesy of doing so yourself."

The crowned head snapped up as if waking from slumber. Their eyes met like twin blades—vital, flashing silver, identical. How could she not see he was hers?

The boy-king stepped forwards, regarding the sorcerer with unusual severity. "Who made the lady come here?" he demanded. "I have no wish to take a sovereign Queen's lands, nor do I have the right."

"Quite, my lord," Merlin said. "But—"

King Arthur held up his hand, cutting him dead. "Why, then, is Queen Igraine standing before me, saying she is here against her will?"

"My lord, if I may finish—"

"*Answer my question!*" he roared. "Why is this woman, whom I have never met, *integral* to my coronation?"

That he had no time for Merlin's cruel theatre was plain, his loss of temper a strange testament to goodness within. The sorcerer, however, was unperturbed, standing shoulder to shoulder with his King like an equal.

"Because, my lord, she is not just any woman." He intoned the words almost by rote, as if the world's secrets were nothing but a tiresome bore. But the glint in his eye was triumph, and it chilled the depths of me.

"Queen Igraine," Merlin went on, "by way of God and the great King Uther Pendragon, is your mother. And you, Arthur Pendragon, are Britain's one true son."

At that, Arthur, our King, beheld his looking glass of a mother and saw the reflection of his own image. All at once she saw it too, her golden son, what was so obvious, inevitable in its way, and it drove into her like a sword, her stately frame crumpling to the floor. Then, in the silence of the Great Hall, she let out a long, anguished howl, a sound so terrible I had never heard its like; the cry of a wounded soul, gutted by lies and loss, broken by the ultimate betrayal.

48

I WAS ESCORTED to a small room just off the King's reception chamber, where I sat, then stood, then paced, and wondered what was occurring down the corridor.

My mother had been gathered from the Great Hall floor by Sir Bretel, staggering out of the room behind the ghost-faced King. I followed, thinking she might need me, but King Arthur's seneschal— a brusque young knight with a sardonic air—shook his curly brown head and pointed to the antechamber instead. He refused to answer questions, but did send wine.

I drank a swift, unwatered gobletful, but it tasted bloody and lay unsettled in my twitching stomach. I thought only of my mother, her collapse, the way her eyes had followed her son as he fled in a daze. Never in her life had she believed she would see him again.

Merlin's explanation to the spellbound congregation was brief, typically reverent towards his old, dead master and devoid of the dreadful, fantastical truths I knew. King Uther had promised him the child when it was still in the womb, he said, as reward for all his service, and honourably kept his word. For the love of Uther and his heir, Merlin had passed the boy into the safe hands of the mild, forest-dwelling Sir Ector, who raised him as his own. Both Sir Ulfin and Sir Ector stepped forwards to confirm this, with talk of dates and signed royal letters. Sir Ector had known nothing of the child's true lineage.

"The High King had no word of his son until his deathbed," Merlin declared. "And much as the boy is still rightfully mine, it is only fair that the realm knows him as their legitimate lord, both by the decision of God and by descent."

No mention of why my mother had not been told—she who bore him and could have ridden to meet him months ago—the final act of cruelty from a husband who cared for nothing but his own selfish wants.

But she had outlived him, and God had brought her reward. Expecting to lose all she had left, my mother had gained a son—a leader, warrior and King, made in her own image. He was also the indisputable heir to Britain. Arthur was hers, and he was Uther Pendragon's, and he was my half-brother.

The door flew open, and the seneschal's bored face appeared. "The High King will see you now."

I followed him down the passageway. Somewhere below, the celebrations carried on: Alys and Tressa, Sir Bretel, Urien, Gore's knights and ladies, a thousand others, eating, drinking and listening to music play, while the man they had come to see crowned contemplated his true parentage in a tower, like a prisoner.

"What of my mother, Sir . . . ?"

"Sir Kay," he supplied. "I know little, my lady, only that Queen Igraine's audience with the King has finished." He stopped at a door, knocking briskly and pushing it open without waiting for a reply. "Her Highness, the Queen of Gore, sire." His voice had changed, gaining a quiet, almost reluctant fondness.

King Arthur turned from the window, hands hooked behind his back. "Thank you, brother," he said.

Sir Kay nodded and left us alone.

"So he is the elder brother," I said. "The one you were raised with." The High King of All Britain took me in with mild surprise.

I should have let him speak first, perhaps, shown more reverence. But quickly, he smiled, a guarded yet genuine expression of youthfulness and charm.

"Lady Morgan, I am pleased to see you." He strode across and kissed my hand. "That is, if 'Lady Morgan' is your chosen address. You prefer Queen Morgan, perhaps, or Lady Gore?"

"Lady Morgan, Your Highness." I had never once contemplated the fact that I could be styled 'Lady Gore' and was quite relieved not to have known it.

"Please sit. Wine?"

I had already caught its iron scent, and my stomach turned over. "No thank you, my lord. And I'd rather stand, if I may."

"As you wish," he said. "Yes, that is my brother, Sir Kay. He is my seneschal now, and a very good one. Or at least, he will be when I am able to settle down to rule."

He moved to a small table and picked up a golden jug, tilting its lion-headed spout at a goblet. He looked younger than in the Great Hall—if still not as young as he was—divested of his mantle and crown, pouring a long stream of wine with an artfulness that told of a less starry past, cupbearing and squiring for his elders. In that dimly lit, low-ceilinged room, he was mortal.

"Though I suppose," he added, "I should say he *was* my brother. Until today."

I felt a rush of sorrow for him—slightly absurd, considering the power he held, but the sight of him tugged at me. It was a sudden existence that had fallen on his head, and a complex one, enough to baffle the strongest of minds.

"He is still your brother," I said gently. "You might look at today as a gain in family, not a loss."

"Yes," he mused. "I'll drink to that, Lady Morgan. Or should I say 'sister'?"

I smiled and he returned it, almost demure, and he resembled my mother so powerfully it felt like a blow to the chest. How like her he was—even more so close up—made from the same pale metallics: gold hair and silver eyes, their skin just rose gold enough to radiate health. His straight-shouldered height too, the proud bearing with which he carried himself—that was my lady mother to her core.

Our, my mind pointed out, *our lady mother*.

It was as if she had produced her son alone, in defiance of his brutal begetting, erasing all traces of his savage father. Uther Pendragon, for all the eye could see, was nowhere in this boy.

"Your sister," I said, trying the idea aloud. Despite everything, it fitted. "I suppose I am. Along with two others—Elaine, Queen of Garlot." (How badly I wished she had stayed, to bring her indifferent calm to this chaos!) "Morgause, I gather, you already know?"

The High King stopped mid-swig. "Yes. We met at Richmond. An exceedingly charming woman, and a shrewd Queen. Shame she is the rebel Lothian's wife." He paused, so deep in sudden thought it was almost audible in the cedar-scented air. "But it is you I'm here to become acquainted with. I've already seen proof of your wisdom in the Great Hall, and my adviser Merlin says you are very learned."

"That is flattering, my lord." It wasn't, in truth, coming from the sorcerer, and I wondered where the devil he had found out anything about me. "I had a lengthy education from my father's good and scholarly chaplain, then I was sent to St. Brigid's Abbey in the Summerland, where I studied the Seven Arts and a great deal of physic."

"Impressive. Do you heal in practice?"

"I used to," I said carefully. "But I was called from the nunnery to marry, and have been occupied with royal life since."

"Of course." There was a lull in the air, and he walked across to the fireplace, gait stiff, self-conscious. "Now we are acquainted, Lady Morgan, I did wonder . . ."

I recognized the cause of his tension at once: my mother hadn't been with him nearly long enough to tell all he must have wanted to hear. He was bursting with questions, and I knew exactly what he would ask.

"You knew my father," he said, and expecting it didn't rattle me any the less.

"Only when I was young, for a while. He was at war a great deal, busy with rule. I have little to tell." So this was where I began lying, hiding Uther Pendragon's unsavoury truths yet again.

"Our mother found it difficult to speak of him," Arthur said. "Maybe because I am seeking a father and she never knew him that way, given I was . . . taken elsewhere." His hands dropped, hanging helplessly at his sides. "She grieves him still, no doubt."

Grief indeed, I thought, *for all she endured, and now she is finally free, there is this.*

She must face it all over again: Merlin's sorcery; Uther's ungodly disguise; his body dominating hers day and night, year after year. My mother's sacrificial silence would save her son from horror; it was not for me to tell him what she kept inside.

And then it hit me, that which had itched in my mind when I saw my mother in the Great Hall. Not the colour she wore, or the wedding necklace, but her body—her wrists, her forearms, her bare neck, her warm skin against my face as she held me close. The difference was that I could see them at all. In Uther's time, she never had more than her face and hands on display; even her jewels were fastened over stiff collars and narrow sleeves, against fashion, regardless of temperature, speaking of all she could not say. My mother was covering her body, and what had been done to it.

Not only had she succumbed to Uther Pendragon's will, she had spent her life taking his punishment for daring to resist—her bones and skin bruised, hidden beneath tightly sewn silks, her body and mind violated while keeping those she loved from the same. And not once did she break—the times I railed against her, refusing to speak to her or believe she loved me—not once did she scream the truth: that, however imperfectly, she was saving me, saving my sisters, by not saving herself.

All this she had survived to find herself in front of the son she had lost, only to be asked about the greatness of his father.

"Lady Morgan, what is it?" The High King's voice came from miles away. "You've gone white as a swan. Come, sit down." I let him guide me to a chair, and he took the seat opposite. "Forgive me. I've asked too much of you."

"No," I managed. "It was a hard journey, a long day. Then . . . this."

He sighed. "Of course. I do not seem to handle shock, or fatigue, in the way others do. It moves me within, but on the outside, I go forth regardless. Are you all right?"

The horror was receding, ebbing slowly as it always did, leaving its scars far beneath the skin. I mustered a smile. "I will be. It's a great deal to take in."

King Arthur looked down, shoulders sagging. Who knew that feeling better than he: a boy in complete ignorance of his impossible destiny until a few months ago, hearing not two hours since that the family he loved were not his, and the blood he shared was with strangers. I considered his pained, fair face; he did not seem a King, before me like this. But my brother? Yes, maybe.

But I couldn't do it; I couldn't conjure my worst memories only to lie to him about his true father.

"I'm sorry," I said.

He nodded sadly. "I understand."

I stood before I could change my mind. "With your leave, my lord, I should go. Our lodgings are a fair ride."

"Lodgings?" he said, rising swiftly. "No sister of mine stays any-where than under my hospitality. I'll have chambers arranged at once."

He was waving away my gratitude when there was a knock at the door. A page came in, bowing low. "I beg your pardon, Your Highness, but I come bearing urgent messages. Merlin the Wise says the banquet requires your return, as several eminent lords would speak with you. And King Urien of Gore asks after his lady wife."

A bitter laugh escaped me at Urien begrudging me as much time as I needed to speak to my own brother. A creature of incomprehensible selfishness as ever he had been.

Arthur found the summons even less amusing. "Tell them I will *not* come presently, or a moment before I am ready." He raised his eyes to the ceiling, as if exhorting some higher power. "Does Merlin *dare*—after all he has thrust upon me today, this great *performance* of his—tell me to entertain? Do they not realize, these people who demand my time, that *they* wait on *me*?"

And there he was, High King once more, his flare of temper swift and regal, less violent than my own, elegant in its deployment and intimately familiar. My mother again—her fiery heart as it used to be, reflected in her anointed son. Arthur's fury was hers, as was his blood; as they were mine; as they were ours.

49

I LEFT MY husband at the banquet, drinking with his men; a test of sorts, to see how concerned for me the news had made him. As it was, I had time to bid goodnight to Alys, don my bed robe and drink half a jug of peppermint tea before he swept into my chamber unannounced.

I was sitting down brushing my hair, and the rhythm of my hands didn't falter, though I tracked his progress carefully in the mirror. He wasn't wine-soaked; his movements were inquisitive and assured, as he padded the room like a sleek, giant cat.

I swallowed the peppermint leaf I'd been chewing, cool, tingling relief spreading over the nauseated tension beneath my ribs. "I checked the almanac," Alys had said earlier. "You were right—you are with child. Almost three months gone." It explained the fatigue, the heightened senses, the aversions, if not what it meant for my future.

Urien paused behind me, drawing my shining mass of hair into his hands and caressing it. I put the hairbrush down and folded my arms, ignoring the anticipatory shiver at the grazing warmth of his fingertips.

His eyes met mine in the glass. "Quite a day it's been," he murmured. "I did nothing but field questions at table."

"Imagine how I must feel, learning it," I replied.

"I suppose. But it's an astonishing story." He trailed a light finger across the top of my shoulders. "And you—once daughter of a King, now sister of one."

I shot up from the stool, pushing past him and his heat. "So that is what impresses you? That I once lived with a King who was not my father, and now I share blood with another?"

Unperturbed, he moved closer. "I married *you*. You've always been impressive to me."

"Hardly. Your thoughts are deep in what you might gain from this." He had come because I knew things he did not, held power that he could not. He wanted to wrench it away and couldn't, but still he wanted to try. And the thought of it lit him up like a torch, just as it did to me.

"True, this is good news for Gore," he admitted. "A chance to restore our fortunes after years in the wilderness. But for now, I can assure you my thoughts are deep on another matter." He brushed his thumb across my lips; I had to resist the impulse to bite it.

"Nothing to do with the fact that I now have the ear of the King," I said. "And you do not."

"Damn it, woman!" Gripping my hips, he pulled me to him, furious with lust and exasperation, jealousy of the simple truth. "I don't *care* about that. I'll swear personal fealty to the boy-king at dawn and have his ear bent to my word by Terce bell. All you have done, my darling wife, is secure a far more comfortable bed than we would have had. And what I want is to lay you on it and be your loving husband, who chose you above all others."

In a way I believed it, in Urien's desire, remembering the earliest days of our union, when I could still feel, and the only wall between me and my grief was the certainty of his body and its need for mine. I put my hand to his jaw and kissed him, savouring his yielding for the slightest moment before pulling away.

"No," I said.

He stared as if he had never heard the word, which in fairness, he little had. "What do you mean, 'no'?"

"Need I have a reason?" I moved away, enjoying his look of perplexity, the surging power of denial.

"I don't underst—" He stopped, eyeing the barely touched platter of food, the half-empty jug of tea. He picked up my cup and took a sip. "This is peppermint," he said, already grinning. "Your illness on the road . . . this reluctance . . . it all makes sense. You are with child."

I could maybe have denied a question, but he had left no space for such a futile lie, so I could only stand mute as he took me in his arms, the mastery I had felt moments before vanishing like the fleeting, dishonest thing it was.

"Good God, I have done it!" he crowed. "Didn't I tell you Gore's heirs take time? Six years—exactly as my mother was with me. It is fated, *glorious*."

His pronouncements made my lungs tight, the true cost of my condition suddenly stark. A successful pregnancy meant being forged to Urien yet further, a bond so inescapable it made marriage seem negligible.

And yet, I could not make myself want anything but to bring this child forth, a fettered chain and shining gift all at once. Already, an instinct ancient and undeniable was working to preserve what was mine, ensuring my bodily sacrifice, my protectiveness, my love for a child I would carry and make strong, and deliver into the arms of a golden future.

50

MY MOTHER CALLED for me three days later, and by then I was anxious to see her. Sir Bretel admitted me to a bright, circular solar, where she sat in the oriel window, overlooking a hedged, ornamental courtyard.

"Uther went back on his word," she said when we were alone. "We married due to my pregnancy, then he waited until just before my lying-in and said the child was not his, that it could have been your father's—or any man's. He told me it was evidence of his Queen's weakness, a treason."

She touched her lips, as if to control an unwelcome feeling. "I knew it was lies, but he refused to accept it, insisting my illegitimate offspring must die. I cried and begged, told him I would do anything to preserve the baby's life. I see now it was what he wanted—he would always be able to say I agreed, that it was my choice for my son to be taken away.

"So when the red-haired girl delivered Arthur, I made my own bargain. I swore to hand over my son if she ensured I never bore Uther Pendragon another child. I knew she was special, her skills unusual. She did something with her hands; it worked, and I felt I had at least done what I could. I never imagined that for all these years, Merlin was plotting Arthur's reappearance, that there was this great Pendragon sword hanging above us. Now we must wait and see who Arthur's blood favours."

She gave a heavy, eternal sigh. "That is the truth. I give it only to you, Morgan."

It was more horrifying than I had imagined, and though I had a hundred questions, I couldn't bear to ask them. I rushed into her open arms. "Mother, I'm sorry. That day, I heard a baby cry, saw a boat sailing away. But they told me I imagined it, I—"

"Hush, daughter," she said softly. "It wouldn't have changed anything."

I raised my head from her shoulder. "But your son lives, and nothing can prevent you from knowing him. I believe Arthur is good, Mother. He is like you, not Uther."

She held me a while longer, but I felt in her bones it was all pause, that there was more. "Morgan, I . . . I am leaving Britain. The King, your brother . . . he asked me to stay, but I've said no. Much as I believe he will be better, that he is not Uther, I cannot watch another realm be formed." She looked past the white towers into the deepening autumnal blue of the sky. "Arthur already has a mother. Sir Ector's lady wife is a good woman, and the only mother he has ever known."

"But you carried him; you bore him."

"Then he was taken from me, and I knew him not at all. I see myself in his face, just as I see you in him—the slant of his cheeks, the half smile you both wear when you're being clever. That same flashing temper. I am drawn to him because of those things, reminders of the children I did raise. But I cannot feel what I should. I taught myself, in those long years, not to feel at all."

I felt suddenly stripped bare, wanting to protest but unable, because I knew exactly what she meant. Had I not used her ways to survive my years in Gore, withdrawing my true self while outside I hardened into stone?

"What did Arthur say?" I asked.

"He was upset, but he'll be busy for a long time and will not miss me. I've given him my remaining lands—I don't want them. He offered me Tintagel, but I cannot go back. I considered asking for your father's tomb, but all he ever wanted was to be laid to rest on that headland, so I must leave him there."

I nodded, swallowing a sob. It was gone then: Tintagel, my birthplace, the castle, the headland, the cove, the chapel where I had taken knowledge into my heart and learned that a game of chess was sometimes more than it seemed. The place I had found love and lost it—once, then all over again. My father's favourite place on God's earth, where he would lie forever now, among strangers.

We could have gone there, she and I, made our fortress unbreachable once more. Yet I could not blame her, knowing what she had suffered within its walls, what it had cost her to keep it sacred for us.

I regarded her sunlit face, the neatly dressed strands of her golden hair. The morning light showed lines whispering around her eyes and the corners of her mouth, as if she had recently learned to smile again.

"Where will you go?" I said.

"To Ireland, to live out my days among your father's ancestral people. Sir Bretel invited me to reside with him on his lands, and I have accepted."

"It's kind of him. Father always said he was the best of men."

She smiled, a gentle, private thing. "That he is. He knelt to me the day of your father's death and has not left my side since. Without Sir Bretel to remind me of the good in the world . . . his boundless loyalty . . . I don't know how—" She wiped a tear from her cheek and was silent for a long moment.

"I can't ever know if I was wrong," she said suddenly. "I was afraid for our lives—a widow and three daughters, with no husband to keep the wolves away, the Duke's knights worried for their heads. Uther Pendragon was so determined to possess me—he would have laid waste to everything else I loved. And when the King himself is unmerciful, where are we then, those of us who must live in this world kings have created? But I'll never forget I had a choice."

"What else could you have done?" I said, an endless, futile question. "What can any of us do?"

She turned her grey eyes on me with an intense, maternal curiosity. "Was it true, Morgan? Was there someone you loved, one you had given yourself to?"

It was harder than I imagined going back to that day, the violent argument with Uther, my confession and retraction; the weeks preceding it, and Accolon's drowsing face those precious few mornings, waking early to watch his skin catch the first glimmers of Cornish dawn.

"Yes," I said. "There was." I would not tell her who, not for the entire firmament. That I would keep within me.

But to my astonishment, she said, "The knight who left. Sir Bretel's former squire, from Gaul." She smiled sadly. "*Your* squire. Even then."

"Even then." I held my breath, awaiting tears, and found I had nothing left. "How did you—"

"Sir Bretel. In many ways he thought of him as a son, and was upset when he left. Much later, I asked him why the boy went, and he said that he believed it was despair, driven by love." She sighed. "It made a certain sense, though part of me hoped to God it wasn't so."

"Well, it is so," I said tonelessly. "It *was*. But he left, and I had to marry. I obviously had a greater love for him than he did for me."

She regarded me directly. "Has it gone away?"

His Gaulish coin, suddenly present, lay warm against my skin.

"No," I said. "It's never gone away."

"Listen, Morgan." She leaned forwards and grabbed my hands, speaking in a low, rapid voice. "There is a place, part of my girlhood lands, that I still hold in secret. A manor deep in the valley along the Welsh Wye, peaceful and secluded, with acres of forest and field, enough income to sustain a comfortable life. I want you to have it."

I could barely take it in, so quickly had she switched from the painful past to an urgent, imaginary future.

"Tell me," I said.

"It's called Fair Guard, believed to be owned by a knight known as the Count of the Pass. To me, he is Sir Cromfach of Rhos—he grew up in my father's household and is a loyal and dear friend." She turned my knuckles upwards, displaying my father's ring with its trio of sapphires. "Show your father's ring to Fair Guard's chamberlain, and he will pass you the keys and the household ledgers." She reached into the purse at her belt, drawing out a small, tightly rolled parchment. "This is a map and written directions—memorize them. If you ever need sanctuary, go there."

The old doubt flared in my chest. "If this place is so safe, so hidden, then why didn't you go after Father died?"

"There was no escape from Uther Pendragon. He wanted his own way so badly that he gave away his own son. He would have found me eventually. The most I could do was keep the manor hidden so another could benefit. And it remains, unsullied, and yours."

"Mother, I . . ." I wanted to say I didn't need this mythical place, that I was as happy as Elaine, or as steadfast in my life's role as Morgause. But I tried never to lie to those I loved, so I tucked the scroll into my bodice and kissed her cheeks. "Thank you."

Too soon, there was a knock at the door, and my mother called Sir Bretel in.

"All is prepared for departure, my lady," he said. "We must away if we are to reach our first resting place by nightfall."

I ran to him, throwing my arms around his unbent frame. Haltingly, he returned the embrace, holding me lightly but safe, as he always had, bearing us up in our darkest hours like the consummate Queen's Knight he was.

"Lady Morgan," he said gently, and I made myself let go. He smiled in his noble, melancholy way, and I wondered if he had ever heard of Accolon, the son of his heart. But as the question formed, I decided it was better if I did not know.

"I will miss you, Sir Bretel. You are the best knight I've ever known."

He bowed graciously. "That means a great deal, my lady. Know that I will do my very best, always, for your lady mother."

He glanced up, casting eyes of sheer devotion over at her. She smiled tenderly and gave a reassuring nod, and he left us alone once more. Before I could decide what it all meant, my mother was clutching me within a final rose-scented embrace.

"I will always love you, Morgan." She leaned back, brushing stray tears from under my eyes. "Please don't cry for me. I am going to a far better place—my own life, my own happiness. You must seek yours, however you can."

I tried not to feel my heart as it sank. "I love you too, Mother. I hope freedom is all you wish it to be."

She kissed me, then regarded me solemnly, smile fading under a sudden pall. "I am sorry for all he visited on you," she said, at long last.

"And I too, for you," I replied. And if nothing else, she knew I loved and believed her; that the fault in our existence was not hers, or mine, but his—Uther Pendragon's—and we had defied him one final time.

He was dead, and now we must live.

51

WITH OUR RETURN to Gore imminent, I requested a private meeting with my brother. He sent his agreement immediately and invited me to meet him in the ornamental garden that our mother's chamber had overlooked.

"Please excuse the lack of formal reception place," he said, as we strolled between fragrant lavender hedges. "I've had little chance to breathe the outside air of late. Everything feels rather . . . stifling, disarranged."

He did not sound like himself, his voice slightly hoarse. His head, too, was bent, face sleepless and clouded—the youthful confusion of a lost boy, not the anointed man who held the world in his palms— a pain I felt as my own. I knew at once how to heal it.

"Your father—Uther Pendragon," I began, though the name stuck in my throat like a burr. "He was a great . . . leader of men. They followed him, looked to him for guidance. He fought hundreds of battles, and I never heard of him losing one."

King Arthur lifted his head, brow clearing, and my heart expanded even though I hated every word of praise I'd spoken for that monster, who I hoped was trapped in the darkest corner of Hell.

"Am I like him?" he said. "A resemblance, anything?"

I considered his face for a long moment, trying to catch even a shade of Uther's cruel countenance, worried how I would feel if I found it.

"No," I said. "But you are like our mother, so very much. Which is a gift, because she is good, and godly, and has always been the best of us. That is what you should be."

"I intend to spend my life trying." Another shadow passed over his face, and he paused in his step, sighing heavily. "But these past few days, I find I am less pleased than I should be to hear of my true father. I am rightfully High King of Britain, but . . ." He trailed off, wincing.

"Before, you felt you had earned it," I ventured. "That men followed you because of your leadership, your great fighting prowess. Now you will wonder if they stay only because of your father's name."

"Won't they?"

"Not if you keep to the ways for which they joined you in the first place."

He stared at me, wanting to believe. "Yet he was still my father. I cannot prevent it."

And there it went: another life, another soul, another possible force for good overshadowed by the scourge that was Uther Pendragon. I could not bear it.

"You *can* prevent it," I said firmly. "You must forge your own path, far from his. You are not him, brother—that is your strength. Be your own man, a King like they have never seen, and Britain will love *you*. It will remember *you*."

He grew tenfold before my eyes, uncoiling, broadening, drawing upright.

"Morgan," he said suddenly, "the time we've had is so short. I am building a new city, Camelot. A beautiful place, with a grand castle where I will keep my main court. I still have wars to fight, but when I settle, you must come, stay for a while. There'll be time to know one another better, and you can lend me the benefit of your wisdom."

"My wisdom?"

"Yes! My clever sister, do not be so modest. For one, your learnedness far outstrips my own. I've had some education, teaching from Merlin, but it's been sporadic at best."

The sorcerer. I had forgotten his role in Arthur's life. It brought my arms up in gooseflesh. "I cannot know a hundredth of what Merlin does. You have him."

King Arthur shook his head. "Merlin is elusive by his very nature, and inconstant. He cares only for his prophecies and disappears for weeks to work on them. He has no interest in the practicalities of ruling. And those who do—my barons, the lords in my service—they're all clinging to their power, blindly appeasing me from morning till night.

"But you are honest—you told the truth about Gore's hesitance, that your advice was ignored. You didn't hide it, which was the natural thing to do. I intend to make a fairer, more just world, establish peace, and decide worthiness based upon deeds and honour, not land, riches or pedigree. And for that, I need the best minds and truest hearts by my side."

He gazed at me with direct, quicksilver eyes, all at once youthful and ancient, compelling in a way that was almost mystical. "Say you will help me, Morgan. Our mother has left; I am at war with another of our sisters. I don't wish to lose you as well."

Happiness washed over me, warm and unexpected, and beneath that, something better: the bright light of possibility.

"You could never lose me, brother," I said. "I stand with you. When Camelot is ready, call for me, and I will be there."

*

IN THE THREE months after Arthur's coronation, I returned to Gore—while my husband helped fight my new brother's

wars—continued my hidden work and eased from the exhausted,
purging stage of pregnancy to the lively "doing" months that Elaine
had described. My mood and health flew high, belly curving forth
as spring crept up around us. One morning, I woke to the first
heart-leaping quickening, child rippling within me like a fish across
the surface of a lake.

Urien's absence was much as expected; from the little information
brought to Chariot, I gleaned he was fighting battles, but alive and
healthy. Two weeks before he was due back, Alys and I were working
on our manuscript in the solar, to make use of the better light, when
there was a great clatter of hooves in the courtyard. I rushed to the
window to see a small band of my husband's house knights skidding
into the courtyard.

"Urien's banners," I said. "He's early. Is he hurt, or . . . ?" *Would I
even save him*, I wondered, *if I was the only one who could?*

Alys put down her quill and came to the window, just as Urien
himself rode under the portcullis. He was somewhat mud-flecked
from the road, but richly dressed and bolt upright, as if parading in
a pre-joust pageant.

"He looks more hale and hearty than when he left you," she
commented.

I took in the sight of him: broad and muscled, at jousting weight,
no visible injuries or stiffness as he dismounted and gestured impatiently to his attendants. It is said men return from war with years
put on them: cold, damp tents, exposed muddy fields running with
blood and disease—it took its toll on the fittest. But not my husband,
it seemed. For a man who had endured weeks of ferocious battle, he
was miraculously unscathed.

"Gather up our work," I told her. "I'll keep him in the entrance
hall while you get safely to the antechamber."

We had just concealed our parchment within a pile of unstitched shirt linen when my husband charged unexpectedly into the solar. Alys had almost edged past him with the wrapped manuscript when he grabbed her by the elbow. My heart stopped, but she merely regarded him coldly, as if he had lost his senses as well as his manners.

"Leave the Queen and me in private," he snapped.

"I was already going, my lord." She extracted her arm from his grip and shot me a perplexed look before exiting.

His demeanour wasn't particularly unusual—the hunt or brisk exercise often inflamed the blood in him—but it was the closest we had come to discovery. Exhaling, I circled a hand around my belly—pride and paternal delight ought to soothe his fraught mood.

He didn't notice. "I've been summoned to King Arthur's court in all haste."

"In Carduel?"

"No, the new city. Camelot. I must leave without delay." He stomped across to the window, looking back and forth. "Why isn't my Seneschal here?"

"Lady Flora isn't in service. Sir Aron left a few days ago to visit her."

"It was *you* who bid him go?" He reared up, cracking his head against the low-slung beam, cursing savagely.

I bristled, jarred by his hostile tone. "Yes. The chamberlain and deputy constable more than have things in hand. Why Camelot? I thought Arthur was fighting the northern Kings."

"He has ridden back south. The rebellion has been defeated, but Lothian fell unexpectedly. There is a great deal of upset."

"King Lot is dead?" I exclaimed. "Does my sister know?"

"She'll hear it soon. Reportedly, she's in Edinburgh with her three youngest sons. The two elder boys were squiring in the battle and are in the High King's custody. The High King himself is distraught. He wanted fealty, not another King's death. He is holding a lavish funeral as a mark of respect, and wants his allies there."

"Then I'll come with you. Arthur wanted me to see Camelot."

Finally, Urien's eyes slid to my abdomen, registering surprise but precious little happiness. "I told him you couldn't on account of your condition."

"I'm perfectly fine," I retorted. "Alys says my health, and the child's, is flourishing."

"I care not what your convent-raised Cymri girl claims. She knows nothing of childbearing."

"Then I will travel on a litter, for the sake of caution. But I feel exceedingly well."

A strange look passed across his handsome, windblown face—a sudden pain, perhaps, overlaid with something like regret. "Indeed, you do look well on it. Beautiful, in fact. Carrying my child becomes you."

Before I could respond, he blinked away his pause. "A litter is much too slow. I am already far behind the High King's train and must not miss the funeral rites." He put his hand to the small of my back, steering me towards the door. "Await me in your chambers. We'll discuss my plans there."

He guided me out of the solar and into Chariot's entrance hall, to the bottom of the main staircase. The vaulted vestibule was bustling, servants and squires back and forth, in disarray without Sir Aron's organizational hand. Knights milled about, shouting for horses and arms.

A particular clamour echoed from near the door. Urien glanced back at it. "Go on up," he said. "I'll return to you presently."

He strode off towards the noise, and I began to ascend the main stair, meeting Alys on her way down.

"Is it true we're leaving for King Arthur's court?" she asked. "Because no one's been told to pack for you."

"Urien's going, not me. King Lot has been killed, and his funeral is at Camelot."

"Won't your sister need your comfort?"

"I always forget you've never met Morgause," I said drily. "I can't imagine her needing anything from me."

"Even still," Alys said. "I'm sure your brother wants you there."

"He's been told I can't risk my condition. I offered to go by litter, but it's too slow, as Urien can't miss . . ." I trailed off, struck by a thought that had been niggling like a bad tooth since I was chased from the solar.

"What?" Alys asked.

"Urien said Morgause would have the news soon, not already. No royal procession leaving Edinburgh this week could reach Camelot in advance of Gore. Arthur won't hold the funeral without her. There must be some confusion." I started down the steps, following my husband's path.

"*Urien!*" The deep roar cut through the hall. Silence fell, and I saw my husband freeze, his shoulders tilted as if he was about to dart away. Only I was permitted to address him by his first name alone, and it rang incongruous off the stone pillars.

Suddenly, Sir Aron appeared, shoving through the crowd of bodies, wet riding cape flying behind him. "So you had the Devil's own nerve to come back here!"

"What in *Annwn* is going on?" Alys whispered.

Dark waves of foreboding inched up my body. "I don't know. I've never seen them have a cross word."

My husband held up an arresting hand. "Be careful, Lord Seneschal. Remember where you are and to whom you speak."

"To whom I speak!" Sir Aron sent a bitter laugh up into the brownstone arches. "A man I have done near twenty years of good service for, through princehood and kingship. A liege lord I swore my *life* to."

"Aron, I'm warning you," Urien said hoarsely. "Come to my Great Chamber and let's discuss this like men."

"*She is my wife!*" the Seneschal roared. "The mother of my *children!* You raised the cup at my wedding and took every ounce of loyalty I had, when for years you've been making me a cuckold!"

It is strange, the sensation of turning to stone, particularly when it's involuntary and you don't know if the hardening of your insides will stop before you crumble into dust. Standing on the stairs, hearing of my husband's lengthy infidelity, I thought I had merely gone cold, when all the while I gripped the stone balustrade, absorbing it, willing myself like it, the final defence against the dread creep of humiliation. Even my belly felt like the burden of Sisyphus, curved and rock hard, though within the child wriggled and dove like a dolphin.

A firm hand took hold of my wrist: Alys. "Let's away from here."

"No," I said, and the word echoed with spite. "He tried to escape, withheld me from my own brother. I *will* hear it." Tearing my arm away, I descended the staircase, parting the crowd. The argument between the men had continued to rage, arms flailing, lurid accusations piling up like slain bodies.

Sir Aron stood seething, hand hovering at his sword hilt. "I'm waiting to hear what is to be done!"

"Let me tell you, as your King and liege lord, what's to be done." Urien pointed at the door. "You will go back to your manor—that which I gave you—consider Lady Flora's pleas for forgiveness, and stay there until I decide what to do with you."

"What to do with *me?*" bellowed Sir Aron. "My *liege lord*, she is with child!"

"She's . . . *what?*"

"Full of a bastard—*your* bastard. Gotten on her during that detour you took after the High King's first battles. She confessed the whole filthy business last night, after I disrupted your tryst." The Seneschal's eyes slid to me, and he scoffed, as if my timing was perfect. "All the while I was here, guarding *your* wife's belly. How proud you must be, my lady, to be wed to a man with the habits of a rampant street dog."

It was only then that Urien, deep in his indignation, looked down and saw me standing beside him. His face drained to a sickly cream, lips working beneath his beard as if seeking a reason, his next excuse, anything to prove he could not possibly have done what he did.

And my God did I will it; I wished in silent, mechanical desperation for him to find an explanation, to save me from the embarrassment, the scandal, the ravening eyes and tongues of the kingdom. I did not want to be what I was becoming—the statue, the bloodless effigy—but I needed his denial at least.

None came, not a single attempt from my husband to utter any words of deliverance. Eventually, Urien shut his mouth, peacock eyes flickering, and I realized he was waiting for me.

I raised my hand, sharp-clawed in preparation to strike, and feel the drag of my nails down his expectant face. I swung hard, but he was quicker, trapping my wrist with a loud slap, like the crack of a slaver's whip.

"*Don't you dare*," he growled. Spinning me around, he threw my arm at Alys, who was there, ready to bear me away.

Halfway to my chamber, I stopped. "I won't stand for this," I said, sinews tight as a drawn bowstring. "If Arthur expects Gore, then it's me he wants to see, not the pig's head that represents this kingdom. Order the stables to ready a litter for the Queen, then send word to my husband. Tell him I am going to Camelot."

52

WE ARRIVED ON a day blazing with spring, meadows and trees fragrant and colourful as we passed through the open gates. The city was still under construction: stonemasons carving and fixing; carpenters hoisting beams for houses and trading posts; thatchers straddling rooftops with their tufted bales.

But the castle was complete, a sight to behold high atop its great walled hill, gleaming gold in the sun, all towers and turrets, light bouncing off an endless rainbow of windows and the cathedral's vaulting spires.

Inside, layers of rooms stood ready to receive fortunate guests, every chamber frescoed or hung with tapestries and filled with artfully carved furniture, rich rugs from the best weavers of the Orient, and hangings and coverlets in the finest fabrics. The plate was gold and silver, the glassware ornate. The vaults were bursting with treasure and the largest collection of spices, oils and incense one could hope to eat, bathe in or burn.

This was Camelot: Arthur's city, his main court and, by reputation, the greatest, most luxurious castle in the world. Its name would ring out, he had told me, for now and all time. Within, he would make new laws and uphold true justice, pay homage to the glory of God with lavish celebrations, and create the greatest knights Britain had ever seen, ushering in a new age of godliness, glorious deeds and unassailable honour.

In a place such as that, one could not help but feel the shift in the world, the kingdom's beating heart contained within its shining walls, under great arches painted with sky. All things seemed possible: the rebellion was defeated, the Saxons almost subdued, peace and prosperity flourishing like the onset of summer. Every mind was on Camelot now, watching, hoping, reaching out for what came next.

And so, when I gazed upon it for the first time, was mine.

*

SIR KAY MET us at the main door and led us promptly to Camelot's Throne Room. Long windows lined the walls, glazed with high-coloured saints and past Kings. Arthur's new standard bedecked the spaces in between—Uther's snarling dragon rampant, but red against its pure-white field. I took it in with slight bitterness but little surprise: absent or not, it was inevitable that men would take on the symbols of their fathers.

My brother greeted us warmly at the foot of the dais. "Lady Morgan, how good it is to see you, despite the sad occasion." He kissed my hand, drawing me aside. "What do you think of my city?"

"Quite glorious," I said. "Exactly as you described."

"I wish I could show you every brick, every garden, and speak of each day since we parted. Unfortunately"—he gestured to the room, where several newcomers awaited acknowledgement—"I cannot catch breath. I'll have Kay set a meeting for when this is over, and we can talk at length. Can you wait for me, dear sister, please?"

I smiled, disarmed by the swift way he slipped from gracious host and ruler to my hopeful younger brother. "You are the only King I have ever known to say 'please,'" I said archly. "I look forward to it."

He had not lied about his time: at banquets and court gatherings Arthur was constantly surrounded by knights and lords vying for his attention. Otherwise, he kept to his council chamber, taking meeting after meeting, negotiating a complicated future.

At the funeral he held the congregation rapt and spoke of his deep sorrow at King Lot's death, his desire for peace, unity, a cessation to the wars that had tied knots in the country's potential.

Later, as the High Priest intoned his lengthy rites, I looked around St. Stephen's solemn congregation and caught sight of a familiar profile. Morgause stood rigid at the front of the cathedral, wearing a blood-red gown and a coronet of twisted gold, flanked by three tall youths. Her eldest sons, I assumed: a russet, handsome pair just like their father and one made slightly darker—still of Orkney but finer-featured, with shades of my sister's haughty beauty.

So she had come. I could comfort her, speak of all that had befallen us in the long years of absence. But her spine was stiff, coiled, and I knew then, as I sensed it as a child—she was poised to leave.

We spoke the prayer as the body was interred, and when I looked up, Morgause had disappeared. I searched for her as the crowd poured forth into the cathedral's courtyard, but she was nowhere. The thought left me strangely bereft.

"Hello, Morgana." The clipped voice I would have known anywhere.

I turned. "Hello, Morgause. If you cannot remember my real name, feel free to call me 'Your Highness.'"

To my surprise, she rewarded me with a thorough embrace. "I see you have not changed, little sister."

She had remained beautiful, hair still black and shining against powdered white skin, rubies glittering at her slender throat. However, the deep-blue eyes we shared with our father were darkened, laced with uneasy lines, giving her a haunted look.

We exchanged vague pleasantries, and I offered my condolences for her husband's death, which she brushed off. "I'm here only to ensure *he* returned my sons." She spoke of our brother with brisk disdain. "Otherwise, I would not have come for all the gold in the Lowther Hills."

"Arthur treated them well, surely?"

She recoiled at my use of his name without title. "Almost too well. My eldest two are quite taken with him and his mighty plans. A trap that is not hard to fall into, granted."

"Of course, you met last year. I heard you rather got along."

She pursed her lips, eyes casting about the courtyard. "All I will say is, take caution with him. Be careful where you place your faith."

"If I have any left," I said bleakly. "You'll hear it from some gossip vine before long, but my husband was recently . . . caught . . . with another woman. His Seneschal's wife."

Morgause sucked her teeth and shook her head, which by her standards passed for great sympathy. "Foolish cur, destroying his own court. And terrible timing, when you're heavy with child. But men are weak, and kings are greedy. Be a good wife, bear his children, then take your own lovers and avenge yourself."

"Did *you*?" I asked, incredulous at such words from the consummate Queen. "Or is it only me you recommend risks burning at the adultery stake?"

She smiled in bitter amusement. "Have you noticed, dear sister, that only we need worry about that? A man might be told to say a few more Hail Marys, or spend some weeks exiled from a bed or two. But only women burn."

"Our view is not so different after all," I said, and we shared a grim smile.

"I have often thought about you," Morgause said. "Half-wild, roaming free, endlessly defiant. I wonder if you were right all along. We can only truly depend on ourselves—I know that now. I wish I had learned it sooner."

"It did me little good."

She shook her head. "You have spirit in you yet. I see it in your eyes, like you will never be done. It always reminded me of Father." Her gaze shifted as Arthur emerged from the cathedral, surrounded and talking. "I must go."

I put my hands to her elbows and held her there. "I hope this is not the last time we meet, sister," I said, despite feeling that fate had it differently planned. "I have missed you."

She smiled again, all edge, as if I was sentimental and absurd, and for once I felt no irritation, only fondness.

"Remember," she said. "Be careful—here, wherever you are. Trust only yourself. Farewell, fox cub."

With another brief and fortifying embrace, Morgause swept away from me, her three towering Orkney sons flocking to her summoning hand, and she left Camelot for good, without taking leave of the King.

53

"SHE SPENT HALF of her reign banished to the wilds of Orkney. After the last child, he never let her south of Scapa Flow."

"Well, you know why that is. You saw those sons of hers— strong-boned, reddish colouring, Caledonian blood and no mistake. But the last boy, the babe, yellow-haired and delicate as a summer breeze. One not like the others, if you take my meaning."

Three days, I thought, since the widow Queen had left with her fatherless sons, and gossip was already spreading like disease in a brothel. I had been placed at the far end of the High Table, among the eminent ladies of the South, none of whom seemed to know that the one they were tattling about was my sister.

"The younger one fares no better," it went on, inevitably. "Uther Pendragon's third daughter. *She* found her merry King in bed with his Seneschal's wife! My uncle heard from his wool merchant that *both* the Queen of Gore and the mistress are heavy with the King's child."

"A royal baby and a royal bastard! Do you suppose they will raise them as siblings?"

My patience tightened like an overtuned lute string. I half turned, preparing to unleash my own tongue, when the banquet hall came to a sudden hush. A shiver ran across my skin, and I knew—a heartbeat in advance—who had come. Merlin appeared on the dais, staff in hand, robes dragging along the floor.

Even better, I thought grimly.

Arthur was already standing. "My lords, ladies and loyal subjects, I am privileged to welcome my guest of honour and most valued adviser, Merlin the Wise."

The sorcerer raised a modest hand. "Thank you, my lord. If I may address the room?"

Arthur stood aside, and I felt a surge of gall at my brother's deference; any rupture between them from the coronation was clearly long healed.

"My lords and ladies, noble guests of the High King of All Britain," Merlin began, the same waspish drone setting my nerves on edge. "I come to share in the grief for King Lot of Lothian and Orkney. However, my purpose is not only to regret a great man's passing, but to look to the dawning age of our own lord, King Arthur. Behold."

With a flourish, he raised his staff and struck it on the floor. A wall of candles blazed into light behind him, lining the entire dais from the left-hand wall into the great curving embrasure behind Arthur's seat and back out again.

"These candles go out only in the event of my death," Merlin told Arthur. "As I live and breathe, my lord, they light your way, whether I am by your side or not. I commend His Highness to God, as your faithful servant."

Such dramatics had silenced the fishwives, at least. As the sorcerer sat, I leaned forwards for a better look at his feat. To all appearances, they were simple candles, snow white and high quality, but nothing more. A fanciful tale, perhaps, designed to solidify Camelot's wondrous reputation and imbue Arthur's power with an air of the mystical. And it had worked; the entire room was buzzing with it.

Yet I knew what Merlin could do. Curious, I rose, making my way to the back of the dais, following the candles into a deep alcove behind a statue of St. Peter. I touched the slow-dripping wax; it looked, smelled and indeed tasted like wax, but did not rub from my skin in the usual way, instead drying like dust and vanishing into the air.

I blew gently at a flame, then again, harder. The blue-yellow point danced but never guttered, almost resisting the idea of air. Next, I passed my fingertips over the top; it gave a narrow blast of heat as it ought, but left no lingering pain or black residue.

A candle that didn't burn, then—certainly an admirable feat. Whether they predicted death was unclear, but they were *something*, a combination of elemental forces changed, made unnatural, controlled in a small but extremely potent way.

"Lady Morgan, inquisitive as ever."

The flames surged momentarily. Merlin appeared in the alcove like a slice of darkness, eyes liquid black in the pulsing light. A silent, familiar mist gathered at the hem of his robes. "Interesting, aren't they?"

How he had got near me without sounding footfall was best left unthought of. He trailed his fingers through the line of fire as he approached, face curving into a blood-chilling smile. "It was a great deal of work, to produce so many. But the effect is impressive. I suppose you are wondering if they truly do what I claim."

"They cannot," I said disdainfully. "It would contravene the laws of nature itself."

The sorcerer smirked, displaying narrow, pearlescent teeth. He drew in a long breath, and the candles shrank in response. "Ah yes, that is what they teach you in the classrooms of convention. They call them 'God's laws' and tell you the elements are immutable, to be used occasionally but never controlled. Never created from nothing."

He turned his hand palm up and uncurled his fingers, a round orange glow forming in the centre. With a sudden *snap*, the sphere vibrated, bursting into flame. I leapt back and Merlin laughed softly, holding the fire up between us like a torch.

"*The elements are our tools, not our slaves*, isn't that how it goes?" he said sardonically. "It's been so long since I've had formal instruction. But as you see, my lady, despite you being fairly well educated, there are limits to what our holy houses can, or are willing to, explore."

"With good reason. To prevent others from becoming like you." But my eyes were fixed on the swaying flame, still alive in his hand. It gave off a definitive but peaceful warmth, like that of a small sconce, but his palm remained unharmed.

"Look as closely as you wish," he said. "Though take caution. Unlike the candles that wait on my death, what I carry here is true fire. One could light a hearth with it, cook meat or burn a whole building to the ground."

Like a moth, I retreated, then returned, feeling its heat, seeking the trick, the flaw that would reveal his lie.

"There isn't a law yet made that cannot be broken, given the correct skills, and enough courage." He snatched out the flame right before my eyes, and it struck me that he was entirely without scent, his only warmth that which, until a moment ago, he had held in his hand. Somehow it made him less threatening, devoid of bodily traits and appetites, concerned only with the mind.

I looked again at the candles, still expanding and contracting with his breaths. "Let's say you are telling the truth. Explain how it is done."

Merlin chuckled. "I beg your pardon, my lady, but such things would make no sense to you."

"There's knowledge enough in me to comprehend a few fairy tricks of yours."

His face tightened, then relaxed into an enclosed, vulpine amusement. "Maybe there is, Queen of Gore. But I wonder if you know as much as you think you do?"

"I won't stand here and listen to riddles," I snapped. "I don't care that you have my brother beguiled. Keep your demonic conjurings, manipulating words and godforsaken trail of mist far away from me."

I gathered my skirts and marched off, but the alcove appeared to have deepened, sounds of talk and clattering of plates distant, as if they were in another room rather than just beyond the wall.

"*You can see the mist?*"

The sorcerer's voice sounded directly in my ear, though when I swung around, he hadn't moved an inch.

"Of course I can see it," I said irritably. "It sticks to you like a moping dog. I followed it on the day you and your red-haired girl took my brother away. And before, coiled around that monster Pendragon when you let him get at my mother. You lack subtlety, Merlin, don't you realize? Anyone can see your damnable mist."

His eyes glittered with interest. "No, they cannot. The mist conceals, not reveals, which is partly how I sent King Uther to your lady mother, and exactly how I carried her son through an entire castle unnoticed. No mortal I've met has been able to see it."

"Am I not mortal, then? Because I certainly feel it." A sudden tiredness descended, the weight of betrayal, humiliation and violent memories pressing on me like Atlas's burden. I slid an arm under my swollen belly, hoping for a reassuring swoop or thrusting kick. But the child, for once, was reticent, slumbering, ignorant to my need for communion.

"You are mortal, make no mistake," Merlin said. "But what you can see is beyond most. Your mind is open, powerful and remarkable."

He moved closer, mist swirling icily about our feet. He gestured back to the candles.

"They take a long time to make. Each candle must be moulded individually, containing some physical essence of myself. Hair or nail suffices, ground up and scattered into the wax. Once set, they are lit and enchanted one by one. Simple, if you have the words, and the ability to speak them."

"Then everyone can know when you have condescended to die," I said wearily. "And they can lament and hold a great funeral feast. That is, if you *can* die."

"I can, and I will, like all men. The candles are less for my vanity than they are politically useful. When I cannot be by the King's side, they remind those inclined to doubt him that I still work in his interests. A powerful tool, influencing the minds of many. But what do you need to know of this? What use such 'fairy tricks' to you?"

"Riddles again," I said. "What use to me something I do not know?"

"But you would know, if I taught you."

My heart lurched. "You already hold sway over Kings. What use could I be to you?"

"Maybe, Lady Morgan, it is what use I could be to you. Everything you have ever wanted to know, I can reveal."

I paused at the thought of finally knowing all: how my father came to die, what passed between Uther and Merlin when Britain's fate was decided. Perhaps even where Accolon was, and with whom.

"You hunger for this knowledge," he said softly. "It would be so easy to give it to you. All you must do in return is learn—powerful things, wondrous things, everything your education would not allow."

Gradually, his image softened into a vision of a young face, angular and distinctive, eyes wide and intelligent, the innocent blue of a summer sky: Merlin as he once was, bright and eager, untouched by time and terrible foresight, before he handed himself over to the seductions of power and lay his abilities at the feet of Kings.

"I don't understand," I whispered.

"Consider it penitence, if you like," the young, hopeful Merlin said. "Teaching you—who would never seek it—will be a gift to the Lord."

"But I have hated you all my life. There is no reason on God's earth why—"

"*Because you can see the mist!*"

The flames surged with his loss of composure. The young face evaporated, blue eyes filling rapidly with black. "I cannot bear to see such power go unexplored. I will not!"

Horrified, I recoiled, but quick as his outburst had come, Merlin smoothed over his demeanour, fingers adjusting the collar of his robe with a strangely human agitation.

"You are one who likes to 'fix' things, are you not?" he continued. "A healer, making right what has gone wrong. Think of that in terms of larger life—using your skill, your prowess, to gain control over your world."

"A pretty thought," I said bitterly. "I learned long ago it is not *my* world to control."

"That is only what you have been told. There are ways, as I have shown you, to bend the world's powers to your own will." With a flick, the fire appeared in his palm once more. "When you have mastered that, it doesn't matter who you are or what body you possess. The world will respect you—I am living proof."

I held up my own palm. "Teach me, then. If this is not a demon's trick, show me how to hold fire."

Merlin laughed, snuffing out the flame. "Impossible. In future, certainly, if you agree to my instruction. But the incantation alone is extremely complex. It is done in the mind, and is far harder than your basic church Latin."

"Still, I will try it, if you are to prove yourself not a fraud."

He stiffened, silky camaraderie withdrawn. "It is no simple thing," he said officiously. "To become master of an element is difficult, and painful. One must learn how to seek darkness within and draw on its reserves. It is deep inside, and not easy to find."

"I know where my darkness lies, Merlin. You may trust that my reserves are endless. *Give me the incantation.*"

Sneering at my foolishness, he leaned forwards and spoke the words into my ear three times, clearly but not slowly, as if it was all a terrible waste of his time. "You will never do it. You have not been taught how. And you are with child, naturally weaker. It's not possible to plumb the depths of hatred and pain when new life moves within you."

"How would you know?" I snapped.

Closing my eyes, I drew a long breath, pulling myself inwards, back through months and years, collecting all I had buried—shards of pain and fear, lost battles and eternal regrets. Soon enough the images formed, memories of grief, horror and futility lining the darkest walls of my mind, a long tunnel of despair, at the end of which stood a laughing Uther Pendragon.

All I had lost stood behind him: my father, my mother and sisters, Accolon and lastly myself, the woman I should be rather than who I had been forced to become. Fear and fury rose like a scream, straining every sense, my mind fighting to break away. But I held firm, letting the darkness seep into my body, feeling it harden in my veins.

I took up the incantation, repeating it in my head, feeling no warmth in my palm, only the anguish within. Nothing was building, or felt like it was about to happen. I had failed, overreached myself, just as the sorcerer had predicted.

You will never do it, he had said. *You have not been taught how.*

And then it came to me, what Merlin had purposely not explained, the motion his hand made as he brought the flame to life. To create fire, one must know how to light one. Put flint against steel, and strike.

I struck my fingers across my palm, eyes snapping open as a flame shot upwards, roaring briefly above my head before winnowing back into my cupped hand. The heat rippled from its edges, but underneath I felt nothing, as if I were the fuel, burning from the darkness deep within. I grinned, but only out of pride; happiness seemed an abstract notion now, a word I had heard but never felt.

It was then I noticed Merlin, rigid and staring, mouth curling into a smile of sheer satisfaction. "Incredible," he gasped. "Impossible. You are a marvel, more remarkable than I first imagined. The power of your mind, its expansiveness; I had no concept . . ."

Whatever triumph I felt dissolved, but I could not bear to extinguish the flame, could not tear my eyes away from this incredible thing I had made. If I had begun with an impossibility, what might I be able to do in six months, a year?

"You must learn it all," he said fervently. "Give your power its head, and those you want to love you will love you. Or, if you prefer, they will fear you. They will behold you at last, Morgan, and tremble before your greatness."

"My greatness," I murmured. "Can it be so?"

"It has already begun," Merlin said.

In a searing moment I was back in the scribe's closet, hearing him speak those same words, telling my mother she could not escape Uther Pendragon, that her fate was sealed because he, the sorcerer, had ensured it. He had done for my father, for my mother and for Cornwall: there was nothing else.

I snatched the fire out. "You disgust me," I snarled. "I will never, *never*, succumb to you. Not for knowledge, not for power, not in my darkest and most desperate hour. Nothing is worth that."

He backed away, stunned. I strode past him, alcove shrinking back to its rightful proportions, setting me free.

"I will never forget the ills you have wrought, Merlin. And if I have my way, Arthur will see you for what you are, then I will watch with pleasure as your candles go out for good."

54

MY PRIVATE AUDIENCE with Arthur arrived late one afternoon, near the end of the funeral celebrations. I had kept to my chambers for days, claiming pregnancy fatigue, when in truth, between the sorcerer, the gossip and my aversion to even looking at my husband, it was the most efficient way of avoiding all I wished to avoid.

Arthur came into the room with only a fond smile and not a hint of curiosity—or sympathy—in his quicksilver eyes. Perhaps great men were too busy to hear rumours, or else found them of vanishingly little importance.

"Lady Morgan, dear sister!" he said. "How glad I am to finally sit down with you. Six days of feasting has done nothing to ease the endless talks and negotiation. How do you fare, with your condition?"

I placed a hand atop my belly, smiling at the kick I received in return. "Very well, thank you, my lord."

"That is good news. I'm happy you were able to come."

"As am I, my lord. I was pleased to see my sister, though she didn't stay long."

He cleared his throat. "I'm not sure if the Queen of Orkney and I will ever be on the best terms. Though I became fond of my nephews while they were here. But even as I solve problems, more arise. One rebellion subdued, still many alliances to be made, and now—" He cut himself off. "I apologize. I came to ask after your health.

When do you expect to meet . . . my nephew or niece, I suppose? How wonderful!"

I smiled. "They could want for no better uncle. Early June, by most reckoning."

"A midsummer child," he mused, then fell silent, as if lost again to thought.

"But please," I said cautiously, "know that I have been asked these childbearing questions a hundred times. What preys on your mind?"

"I should not complain, successful as I've been. I thank God more each day for His grace. But it is a great deal for one man."

"Then share your burden."

He smiled gratefully, followed by a deep sigh. "Where to begin? I almost have the treaties signed with the northern Kings, only to hear there is unrest in Gaul and Benoic. The men they sent helped defeat the rebellion, and now I may have to return the favour sooner than expected. If news gets out I am fighting overseas, the rebel lords may not feel quite so subdued. Then Merlin declares he is leaving. He says my way is clear for now and he has much to do, seeking what will befall the kingdom in future."

"If your way is clear, what did he advise?" Perhaps whatever Merlin was doing would have been part of my learning. The thought made me shiver, whether in revulsion or regret I could not be sure.

Arthur gave a hopeless scoff. "It's never so simple. He is satisfied I will hold on to power until he gets back. As for the life I must live in between—he has no interest in that."

"Perhaps you need better advisers."

"I certainly feel compelled to find some. Decent, trustworthy knights to aid me in the daily running of a kingdom, then I can leave Merlin to his prophecies without qualm. But absolute loyalty is not easy to come by. A hundred new men swear to me every day, and most of them I don't know from Cain."

"Then begin with the ones you love best," I said. "Sir Ector, Sir Kay, men you trust with your life. Ask them who they trust in turn. Seek those who believed in you—Neutres of Garlot, Leodegrance of Cameliard—the men the rebel Kings claimed were mad. Reward honour, and true loyalty will follow. That is what I would advise, if you asked me." I gave a rueful smile. "Which, of course, you did not."

"But by God, Morgan, you're right! You—" Suddenly, he cut off, his eyes squeezing shut as if in great pain.

"Brother, what's wrong?"

"I've had a head like thunder on rocks for three days now," he managed. "It'll pass—it always does."

"That sounds concerning. You should see your surgeon. Or Merlin."

"By God, I'd never tell them of something like this. A mere sneeze sends Merlin flying off to his astrological charts." He attempted a smile, but it turned into another grimace. "I know you are learned in healing and I should heed you, but the slightest twinge or bruise and everyone panics. I'm only hoping they don't notice how *tired* I am."

My hands tingled in anticipation. But Arthur knew nothing of what I could do; perhaps he imagined tonics or potent prayers, not the golden force I had mastered, which represented, depending on who you asked, either miracle or witchcraft.

Arthur pressed a hard palm to his forehead as another pain took hold, groaning unintelligibly, something about flashes of light.

"Here, quickly." I stood, holding my arms high, beckoning.

Gingerly, he rose, then stood like a placid horse as I placed a palm on each temple, laying my fingers snugly along the sides of his skull. I had barely focused before the old heat took up in earnest, life force rushing pleasantly to my fingertips, seeking the dark obstacle of pain. In the head it was usually stone-shaped, or sharp and twisted like a thorned vine. In him it was a wall encircling his skull, formidable and obstinate, but as yet untested. I drew a few long breaths and let my mind work at it, tendrils of warmth seeping in under my hands, pushing, clearing, crumbling its resistance like mortar, a slow release of tension beneath the bone.

Arthur's eyes snapped open. I dropped my arms, savouring the old thrill of success. One thing in my life, at least, was still simplicity itself.

My brother touched tentative fingers to his forehead. "Good God in Heaven—it's gone! There isn't a trace! Do others know of this?"

I swallowed, euphoria rapidly chilling. "Not . . . particularly, my lord. As I said before, I never much practised. Nor do I tend to speak of it."

"That's a shame, and should not be. Between your knowledge and your skills, what a boon you could be to this court."

Then let me stay, here and now. I'll simply never go back to Gore.

I had half opened my mouth to repeat the thought aloud when Arthur added, "Of course, there is much to do first. I must settle this trouble across the Channel, and you have a child to bear in its homeland. Perhaps in a year or so, the stars will align for us. Then just imagine the good we can do!"

A knock at the door interrupted us, followed by a liveried page. "Excuse me, sire, but the King of Gore asks if he might pay his respects."

"Certainly! Send him in."

Hearing Arthur's permission made my throat dry; light-headed, I took hold of his elbow. "Brother, what we've spoken of—me at Camelot, the healing—don't mention it to my husband. He won't . . . understand."

He frowned. "You want me to lie?"

"Not lie, but . . . keep it between us. Please, Arthur."

He gave me a long, searching look as Urien sauntered in, smiling with affected charm. I scowled and turned my face away.

Urien bowed deeply. "Your Highness, to what do my wife and I owe the pleasure of your private company?"

Arthur looked down at me, jaw set, then back to my husband. "I simply wanted to extend my congratulations, as a brother, on the forthcoming birth of your child. And to commend your wife to you, King Urien. She has been a great help to me. Camelot's loss is Gore's gain."

Urien laughed heartily, only ceasing his mirth when he saw neither I nor the High King had reciprocated. "Forgive me, Your Highness. I thought you were in jest."

Arthur inclined his head. "Indeed not, King Urien. Best we say no more about it." He placed a hand on my shoulder. "Dear sister, may time pass swiftly until you are here again."

"I share that wish deeply, my lord," I said, and watched him go, restlessness aching in every bone.

"What in Lucifer's name was all that about?"

I had forgotten Urien was there, so used had I become to not having him in my vicinity. His broad presence filled the space between me and the door.

"You can leave now," I said. "The King admitted you, not me."

He spread his arms wide. "Nevertheless, I am here. Finally, a husband gets to converse with his own wife, with no Welsh shrew to tell me I cannot do what is my God-given right."

I rolled my eyes. "Don't bring Lady Alys into this. She acts on my orders. Her opinion of you has nothing to do with it."

"She dares have an *opinion* of me, does she?"

I threaded my fingers together, straining with the impulse to strike. "Her view is nowhere near as low as my opinion of you."

He regarded me with mild suspicion. "Why was the High King here? You were telling him of my missteps, I suppose."

"You flatter yourself," I retorted. "Your lies, your tawdry betrayals, are beneath the King, as they are beneath me—only I am stuck with them by law. But do not mistake my silence for compliance on my part—take it as a warning of what I could yet do to your reputation."

His arm shot out, grabbing the twisted braid at the back of my head and yanking it backwards. He put his face so close to mine I could smell the metheglin on his breath. "How dare you threaten me with that serpent's tongue. I ought to thrash the poison right out of your mouth."

I ignored the nausea, the burning pressure on my spine beneath my strained belly, and kept my eyes steady on his.

"Do it," I told him. "Strike me and I'll wear it as a mark of your honour at the High King's table. Break me in half and send your child to the Devil. Do as you wish then *get out*."

Urien paused, jaw muscles twitching. Abruptly, he let go and straightened his shoulders, looking down at me like I was a boot he had just stepped in dog mess with.

"You are unnatural," he growled. "A woman formed in the fires of Hell. I dread to think what your black maw will birth when the time comes, what demon spawn will spring from your vicious loins. God help us all."

55

WHAT I BIRTHED was not a demon but a son—a milk-scented, tiny-fisted cloud of pink skin and dark-gold curls, a creation so cherubic and contented it seemed I had instead brought forth an angel.

Yvain, Prince of Gore, came into the world not without blood or pain on my part, but swiftly, safely and was laid against my breast, bawling and alive. Enormous blue eyes stared dark and endless as he suckled from me, seeming to contain the entire cosmos. Already I had forgotten the hours of labour, the resurging sickness and the hot pressure of my body splitting apart. As he lay there, full and sleepy, taking quick, feather-light breaths, all else in the world vanished, irrelevant now against the torrent of my love.

A full night and day later, I was still looking at him, hardly noticing the midwives fussing around me, bathing my skin and arranging my hair, when the chamber door swung open and my husband came in. The women left, paying their respects to the presence of the father.

Urien had been elsewhere, hunting, when my labour pains began, and it was strange to see him now, approaching me with an almost reverent caution. He paused at the edge of the bed, saying nothing. We had spoken fewer than fifty words since Camelot; upon returning to Gore, I went directly to my lying-in and was happy to see nothing of him or his prying court.

I took in his dark-circled eyes; he must have ridden non-stop through the night, which in my heightened state I found somewhat affecting, his arrival signifying a painful odyssey, finally concluded.

"You have a son," I said. "Sit, meet him."

With exaggerated delicacy, he sat on the bed and looked down at the yawning face of our child. One small pink arm had fought its way free of its swaddling, straining upwards like a baby bird. Urien reached out to touch the soft, almost translucent skin, and the baby's tiny fingers hooked on, curling tightly around the thumb of a hand that could have held him in one palm.

Father smiled at son, impressed. "He is strong."

"Healthy as they come, says the midwife."

"And you?"

"I am well." The baby yawned again, eyes closing. "He made it easy for me."

My husband nodded, seemingly agreeable to the idea of a still-living wife. He tucked the child's arm back within the swaddling with surprising care. "Yvain, then," he said.

It was his great-grandfather's name—he of the map room—a legendary ruler who had raided at will and frightened all comers from his borders, making Gore rich and formidable all at once. We had agreed upon the name's use many years ago, when a swift heir was expected and Urien still solicited my opinions.

"Yes," I murmured. "I think it rather suits him."

"It is all I have wanted—to have a son and bestow on him a name of greatness."

We smiled at the sleeping face. It was early to seek a resemblance, but something of the creased, contemplative brow whispered to me of my father. If I could only remember enough to teach my son to be like he was—but it was so long ago, my memories unspoken, and sometimes I wondered if I had known him at all.

"You've done well." Urien put a hand to my cheek, his palm rough from years of sword wielding and hunting in harsh weather. But his wrist smelled sweet, like the flowers of the woodland, wholly unusual. I wondered if he had new bath oils, or if I had not lain with him for so long I simply could not remember him at close quarters. "You bore a child, defeating whatever curse dogged your body, and we can now move forwards with greater harmony."

He made a quick, muscular movement and kissed me full on the mouth, gentle but purposeful. Shock ran through me like ice water, followed by a mix of revulsion, indignance at his presumption and a faint, unwelcome recollection of pleasure. It had felt good once, to be touched this way, and could again, so easily. But not with this man; never again.

I broke free, and he sat back, preening like a cockerel, leaving behind the same scent, which I now recognized as primrose. "You have made me happy indeed," he said, fingers toying with the end of my braid. "Once the boy is with the wet nurse, I look forward to returning to your bed."

I pulled my hair from his hands and shifted uncomfortably against the pillows. God, I hated him.

"I'm very tired," I said. "Will you send the women back in on your way?"

"Of course." He jolted up, and I gripped the child tighter, holding him out of his father's careless wake. Urien got halfway to the door and turned, glowing with the pride of one who is never kept from his will for long. "You are to be congratulated, my Queen. Now all is forgiven, I see a bright future ahead. A reward is due—what gift will you have?"

Peace, I thought, *a way out of this maze of lies, escape from capitulation to those I do not love and cannot trust. Freedom.*

I said, "Best you choose, my lord."

He nodded, pleased, and I watched him go, wondering when in God's name I had said I'd forgiven him.

*

LATER, WHEN THEY took my son to be freshly swaddled, I turned my palm upwards, as I had every day since leaving Camelot. *Like flint on steel*, I thought, snapping my hand open. Nothing happened. For months now, no amount of focus, determination or plumbing the depths of my darkness had produced a single spark.

I looked into the fireplace; the flames mocked me with their ease of burning.

56

"IT'S HARD TO believe this wondrous boy will be three months old tomorrow." Alys leaned over and stroked Yvain's silky head. "It's gone so quickly."

My son gave us each a cursory glance and returned to watching the flame shadows dancing on the wall. I had finished feeding him, and he was contented but resisting sleep with the determination of one who is far too busy. *Exactly like his mother*, Alys liked to point out.

"It seems impossible he hasn't always been here," I replied, turning his warm, compact body to face me. "Though he will not rest until there's nothing to see, will you, my keen-eyed eyas? You must sleep sometime."

Yvain wrinkled his brow, as if he understood but did not approve.

There was a soft knock on the solar door.

"That'll be the nurse to take him to bed," Alys said, lifting him from me. "Say farewell to your lady mother, Yvain. How many times will you wake up hungry tonight, I wonder—*un, dau, tri*?" She counted on her fingers and pulled a comedic face. Yvain grinned, giving her braid a happy tug, and they goggled adoringly at one another all the way to the door.

Alys rejoined me at the fireplace, and we stood for a long moment, alone in our peace. "I heard from the women that a wet nurse has been found," she said eventually. "Apparently, when we reach Sorhaut, she will be there."

I had dismissed my women hours ago; the Royal Court was due in the capital for Michaelmas and had largely left, but Urien had charged the ladies to travel with me. I wanted none of it; they were the same old gossiping flowers—less Lady Flora—and I could barely be in the same room with them without wondering who was complicit in my husband's subterfuge, or if others had gone to his bed.

"They've been trying to snatch Yvain from my breast since I delivered him," I said scornfully. "Telling me queens cannot possibly feed their children because they have duties elsewhere. But I know it's all Urien's doing."

I put my hands to my shrunken belly, against the nauseated ache that had taken up there. By all appearances I was back to normal, queenly life beckoning like a purgatorial fate, but inside I was edgy, unmade, wracked with a disquiet, deep and unnerving.

"And for what?" I continued. "So I can sit in a drafty hall, listen to him hold forth and never be asked my view? Or so they can strap me tightly, dry up my milk and make my body palatable enough for him?"

I had held on tooth and nail, insisting I would feed my own child, that the Holy Mother had done it and many noblewomen never had wet nurses at all. But Urien would only indulge it for so long, and the inevitability of him made me burn. Did he truly expect to be let back into my bed—into my body—after all he had done?

My gut twinged, and I let out a low groan. Alys ushered me back into my chair. She took up Yvain's small blanket, which had been warming before the fire, and laid it over my abdomen.

"Thank you." I smiled; her fussing soothed me in a way I would never admit.

Alys knelt and sat back on her haunches. "How will you do it, Morgan? First the wet nurse and then—your husband calls you back to his bed? What he might visit on you . . ."

My breath caught in my throat. I had never told her about Urien's escalating aggression, the casual violence with which he felt he could grab my wrists, my arms, my hips; the threats and epithets he slung; the hard grip on my hair and sickening pressure on my pregnant body when I had dared challenge him. But Alys had always sensed his underbelly, long before he had shown it to me.

"Isn't there another way? King Arthur is back in Camelot."

By all accounts he was. Arthur had married unexpectedly at Pentecost, around Yvain's birth—a hurried ceremony for a sudden and all-encompassing love. Word had it he had formed quick alliances overseas and sent an impressive army to Benoic with his most trusted commanders, so he could stay in Camelot with his Queen.

"I can't simply go without being summoned. Besides, Arthur's trying to form a new, honourable realm. Do I really want to bring trouble and a spurned husband to his door, with all the scandal that accompanies it?"

"He's your brother. I'm sure he'd understand."

I shook my head. "In any case, it's the same problem that stops us from riding to my mother's manor. She didn't dare attempt going there to hide from Uther, and she had Sir Bretel, Sir Jordan, a whole host of loyal knights. If I ran anywhere now, taking Urien's heir, he'd chase us down and capture us back before we reached Gore's southern border. Then I *would* be treasonous. Goodness knows what he would do."

Alys nodded, eyes brimming. She stood and wandered over to the long table, taking the crumpled work from the ladies' sewing baskets and methodically folding it.

No tears pricked my own eyes: masks do not cry. I rose and followed her. "I'm sorry, dearest heart. But all I have—all I've ever had—is you and Tressa. And while you give me the will to live, none of us are enough to escape, or get to Fair Guard, or keep us there in safety. One day, perhaps, but not now."

She brushed away a tear. "No, I'm sorry, Morgan. I know the bind you're in, just as I know you'll find a way around it. You've always been remarkable with taking difficult circumstances and using them to create something better. I just wish there was something I could do now."

"You're still with me; that's all that matters," I said. "And Arthur will call for me before long. In the meantime, we'll go to Arrow Castle for a while—you, me, Tressa and Yvain. Take our manuscripts, spend time in peace and study. Urien will be hunting the entire boar season and won't care where I am."

The linen she was holding fell to the floor. "Damn my bones! I can't bear this. You *can't* go to Arrow Castle."

"What?"

Sighing heavily, she took my hands. "The wet nurse wasn't all I heard of. Yesterday, when you left us, Lady Lily let slip that the King . . . he has . . ."

I felt the blood rising up my neck. "What? More women, another dalliance?"

"Not . . . another," she said tremulously. "The same. Lady Flora. She . . . never left Gore. He's been keeping her at Arrow Castle, visiting her and, lately . . . their new child. Word is, he intends to keep her there, as his mistress."

"*Arrow Castle?* You know this without doubt?"

"That's just it—I don't. I meant to corner Lady Lily privately, confirm it before I brought you another burden."

"It's almost certainly the truth." A sudden, unlikely memory reared within me. "Primrose!" I exclaimed. "The scent Lady Flora wore. I have long hated it, fugging up my rooms with that sickly sweet oil."

Alys regarded me with confusion.

"I smelled it on him," I said. "Urien is so scrupulous, so clean. But he hurried in, must not have had time to wash. God's blood! It was the day after I gave birth. That blackguard, that *cur* . . . As I laboured and brought forth his heir, he was with *her*. *How could he?*"

"I'm so sorry, Morgan," Alys groaned.

I drew a deep breath. "The child. What did they have?"

There was a long, agonized pause. "Oh God . . . they have a son. He . . . they named him . . . Yvain."

Another bolt of fire hit my gut. "*Yvain?* As in my son's name? Urien gave his heir and his bastard *the same name?*"

"Yes. No one knows why."

"He must have lost his senses!" I stalked to the window. The sun was slipping towards evening, leaving a violent sky of molten copper. "Who would *do* such a thing?"

The neckline of my wool gown chafed. I tugged it away from my neck, and the fine gold chain caught on my fingertips—the Gaulish coin, still nestled against the cage surrounding my heart. It was more than Accolon now, more than the beauty of what we had, and the promises he failed to keep. His coin had become mine, a symbol of all I once was and what I had lost, an anchor, a touchstone, a reminder that shining things can still be found, even after hundreds of years buried in the dirt.

"*Cariad*," Alys said, "are you all right?"

I sighed. "What should we do, Alys? I know what I feel, but it's your life too. You are the bravest person I know, the love I am most sure of—tell me your mind."

Alys hesitated, but her voice, when it came, was clear, determined. "As long as I have those I love, Tressa and you, I want for nothing. But *you* should be able to exist as yourself, with those who appreciate your heart, your brilliance, all you have to give. I will stay or go wherever you wish, Morgan, but you deserve to live in the light."

I turned to face her, the steadfast, eternal thereness of her, her deep faith in me gleaming from her amber eyes. What had she said? *Taking difficult circumstances and using them to create something better.*

I went to the writing desk, scrawling two quick notes and sealing one of them. Next, I reached behind my head and pulled at my hair; the tightly woven coil fell down my back with a thump, unravelling. It had been held by a cage of wrought gold studded with emeralds and diamonds, one of the glittering rewards Urien had bestowed on me for bearing my son, and worth more than most knightly manors earned in two years. "Will you do something for me?" I asked.

"Anything. What?"

I tied the jewelled cage into my kerchief, pressing it and the notes into her hands. "Find a fast messenger. Tell him to ride to the place in the unsealed note, give the recipient the sealed letter and kerchief, and not leave until he has a reply. Then get Tressa to bring Yvain to your bedchamber and await me there. I will explain everything when I return."

"Of course." Alys slipped the notes into her purse, chewing worriedly on her bottom lip. "But where are you going?"

"I," I said calmly, "am going to speak to my husband."

57

URIEN'S BEDCHAMBER WAS as alien to me as the first time I'd
seen it on our wedding night: tall-ceilinged but somehow cavernous,
dominated by the enormous bed, draped in varying shades of crimson. Above the huge stone mantelpiece hung the usual Goreish arms,
surrounded by a starburst of swords.

I awaited him by the fireplace, keeping my eyes fixed on his
dressing room door, from which came the faint, heavily spiced scent
of his bathwater. At length he emerged, handsome and swaggering,
dressed in a pristine white shirt under a tunic of gold-edged green,
skin glowing with care, hair glossy, his beard groomed so neatly it
looked painted on.

He saw me stood sentry against the fire and grinned. "So it's to
be now? My lady, you do surprise." He strode over to the wine table.
"I like your hair that way, loose and wild, as if you were young again.
Some wine first?"

"No," I said. "I know what you're assuming, my lord, but the
reality is *very* different."

"Come now, what can it be this time, when things have been so
much better between us?" He shoved a goblet into my hands, and I
was forced to accept it lest it spill.

"You lied to me, yet again," I said measuredly. "You swore on your
son's eyes that Lady Flora had left the country."

He sipped at his wine, unmoved. "She has. Gone to relatives on her mother's side, I believe."

"Then why is she at Arrow Castle? Where I could not go all these years so you could tryst with her when you claimed to be hunting, or fighting battles."

"That was *before*," he replied. "Old news. We're beyond that now, aren't we?"

His continuing lies tore through my composure like a longsword. "She never *left* Gore!" I exclaimed. "Your precious mistress remains, kept at Arrow for your convenient use!"

He flattened like a trapped hare, eyes darting around. "Where did you hear that?"

"Did you expect me *not* to hear? You are neither careful nor clever enough to conceal it. It is a kingdom-wide scandal—your Seneschal of almost twenty years renounced you! It is *all anyone talks about*."

Urien hesitated, grasping for the cleverness he had long lauded himself for.

"Perhaps you thought," I forged on, "that I was so weak, so beaten down, that I would simply accept it?"

"I thought maybe you . . . weren't that callous," he attempted. "Given she was with child and her husband wanted nothing to do with her."

"*I* am callous? Is it too much to ask that, while you provide for the child, you don't keep her in the home you once gave me, to make me *happy*? You were with her at Arrow the night I gave birth to your heir, yet *I am callous*? What will your son think when he discovers that you betrayed your closest knight and humiliated your Queen, and were long gone the night he was born?"

"Yvain needn't know any of it. He will know only of my love and pride as a father."

"Oh, really?" I snarled. "*Which Yvain?*"

The shock on his face was almost worth the seven years I had wasted, his expression as raw and horrified as if I had just hacked off his sword arm.

"That's right," I said. "I know you gave your bastard the same name as your legitimate heir. It is the one thing, in all of this, that truly beggars belief. What sort of pathetic, cowardly father would do such a thing?"

Urien stood rigid, dumbstruck. Suddenly, his jaw clenched and he slammed his empty goblet down. "I don't have to listen to this—your high and mighty judgment all the damned time. *Years* I waited for you to bear me a child, years and *nothing*. I had to ensure my great-grandfather's name was commemorated somehow. She has three living sons; it seemed probable. Who knew what you would have produced—a daughter, a corpse?"

"So you *excuse* it? Our child was born first! And when he is old enough, I will tell your legitimate son that his lying, duplicitous father thought so little of him that he threw his ancestral name upon an unfortunate by-blow. My Yvain will know you, Urien. I will spend my whole life making him see what you are."

I expected anger, violence, some sign I had provoked him, but there was nothing, only his giant frame, granite against my hurled threats.

"In fact," I spat, "keep your mistress. Let the whole realm see the truth of their vain, shallow ruler. Keep her, and any of the other women you've doubtless had over the years."

"I *intend to*," Urien growled, leaning towards me. "Now listen to me. I'll not spend the rest of my days hearing the same old complaints, as if I am not King of this country, master of my lands, my men and you. I will take *anyone* I want into my bed, and keep them wherever I see fit. You are my Queen, bred to beget my heirs, obey me and sit quietly by my side, to my glory and that of my Crown. A figurehead, nothing more. You have no say in what happens in this kingdom, or anything I do."

"I have *never* obeyed you," I shot back. "Everything you forbade I've done. I've read, studied, accumulated books you didn't know of to burn. While you were whoring, slaying beasts and betraying your men, this *figurehead* healed the sick, helped your people. I've saved lives."

"God's nails, of course you have," he scoffed. "Your petty, secret freedoms, thinking yourself so wise. Well, you tricked me. I am shaken to my core. You've had your woman's rebellion—can we move on with our lives?"

"I will, have no fear of that," I said. "I am leaving."

Urien started forwards, then stopped, descending into slow, joy-less peals of laughter. The anger that coursed through me felt like it came directly from the depths of Hell. I lifted my goblet of wine and threw it in his laughing face.

His eyes snapped wide, rivulets of red dripping down his cheek-bones, staining his chestnut beard and spreading darkly across his tunic. He dragged his shirt sleeve hard across his face and lunged, snatching up my forearm. I tried to pull away, but his grip was iron.

"Let me *go*," I said, voice low and forceful. "*Now*."

He sneered. "You are going *nowhere*."

The lies and betrayal, his brutishness, the mocking assumption that I had no choice but to submit to his will: it had been my mother's existence, only I was not her—the self-mastery she had was far greater than my own. My mother was marble, her strength cool and smooth and patient; I was dark and made of shards, formed under pressure in places light did not reach. I was flint, and always had been.

And I was also steel: hard, forged in blazes, bright and glitter-ing sharp.

I struck my fingers across my palm and knew without looking what I had done. Flint and steel, brought together, creating one thing.

Quick as damnation, I brought my free hand up to the side of Urien's face. Momentarily, his eyes widened in confusion, then the heat took up and his skin began to sizzle, wine on his face set alight, and I felt it reach him: true fire.

Pain shuddered through his body, all that he needed to feel, all that he deserved. The hiss of blistering skin was quickly drowned out by his agonized roar, the scent of expensively oiled flesh filling my nostrils as he dropped my arm and reared backwards.

He stumbled across the room, arms flailing, flames catching in his hair and beard. Ashy clumps of skin fell onto his shoulders as he beat desperately at his face. Eventually, he reached the window drapes, wrapping his head up and extinguishing the fire. It felt like an age I had watched him burn, and I could have done so forever.

Untangling himself, Urien stared at me in horror, at the flame still dancing in my hand. "What have you done to me?" His breath came in gurgling, laboured gasps. "I'm seeing things."

"You have *no concept* of what I can do, the power I possess," I said. "Skills you could not comprehend if I showed you a thousand times. You made a grave mistake thinking you could break me. You almost did, but not quite. And this ends here, King Urien of Gore. If you come near me or anyone I love ever again, I will burn the rest of you without a second thought. I will burn you, this room, this entire castle if I have to."

"W-witch," he rasped. "She-devil."

"*My name is Morgan,*" I said. "And there aren't enough words for all that I am."

Then, with a flick of my wrist, I lit fire in the other hand and held them up on either side of me, like a goddess of discord bent only on destruction. I flexed my fingers and the flames surged taller, roaring, burning, my own inferno.

Urien's eyes widened, fluttered upwards, and he fainted dead away.

58

"WHAT HOUR IS it?"

I leaned my forehead against the cold glass. First light had widened into morning, and the courtyard was awake: blacksmiths early at their anvils, the last of the grain harvest coming in, stableboys grooming horses among wandering hens.

"Barely any different to when you asked me moments ago," Alys said, attempting brightness.

After I had summoned the Royal Surgeon and explained Urien's "terrible accident" with his wine and a candle, I had been assured he was bandaged up in bed under heavy sedation and would not wake for a day or two. Still, Alys, Tressa and I had spent a sleepless night locked in my bedchamber, waiting desperately for dawn.

I turned away from the window. "How do we fare?"

Alys patted the two large packs, tightly rolled and strapped with belts. "We're ready. Tressa has gone to get Yvain and ensure our mounts are prepared. Everything we need is packed; all else can be bartered for on the way. I've fitted the *Ars Physica* and our own manuscript in the middle."

I crossed the room and embraced her, shuddering beneath her arms. "I'm so sorry, Alys. It wasn't supposed to be this way, taking to the road under fear of treason."

"Hush. Better this than staying with him. All we must do now is reach the border and your husband won't dare follow."

"He might," I said doubtfully. "I have no measure of Urien anymore; maybe I never did. He could do anything."

"He *won't*. He's a coward above all things. Now take courage. I'll summon pages for these packs, then we'll go to the courtyard and wait."

After the pages had gone ahead, Alys picked up Yvain's meagre possessions, rolled up in the vibrant tapestry she had woven for his birth. I sighed, following her along the upper gallery and down the main staircase: this was no decent start for one as precious as my son, but the important thing was that we were together, and heading for brighter skies.

The entrance hall was empty, most of the household having long since left for Sorhaut, aside from a small gang in the centre, between me and the front door. A figure stepped forwards, stopping us dead. Urien stood before us, a quartet of guards behind him, hands on his hips as if he had been waiting.

Panic churned within me, but outwardly I didn't flinch. "I thought you were in bed," I said carefully.

"Yes, you'd like that, wouldn't you?"

His face twisted into an unpleasant smile. The burned half was entirely swaddled, bandaged thickly over the foul-smelling poultice they used on horses shot with fire arrows. Not how I would have treated it—in fact, I could have restored him with one sweep of my hand—but he had never cared enough to know it. He wore a mail shirt and an edgy demeanour, the gleam of opiates lying thickly over his uncovered eye.

"I am leaving," I said. "And taking my son with me."

"*Our* son, you mean," he replied. "Or, more accurately, *my* son. The Crown Prince of the Realm."

He wasn't wrong, legally—I had read more of his kingdom's laws than he ever had, and mothers were mere vessels, if they were mentioned at all. But I didn't care.

"I'm not afraid of you, Urien," I warned. "I bore Yvain, I feed him, soothe him when he cries. I'm taking him with me."

"One more step and your head will be on a spike," Urien snapped. "Even your devilry cannot overcome that."

"Don't you dare threaten me!" I said dangerously, and felt Alys hold my arm.

"Let's go, *cariad*," she murmured. "There's no gain in this. If he wants to speak to you hereafter, he must go through King Arthur."

"Ah, here she is, your determined Welsh scold." Urien attempted another grotesque smile. "Unfortunately, the question isn't whether I let you ride into the arms of your beloved High King brother. It is whether I release you at all. *Seize them.*"

Two guards grabbed Alys and me, crossing our wrists fast behind us. "What in God's name do you think you're doing?" I snarled.

"What I should have done when your treason began." Urien's tone was barbed, but then softened into something more persuasive. "Of course, my darling wife, there's always a peace treaty to be made between us. Your pedigree *is* unparalleled, and we have always rubbed along well in . . . certain ways." He gave me a one-eyed, pointed look. "Return us to our proper marital state, swear complete obedience, and I will let you both live."

"I'd rather die a thousand times than be within a bowshot of you ever again," I told him.

"Then death it is," he said, almost disappointed. "Upon reflection, it's probably for the best. I can seek a new, less difficult wife and have done with it."

"You will unhand her and have done with *that*!"

A gruff, commanding voice echoed down the hall. Urien swung around as Sir Aron marched into view, flanked by several knights.

More filed in, until I counted twenty in all, heavily armed, tunics bearing the ram and stars of the former Seneschal's personal standard, not the pig's head of Gore.

"Release the Queen and her woman," Sir Aron called to the guards. "Wouldn't want to cut you lads up, but we will if needs be."

The guards looked doubtfully at their King.

Urien held up a halting hand. "What are you doing here, Aron? I charged you never to come into my sight again."

"It gives me no pleasure," Sir Aron replied. "But I'm here in service of the Queen. Are you ready, my lady? We have your Cornish girl mounted safe with the child."

"Ready, Sir Aron." I wrenched my arms free. "I'm sure no one wants the bloodshed your men could exact. Come on, Alys. Let her go." The second guard obeyed, releasing her.

"So it's her bidding you do now, Aron?" Urien scoffed. "The Queen you didn't have a decent word for all the years she was ill-serving me?"

The former Seneschal didn't flinch. Sir Aron had never offered me more than cold civility, but Urien had done the most definitive job of casting their bond asunder. For that reason alone, I knew the knight would come to my letter and guard us on the road to Camelot, bringing the men my jewelled hair cage had paid for. That, and the fact he had always been shrewd—the promise of a place in Arthur's service with my ringing endorsement too great an opportunity to ignore.

I glided into place within my steely crescent of knights. "I think you'll find, husband, that a common enemy can build many bridges."

Urien's half a face twisted into a sneer, one I hoped pained him greatly. "Enjoy your victory, Jezebel. It will be short-lived. You'll hear from me."

I shot forwards, flame half lit in my hand, tingling with the desire to burn the rest of him. But then the others would see and know what I could do; they would wonder if he was truly to blame, reconsider if I was worthy of help. They were men, after all, and I was still at the mercy of what they chose to believe.

So instead, I thrust my unlit finger in my husband's face, feeling a last rush of satisfaction as he recoiled in fright.

"Don't forget me, Urien," I said. "Check the darkness and pray to God before you sleep at night, because one day, when you wake, alone and chilled to the bone, I'll be standing there—without fear, and without mercy—and I will be the last thing you see. Or the Devil take me."

IT IS STRANGE, the sensation of turning to stone, superseded by only one thing: when the process halts, suspends and begins to reverse.

In the instant we crossed Gore's border I felt it: the hardened shell I had formed began to shiver and crack, fracturing day after day, road after road; crumbling ever faster when I looked at Alys and Tressa beside me, laughing in unison, cheeks flushed with love and joy, and at my son, snug in his sling within Tressa's safe embrace.

By the time we stood at the gateway to our future, gazing up at Camelot's sheltering golden walls—when Arthur ran down the castle steps, more brother than King, all smiles and surprise, his arms open wide—I was what remained: Morgan, sea-born and uncaged, shattered but soaring, returned to life.

More was to come, I knew, decisions and challenges there had not been before. But at long last they were only my own, pointing towards freedom, and I was ready.

It was not the end of me, but the beginning.

ACKNOWLEDGEMENTS

My greatest debt of gratitude is owed to my wonderful agent, Marina de Pass, who believed in this book—and me—from the very first day, and has been a constant source of wisdom, kindness and understanding. Thank you for being my guiding star.

I am also incredibly grateful to my editors, Harry Scoble from Audible, Jenny Parrott from Oneworld, and Amanda Ferreira from Random House Canada, for making this book's existence possible, and providing the insight, patience and enthusiasm required to make *Morgan Is My Name* the best she could be.

Huge thanks to Alex Mackenzie, Vanessa Kirby and the entire Audible production team, for bringing Morgan to life so beautifully in audiobook form, and to the teams at Oneworld and Random House Canada, who have worked tirelessly to get the printed book perfect and out into the world. Thanks also to Ben McCluskey at Midas PR.

I would not have come half as far without my earliest readers: TC, who first told me I could write; Emma Darwin, who taught me so much about writing, language and structure, and showed me how to turn words into a book; and Fiona Mitchell, whose insightful feedback gave me the confidence to keep going at exactly the time I most needed it. Endless thanks to all of you.

I am also forever grateful to the online writing community and the wonderful writers I've found there—you know who you are.

Special thanks to Jess Lawrence for the craft talk, accountability, and solidarity through the ups and downs of this writing life—I couldn't want for a more brilliant critique partner. Thanks also to Karen Harris, for listening to my never-ending chatter about writing, characters, and every wild book idea I've ever had.

Much appreciation to my family, both my own and my in-laws, for being supportive, proud, and for always believing I was capable. And to my cat, my constant writing companion, for keeping a quiet vigil while I did the work.

Thank you to my parents for their love and care, and for filling my life with books, paintings, music, museums, castles and stories. To my mother, for always telling me I could do anything I set my mind to, and to my father, for the birds.

Most of all, I am eternally grateful to the two halves of my heart: to Milo, for being the very best, and to Jason, for everything. I love you.

SOPHIE KEETCH has a BA in English Literature from Cardiff University, which included the study of Arthurian legend. She is Welsh and lives with her husband and son in South Wales. For her debut novel, she was drawn to Morgan le Fay because of the progression of her character through time, becoming ever more villainous as she was written and rewritten in the words of men. But beneath the infamy, Sophie felt there was an unsung story and was compelled to seek out the woman behind the myth and give a voice to her contradictions.